I0761100

One & Only

Also by Maurene Goo

YOUNG ADULT NOVELS

Throwback

Somewhere Only We Know

The Way You Make Me Feel

I Believe in a Thing Called Love

Since You Asked

One & Only

Maurene Goo

G. P. PUTNAM'S SONS
NEW YORK

PUTNAM
— EST. 1838 —

G. P. Putnam's Sons
Publishers Since 1838
An imprint of Penguin Random House LLC
1745 Broadway, New York, NY 10019
penguinrandomhouse.com

Book design by Kristin del Rosario

LIBRARY OF CONGRESS CATALOGING-IN-PUBLICATION DATA IS ON FILE.

Hardcover ISBN: 9798217181162
eBook ISBN: 9798217181179
International edition ISBN: 9798217184002

Printed in the United States of America
1st Printing

The authorized representative in the EU for product safety and compliance is Penguin Random House Ireland, Morrison Chambers, 32 Nassau Street, Dublin D02 YH68, Ireland, https://eu-contact.penguin.ie.

For the people of Los Angeles

1

Depending on the season, the office on a Monday morning smells like roses, lilies, or peonies.

Because it's May, the month of my birthday, it smells like lilacs.

Like I need the reminder.

The flower delivery always arrives just as I've disarmed the security system. The delivery girl, Katie, brushes by me quickly and places the first arrangement—lush lilacs and seeded eucalyptus—on the marble entryway table. "Morning, Cass!" she says on her way out to fetch the rest, her Land Cruiser parked along the curb.

"Morning," I call out as I walk through our waiting room—a large space filled with floral-patterned sofas and chairs, high-piled cream rugs, and oak tables. Sunshine streams through a row of windows looking out into a courtyard set up with white iron benches and giant potted ficus. A black walnut tree shades it all, its skinny leaves shedding onto the dark-green cushions of the benches. The morning light is soft, and I take a moment to appreciate it before the day gets away from me. I close my eyes against the sunshine, willing myself into the present moment. Not the coming birthday.

When the last of the flowers are placed on the front desk, Katie leaves and our office manager, Shreya, arrives. "Please let me take over," she says to me, brusquely, at the espresso machine where I'm starting to make myself a cappuccino. Shreya is young but bossy, because she is the eldest daughter to Indian immigrants, or so she tells us in all the memes she posts. She nudges me out of the way as she sets out delicate cups and saucers on the counter.

I let her, because her drinks are so much better than mine, and lean against the counter. "How was your weekend?"

"Good," she says, keeping her eyes fixed on the milk frother. "Oh, I got an update from the private investigator. About . . ." She glances around before whispering, "Daniel."

I lean in close, my heart jumping into my throat. "And?"

She shakes her head once. "Sorry. He ended up being a college student. In Florida."

Damn. "Thanks, anyway."

She softens for a minute and even makes a move to touch my shoulder before stopping herself. "We'll find him. I know it."

I nod tightly, trying not to acknowledge the little flare of hope I had that maybe I'd get this one big thing—the biggest thing—off my list before I turned forty. But I don't want to make Shreya feel bad so I joke, "At least I can cancel that bikini wax, huh?"

"Cassia."

"Gotcha. Regressive, internalized misogyny alert."

She gives me a wink and hands me my latte. "Proud of you."

A chaotic jumble of noise echoes through our lobby and I know the interns have descended. Matteo and Lila walk in wearing sunglasses and various low-waisted bottoms. Lila is drinking something out of a giant 7-Eleven plastic cup and Matteo is eating a powdered donut, the sugar dusting his Fair Isle sweater.

"The nerve of your metabolisms," I say as Shreya hands me my cappuccino, the cup clinking against the saucer. The delicate bone china is at my grandmother's insistence. We've broken about half of the beautiful cups, but I have secretly replaced them with eBay finds over the years. I now know how to spot an original Spode Italian Blue from a mile away. Halmoni never has to know.

"Coffee's gross," Lila mutters as she grabs a banana out of a fruit bowl. Also at my grandmother's insistence.

While I balance my coffee and red suede tote on the way to my office, the front door flies open again.

"I almost rammed into one of those damned robot cars," Sunny says in greeting. She shakes out her Burberry trench and hangs it on the coatrack. My aunt's bob is streaked with gray and impeccable, as are her gingham capri pants and red cashmere sweater. As the marketing and publicity director, she is our most public-facing employee and always looks the part.

"On purpose?" I ask, my lips hitching into a smile.

She rolls her eyes as she walks by me, reaching out briefly to squeeze my upper arm. "Morning, Cass." Then she heads to her office, leaving behind a scent of something expensive and subtle.

The phone rings and Shreya rushes to the front desk to answer. "One & Only Matchmaking," she answers. "How can I help you?" She hands me a folder wordlessly as I sidle by and I add it to my load.

My day really begins with my calendar—my ride or die. I keep calendars for not just my work life, but a shared one for my family (so I can keep track of their endless old-people doctor appointments), and one for me and my best friend, Marcella—which includes her kids' various doctor appointments and extracurriculars on days she needs me to help her out. I wake my computer and check out the day's schedule. Four readings, oof. Then a meeting with our Web designer about some changes we need on our website. Once the calendar is sorted, I make my to-do spreadsheet. This is a list that would, in Marcella's words, make Microsoft Excel's creator jizz his pants. Since I'm director of operations at One & Only, meticulous spreadsheeting comes with the territory. And an unhinged obsession with schedules and routines doesn't hurt, either.

A small figure pops into frame. It's my grandmother's sister—who I call Emoni, a nonsense honorific I made up as a child because I couldn't actually pronounce the proper Korean name for Great Aunt, "Emo Halmoni."

"Cassie-ya," she says with urgency. "My computer is doing the thing again."

We have an on-call IT contractor, but I get up anyway, never able to deny Emoni anything. "You need to stop clicking on YouTube ads."

"I didn't!" she insists, her perm bouncing in indignation as we walk down the hall to her office. "At least, maybe I didn't." Emoni is technically the VP and chief financial officer of One & Only, though her hours are pretty much part-time now. But Emoni was never one to sit still so she remains very much a part of the business—a family business run under the thumb of a true matriarch.

We pass the bullpen with the interns. "I tried that poker strategy you taught me," Matteo calls out to Emoni. "For the first time ever, I made out like a bandit on poker night." Emoni truly loves money. Any time she doesn't spend in her garden is spent at the casinos. It's not a gambling *problem* per se because she always manages to win.

Emoni sniffs with satisfaction. "I have so much more to teach you, let's meet at lunch. Lila, did you try that egg soufflé recipe? Because you need more protein. Your arms—"

I steer her away. "All right, back to work, minions!" Farther away, I look at Emoni. "You can't talk about people's bodies."

"I'm old, I can do anything."

After her computer is sorted out (YouTube ads strike again—

this time from a video about a penguin who delivers groceries in a small Japanese town), I head back to my office.

"Cass?" Shreya motions to me discreetly from the front desk.

I walk over. "Yeah?"

"You have a last-minute reading scheduled for, well, *now* if you can do it."

"I already have four readings today, you know they take a lot—"

"You might want to see who it is." She jerks her head toward the waiting room. There's a woman sitting on the sofa, flipping through a magazine. When she tilts her head up, I catch a glimpse of a very familiar face. Celebrities are not foreign to us here at One & Only—we're in Beverly Hills and our reputation as the best *discreet* matchmaker in Los Angeles is pretty sterling. Still, the woman in our living room won a Golden Globe this year and is the latest spokesmodel for Dior. It's been splashed all over the internet that she had a messy breakup with her equally high profile musician boyfriend. The latest in a string of bad romances.

I'm pulling up my calendar on my phone, to see if there are any conflicts, when someone says with full authority, "Send her to the reading room in five minutes."

Shreya's back snaps into an impossibly straight line. "Yes, Mrs. Park."

I turn to see Halmoni—my grandmother. The boss. She has made a fashionably late entrance, as always. She's grown shorter, but her presence is still intimidating at eighty-eight years old. Her hair, still fairly dark for her age, is twisted into a low knot on her nape. Her big Chanel sunglasses are still on, and her cheekbones are still on a level with Audrey Hepburn's. She hands her Hermès bag to Shreya, who takes it wordlessly, then lifts an eyebrow at me. Challenging. "Can you handle this reading, Cassia?"

Halmoni has no cute nicknames for me. To her, I am always

Cassia. The name my mother, her daughter, gave me. A daughter she can now only see in the shape of my eyes, the stubborn wave in the back of my long hair, and the large feet that accompany my tall frame.

"Yes, of course," I say easily. "You sure you don't want to handle it?"

She waves her head dismissively. "Your halabuji snored all night. Too tired."

I laugh but look at her closely. She is impossibly spry for her nearly ninety years, but age has been creeping up on her and I'm always on high alert. Halmoni notices and scowls. "Go take care of our client."

Right below the surface of my adult veneer is a surly teenager and I roll my eyes. "I was *gonna.*" She makes a quick *tsk* sound and digs a knuckle into my upper arm. I pretend it hurts but we both know it doesn't, and I make a face at her before she walks away. Halmoni has a hard shell for everyone in the world but her family. And, although you wouldn't necessarily know it at first glance, she saves the softest parts of herself for me.

When I walk into the waiting room, Gemma Flores looks up at me. She is beautiful and tiny like a hummingbird, like all actresses when you see them in real life. Her clothes are very celebrity incognito—a matching set of soft lounge pants and a sweater with a black cap. "Ms. Flores? I'm Cassia Park, it's so great to meet you."

She stands up and shakes my hand, her tennis bracelet pressing into my wrist. "So nice to meet you, too!" She laughs nervously, a husky sound that is familiar to me from watching her on a long-running hospital drama for years. "I kind of can't believe I'm doing this."

I tilt my head. "Why?"

Another nervous laugh. "Just . . . If it got out that I went to a matchmaker, I'd be skewered online. But I can't take any more of the heartbreak, you know?"

Something in me loosens. Gemma Flores may be famous, but she's familiar. I get her. "I know."

Halmoni walks in, her expression warm and serene. This is her client-facing side. "Ms. Gemma Flores, we are such huge fans of yours. We're so happy you've decided to join us here. I'm the founder, Mi-Kyeong Park."

"Thank you, and so nice to meet you, Mrs. Park," Gemma says, everything a bit more relaxed now. "I heard about your agency and your face-reading methods and thought, well, that's something new, right? I'm a little nervous."

Halmoni takes Gemma's hands in hers, grasping them tight. "Don't be nervous. Our family has been matchmaking for centuries. It's a skill that runs in our family, and we were known for it in Korea. We brought it here to Los Angeles in the seventies. So, you're in good hands." She winks and Gemma is charmed. "And yes, we use face-reading, but we blend it with traditional matchmaking practices. This form of matchmaking is unique to our family."

"How does it work? Face-reading I mean."

"Well, you know palm-reading?"

Gemma nods.

"It's like that—but for the face," Halmoni says with an impish smile. "A face is very revealing about a person's character—their strengths and flaws. But it also reveals interests, temperament, and even their future."

Eyes wide, Gemma says, "Wow. But how does that help with matchmaking?"

Halmoni places gentle hands on Gemma's arm. "All this information helps us determine who would be the best match for you. Who we call your 'fated.'"

I've heard this speech so many times but each time it stirs something in me, fills me with an overwhelming emotion that catches in my throat. "And we *will* find a good match for you. We believe that there's someone out there for everyone. Happiness guaranteed."

Gemma looks properly convinced when she says, "Well, okay! I'm so excited to start this . . . journey!" She follows me through the office, past our brass plaque that reads: WE HAVE A 100% SUCCESS RATE FOR TRUE LOVE. GUARANTEED. We've had this guarantee since the business opened and it's one of the reasons why our reputation is so solid. Because it's true—everyone we match stays together.

I take Gemma upstairs, and we pass by a wall of photos documenting the nearly five decades of One & Only's existence. There's an old photo of the first office in Koreatown, a nondescript storefront in a strip mall, next to a billiards hall and Chinese takeout. The leap from that spot to where we're standing today, in a beautiful colonial building in Beverly Hills, feels like a miracle. In the photo, standing in front of that first storefront, are Halmoni, Emoni, my grandfather, and a young Sunny. Holding her hand is another little girl—Evette, my mom.

We enter our reading room—a relaxing space with plush sofas low to the ground, dim lighting coming up from the baseboards, and woven Korean textiles on the walls. String music, played by the traditional Korean instrument called the gayageum, is piped in quietly in the background.

The vibe is very much *fancy ancient magic*.

Adding to that is the ancestral shrine we keep tucked away in a corner. It's nothing flashy—just a small wood table with two (electric) candles, a stick of incense, and a brass bowl of water. Most Koreans don't keep an ancestral shrine year-round. They only put them up for special holidays like Chuseok in the fall or Lunar New

Year if they do it at all. But our family? Well, we're not like most families.

Gemma and I sit across from each other. She looks around, absorbing it all. "Wow, this is such a cool space."

"It's where the magic happens," I say with a smile.

Gemma uncrosses her legs and lets out a breath. "To be honest, I'm not sure if I believe in all this"—she waves her hand around the room—"but at this point . . ."

"You'll try anything?" I finish for her.

She nods. "Yes. No offense."

"I understand. Let's make you a believer, shall we?"

2

Please focus on the charm over my shoulder," I say.

Gemma's gaze shifts to the little jade bird hanging on a cord of red silk from the ceiling, hovering just behind me, and I wait for the moment her features relax.

My eyes skim her face, landing on each spot briefly—eyes, nose, mouth, chin, cheeks. "You have a very symmetrical face, which implies harmony."

Gemma smiles a smile that is automatic for someone who is complimented about her beauty regularly. "Thank you."

"Your brows have a high arch—cleverness." Another polite smile from Gemma.

I take in her eyes. "Your eyes are close-set, which implies suspicion. You don't trust easily." The smile stays on her face but doesn't reach her eyes. "You need someone honest, someone who will not play games." It's the first time there's a break in her composure, a little wobble. I know I've hit on something real.

"Your nose implies fortune," I say, not giving the reason—large nostrils. "And your wide mouth indicates generosity. Whoever you end up with will be entrusted with both your heart and finances."

There's a beat of silence and then she lets out another low, nervous laugh.

"And now I'll just be reading silently, so please sit through the initial discomfort." I try and sound warm when I say it, and not like a gynecologist. I look at her again.

As my focus becomes laser sharp, it happens. The room around me dissolves. And with neck-snapping speed, I find myself on a busy street. Filled with horse-drawn carriages and people rushing around me, dust kicked up from the dirt-packed road. The scent of horses and trash and food mingle together in a way that screams "before modern-day plumbing."

A quick look at the outfits—hats on the men, bustles on the women—and I know I'm in a turn-of-the-century city. There's a boy nearby holding up a newspaper and yelling something in Spanish. The sound of horses clopping is overwhelming and I try to orient myself, to ground myself and not feel overwhelmed by what's surrounding me. I look up at the sky—blue behind all the industrial smoke—and take big breaths. When I look back around me, I see her.

Gemma, or whoever she is in this lifetime, is rushing down the street, dodging the busy traffic. She's wearing a long brown-patterned dress with a bustle and a dusty-rose velvet bonnet with black ribbons floating behind her as she dashes down the sidewalk. I follow her, careful to keep my eyes on her hat. She eventually pops into a shop—a dressmaker, the cheerful bell above the door chiming as she sweeps inside. And, as if I'm watching a movie, I am now in the shop, too. Gemma is behind the glossy wood counter, busy putting on a striped apron over her dress, speaking rapidly to another woman in Spanish, and they are both laughing.

I catch her reflection in a mirror, and it's the face of a different woman. Our past lives don't embody identical bodies, but while I'm here, I am able to see them as I know them. No matter how many readings I've done, the magic of this never ever gets old. I look at the details of the shop—the neat rows of colorful thread behind the counter. The glass display case filled with various sewing notions. The open cupboard filled with spools of ribbon—thick velvet, creamy lace, saturated grosgrain, pastel satin. I want to reach out and touch them.

The bell chimes again and the chatter stops.

Gemma stares at the man who has walked in. He's got salt-and-pepper gray hair and impeccable tailoring. Before I can process him, a woman enters and lays her hand on his arm. Gemma looks away, her face red.

And then.

A strand of glowing red thread unspools from her hand, wrapping around her wrist, until it finds its way to the man, and wraps around his wrist. No one sees this but me. The red thread of fate.

I know I have about ten seconds, so I focus on the man's face—following the map of patterns on his features until I feel it. The tug in my chest, the *click* of recognition.

And then as quick as a blink, I'm out and back in the room with Gemma. It takes a few seconds for me to adjust and wait out the wave of nausea. The jade cuff I'm wearing on my right wrist is warm.

"Your future has been laid out in my mind's eye," I finally say, placing my hands in my lap. "And in it, I've found your match." The words are so familiar to me that I barely register saying them as I twist my still-warm bracelet around my wrist.

"You have?" Gemma is both hopeful and skeptical.

Dispelling people of this skepticism gives me a high that's better than any drug. "Give us one week and we'll find you an array of potential matches."

When Gemma leaves, I head to Halmoni's office, which is next to the reading room upstairs. Her office is where a crucial part of our process happens. I find all the Park women gathered there, drinking coffee. All their shoes have been kicked off.

I hand Halmoni my cuff and she wraps her delicate fingers around it. All of us wear a piece of jewelry made of jade: Sunny wears dangling stones in her ears, Emoni a pendant on a necklace, and Halmoni a ring. These pieces of jewelry—they've been forged from the same piece of jade handed down in our family. And they all hold the same power. Every woman in my family is born with the same gift I have—inexplicable yet reliable: the ability to see past lives and past loves.

Halmoni's eyes close as she holds my bracelet. "Yes, you found him."

Behind her large redwood desk is a floor-to-ceiling apothecary cupboard—a piece of furniture that has been in our family for centuries. Halmoni opens one of the drawers and pulls out a piece of paper, handmade by Emoni, an almost-transparent sheet. The "recipe" for the paper has been passed down through our family as well. Regular old paper will not do for this job.

Halmoni places the bracelet on the scrap of delicate paper and we watch as a name appears, stitched in red thread:

Peter Cruz

"Gotcha," I whisper. Halmoni picks up the scrap of paper and places it back in the drawer. On the placard placed on the front of the little drawer, I write Gemma's name. This piece of paper will be kept in the drawer for as long as the courtship, until we know the match has been successful: when the red thread turns white—the final step before we take the name out of its drawer and place it in our archives, a compartment in the back of the cupboard, hidden by a false back.

"I'll get the interns on finding Peter," I say, putting my bracelet back on. When I reach Lila's and Matteo's desks, they each have about three devices open, toggling between all of them.

"Gemma Flores is our newest client," I say, grabbing a Post-it off one of the desks. They gasp. "I know, I know. We have to be discreet, okay?" They nod.

"I just did her reading and we're looking for a 'Peter Cruz' to add to her matches. Los Angeles." I write the name down and hand it to Lila. This would seem like an impossible task—to find a single human in the entire world. But what my family has learned over the centuries is that fateds always wind up in the same area lifetime after lifetime. They cannot help but be drawn to each other. That helps us narrow it down incredibly. And the one thing I've learned with interns is that there is no human being that a twenty-three-year-old cannot find.

Well, almost no human being.

"Peter Cruz," Lila repeats out loud, looking at the Post-it. "Sounds hot."

No one else at the agency knows how we get these names. They think we draw it from some database that only the founders have access to. It's taken as part of the whole "secret sauce" vibe of this business.

The secret sauce being, of course, the gift that runs through the women in my family.

"God, I wish we could post this on socials," Matteo complains. Then he slides a look at me. "Too bad."

We don't have a social media presence, at my grandmother's insistence. The secret behind our matches must be protected at all costs—even if it means missing out on an entire customer base. Also, the shamanistic roots of our business might rub some in the Korean community the wrong way. There's a bit of fear and stigma surrounding some of these ancient traditions. Our altar, for example, would freak some people out.

"Actually I've been meaning to talk to you about social media," I say to the interns. They both perk up comically, like cats hearing a can opening. "Create an Instagram account. Let's test it out."

Matteo clutches his chest. "For real?" Lila is unnaturally still, as if she doesn't want to scare me off.

"For real," I say. Then lower my voice. "Keep it on the down-low, just between us. Basic info and imagery. No posting about Gemma, obviously. Create an initial grid and then review it with me by end of day, okay?"

They nod enthusiastically, and as I walk away I hear them squealing.

When I get back to my office, I see that Gemma's already emailed me.

> Thank you so much for that incredible experience.
> You've made me a believer! xx G

I remember the moment when amusement turned to hope in Gemma's expression. The complete vulnerability of saying you believe in love.

It's the common denominator between everyone who comes to One & Only, the thing that ties everyone together.

Ties *us* together.

The jade cuff feels warm on my wrist once again. Everyone has big feelings about big birthdays, so mine are nothing new. But for me, forty marks ten years of knowing who I'm supposed to be with.

And ten years of not being able to find him.

Halmoni's not in her office when I creep in. The sunlight filters through a row of fig trees planted outside the bank of windows, and shines onto the apothecary cupboard.

I find the drawer with my name on it: *Cassia Park*

Third row from the top, almost dead center. I pull the drawer out, beautifully lined with red floral-patterned silk. A small scrap of paper lies right in the middle. The edges have curled slightly so I need to flatten it out on the table to read the name stitched into it:

Daniel Nam

I've seen it a hundred times, and yet something still stutters inside of me when I read his name. This was the name Halmoni drew for me. At my insistence, I had never let my grandmother or aunts do a reading for me. My mom got her face read at a young age and it led her to rebelling and dating my deadbeat dad—a fate I wanted to avoid. But when I turned thirty, after a terrible breakup with yet another damn musician, I asked my grandmother to read my face and enter my past life.

Almost ten years I've known my fated is Daniel. Ten years of searching for him.

All our methods here at the agency have come up with nothing. At first, it wasn't a big deal. *I'm only thirty! Be patient. What am I, a child bride?* At that age, marriage and children were nebulous desires. But the one clear goal I've had is this: I want to be so in love that the entire world around me dissolves. I want to go through life with someone beside me. My mother died young, and I don't take this future available to me for granted.

With my thirties coming to a close, I've spent the past year doubling down on my efforts. Shreya has this side gig that is Daniel

Nam focused—she's working with a private investigator and sends me updates every week. This week's update was the same as the last. I'm trying to stay determined—but a feeling of restlessness has been growing.

Because beyond having a partner, I want to feel that magic. The magic of falling in love with the person whose fate has been intertwined with mine many lives over—overcoming time and space and all else.

I want to begin a love so fated that it is *inevitable*.

And it's not lost on me that I'm the last woman in the family with the gift. Sunny has no children, and Emoni only had two sons, and *they* only had sons, by some goddamned curse (I love those boys, it's fine). With my possibly last male relative, Wally, born only eight months ago, it's getting increasingly clear to me that if I don't have children, the gift might be lost. So that once-nebulous desire to build a family has become clearer. It's here now. I guess I really am growing older because I truly cannot believe it's snuck up on me like this. This big decision that had always felt so far away.

Forty. A milestone birthday for many, but especially heavy with expectation for me.

Maybe this will be the year. A milestone gift for a milestone birthday. I close the drawer and carry this hope close—willing it into the world with yearning alone.

3

The night before my eighth birthday, I had a dream about a fire in my house. The next morning, my mom told me it was auspicious—that fire dreams mean all your troubles and worries will go away. That was the day my mom had a brain aneurysm and died while doing a load of laundry.

So I don't put too much stock into dreams.

And thank god. I wake up to my alarm and tiny talons poking my scalp on Saturday morning after a bad night of weird dreams about my middle school crush being in the circus.

"For crying out loud, Betty!" I yell and my cockatoo flies off my head. I touch my scalp and see that she drew blood. "You are a fucking demon." From her perch on my nightstand, Betty stares back at me with her soulless black eyes.

I shake off the rough night in the shower, and head to the kitchen to get coffee started, trying not to let the specter of birthday week dreams throw a shadow over everything. My bare feet slap on the Spanish tile as sunlight fills the kitchen, the windows left open all night to let in the cool spring air. I stand by the windows, looking out into the sunlit canyon, inevitably thinking about my mother.

Our mornings would start chaotically—her barely getting dressed in time to make me breakfast, in this very kitchen. Breakfast usually consisted of whatever we ate the night before: a cold chicken leg with a tortilla or spaghetti warmed up with a glass of milk on the side. But we'd be blasting music the entire time—Blondie was a favorite—the windows open wide. Bringing in the same sage-laced scent that comes into the kitchen now.

The garage is cool and dark when I open it to grab my bike from its rack on the wall. My grandfather installed it for me four years ago when I started my bike rides. His joints aren't what they used to be, but he can still build almost anything anyone needs. Although he immigrated here with a medical degree, my grandfather started doing construction work when he first arrived in L.A. While Halmoni built One & Only, he built his own contracting business and did that for decades before retiring. My little bungalow in Mount Washington reaps all the benefits of his skills—from a deck overlooking the hillside to the cabinets in my kitchen. Betty benefits most. He built her a giant cage in the backyard so she could commune with the hawks while being very safe from them. That said, many mornings I'm tempted to accidentally leave it open.

My grandparents raised me after my mom died. When people would remind me that I was an orphan because I lost both my parents, I would always bristle. Because in my mind, I only ever had one parent. My dad was a nonentity. He left us when I was only two, and while my mother raised me alone in this house, I had never felt the absence of a parent until she died. The pitying looks when people found out about me would make me sad until they made me angry.

For a bike ride, the weather is cooperating in L.A., which seems like a no-brainer but you'd be surprised. We have humidity and summer storms now—this isn't the steadfastly mild L.A. I grew up in. I only need an oversized Sade concert T-shirt and bike shorts for today's ride. I put my long hair into two French braids then strap on my helmet, secure my giant water bottle on the frame of the bike, and pop in my AirPods.

A podcast about scammers blasts in my ears as I take the easy ride downhill, coasting by the mid-century homes tucked into the scrubby hillside. The ancient, leafy oaks and shaggy pepper trees shade me as I zoom under them. People walking their dogs and pushing strollers wave hello to me and I wave back. Parts of L.A. can feel like a small town sometimes.

By the time I reach the street traffic of San Fernando, the sun is a little stronger and I take a break to drink a giant swig of water by a gas station under a freeway overpass. Cars almost clip me and I'm not even mad. This is a car town, I get it. I'm a little insect on a bicycle huffing along.

But riding my bike on Saturdays has been the joy of my life. It reminds me of being a kid, riding up and down steep hills in my neighborhood. Before all the heavy things became heavy. How easy it was to feel light as air, free as a bird.

When I finally reach Frogtown, my riding group is already at the coffee shop that sits alongside the L.A. River. Which, thanks to torrential rains this winter, is still flowing in May.

Marcella has my flat white waiting for me with outstretched hands by the time I reach the group.

"My baby," I say. "Thanks."

"Mm-hmm," she says, distracted. "Do you think my neck skin is looking saggy?"

I glance at her neck before I catch myself. "What? Shut up."

"Pardon, but Nora Ephron wrote an entire essay on this very topic," Marcella says. "It's valid."

The flat white is creamy and hot and exactly what I don't need after a four-mile bike ride, but I appreciate the second shot of caffeine. "Mar. Your neck looks fine."

"I bet you've never even looked at your neck," Marcella says with deep distaste. "You have the skin of a toddler."

"My fave beauty products *are* endorsed by preschoolers," I say. "And when I say your neck looks fine, I mean it."

She pulls out her cell phone and turns on the selfie camera to inspect her neck. "Hm. Maybe. For your birthday this year, let's go to Seoul and just get a ton of treatments done for ourselves. You can be my translator."

I'm spared from this conversation when our bike group starts getting a move on. A ragtag group of adults with varying athletic abilities, we take the path that follows alongside the river, which runs about nine miles from Burbank down to Elysian Park. Here, in Frogtown, the river is filled with greenery and wildlife, one of the few areas of the river with an earthen bottom. Thick groves of shrubs and trees dot the center of the river, which has a concrete basin on its sides. It's one of those mornings when everything feels exactly right and you can't imagine ever complaining about anything ever again.

"My thighs are feeling *the burn*!" Marcella shouts, making several other riders around her laugh. She's never given up her class clown mantle. Mar and I met in a run club almost eleven years ago and we bonded because we both immediately hated it and ditched halfway through our first run to grab martinis at a dive bar. She made me laugh so hard I almost peed in my overpriced leggings. We started this bike club as a bit of a jokey nod to our friendship origin story, but the joke's on us because now we're obsessed.

The wind whips a long strand of one of my braids into my face and I try to bat it away at the exact same moment someone in front of me slows down on their bike. I grab my handlebars with both hands to avoid them, but I overcorrect and find myself veering off to the right—on the side of the river.

The bike tips over and I instinctively curl my body into itself as I hit pavement. Hard. But it doesn't stop there—the momentum of the fall sends me rolling down the concrete incline toward the river. After a few painful seconds, I'm stopped by something leafy and green.

I hear shouting voices as I lie there and register what just happened. Shooting pain starts in my right side and my arm feels like I seriously shouldn't move it. Fuck.

When I try to lift my head, the world spins and my eyes tear up from the disorientation. In my blurry view, I see a pair of feet jogging up toward me. I think it must be one of the other riders, but I realize I'm facing the river.

The feet—in men's boots—stop by my head. "Hey, you okay?"

It's a man's voice and he's concerned. I wonder if I look busted up. I blink to clear my eyes and try and move to look up at him. "Um, kind of?"

"Don't move!" He crouches down. I register blue jeans and bright yellow socks peeking over his boots. "Okay, I don't see any blood."

I smile and it hurts. "Amazing news."

A low huff of laughter. Then he says, "Just in case, though, I'm going to call nine-one-one."

Something about this delivery is very considerate and I feel instantly soothed. "Okay, thank you."

"You're welcome." There's an amused tinge to it before I hear him on the phone with the operator. The call is quick and the guy is talking to me again before I can zone out. "I'm Ellis, by the way."

Ellis. Somewhere, buried deep under panic, I understand this name is cute. "Cassia. Hi."

"Hey, Cassia. So, you'll be getting some help soon." He's crouching down now and when he leans over, I catch a flash of a silver chain beneath a white T-shirt. Then I see his face.

I blink at the sight.

"Thanks, again," I say as I try not to stare at the devastating combination of wholesome and beautiful in the features of a mixed-race Asian guy in his twenties. Not a day over thirty, that's for sure.

"Of course."

Something occurs to me. "Did you run down here? Or are you a river troll?"

Again, the huff of laughter, but now it's matched with two incredibly deep dimples. "I was working down at the river, actually."

"Working?" I automatically turn my head to look and wince. His hand shoots out and touches my chin.

"Sorry!" he says as he pulls his hand back. "I feel like you're not supposed to move your head when you get injured?"

"You're probably right."

"Anyway, yeah, I was working and I kind of saw you . . . *roll* down here."

I laugh and it hurts, again. "There was no way that wasn't funny."

A pause. "Well, I don't want to say it was funny until I know you don't have any head trauma or, like, internal bleeding."

Then I hear my name being called and thundering footsteps. Marcella.

"Cass!" she shouts as she reaches me, flinging her body to the ground, her helmet thrown off, blond curls flying everywhere. "My god. Are you okay?"

"Yeah, I'm in some pain but I think I'm fine. Ellis called nine-one-one."

I see her register Ellis then. A tiny lift of a dark brow. "Thanks, Ellis."

He gets up and steps back. "Of course."

Marcella's hand strokes my forehead. That mom touch. "That was fucking gnarly."

Marcella's kids have said "fuck" since they were able to talk. I sigh. "I'm kind of embarrassed but mostly too worried I broke several bones and my brain."

"You look cute despite having rolled down a hill like a Homer Simpson GIF," she says tenderly.

I try not to laugh, and she slides a look at Ellis again. "Only you would get hit on by a hot guy after a humiliation like that." For once, her voice is blessedly quiet.

"Get out. He's, like, twelve." I also keep my voice as low as humanly possible.

"Who cares? You'll be done with him before he has to buy school supplies."

Marcella knows why I don't date men for longer than a few months at a time. For many years, she didn't, and thought I was just delightfully slutty. Other than my family, she's the only person in my life who knows about Daniel and the whole past-life-fated deal.

We hear sirens in the distance. Suddenly, I *am* super embarrassed. More than when I actually fell. Am I really hurt enough to call an ambulance? It seems like a lot for what's possibly just a few scrapes.

"You can't be too safe."

My eyes whip over to Ellis, who's gotten close, again. Dimples, again. "You looked like you regretted me calling nine-one-one."

This is a level of perceptiveness I am not used to from any man and I'm so startled by it that embarrassment melts away to curiosity. "Do you read minds?" It sounds like I'm joking, but I'm not. If I can see past lives, he could one hundred percent read minds.

But he just laughs and runs a hand over his chest. A weirdly confident "aw shucks" gesture. "It's just how I would be feeling. I'm sure your girlfriend agrees."

Mar and I look at each other before Mar says, "She wishes. We're just friends, sorry. I'm married. She's single."

Before I can absorb the embarrassment of that pointed remark, an army of medics descends on me and I lose track of both of them in the chaotic good intention. Authoritative and comforting, they check my body, ask me questions, and gingerly touch my arm and head. After what feels like forever, it's determined that I might have a concussion and a sprained wrist. They load me up in the ambulance and Marcella hops in with me. Before the doors close, I see Ellis standing back, his hands in his pockets. Sitting up with my vision no longer blurry, I can see him clearly—relaxed posture, broad shoulders, and a great head of wavy brown hair. His jeans are covered in dirt smudges, as is one part of his cheek.

"Thank you!" I shout out.

Dimples. "No worries!"

The doors shut and Marcella rolls her eyes. "Just bone already."

The medics laugh and I rest my head back, the movement reminding me of Betty's morning scalp assault. Birthday week, as per usual, is off to a great start.

4

Despite every woman in my family threatening me with death, I go back to work on Monday. I didn't even actually sprain my wrist, just bruised it pretty badly. And the concussion was mild enough that I could drive. In sum: I simply fell off my bike like a dweeb.

I watch Sunny and Emoni shuffle furniture around in my office. Sunny places a cushion on my chair.

"Guys! I hurt my wrist, not my ass."

Emoni tsks. "That mouth."

"Always so foul since you were little," Sunny says as she lowers a blind so that the beam of sunshine on my desk disappears.

"Well, geez, guess who I picked it up from?" I say as I reach to help Emoni pull an ottoman under my desk. She swats my hand.

"Nice try." Sunny helps us. "The bad influence was always Evette."

There's a familiar beat of silence, a pause in the buzz of energy whenever Mom is mentioned. Mom was the glue between all of us: Sunny's sister, Emoni's niece, Halmoni's daughter. We feel the pain of her absence acutely.

"Your mother would have been the worst matchmaker," Emoni finally says.

"Evette was the most cynical romantic I knew," Sunny confirms, perching herself on my desk.

"Because she didn't choose to be with her fated."

Halmoni, with her soft ballet slippers and tiny bones, has slipped into the room without us noticing.

"Subtle as always, Halmoni," I say.

"It's true. We all knew your dad was wrong for her from the beginning. But she never listened to me." Fondness crosses her features rather than vexation. Halmoni has long since come to terms with her daughter's rebellious nature. "But we got a pretty good granddaughter out of it, I suppose."

"Thanks," I say dryly and roll my eyes. It's a joke and I'm reacting to it as a joke, but somewhere inside me, a tender spot feels poked. My mom rejected her fated and picked my father. She was a romantic, a rebel, and just as stubborn as her mother. My father left us. Maybe because he wasn't her fated, but definitely because he wasn't able to handle fatherhood. We have no relationship and never will. He didn't come to my mother's funeral and that was all the closure I needed. He's more dead to me than my mother is.

Halmoni touches my brow. "I heard you hurt your head," she says with a frown. "We can't have you hurting your head. It might affect your readings."

"It was just a little concussion."

Halmoni inspects my face further, her eyes incredibly sharp. "You also have some scratches here." She touches my right cheekbone. "A woman should take better care of her face."

I bat her hand away. "Okay, okay. Enough, I'm fine!"

I shoo them out and have about a second of peace before Shreya knocks on my open door.

"Come in."

Her eyes scan my face behind her metal-framed aviator glasses. "How are you feeling?"

"Oh, god, I'm fine," I say, pushing my chair back to look up at her. "Everyone's fussing over a few scrapes."

She sits down across from me with a folder in her arms. "Oh, good. Today's going to be a little hectic."

"My favorite," I say, without a trace of sarcasm. Being a workaholic is a no-brainer for me. I love this job—One & Only has been a part of my life since I was born. When Mom had to go back to her freelance illustrator work six weeks postpartum, the Park women toted me to the K-Town office and took turns wearing me in baby carriers. When I learned to crawl and walk, they set up a playpen for me in Halmoni's office. Once I went to middle school, Sunny would pick me up after class—blasting Fleetwood Mac in the car—and drive me to the office where I would do my homework in the conference room, a plate of mandarin oranges and chestnuts delivered to me by Emoni. The table made it all the way to our Beverly Hills office—if you look closely at it, you can still see where I scratched in "LEO" surrounded by a heart. Because I knew my fated was going to be Leonardo DiCaprio.

My life and One & Only were always intertwined and the business runs in my blood just like the magic does. I know people think romanticizing workaholic lifestyles is bad, but matchmaking energizes me. And it never gets boring—because no two love stories are ever the same.

I ask Shreya, "What's first?"

The folder is pushed across the desk. "The interns populated a few matches for the name Peter Cruz." I open it to find printouts of photos and social media profiles for twelve different Peter Cruzes in the L.A. area. Since Shreya's watching, I take my time reading each one, even though by the time I see the third choice, I know who the correct Peter is—the man with the strong jawline and serious brows who I saw in Gemma's past life.

Shreya leans in. "Well?" Her fingers tap in her lap, excited to see what I have to say. This is always a little tricky, as I have to convince her that I'm able to do a match based on photos of the candidates' faces.

"Hm, well these five are definitely out," I say, placing a pile aside. "Ages are not a match for what she's looking for." I grab two more. "And these two are not quite right."

"Why?" Shreya looks at the photos and profiles, squinting as if trying to find the info herself.

"Noses." I tap on them. "Not a good financial match." It's true, even though I am definitely looking for reasons to discount them.

With the five left spread out in front of me, I look at each of them intently. "Gemma's jawline indicated a stubborn nature; she will need to match with someone more yielding." I push two more matches out. "They're not going to be that for her."

Three are left. I pause, trying to weigh whether I keep my cards close or show my certainty. Shreya is so absorbed that I decide to keep it closer to the vest. "Let's invite all three of these Peters to the next event for Gemma's matches."

Shreya nods, looking slightly disappointed. "So none stuck out as, like, 'the one'?"

I shake my head. "They're all good possibilities."

When she gets up to leave, she rotates her head a little, as if getting out a crick. "Did you ever talk to that physical therapist?" I ask her in my sternest boss voice.

"Ugh, no. I haven't had time with my parents in town," she says with a grumble. Shreya's parents moved to Canada when they retired, but they've been camping out at her place for the past couple weeks while visiting.

"Take it from me, you don't want to mess around with your upper back," I say as I start opening up a website. "Check your email in five minutes."

She gives me a suspicious look. "Okay, boss."

When Shreya leaves, the door is left open and I hear her talking to Matteo and Lily.

"Let's send invites to these three guys," she says.

"It's totally this one," I hear Lila say. "Biggest nostrils."

"No way, it's this one," Matteo argues. "He's tallest. The tallest guys always beat out the shorter ones."

I smile to myself. The employees at One & Only believe in a mix of our fortune-telling and pragmatism. Like I would if I didn't know about our ability to read past lives. During our hiring process, we read applicants' faces and, depending on their reactions to it, we make our decision on whether or not to hire them. Because the main thing we are looking for are the believers. Not fanatical about mysticism, but those who believe in love. A love that can feel fated—that one person is out there for you. A couple of former employees have been successfully matchmade by us. As small as we are, I take the responsibility of our few employees and their livelihoods seriously, and I take a few minutes to buy Shreya a massage gift certificate.

I have two reading appointments that morning (a finance bro whose past love was a man bootlegging alcohol during prohibition; the other a woman in her fifties whose past love was a lover she had on the side as a duchess in Regency England), then I meet with Sunny to start planning for this season's big matchmaking event—the one I'll be sending Gemma and Peter to.

Sunny and I have kicked off our shoes and are sitting on the sofa in Sunny's office. She has a diffuser and humidifier running with Joni

Mitchell playing in the background. Even though, on the surface, she and my mother seemed like polar opposites, so much of Sunny reminds me of my mom: their need to always have music playing, the way they cross their legs when sitting down, and of course, the way they laugh. That throaty cackle.

"LACMA confirmed the date," I say as I scroll through my to-do list on my tablet. "We just need to put down the deposit."

Sunny raises an eyebrow. "Good job, kiddo."

"You can thank Connie, who's pregnant with her second child," I say with a wink. Connie was a client who we matchmade several years ago. She's also the director of Curatorial and Exhibitions at the Los Angeles County Museum of Art. Very handy.

We have our client list printed out and make sure that everyone has their fated matches invited. Double-check, then triple-check. We absolutely cannot get this wrong. Let's just say it's happened in the past and I still have wounds from the absolute burning we got from Halmoni.

"Open bar and catering, right?" Sunny says as she pushes her reading glasses up—a beautiful pair of oversized clear frames.

"Yes, and I have just the spot for the food," I say. "Mar's too busy this month so she gave me a good rec for a place near the museum." Marcella runs a very popular oyster bar in Echo Park, and she's opening a sister location in Venice. I make a mental note to get her a bottle of chill-out-don't-kill-your-contractors wine because construction is the worst.

"Oh!" I sit up. "I forgot to say that Connie is going to hook us up with a couple open galleries. It'll be a great way for couples to walk around fairly privately, and a great icebreaker."

"Look at you," Sunny says fondly. "You're killing it."

I bask in her compliments. "Thank you."

"You really remind me of your mom sometimes," she says with

a bittersweet smile. "She was always so much more fearless than me—willing to put herself out there and get stuff done."

"In so many ways she wasn't eldest-daughter material," I say with a laugh. "She didn't listen to Halmoni at all."

"Yeah, but she did all the bad stuff so that I had an easier go of it," she says.

"How?" I love when Sunny starts talking about Mom. She knew a side of her that no one else did, not even my grandparents. I soak up every story greedily.

"Everything!" she says with a laugh. "I mean, tattoos, getting caught sneaking out of the house, refusing to be a matchmaker—anything I did after paled in comparison."

Halmoni appears in Sunny's doorway wearing her purse and sunglasses. "I have to go get my nails done. I'll see you all later for your birthday dinner?" she says.

I get up and grab my purse, too. "I'm getting coffee, let me walk out with you."

"How are you feeling, Cassia?" she asks as we walk downstairs, arms linked.

"Hm? What do you mean?"

"With your birthday." She squeezes my arm.

The question hits harder because I know this is a difficult time for both of us, not just me. "Oh, you know. I'm good, don't worry about me, Halmoni." But she does. All the time—whether it's fretting over my bike accident or the carbon monoxide detectors in my old house. She only had eight years to be a carefree grandmother before she had to become a mother again.

"Just make sure you don't work too much."

I start laughing. "Look who's talking!" Everyone thought she would retire ages ago. Yet here she is, approaching ninety and still coming in most days. I very much take after her. We're in the lobby when Shreya calls me over from the front desk. "Cass, someone's here to see you."

I check my phone. "Do I have another surprise reading?"

"No, he didn't make an appointment. He just wanted to see you but I couldn't get any other info . . ."

I stare at her. "And . . . ?"

She flushes. "He's *hot.*"

Halmoni rolls her eyes and says bye to us as she heads to the door.

"He's in the waiting room," Shreya says in a hushed voice.

When I turn around to see who this person is, I find myself face-to-face with Ellis. "What!" I exclaim. Happily.

Dimple time. He glances down quickly before he looks up at me. "Okay, don't be freaked out."

I tilt my head. "Okay. I'm not."

"Oh." He looks embarrassed. "Um, hi. Do you remember me, then . . . ?"

"Of course. Ellis. You saved my life." I smile widely. Flirting with young guys is always so low stakes.

He just looks at me for a second, then he seems to snap out of it. "Oh, ha. I didn't really do anything." It's as if he's seeing me for the first time, his eyes sweeping over me, drinking in the details of what I look like in my element. I remember what I looked like when he last saw me, wearing a bike helmet and nineties-coded workout clothes. Sweaty and mildly humiliated.

Today, my long hair falls over my shoulders in natural loose waves. I'm in a crisp, oversized men's shirt, the sleeves rolled up to my elbows, thrown over a mini, lace-trimmed slip in butter yellow. Under Ellis's interested gaze, I'm glad I shaved my legs this morning.

"Saved your *life*?" Halmoni is back outta *nowhere.*

Ellis looks over at me with a little bit of alarm.

I summon patience. "Halmoni, this is Ellis. He was there when I had my bike accident. He was the one who called nine-one-one."

With a loud clap of her hands, Halmoni rushes over to greet Ellis. "Omo, omo. Thank you *so* much. She's the most precious thing in my life." She's gone from elegant matriarch to cartoon Miyazaki crone.

I widen my eyes at Ellis; he catches it, hiding a smile. Sunny, then, marches in. Oh, god.

"What's with the ruckus?" she snaps. But her expression immediately shifts after spotting Ellis. She sends a sweeping, appreciative look down his tall frame. "Hi."

"This is the young man who helped Cassia after her accident," Halmoni says.

Emoni joins in the mix, head popping out of her office, and she's fumbling with her reading glasses before squinting at Ellis. "Oh, handsome!"

Sunny looks at him curiously. "Why are you here?"

Ellis looks overwhelmed and trapped and exactly how most people feel when confronted with the combined focus of these three women.

"All right, good job, family. We'll see you all later," I say as I push Ellis out the door. He does an awkward bow-and-wave hybrid as we duck out.

5

I have to adjust my eyes to the sun when we step outside onto the pristine streets of Beverly Hills. When Halmoni had first told me where the new offices would be located, I had recoiled. We were not Westside people. And *Beverly Hills*, of all places?

But then Halmoni had said, "Do you remember that car accident we got into when you were five?"

I did. Halmoni had accidentally put the car in drive instead of reverse when we were pulling out of a parking spot in front of a building. We had crashed through the lush hedges and barely avoided smashing through the entire building.

The people inside, white people wearing suits, had run out and yelled at Halmoni, whose English then wasn't as great as it is now. She had apologized profusely until she could feel their shock turn into contempt for us and our beat-up old Toyota. Then she had gone deadly silent and put me back in the car. We ran over the hedge one more time, sending people scattering, and then drove home.

That building is the building our offices are in now.

It was Halmoni's "Big mistake, big, *huge*," Julia Roberts moment. It's important to know that this level of petty runs through my blood.

Ellis and I walk out of the gate onto the sidewalk. "So sorry about that," I say, closing it behind us, squinting in the harsh light.

He takes a wide step to the left and suddenly I'm not squinting. "No need to be sorry at all. I'm half Chinese, I get it."

Did he step to block the sun for me? "Half? What's the other half, if you don't mind me asking?" I'm distracted when I ask.

"Jewish." Quick pop of dimples before he says, "So, yes, I happened to reach out to your riding group online because I wanted to make sure you were okay? I hope you don't mind that one of them told me you worked here. I couldn't find you online, otherwise I would have just messaged you like a normal person. Ha, ha."

This kid. I pull on my sunglasses. "Totally fine. I believe you. You *did* help me when you could have killed me instead."

He swallows a guffaw of laughter. "Yeah, murder."

"You'd be surprised at how top of mind murder is for women." I realize we're just standing on the sidewalk and start walking briskly. "Want to grab a cup of coffee? My treat, obviously."

"Sure," he says, taking big steps to catch up with me. "So, you look like you can walk okay?"

"Oh, yeah. I just had a mild concussion, and I need to wear this." I hold up my right wrist, showing off the ACE bandage wrapped around it.

He winces. "Oh, no. I hope you don't need your wrist for work."

I throw a sidelong glance at him as we reach the corner and stop for traffic. "The very cushy office job isn't in danger, no."

"Matchmaking, huh?" Ellis does this little thing then. He steps to my other side—which is the side close to traffic. It nudges me away from the street.

I'm so distracted by that little chivalrous maneuver that I don't respond to him right away. The light turns green and we start crossing, passing by a woman in athleisure and a fur coat. "Yeah. Been in the family for decades, well, centuries really."

"That's so cool. I've never heard of that being a family business before. It feels like . . . like, folklore."

I look at him when we reach the other side of the street. The wonder in his voice makes me look at him carefully. "How old are you?"

His expression shifts into wariness. "Why?"

"I need to place you in history."

He laughs. "Wow. Never heard it phrased that way."

"Do you want to know how old I am?"

His eyes drop down briefly, his body instantly uncomfortable. Then he looks up. "I wasn't particularly curious."

I laugh as I lead us toward a side street that is quieter, with less foot traffic. "That's only something a young person would say."

There's an entrance to a small café tucked into an ivy-covered brick wall. We enter when he finally says, "I'm twenty-eight."

I almost snap my neck looking up at him. He grins. "Too old for you?"

This guy. "I have no age limits on friends." *Keep it breezy, Cass.*

The smile stays on his face, his eyes never leaving mine. "Oh, good. Good to know. I'll bring my three-year-old nephew around for the next wine night." I laugh, feeling a familiar lightness float through me. *Crush* lightness. Oh boy. But I have to admit, it's the lightest I've felt all week—a particularly heavy week.

We're seated at a bistro table out in the brick-paved alley, tucked behind potted olive trees and shaded by a yellow-and-white striped umbrella. I order an iced latte, and he gets a black coffee and about eight different pastries. When they arrive, they're spread out in front of us like a buffet.

"Are you secretly a coffee-shop-pastry critic?" I ask, taking a sip of my creamy ice-cold drink.

He breaks off a piece of cheese-filled Danish and holds it to me questioningly. I take it even though I've already had breakfast and I'm pretty disciplined about snacks and sugar and all that as I get older. But there's something about him. I can't say no, and that lightness guides me.

"I just like sampling things," he says. This sends a zing straight into my belly.

"Are you actually able to eat all this?"

He nods. "Probably. But I won't, I'll save some for later."

"Well, you're a growing boy, after all. Need those calories."

He shakes his head and laughs while taking off his deep-blue chore coat. He's wearing a light blue T-shirt underneath, worn thin and fitting him like a freaking dream. There's that glimpse of his silver necklace again. I resist reaching out and touching it. His long, tanned forearms brace the table as he leans forward. "So, how do you like biking with that group?" Ellis asks.

"I love it." I can feel myself light up as I say it. "I only started doing it a few years ago. I've never been very athletic or particularly outdoorsy, so I was surprised by how much I enjoyed it. It was just . . ." My gaze shifts to a spot behind Ellis, my mind wandering. "It was like finding this other part of myself that was lying dormant for four decades, you know?"

Shit. Cat's out of the bag.

Ellis doesn't bat an eye. "That's incredible. I haven't had that in my life yet."

I wink. "Just give it another fifteen years, sonny."

He sits back. "Okay, enough. So, you're what—forty?"

"How dare you. I'm thirty-nine."

"Thirty-nine. What's the big deal?"

"When you turn thirty-nine, come back and tell me."

"I will." His voice is even, and his gaze is serious. It's pretty hot and I bet people fall over themselves when confronted with this face.

"Ellis, what's going on?" I ask, wiping my mouth with a napkin. "This feels like more than a casual check-in on an injured biker you saved."

His high cheekbones turn slightly flushed and he takes a sip of his coffee. Then he levels his gaze back on me. "Yeah, well, um, I'd like to hang out."

"We are hanging out." Is this how the youth describe fucking? *Hanging out?*

"This doesn't . . . I mean, it's nice. But, like, I'd like to take you out. On a date."

I take a sip of my drink to give myself a beat. "I'm really . . . you seem great. But—"

"But I'm too young?"

"Yes!" I exclaim, laughing a little. "Eleven! Years!"

"But we're both adults. Who cares? I feel like millennials are kind of obsessed with aging." He says this with a raised brow. He is challenging me. I can't even be mad. Somehow everything this guy does is just kind of, fucking *endearing*.

"We are. Because we're the first people in the history of humans to age, didn't you know?" I'm about to reach for a croissant when he intercepts me and hands it to me. I take it. "Stop being so damn considerate."

"No, I won't."

"Even that's cute. Stop." I busy myself with making sure I don't get croissant crumbs all over myself. "I'm turning forty this week."

He drops his pretzel roll dramatically. "It's your *birthday* this week?"

"Yup."

"What are your plans for the big day?"

There's no reason to go into my birthday angst and grief with Ellis. This sweet cinnamon bun of a guy. No need for him to know that I usually leave town on my birthday, just me and a playlist from 2001 blasting in my car as I drive to some random California destination in the vain pursuit of peace. Of a moment of enlightenment—still waiting to be okay with my mother dying on my birthday when I was a child.

"Not sure yet," I say breezily. "I'll probably head out of town."

"Ooh, where?"

"You are a very curious person." I try the lemon scone next.

"I'm curious about you."

The scone threatens to choke me when I swallow. "Well, not sure yet. I usually plan my birthday trip really last-minute. The only time in my life I do anything last-minute, honestly."

He leans closer. "You do this every year?"

"Yeah."

"Fun tradition. Do you go alone? Or with, like . . . a boyfriend? Girlfriend." He does that kind of crooked, hot-guy smile—another challenge.

I look at his eyes—dark brown with a hint of amber. Thick lashes, a dusting of freckles on his very nice nose. And without being aware of what I'm doing, I look down at his mouth. He's absent-mindedly biting down on his bottom lip. There's a little scar between his upper lip and his nose.

Shit. I'm doing it. I stop myself from reading his face. I never do it with men I date. I never do it with anyone who doesn't give me explicit permission, in fact. It's a code that we have.

"I go alone. Sans boyfriend and girlfriend because I don't have one. Which Mar so obviously pointed out to you."

The check arrives before he can respond, and I reach for it—but he grabs it before I can. "No, no way. This is for saving my life," I say.

He scoffs. "I didn't save your life. I called nine-one-one a minute before your friend would have."

"You helped me," I say sincerely. "You kept me calm. I really appreciated it."

The flush returns. "It was nothing. And—well, if you're not going to let me take you out on a real date, this is my treat." He keeps the check out of reach while he digs out his wallet. The server takes it before I can make any real attempt at paying.

"But—but I'm also your elder," I say pathetically, having lost the battle.

He laughs. "I am an adult with a job, it's fine."

"What's your job?" I brace myself for *actor* or *influencer.* There are so many hot young Asian dude chefs on TikTok.

"Landscape architect," he says, surprising me. "That's why I was at the river that day. My firm is in charge of the big restoration project there and we had a deadline to hit, so we had to be on-site."

"Wow, really?" A few years ago, the city had earmarked a ton of money to rehab the L.A. River, creating more green corridors for wildlife and a series of parks and paths to increase foot traffic. Basically, *make the L.A. River cool again.* "That's awesome. I've been watching the progress for the past few years while biking."

He nods, immediately animated. "Yeah, it's really exciting that we got the project. I mean, my company."

"So, you design the landscaping?"

"Yeah, we're part of the team in charge of creating the paths and one of the parks."

"That's very, very cool," I say with a big smile. "Can't wait to see the fruits of all your labor."

We get up to leave, and I can't help but notice the way Ellis does it—his movements easy and fluid. He stands and waits for me to get my bag before moving an inch.

We walk back toward the office. "So, what does matchmaking work entail?" he asks.

"Oh, it involves a lot."

"I'm serious," he says.

"I'm serious, too. We're not a conventional matchmaker."

"In what way?"

This is always when I have to make the decision about whether or not to be honest about what I do and how I do it. The past lives—we never reveal that. That's a secret. It's the face-reading that I'm considering, weighing all the possible complications and questions. But Ellis's curiosity feels like a gentle prodding that will not be appeased with a hand-wavy answer.

"Our matchmaking is based on the 'ancient Korean art'"—I am using my old-crone voice—"of face-reading."

"Face-reading?"

We cross the street. "Yeah. Are you familiar with it?"

He shakes his head.

"Well, it's kind of like palm-reading? I read fortunes by facial characteristics."

"No way, really?" He's looking at me with surprise.

"I know, it sounds wacky."

"Not really," he says with an easy shrug. "It must work, though? If you've made a family business of it?"

Yes, and it's worked for hundreds of years—that's how long my family has been practicing this. We have a record of it going all the way back to the early 1700s. I imagine that the gift may have even predated that, although I wonder how many past lives people could have had at that point. My imagination always takes me to weird Neanderthal places when I do, and I have to stop thinking about it.

The agency is within view, and the sight of it fills me with something close to peace—a steadying hand.

"Yes, the face-reading works," I say. "And no, I haven't read yours. I don't do that without permission."

Ellis raises his eyebrows. "Serious stuff. Ethics and everything."

"We have our own rules. It's very private, what your face has to say."

We stop outside of the agency. The sun is less bright but still gilds Ellis's face in a way that makes me feel restless. "Anyway, thank you for the chat even though I was supposed to treat my savior."

"You're welcome." He puts his hands into the back pockets of his dark gray jeans. "What if I gave you permission to read my face?"

This is leading to something. "No, it's my job. Not something I do as a party trick."

He looks a little devastated. "Oh—god, sorry! I was trying to be . . ." He sighs and runs a hand down his face. "I was trying to be, uh, cute. Basically, hoping my face says that I want to see you again."

A car honks behind us and the moment is made more awkward. I save him. "Ellis. I don't know."

He nods. "Okay. I will not push this, because I am an evolved male who respects boundaries." Then he pretends to throw his head back and wail. When he's facing me again he grins. "See you around, Cass."

That nickname coming out of *his* mouth does something to me. "Bye, Ellis." I wave, trying not to smile but finding it impossible as he walks away, his steps unhurried and long.

I have a reading scheduled so I make my way up to the reading room to have a little time to prepare. When I enter, the fresh scent of newly lit incense hits me, and I see that someone has refreshed the shrine. And now it includes a framed photo of my mother. At first, it startles me, until I remember that my birthday week is also the celebration of my mom's death anniversary. After thirty-two years of my mom being dead, you'd think I'd stop being surprised by this realization.

But there are some things that you can never get used to. They refuse to feel normal—because they're sharp and painful every time.

6

"Auntie Cassie, can you please play Billy Joel?"

I'm on the 101, somehow stuck in traffic on a Saturday, headed to my grandparents' house in Hancock Park. I glance in my rearview mirror at Marcella's youngest child, Ozzie, a three-year-old girl permanently encased in an Elsa frock. She is currently kicking the back of her mother's seat from her car seat and Marcella's hand whips out and stops the movement without a blink.

"Sure, Oz." I select "Uptown Girl," and it immediately gets everyone in the car shaking and grooving, including Marcella's son, Mica, who is seven and usually only responds to Minecraft sound effects. Their dad and Marcella's husband, Logan, is wedged between the car seats doing a limited-movement dance with his upper body. Billy Joel is always the right move.

"I can't wait to see what new massage chairs Halmoni has," Marcella says over the music. The way she says "Halmoni" is so phonetically accurate that I'm always a little proud of my white friend. "I need it really badly."

Something in her voice makes me look over at her sharply. "You okay?"

"Yeah," she says wearily. "Just, you know, opening a new restaurant is sapping my will to live."

"Is it the clown-town contractor again?"

"Just one in a long line of offensive men," she says with a groan, leaning her head back and closing her eyes. "I wish someone could knock me out until everything's over."

"You for sure get first dibs on the massage chair."

There'll be a line of people waiting for it. My birthday dinner involves my entire extended family: Emoni and her kids Josh and Brian and *their* kids and spouses, plus Sunny and Stu, and my grandparents. Mar and Co. are also my fam, so they always come, too. This pre-birthday birthday dinner is a tradition that started when I began bailing town on the actual day years ago.

When we get to my grandparents' house, Ozzie and Mica are instantly suffocated into big hugs and words of praise from my grandparents.

"Such a beautiful dress!"

"Look at this tall, big boy!"

I don't bother giving them the "less-gendered compliments, please" lecture because these are old Korean people I'm dealing with. Then Emoni's grandkids come storming in—ten-year-old Griffin, seven-year-old Hayes, and four-year-old Aidan.

They are definitely more excited to see Ozzie and Mica than me, but their meticulous manners force them to halt in front of me and give me kisses and hugs.

"Why are you *so* tall?" I complain to Griffin. He can't even hide his pride as he stands straight on his sock-clad toes. He's wearing cool skater pants and an ironic T-shirt of some kind and my heart squeezes. I don't see them as much as I want to. They're all scattered throughout California—Griffin and Hayes live in the Bay Area with their parents Josh and Lisa, and Aidan and baby Wally live in Orange County with their parents Brian and Wes.

Technically, these kids are the same generation in my family as me. We live on the same height in the family tree. But because Emoni is almost a decade younger than Halmoni, and Mom had me when she was just twenty-two, we're all a little staggered age-wise. Growing up without siblings, and then later without parents, I never quite fit in with Josh and Brian, technically my second cousins, and then was way too old to connect with their kids except as an aunt figure. But as I ruffle their hair, sniff their necks as I squeeze their little wriggly bodies—all the loneliness feels overshadowed by my intense love for these kids.

Ozzie and Mica are absorbed into this kid-ball as they roll out into the house and Marcella asks after the massage chair.

I walk into the kitchen—a sprawling, tiled dream space with giant casement windows and a view of the pool—where the rest of the family is gathered.

"Happy birthday, Cass!" Lisa, Josh's wife, says as she throws her arms around me.

A drink is shoved into my hand. "Here," says Josh dryly. "Numb yourself to the chaos."

"And the impending four-oh," Brian's husband, Wes, says with a grimace. The newest member of the family, eight-month-old Wally, is strapped to him like a baby possum.

Brian swats him with his arm. "Come on."

It strikes me again: I am the only childless and unmarried family member here. I take a swig of my chilled white wine before kissing the soft downy cheeks of the baby. "I've missed you guys," I coo.

"Not really," Brian says. "You miss the kids."

"Why not both, though?" I say with a grin. Halmoni walks in and everyone straightens. Wes and Josh hide their beers for some reason.

"How was the drive?" Halmoni asks me as she pats my back.

"Fine," I say as I take baby Wally from Wes. "Can I help with dinner?"

"No. You're not allowed." Emoni has popped in silently like an assassin, as is her style. She lives here, too—ever since she was widowed. If my grandparents had their way, the entire family would be shoved into this house. It's a large Spanish-style villa and they've lived here since I was a child, but before I was born they had lived in K-Town, which was just a few short but significant blocks to the south.

This house hosts every gathering. All major holidays, and one very important occasion: my mother's death anniversary. Which, of course, happens to be my birthday. Emoni's kids roll into town for it, without fail, every year. I love them for that.

Emoni takes Wally from me, and Sunny and Uncle Stu walk in from the French doors leading to the yard—Sunny holding rose clippings and Stu carrying an empty cooler. Sunny and Stu live a few blocks over in a house that inexplicably looks like the cottage from *The Holiday*. Everything about them is aesthetically pleasing—their home, their handsome labradoodles, and their own physical appearances. Uncle Stu gives me a hug, his thick salt-and-pepper hair voluminous and his peacock-blue cashmere sweater softer than a baby lamb.

"New glasses?" I ask, tapping his tortoiseshell frames.

He grins, his face impossibly handsome with its eye crinkles and glass-cutting jawline. "Never miss a thing, Cass."

"I follow your every item of clothing like unhinged people follow Taylor Swift's private jet travel," I say.

He laughs and throws his arm around me. "That is unhinged, but happy birthday, favorite niece."

"Only niece."

When Sunny first matched with Stu, we had all been holding our breaths. She had waited so long to find out who her fated was—was he going to live up to her expectations? This was a woman who only stayed in hotels that didn't allow children and had sheets with thread counts over five hundred.

When she came back from her first date with Stu, I was twenty-four years old and staying up late watching TV with my grandparents. We were trying to act casual while watching a Korean variety show when we heard a car pull up. Halmoni and I made eye contact and she lifted an eyebrow. I knew what she wanted me to do, so I casually walked over to the window and peeked out the curtain.

A car I didn't recognize was idling on the curb. But I could see Sunny's face in the passenger seat. Oh, god, was I about to witness a make-out session by my aunt? Luckily, I was spared that, and instead I saw a man get out of the driver's side and open the door for her. He was handsome and dressed like an old-fashioned movie star—light suit, white shirt unbuttoned at the top on that warm evening. Check and check for Sunny. And the way he took her hand when she got out of the car—impeccable. I felt my heart racing for Sunny as the two walked toward the front step, it was all just so *romantic* and dreamy in the L.A. moonlight with the white roses blooming along the path.

Then Stu tripped on a step.

And fell into a rosebush.

Still holding Sunny's hand.

I gasped and covered my mouth. My grandparents were next to me in a second. "What happened?" Halmoni asked, shoving in next to me. Halabuji's head bobbed around trying to see over us.

"He just *fell*," I whispered—mortified for him.

Sunny, in her beautiful Missoni wrap dress, was horizontal on the concrete path and Stu was disentangling himself from the thorny bush. The three of us held our breaths as these two impeccably dressed, dignified humans found themselves sprawled in front of the house.

Then Stu fell back into the bush and started laughing hysterically. Sunny looked paralyzed for a second, sitting up as she stared at the man across from her. He was laughing so hard that he clutched his chest with both hands. *Is this guy off his rocker?*

Then Sunny's face cracked into the biggest smile I had ever seen on her—it actually took my breath away. Had my aunt ever been this happy? She got to her high-heels-clad feet, hiked her dress up, and held her hand out to him as she laughed. He looked up at her, and he was dazzled. Actual stars in his eyes. He took her hand and she heaved him up. As they stood next to each other, laughing and trying to catch their breaths, I closed the curtain.

"Let's give them some privacy," I said in a hush, pushing my grandparents back to the sofa. But things were changed in the room—we knew Sunny had found her fated. And the sheen of tears in Halmoni's eyes expressed a relief so profound that it made me reach over and squeeze her hand. This was the power of love.

In present day, Stu squeezes my arm and says, "Welcome to another great decade, Cass."

After being properly plied with wine and massage chairs, we all sit down to dinner in the backyard. Twinkly string lights drape across the pillars of the stone terrace, and the water feature, a small babbling brook that feeds into their pool and hot tub, is lit up as well. White roses and lavender bloom around us and I feel incredibly lucky for all of it.

Before we dig into the food, Halmoni stands up with a glass of prosecco in hand. "Thank you all for being here. Another year of Cassia." She looks at me with love, but there's sadness in her eyes. "And another year without Evette. Let's take a moment to remember her and feel her spirit around this table with us."

Everyone quiets and Mar catches my hand under the table and gives it a squeeze.

A beautiful salad of butter lettuce from Emoni's garden is passed around, bright orange nasturtium scattered on top. It makes the kids giggle at the thought of eating flowers. I watch Marcella's husband, Logan, pretend to be a cow gnashing at his, and smile. He's this quiet (literal) rocket scientist who, around his children, becomes a playful goofball willing to put aside all dignity for a quick smile. Ozzie and Mica have their mother's wild, curly hair and their father's brown skin and all together they look like an idyllic future of humanity. We should be so lucky, honestly.

Marcella gives herself a heavy pour of prosecco. "And now, a toast to the birthday girl, please."

"No need," I say, scooping some salad onto my plate.

"Please." Marcella scoffs. "You're turning forty and we're not going to toast you?"

"Save it for my funeral."

Indignation erupts around the table, with Emoni crossing herself. I laugh. "Okay, okay. I'll allow a toast."

Halabuji clinks his glass with chopsticks. "More than one!"

"I'm going to start," Marcella says, standing.

Ozzie squeals, "Mama!"

I grin, looking at my best friend. A tall blonde with broad shoulders and impeccable style, Marcella is a force to be reckoned with. She has a scratchy voice and would have probably been called a "broad" in the golden age of Hollywood. I would say she's superhuman for doing all she does with two young kids, but the reality is she's worked hard to make it happen: saving up money to have childcare. Waiting until her parents retired and could help out before having her second child. Scheduling regular marriage counseling to make sure she and Logan remain a functional team. None of her success is an accident, and it's one of the many things I admire about her.

"Welcome to the fourth decade, darling," she says. "It's great.

You will no longer care about young people's ugly clothes nor their shitty music. You will no longer have FOMO about literally anything except people who get to drink a lot and wake up without hangovers. You will be"—she glances around the table full of Korean geriatrics—"ah, your needs will be much more clear." My cousins are dying trying to hold in laughter, so she rushes through. "And you will manifest the things you want."

My family all look at me, something behind their eyes. Hope. They hope I find Daniel before I become a withered old husk of an ovary. It would stress me out except I froze my eggs when I was thirty-two. Just as insurance, and to ease my grandmother's worries. And maybe a little bit because it was the age my mom was when she died.

I also don't squirm under this pressure because I know I'll meet Daniel. We have a 100 percent guarantee for a reason. I just don't know when.

"So, cheers to Cassia. The most type A person I know. Who takes care of those around her but knows how to take care of herself, too. The world would be better if everyone was like her. We'd have no wars and no bad dates. Happy birthday!"

Everyone raises their glasses, and I feel the flush of wine hit my cheeks with the overwhelming sense of gratitude I always get whenever I'm with these people. "Thank you, Mar. The tallest woman I know."

Mica bursts into laughter and Ozzie copies him instinctively. Emoni takes a sip of prosecco. "You are *very* tall. And a very good friend to our Cassia."

"She is." I signal my love to Marcella with my eyes and she accepts it with a slow blink. "Thank you, all, for gathering again for my birthday. Special thanks to Emoni and my grandparents for cooking and hosting, as always."

"It's one of the few times all my kids make the trip out to L.A.," Emoni says with winks at Josh and Brian. "So, I look forward to it every year."

They all groan, Korean-mom guilt in full effect. But I know later they will make sure to take home her leftovers, to update all her apps on her phone, and probably one of them will buy her a new car.

"I'm sure I'll be dreaming of this meal while I'm eating a can of beans in a few days," I joke.

Sunny frowns. "No. Are you camping again? With your injuries?"

I shrug. "Not sure yet, I haven't decided on where I'm going." A very weird thing for me to say, but everyone knows it's the one time of year I am spontaneous. "Also, I don't even need the bandage anymore." I hold up my naked wrist as proof. The cousins all start talking at once.

"What happened to you?"

"Couldn't you do a five-star resort for your fortieth?"

"Can I see your wrist?" This from Lisa, the doctor.

Uncle Stu pulls out his phone and squints at it. "We're supposed to have Santa Anas this weekend."

My grandfather gets up from the table. "I need to make sure your tires have good pressure."

"No, no. Sit down, Halabuji." When he won't listen I get up and drag him back by the arm. "We can do that after dinner. Everyone—chill!"

He looks unhappy about it but stays put. Halmoni asks, "Can't you just stay in town this year?" There's an edge of sadness to the question. We all know the reason for me bolting, but we rarely talk about it. It's too painful and no one wants to ruin my birthday. Even though it's always ruined, for eternity.

I tear my barbecued short ribs apart carefully. "The woods are calling and I must go."

"Maybe Daniel will be in the woods," Marcella says.

"Mar." I shake my head.

"What! I'm supporting you."

"Daniel Nam?" Griffin asks.

My mouth drops open and I look at Josh accusingly. "You all are just talking about this guy now?" I'm kidding but Marcella takes it seriously.

"Yeah, we are. You won't even date a hot young guy because of Daniel. Of course we talk about this cockblock!" She glances at my grandparents before her own children. "Sorry." Griffin laughs so hard that Josh has to smack his arm.

Halmoni's unfazed. "Cassia knows her fate." Then she frowns. "Wait, who is this young guy? That handsome boy who came into the office the other day?"

Marcella almost drops her rib. "Wait, *what*?"

Cousins start shooting questions at me and I pour wine directly down my throat, barely tasting it along the way.

"Ooh," says Mica gleefully. Logan reaches over and covers his mouth with this hand, his face holding back laughter.

"What guy?" he asks, glancing at Marcella.

Marcella leans forward. "The guy who helped Cass after the bike accident. Ellis."

"Ellis-euh?" Halabuji's accent comes out full force.

"He came into the office?" Marcella prods, looking at Halmoni.

She nods. "Yes, they went out together. But, of course, I thought nothing of it because he looks like a baby."

"You went *out* together?" Marcella's voice is at a pitch that would summon Betty the bird from her cage in Mount Washington. Everyone starts squealing.

"Calm down, please. He showed up yesterday making sure I was okay. Somehow he found out I work at One & Only since I'm practically invisible online. Anyway, I took him out for a coffee, no big deal." I pause. "Well, I wanted to take him, but he ended up paying."

Everyone looks smug, even Ozzie.

"Okay, okay. So, he's into you. I knew it. He was *so* concerned when all you did was scrape your knee." Marcella waves a finger in the air. The sign of drunk authority.

"Excuse me? I thought everyone here was concerned that I was going to *die*."

Marcella waves more aggressively. "You were fine, but Ellis was at your side like you were a Victorian maiden. How old is he, did you find out?"

"It doesn't matter because we won't see each other again." I reach for the kimchi. Everyone just stares at me, waiting. "He's twenty-eight."

A few gasps. Wes bellows, "Noice!" Baby Wally next to him screeches and throws a corncob into the middle of the table.

I laugh. "Exactly. So, let's all just drop it."

"Why? Twenty-eight is nothing," Marcella says.

Logan nods. "Yeah, a man your age wouldn't blink twice at dating a twenty-eight-year-old."

Marcella looks at him with fondness. "Good answer." He tilts his head to the side, and she plants a kiss on his cheek. That familiar tug in my chest.

"None of this matters, okay? He's not Daniel, he's too young, et cetera, et cetera."

"Since when does that stop you from having fun, though?" Marcella asks.

I think about it for a second. "I think turning forty is since when."

Logan nods. "I see that."

Marcella swats his arm. "No! Wrong answer. Forty is *nothing*."

"You just gave a huge toast about how forty means letting your boobs sag in the wild," I shoot back.

"Literally *when* did I say that?" Marcella ignores all the giggling children. The souls of the men at the table have left Earth. "I said forty is when you stop caring about what other people think. Which is what dating Ellis would be. Halmoni, don't 'at' me."

Halmoni shrugs as she eats a spoonful of rice dotted with purple beans. "Whatever that is, I won't. Cassia knows her fate. I will say nothing else."

Sunny and Stu exchange a glance that I catch because I notice everything. When you're a face reader, you learn to pay attention to the most minute movements in the face. Sunny looks at me then. "If he's cute, go for it. You're not forty forever. When you're sixty-six, you're going to wonder what the hell you were so hung up about."

"Thank you!" Marcella and Sunny clink their glasses loudly, sloshing their wine onto Mica's head between them.

Ellis's earnest brown eyes flash in my mind. His hands in his back pockets. That spark of awareness that crackled between us. A guy like that wouldn't be *serious* about dating, right? He's part of the Tinder generation. And also, *look* at him.

And then, like with most things in my life, destiny strikes. My phone vibrates, and when I look down I see that One & Only has a new follower on Instagram.

Ellis Yang-Cohen.

I catch Marcella's eye across the table. "I blame you if this all goes south."

She grins. "I am happy to take the credit when it all comes up roses, baby."

7

Ellis is active on social media. He posts at least every week, and mostly about plants.

I'm in my big reading chair by the window overlooking a canyon dotted with oaks and chaparral. I've lit several scented candles and am sipping from a mug of steaming decaf coffee. My foolproof method for sobering up before crawling into bed.

Betty is grooming herself and chirping happily for once as I scroll through Ellis's feed. He likes to document the progress he's making on the river restoration project. But he also likes taking pictures and videos of him and his friends going out, playing D&D, and eating food. His life looks full and wholesome and if I was thirty I would have dated the hell out of him. Daniel be damned.

But I am feeling time passing, that restlessness of wanting to get started on this lifetime partnership thing. It's a new feeling. My twenties and early thirties were busy and fulfilling—like the life Ellis shows on social media. I was too focused on having adventures and building my career to think about settling down.

In a way, the "when" of finding my fated is the only big unknown of my life. Other than, let's say, death. I've always known what I would be when I grew up—a matchmaker. I never had a moment of rebellion with it, like my mother. When Mom went to art school instead of working at the agency, Halmoni and she barely spoke to each other until she was pregnant with me. But with me, it was always clear what I wanted to do. I knew I wanted to end up with my fated—to have a love like my grandparents. Like Emoni and Sunny had. After I graduated high school, my grandparents sent me to travel around the world for a couple years and when I got back to L.A., I was ready to commit to the business.

According to his feed, Ellis has traveled some. One picture catches my eye. Mongolia? I look at the deep green meadows, the charcoal smudge of a sky. Mongolia is one of the more magical places I've visited, and I feel the sudden urge to talk to Ellis about it.

I assess the temperature of my cheeks with my palms. Am I still drunk? Logan drove us home after dinner because I was definitely drunk then. My cheeks feel warm to the touch. But not *hot*.

Suddenly I'm thirteen again, nervously gripping a phone before calling a crush. *Cass, get ahold of yourself. You are, like, middle-aged now*. Before I can rationalize myself out of it, I leave a comment on the Mongolia photo.

One of my favorite places in the world—C

Since I don't have a personal account, I have no choice but to comment from the agency's new account. Hopefully the "C" makes it clear it's me and not my grandmother.

Betty squawks like she knows I just did something embarrassing.

I'm putting my mug in the dishwasher and turning off the lights, when I see my phone light up on the counter. I grab it to see a DM waiting for me. My palms immediately start sweating.

"Grow the fuck up, Cass!" I actually say this out loud. Betty chirps in agreement.

Hi, C. You've been to Mongolia, too?

The worst thing about DMs is that the sender can see the exact second you've read it. Shit. The jig is up, I don't play things cool. I reply right away.

Yeah. Beautiful country.

He also replies immediately. I felt weirdly connected to it. Does that sound like an obnoxious thing a privileged white guy would say?

Maybe, but thank god your peasant Asian roots keep you humble

He sends me a crying laughing emoji in response and I can't help but smile. At my own joke, but also at making him internet-laugh.

I reply again: My grandfather is obsessed with Mongolian history because of our shared ancestry.

That shared ancestry being . . . invasion? 😬

What else?

There's a pause as he takes his time with his reply. I refuse to sit around for it so I start brushing my teeth. But then my phone buzzes.

Did you eat goat?

I reply immediately: Absolutely not.

Another laughing emoji. Fair. It was okay. Just had to get over it mentally.

I'm not an adventurous eater for an Asian. Kind of embarrassing. I like ordering kung pao chicken. I smile as I type this, knowing that somewhere the Asian foodie gods are disowning me.

Sometimes kpc is the only thing that will hit the spot.

100%

My toothpaste drips down my chin. I wipe it off and look at myself in the mirror. It's ten p.m. and I'm texting—no, not even texting, *DM-ing*—a twenty-eight-year-old. The weekend before I turn forty years old.

But I've spent a decade looking for Daniel. The past year with a private investigator. I'm not only feeling restless . . . but reckless, too.

Oh, hell.

What are you up to right now? My hands are clammy after I type it.

He takes a second . . . and then, Talking to you.

Shortly after, I send him my address and the lazy night routine takes a sharp U-turn. I dry brush my body vigorously before hopping in the shower and slathering myself with my most decadent and moisturizing bodywash. I want to smell like the most delicious thing this guy has ever had the pleasure of smelling. As I wash my hair with shampoo that costs more than wine, I realize I'm smiling. *Wow, ever get laid much, Cassia?*

But this birthday has just been so *heavy*. And everything about Ellis and this spontaneous hookup feels *light*. I hadn't realized I needed this until now. I take my razor and shave carefully under my arms. A routine that has gotten rusty, I admit. I know that I'm not supposed to care about body hair in this day and age, but I grew up in the nineties, the toxicity runs *deep*. And while I'm comfortable with how I look—I am still about to be naked in front of a guy twelve years younger than me.

"Stop saying twelve years," I say out loud to no one.

Because he's coming over, and there's no turning back now.

When I open the door, the first thing Ellis notices is Betty.

"Whoa. A bird."

She's on my shoulder, to be fair. "Say hi, Betty."

Ellis waits expectantly but she just stares at him. I laugh. "Sorry, she would never in a million years say hi to you. But, hi."

His eyes are immediately on mine. "Hi." His lashes are stupidly long and they lower slightly as he sweeps his gaze over me, drinking me in, like he did the other day at the office. My bare legs suddenly feel downright indecent, and I let out a nervous giggle. Like this is the first time I've ever invited a man over after bedtime.

I think about when I last did that and can't remember. "Come in."

He takes off his sneakers and while he's looking down, I get a good look at him. He's wearing a gray sweatshirt and slate-blue pants. His socks are orange. His hair is a little wet—like maybe he took a shower before he got here, too. When he straightens up, it's confirmed. He smells like soap.

"Would you like a drink?" I ask, already headed to the kitchen. Portishead is playing, sexily and obviously.

Betty swoops away and Ellis keeps his eyes on her when he says, "One, you having a free-range bird is awesome. And two, sure."

"What would you like?" I open the fridge, taking out a chilled bottle of pét-nat for myself. "I have wine, but I could also make you a martini or something with whiskey?"

He leans forward on the counter, his elbows sliding on the butcher-block countertop, watching me as I pull out a glass. "I'll have what she's having."

I feel his eyes on me every second I pour the wine in delicate tumblers and slide his across the countertop. "Have you even watched *When Harry Met Sally*?"

He clinks his glass against mine before answering. "Once."

"Mm," I say before taking a sip of the effervescent liquid. "I'm just grateful you know what I'm talking about."

"I'm not an alien." His eyes flash in amusement over his glass. Something about him maintaining eye contact while drinking is very charged. But maybe it's all charged because I clearly asked him to come over for one reason.

"So, what were you doing before I so rudely interrupted your evening?" I ask. "Playing beer pong?"

He laughs, low in his chest. "No, I was playing a video game."

I laugh then stop. "Wait, for real?"

He rolls his eyes with a lopsided grin. "Get over it." Then he looks around, taking in the house. "You have a cool place."

"Thanks," I say, looking at everything through his eyes. The plentiful windows I refuse to cover with curtains, the dark wood beams, the warm light of my many lamps reflecting off art and objects I've collected over the years. "Want a tour?"

"Hell yeah." His enthusiasm makes me smile.

We walk through the house with our glasses in hand, stopping at various spots where I point out fun architectural details, like the built-in nook in the hallway where telephone calls were made. Or the hidden little cubby in the laundry room for the iron. He does this thing where he runs his hands over everything, murmuring his appreciation. It's something I noticed at the café, too, the other day. This guy is very tactile; he likes to touch and taste and enjoy things.

This observation being, of course, absolutely inconsequential in any way.

When we reach my bedroom, I am properly fuzzy headed and from the pink in his cheeks, so is he. We kind of hover in the doorway, looking at the navy-painted walls, the brass light fixtures. My bed is large and soft and the sexy music from the living room is a light strain in this part of the house.

My bare feet touch the edge of my soft antique rug. I feel nervous suddenly. Ellis obviously showed interest in me the other day, but is it still there now that he's here? With me—a lady with her own house on the cusp of her fortieth birthday?

He reaches out and touches the tip of my nose. "Hi." It's playful and also like he's reading my mind somehow. Ellis knows how to relax, how to be normal. He's been quietly confident since the second he walked into my house. It makes me relax.

I reach out and touch the hot surface of his cheek. "Hi."

He tugs my ear, sending a zing down my body. "Hi."

I take a step back into my room, and tap both of his hands, then pull him along with me. "Hi."

He follows, and then runs his hand up my arm, cupping my elbow. "Hi."

I step closer and push my thumb into his generous bottom lip. "Hi."

His voice is less playful when he catches my thumb with his teeth. "Hi."

We're together in an instant, my hands in his hair, our bodies pressing into each other with an urgency that is, quite frankly, startling. Ellis kisses me with enthusiasm, putting his entire body into it, his lips warm and searching. His hands run over my back, my arms, and then cradle the back of my head. He slips his tongue into my mouth at the same time he pushes his fingers into my hair. I feel like I might burst into flames.

I didn't think it would be this good. He kisses me like it's his life's singular purpose.

I slip my hands under his sweatshirt. His skin is hot to the touch, and he jerks forward when he feels my cool fingers on his lower back. But then he steps back and pulls his sweatshirt off. It leaves his hair mussed and I reach out to touch it. "You have good hair," I murmur. Then I run my hand down the side of his face, down his neck, over his broad shoulders. He has the body of a guy who swims—lean but decidedly strong.

He pulls me in by the hips, until they bump against his and I feel exactly what he's feeling.

"So do you," he says as he grazes his lips on my hairline. I feel a firm tug on a lock of hair and it makes me feel crazy. Then one of his hands drags down and grazes my collarbone, dipping into the hollow of my button-down shirt. He touches the sky-blue edge of my lace bra then looks up at me, his eyes asking for permission. I nod.

He undresses me, in a hurry, so much so that he messes up the buttons and we both start laughing.

"Here, I've got it." I cover his hands with mine and push them aside. He plops onto the edge of the bed and watches me as I undress. I slide my shirt off and let it drop at my feet. His eyes rove over my body with appreciation, dark and serious. And it makes me feel good as I bend over and pull my cotton shorts down, leaving my scrap of lace briefs on. I walk over to him and he leans back on his hands, head tilted back to look at me with a soft smile.

"Hi, again." I straddle him, but he flips me over in an easy move that makes me catch my breath. He lays me down on the bed and we explore each other's bodies with a little less urgency, and I feel drunk and heavy as his lips skim over my skin. His very assured hands run up my legs and linger near the edge of my underwear. I lift myself up ever so slightly and he drags them off, his face buried in my neck. He lets out a little groan with a laugh. "I can't believe you're letting me do this."

I laugh back, and I'm surprised by it because everything we're doing is so absolutely hot that I couldn't have ever imagined little comedy breaks. "Yes, this is pure charity," I say before I suck in a breath, his fingers exploring, gentle but very, very confident. These aren't the fumbling, eager hands of the guys I dated in my twenties—this is someone who is taking his time, who is enjoying the experience.

Like he does with everything else.

His cheekbones are flushed, his eyelids at half-mast. His golden torso is tense, and I can feel his desire like a taut string. Something about seeing this beautiful guy so turned on makes me feel like the first woman to have ever done this, and it's heady. Then he drops down to the floor and pulls me to the edge of the bed and I let out a surprised "Oh!"

He grins at me from below, one of his incisors crooked and appealing. His hair is mussed and his chest red from my hands on him. "You okay there?"

"So okay," I say. We both laugh again, and he kisses the inside of my thigh with affection. Something about it is so sweet, not just sexy, but sweet, and my heart does a thing that I didn't expect—some squeezy skip that makes me feel like a teenager again.

He takes his time, way too languorous, and I can't stand it anymore. "Please," I gasp, grasping his hair.

I can feel his soft laugh on me, and it sends a wave of desire up my body. I'm about to lose it when he crawls back over me, pulling a condom out of thin air. His eyes ask the question and my body answers.

His teeth graze over a tender spot on my neck as our bodies move together, and I am done. My entire world narrows to the rhythm of our breaths, the taste of his skin, an overwhelming sensation of *yes*. There's nothing else—no past, no future, nothing—a sense of pure freedom. When I come undone, he's right there soon after and we find each other's lips at the same time.

8

Nothing goes according to plan.

I was going to gently kick Ellis out the next morning, with the grace of a seasoned lover, then go about my usual Sunday-morning routine: coffee (drip, healthy heaping of half-and-half, no sugar) and breakfast (scrambled eggs with chives and a slice of sourdough) by nine a.m.; yoga on the deck; laundry and a deep clean of the kitchen and bathroom before lunch. All while thinking back fondly on my hot one-night stand with a twenty-eight-year-old.

But I didn't know we'd reach for each other in the middle of the night, that he'd have me gasping on my back more than once in the early hours of the morning. That, at the crack of dawn, feeling him curled up behind me, we'd move together in a dreamlike state, until both of us were exhausted and passed out.

It's been a while since I've slept with someone, so I want to chalk up this obsessive state to neglect. But a voice in the back of my head is telling me that this is *good*. That this level of good has maybe never happened to me before.

When we actually wake up, it's almost noon. And we only get up because Betty is literally screaming at us from the other side of the closed bedroom door.

"Oh, shit." I scramble into a sitting position, the light unnaturally bright in my room. "I have to feed Betty." It's been years since I've overslept this hard. I didn't even know my body was physically capable of it.

But I'm gently pushed back down. I'm about to protest, like, I really need a sex break, my guy. But he just presses his lips to my forehead and gets up from bed, pulling on his crisp cotton boxer shorts. "Where's her food?"

He proceeds to feed my horrible bird, then makes coffee in the kitchen as I stretch out under my soft comforter, my body a giant relaxed noodle.

I'll take the coffee, then politely nudge him out.

The coffee arrives in a hand-thrown mug, a speckled brown and white one with an enormous and uncomfortable handle. A souvenir from Marcella's ceramics phase. I take it from Ellis with a grateful smile. "Mm, thank you."

He places the half-and-half and sugar bowl on my nightstand. "Not sure how you like it, so brought the usual suspects."

"Thanks," I say, pouring some cream into the mug, then peer at him over my cup. This guy looks great in the morning. His hair is tousled, shirtless in white boxers. Who even wears white undies? Risky as hell. His cheek has a red crease, and I reach out to touch it without thinking. He leans into it and something tugs low in my ribs. I try and ignore it.

"Your house is a real house," he says as he stretches with zero self-consciousness and I tear my eyes away from the delicious sight. "You have an espresso machine and a wine fridge. What else is lurking in your bespoke cabinetry—cloth napkins?"

His tone is teasing but not mocking and I smile. “I might even have scissors specifically for cutting poultry.”

His eyes roll back in bliss, and I laugh. Suddenly, Betty swoops in. “Hey!” I yelp. “How’d you get out?”

Ellis looks sheepish. “Um, I let her out. She looked so sad when I pet her.”

“Don’t let her fool you,” I say. Then pause. “Wait, she let you touch her?”

“Yeah.” He looks at her fondly as she lands on my dresser, preening in front of my mirror.

I look at her, at how comfortable she is around a new person. “That is very strange. She never lets anyone but me touch her. Many a friend has left here with broken skin.”

Her feathers fluff up in pride. Ellis looks surprised. “Really? She let me hold her, too.”

“What?” I am quite literally shook. “That’s . . . she barely tolerates my touch.”

“What can I say? The birds love me,” he says, joking.

But I assess him. Something about him brightens up every space he’s in. My room feels different with him in it. Betty is certainly basking in it. And try as I might, I can’t quite kick him out.

So we end up spending the day together. Even though it’s legit afternoon by the time we get out of bed, we make eggs and eat them on the deck, the afternoon sun feeling good. He marvels at the views of the canyon, the comfort of my red loungers. When a hawk flies overhead, his jaw drops. “It’s fucking incredible that you found this house.”

I think about people his age and how impossible it is to buy a house in Los Angeles proper unless you are obscenely wealthy. My house is modest, but it’s special. “I didn’t actually find this house. I grew up in it.”

He looks at me in surprise, one of my baseball caps shielding his eyes from the sun. "Really?"

"Yeah, with my mom." I realize that it's impossible not to talk about the big things when someone's in your home and very curious about everything about you. He's worn me down, this one. The food coma and sun conspire to make me talk too much. "Well, I kind of grew up here. She died when I was eight, and so I had to live with my grandparents after that. But they kept the house and saved it for me so I could decide whether to keep it or sell it once I was an adult. I kept it."

I don't look at him, but I can feel him looking at me. He's quiet for a moment. Then his hand reaches over and squeezes mine. "I'm sorry."

"Thank you," I say. And even though I'm used to people's sympathy and I've had decades of training for it, Ellis's gesture still touches me. That tug in my ribs is pulled tighter. "Maybe it's weird to live in the house that you grew up in with your dead mom, but it's also my strongest connection to her." I point to the hillside full of blossoming shrubs. "Those plants, for example—her favorite."

His eyes get wide. "Oh. I get it—that's why you're named Cassia."

"What?" I look at him in confusion.

"That plant, it's called Feathery Cassia."

I look at the yellow flowers, my throat feeling tight. "Really?"

"Yeah. What a cool name for you."

My eyes catch his and we smile at each other. I feel the tug in my ribs again and try to distract myself from the feeling. "What are your professional thoughts on my very remedial gardening skills?"

He looks at the various potted plants I have on the deck—some olive trees, bougainvillea, and tomatoes. There's a seed tray of geraniums waiting to be put into a bed. "It looks great. Very, uh, color coordinated?"

I laugh. "Listen, I have systems."

"I can tell. You had your records organized alphabetically. Which I noticed because you have them shelved with labeled dividers like a very normal person."

"Thank you," I say with a sniff.

I find him gazing at the geraniums. "Why don't we plant those today?"

"What?" I ask. "Oh, no. I don't have the right soil and the ones that haven't bloomed yet—I forget what color they're going to be so I don't know where they go."

Ellis stares at me.

"What?"

"Get up, we're doing this." He stands and holds his hands out to me so I'll take them. "We don't need fancy soil and it'll be fun for the blossom colors to be a surprise."

"Um, I don't know . . ."

He takes my hands and pulls me to my feet. "Listen to the professional." I grumble but follow him over to the plants, where my gardening supplies are laid out. He tosses me some gloves but doesn't wear any himself. When he pushes his bare hands into the dirt in my bed, I gasp. "But your hands!"

"Cass, god made dirt so dirt don't hurt."

I laugh. "Wow, haven't heard that one in a while."

He loosens up the dirt throughout the bed, the baseball cap pushed low on his forehead. "Nothing feels better than this to me." It's weirdly sensual the way he is touching the soil, and I clear my throat and grab a cobrahead to help him loosen up some of the roots that have managed to stay in the bed.

After we do that, he has me take out the geraniums and place them where I want them on the bed. "And remember, they don't have to be tidy rows. Just try to have them spaced out evenly."

He's very confident as he orders me around, but it's not annoying somehow.

When we're done, we stand and look at our handiwork, sweaty and a little out of breath. He has dirt smudged across his forehead and up his arms. That was a lot of geraniums. "Now, you just need to water these every few days and watch them thrive."

"Even in this old soil?"

He shrugs. "If they look like they're struggling, we can add some compost and stuff." The "we" isn't lost on me, and I wonder, just for a second, if there will be another time when he's over again. After that manual labor, I'm starving. So, dusting off my old spare bike for Ellis, we ride down to a taco truck at the bottom of my hill. Then the tacos make us want beer, so we swing by a liquor store and grab a frosty six-pack of Modelos and crack them open on my front porch. We talk about his childhood growing up in Queens, his older sister who used to beat up kids who looked at him funny. She's now a personal trainer with a wife and three kids.

"Ah, that explains it," I say when he talks about her.

"Explains what?"

"You have little-brother-of-a-sister energy."

He laughs. "Okay."

"It's a compliment. They are the best guys to date," I say with a grin.

"Date?"

"You know what I mean," I say with an eye roll.

He shows me photos of his nieces and nephew, and I genuinely look at each one with interest. They have his amber-flecked eyes and sweet expressions. And, in a moment of complete surprise, I see a future for him with his own children, and I know he'll be a wonderful dad. I can't tell if this is a face-reading thing or just an intuition thing. Either way, I am spooked by it and change the subject to his pet turtle who enjoyed swimming in the toilet.

In turn, I talk to him about my grandmother, Sunny, and Emoni. He wants to know everything about them and then admits to me, "I might be a little obsessed with old Asian people." I find out his Chinese grandparents died before he was born, and he's always had this idea of an extended family that would nourish his Chinese roots. He's envious that I had this matriarchal force my entire life, that my Koreanness is woven into me naturally. That I keep a rice cooker on my counter all the time, that I can understand Korean fluently even if I speak it like a toddler.

As the afternoon sun grows low in the sky and the bougainvillea starts to turn golden in its light, he sets me on top of the kitchen counter and reaches under my linen dress. He gets down on his knees, and I feel the breeze kick in through the open windows as I press back against the vintage cornflower-blue tiles and close my eyes. Which means that it's impossible, yet again, to kick him to the curb.

This is my birthday treat, I tell myself. This is what turning forty deserves. When it turns dark, I turn on the firepit on the deck and we sit in a chair together, me in his lap with a giant blanket wrapped around us. I've made us martinis with thinly sliced lemon peels curled into them, the glasses frosty and beading by the fire. We inevitably start kissing, under the stars with an owl hooting from a treetop deep in the canyon. The cold air feels like a baptism on my skin, the surface of my body intensely hot. I welcome it.

9

I drive us to K-Town that night and I worry that the spell of our fun weekend will be broken if we leave the invisible boundaries of my L.A. neighborhood. But we're both famished in that way that only a solid twenty-four hours of boning makes you and nothing but good Korean food will do the trick.

We park in a strip mall that is packed to the brim with cars even at ten p.m., leaving my car with a valet who has to be a Tetris master in order to make this work. The valet will cost three dollars, and I will tip heavily from bougie guilt. But it's all worth it for the hand-cut noodles that taste like they are pulled from the dreams of a starving person.

When we finally get seated in a booth, surrounded by drunk college kids and senior citizens alike, Ellis asks, "Okay, what should I order?"

"You only order the chicken kalguksu," I say bossily. You don't "experiment" with perfection. You don't "try out other things on the menu." I am evangelical about my Korean food. Don't you dare try to add cheese to anything related to kimchi or I will cut you. When our taciturn server comes to take our order, I order for us—two giant bowls of hand-cut noodles with shredded chicken, chunks of potatoes, and julienned curls of squash.

The side dishes arrive—thinly sliced pickled daikon radishes, marinated soybeans, and a potato salad with apple slices. Ellis's forearms brace the table as he leans forward to get a good look at all the banchan. "What are your favorites?"

"Favorite banchan?" I ask.

"Yeah. I love these guys," he says as he pokes his metal chopsticks into the sesame oil–marinated soybeans.

"What? *Those*?" I say with disgust.

He holds up a healthy amount between his chopsticks and waves them at me. "Yo, these are underrated af."

I close my eyes briefly. "Wow. Kongnamul described as underrated af. Never thought I'd see the day."

"It's true," he says between chewing. "They are the baseline banchan. Just a perfect light marinade *and* protein? God's gift."

His enthusiasm is contagious, and I laugh as I slide the kongnamul closer to him. "Help yourself. Me, I'm all about that potato salad."

"Oh, the workhorse of the banchan." He swipes a bit of the potato salad. "Really fills you up when the food's taking too long."

I point my chopsticks at him. "Exactly." I'm impressed by his Korean-food knowledge but honestly, anyone who lives in L.A. long enough becomes a Korean-food expert.

Our noodles come out in two giant metal bowls, steaming in glorious heaps. For a few seconds, we're quiet as we attack our food—pulling up scorching hot noodles and cooling them off, taking delicate sips of the cloudy chicken broth, making little piles of noodles topped with the pickled radish slices on our spoons.

"So, you had no plans today?" I finally ask between mouthfuls.

He makes a funny face at me. "This is my plan."

"You planned on . . . this?" I raise my eyebrow suggestively. "Pretty bold."

His cheeks turn red. It's adorable. "No, I mean . . . I don't really make plans. I go where the wind takes me."

A sobering wash of cold comes over me. Right. This guy has no obligations, his entire life is spread out before him like a wonderful buffet o' potential. Suddenly, the harsh lighting, the voices of the servers and diners—they all wake me up from the Ellis stupor I've been floating in for the past twenty-four hours.

"Mm, the wind," I say, distracted by the sudden jolt of reality. He seems to sense it immediately.

"But that doesn't mean that I wasn't really happy to hear from you last night," he says. "I was hoping you'd change your mind."

"Did I change my mind?" I raise my eyebrow, the playfulness not quite coming through.

A little line appears between his eyes. A line that will not take root in his face for another decade, at least. Mine is removed by an injection every few months. "What do you mean?"

I regret my sharpness. "I'm sorry, I didn't mean to be flip about it. But . . . this weekend. Will probably just be this weekend, right? I know you think it's silly for me to beat the 'but I'm turning forty' drum, but it's real. I personally can't go where the wind takes me. Certain biological things dictate decisions in my life." There's a tenseness in my body when I say this. It's the first time, ever, when dating anyone, that I've admitted to the fact that I probably want to have children one day. That, at some point, I have to commit to the idea and stop fucking around. And I've never admitted it because unless I was talking to Daniel Nam, it wouldn't matter. But something about Ellis makes me feel like I have to explain it. That he does matter, a little bit.

He is completely calm and serious when he says, "And what makes you think that I don't fit into certain biological things?"

The unintended euphemism makes both of us pause for a second. Then I say, "There's no way you want to have kids anytime soon."

"You don't know that," he says with a shrug. And it's so easy, so casual that it only reaffirms that he doesn't understand the weight of these kinds of decisions. Because when you're twenty-eight, they are still abstract.

"Even if you did, I can't gamble on the hope that maybe sometime in a few years, the guy I'm seeing might want to have kids," I say. "It's a really sobering reality for a lot of straight women. If we want a family, we have to be five steps ahead of men. We don't have the luxury of figuring it out as we go."

"I get that, I really do," he says earnestly. "But there's also room for romance, for the falling in love of it all."

The words are jarring, and then the tug in my ribs feels like it's yanking me forward and I physically sit back to put distance between us. His foot had been hooked with mine under the table, and I pull it away in the movement. Because what he's revealing is an intense belief in romance—the same that I have.

He puts his chopsticks down. "Listen, I'm not trying to coerce you. I just think that, even when you need to get down to business because of, ah, biological realities"—I make a face and he looks exasperated—"you know what I mean. Even then, there's a certain alchemy that can happen, and that sometimes it takes time to see if the experiment works." He pauses. "That sounds unromantic. Replace experiment with *magic*."

I laugh. If only he knew what I know about magic. "Do you think I don't believe in love? That's my literal job."

"Is it? Or is it matchmaking?" He also sits back and crosses his arms. Our food is getting cold between us.

The challenge in his tone is the first real bit of friction I feel from Ellis, and it's kind of intriguing. Is it about his male ego? Or something more deeply felt in his value system? "Matchmaking is ultimately about love. That's the whole point. Especially my agency—it's called 'One & Only' because we believe there is one right person out there for you."

"Just one?"

I hold back from being too adamant here, not wanting to hint at the truth. "Well, if there is more than one—the one we find you will be the last one."

"Pretty confident there," he says, a bit of cheekiness sneaking back into our serious shift.

"The one thing I have earned by living almost four decades is confidence in this one thing," I say with a smile.

He nods, his face softening. "I admire that. I wish I had it."

"You will."

"How do you know I'm any good at what I do?"

I stare at him, intently. "Hm. You've shown an incredible work ethic and, ah—quick ability to learn new skills in the time I've known you."

His face flames red and he ducks his head down to fiddle with his chopsticks. "Yeah, well. I think my parents would have something to say about my work ethic."

I tilt my head. "What do you mean?"

The chopsticks in his hands are turning into whittled-down pieces of wood. "Ah, nothing."

"You can't just bring up parental disappointment and not elaborate."

"They're not disappointed," he says quickly. "They are annoyingly always supportive."

"Wow. Big problems."

He flicks the chopstick wrapper at me. "But you know, they were worried for a while because I was kind of nomadic. Going from one job to another until this one."

"You seem really into your current job, though," I say, remembering the way he lit up when he talked about it at the coffee shop.

"I am into it," he says with assurance, voice earnest again. "But it's something I discovered, didn't pursue. Anyway, I'm the baby in a family full of very type A people."

"Does that bother you?"

He looks thoughtful. "No. Sometimes the role you play is a burden, but mine is pretty true to me. Life is short—I'm okay with the unexpected. I think the unexpected brings some of the most meaningful experiences."

My mouth hitches up in a smile as our eyes catch. The subtext isn't lost on me.

When we get back to my house, suddenly I see it: his sweatshirt thrown on the floor. The way he kind of kicks his shoes into the general vicinity of my shoe rack. This guy does go where the wind takes him, and I feel his youth like it's a palpable thing I can hold in my hands. There's a little warning bell there.

But that's a problem for Tomorrow Cassia. My clothes end up next to his, leaving a trail to the bedroom.

10

My birthday begins with realizing that Ellis is curled into an angle that has his head at my hip level. My fingers graze the silk of his hair. It is whisper soft—his entire face is soft, relaxed in its easy sleep.

I slither each limb out from under him and then silently walk to my bathroom. When I close the door with the gentlest of *snick*s, Betty starts her devil's cry. Damn it.

When I'm done with the bathroom, I step out to see Ellis is sitting up, my crisp linen duvet bunched around his waist. His face cracks into a smile that makes me want to jump back in bed with him. But I resist. It's Monday. Birthday road trip day. Enough is enough. Time to end this cold turkey.

"Hi." His voice is scratchy with sleep, heavy with intimacy.

I lean against the doorway, in a scalloped cami and boy briefs set. "Hi. Would you like some coffee?" I ask, heading to the kitchen. But his hand reaches out and rests on my hip. A little tug.

"Hey, come here." His head is tilted back ever so slightly. It's so cute I cannot resist and walk over to him until both his hands are on my hips, his thumbs lightly stroking the skin above my bottoms. "Good morning."

"Good morning." I run my hand through his hair then, and I feel the softest of sighs against me as he closes his eyes.

"Black coffee?" I ask.

He nods and presses a kiss into my palm and I'm surprised by my reaction to it—the surge of pure affection. My heart does that squeezy skip thing again.

I give his silver chain a little tug, then pull away and pad into the kitchen.

A few minutes later he joins me, having put on his sweatshirt, but still in his boxers on the bottom. We take our coffee on the deck again, enjoying actual morning today.

After a few peaceful moments, the sun starts to feel hot, and I take that as a sign. "Hey. Let's get you dressed for work. I have to head out for my road trip soon."

"Wait. Your *birthday* road trip?"

"Yup." I stretch my arms, and he glances at the stretch of skin exposed above my shorts for a second before his eyes slide back up to mine.

"Does that mean today's your birthday?"

I touch the tip of my nose. "Ding-ding."

We get inside and put Betty back in her cage. "I feel like we need to celebrate somehow," Ellis says putting his mug in the dishwasher. So comfortable and easy like he's lived here his whole life.

"We did."

Ellis grins—dimples appearing along with an adorable pink on his cheeks—but quickly shakes his head. "No, I mean, that was a mutually beneficial—argh. You know what I mean. I would have made us breakfast, or gone out and bought some flowers—"

I stop him. "Hey. This is fine. You're not my boyfriend, I don't have any expectations from you, okay? You're good."

Something flickers in his expression, a flash of hurt. I have to ignore it. "Thank you, though. You're very sweet."

He must feel the door close on this discussion because he goes to change without any more resistance.

I already packed for my trip so once I'm dressed, in denim overalls over the same white cami with my high-top Chucks, I'm ready to head out. Betty is safely back inside, and my next-door neighbor, a surly teenager with a perplexing affinity for Betty, will be taking care of her for the three days I'm gone.

I'm loading up my hybrid wagon with my duffel, camping gear, and a cooler full of La Croix and white wine, when someone lets out a quick succession of staccato honks as they drive up to my house.

"Get in loser, we're going camping!" It's Sunny in her outrageously fast convertible, idling at the curb.

Shit. I glance back toward the house. The perils of having family all up in your business all the time is the unannounced goddamn drop-ins. "Sunny, what the hell?" I say it with a smile, trying to keep the irritation out of my voice. "You're on the east side before noon?"

She makes a face. "I know. But I wanted to see you off for your birthday trip." And then she reaches over to the passenger side and hands me a single, beautiful chocolate cupcake.

"Thanks, Sunny, you really didn't have to," I say. It's sweet and I feel bad, but I really need her out of here before—

Sunny's eyebrows lift, and she pushes her sunglasses onto the top of her head. "Oh, hi there."

Damn.

Ellis walks up behind me. "Hi." He looks nervous. He's arranged his hair a little more neatly, now wearing his gray sweatshirt with his artfully slouchy pants. His sneakers are something cool and mysterious to me. He looks like an ice-cold glass of sparkling water come to life.

I try to look easy-breezy. "Sunny, this is Ellis, you might remember him—"

"Of course, the strapping young man who rescued you," she says with a shit-eating grin.

Ellis flushes and I rescue him. "And, Ellis, you remember my aunt, Sunny. She was just on her way, right?"

She's still smiling. "Yeah, yeah. Did you figure out where you're going this year?"

"Yeah, heading to the desert," I say.

"Wait. Joshua Tree?" Ellis asks, his expression very alert suddenly.

"Yeah. Did I mention that already?"

He laughs, low and ironically. "You didn't. But we're taking a work trip there this week."

"What? Are you serious?"

"Yeah. We do one of these every year for bonding but also for checking out different climates and landscape ideas."

I take a deep breath. My birthday road trip is supposed to be one of extreme loner hermit vibes. Just knowing Ellis will be in the same area will put things off kilter. Suddenly I very much regret listening to Marcella's "slut around" advice.

Sunny lets out a laugh. "That's my cue to run. Happy birthday, Cass. Love you."

I reach over to give her a kiss on the cheek and then she's off in a zippy zoom around the bend.

When she's gone, Ellis turns to me. "Hey, I won't come looking for you, if that's what you're worried about." Ellis says this lightly, but I can feel the strain behind it. I've probably hurt his feelings. Again.

"I'm not," I say with a smile. "Have a good trip."

"You, too."

I'm about to step into the car when he says, "Wait."

When I turn he's right there. He slides his hand behind my neck, cupping my head. "Happy birthday," he whispers, his lips hovering right above mine.

I make a slight movement forward to encourage him and he presses his lips to mine in a confident, soft kiss that hits me like a wave—reminding me immediately of how he was last night. Completely focused and enthusiastic.

When he pulls back, I almost say, "Fuck it," and pull him back into the house. But it's almost nine and I really have to hit the road. "Bye," I say, touching his cheek briefly.

He's waving at me while I back out. And then he stays there in my driveway. I roll down my window. "Where's your car?"

"I took an Uber here the other night," he says somewhat sheepishly. "I was kind of drunk already when we were texting."

That feels like a million years ago. "Are you waiting for one right now?" I ask, looking down the street. He nods.

"Cancel your ride. I'm dropping you off." I park and unlock the doors.

He hesitates. "Are you sure?"

"Yes! In my day we didn't take Ubers, we made our friends pick us up from LAX during rush hour. Get in."

We drive down the windy hillside with the windows open. "I appreciate it," he says. "I know this is cutting into your birthday trip."

"Hardly, don't even worry about it." I point to the car's touch screen. "Want to plug in the address? Your work, right?"

"Oh, you can just take San Fernando all the way to Fletcher. We're in Silver Lake, I can just tell you how to get there."

I appreciate this, a guy who knows how to navigate. And he does it well, with patience and competence. All these moments of appreciation add up to a realization: If, and it's a big if, I don't find Daniel anytime soon . . . Ellis. Ellis is pretty damn great. It's a little scary to think of another option, but there's no denying we've had an amazing weekend. That maybe we could have many more.

We're driving alongside the Silver Lake Reservoir when he asks, "When did you start this birthday trip tradition?"

"Hmm, twenty years ago, I think? Wow, that's a long time." I am about to do the math to see how old he would have been then but stop myself from that particular torture.

"Can I ask why you do it?"

I'm not ready to give him the answer and my silence is met with understanding. He nods. "We don't have to get into it."

"Thanks."

Soon after, we pull up to his office, a tasteful two-story mid-century situation tucked behind greenery on a corner off of Sunset.

"Thanks for the ride," he says. "And happy birthday again."

"You're very welcome. And thank you."

There's a moment where we both wonder if we should kiss or if that would be overkill at his place of work. He makes the decision—he gives me a quick, firm kiss on the lips then swiftly gets out of the car. He's about to close the door when someone shouts his name. It's a man walking toward the building in efficient, hurried strides. He's wearing black wayfarer sunglasses and a crisp white shirt rolled up at the sleeves. When he reaches Ellis, the two exchange a fist bump and I can see that the guy is Asian, as well.

"Morning," he says to Ellis, then peers into the car at me. "Hello there." He has a British accent.

I wave. "Hi."

"Oh, sorry, this is Cassia," Ellis says, his arm sweeping toward me. "Cass, this is my boss, Daniel."

The world stutters around me. I push my sunglasses to the top of my head to get a good look at this man. “Daniel?”

Daniel smiles uncertainly. “Yes? Have we met?”

My extremities are starting to go numb. “Possibly. Daniel . . . ?”

“Nam-Watson.”

11

I was thirty when Halmoni gave me the piece of paper with Daniel Nam's name stitched into it.

"Do you want to know what I saw? To know more about your past life?" Halmoni had asked as I held the piece of paper in my hands, my heart beating so furiously that I thought I might actually have a heart attack.

I wasn't sure. It seemed like a no-brainer. Who *wouldn't* want to know about their past life? But I also felt a warning rolling into the atmosphere, like the moments before a storm. A voice whispering, *This path leads to destruction*. Well, close to that, maybe not as dramatic. So, I shook my head.

Halmoni pushed my hair back from my face. "You're going to have a wonderful love story, Cassia."

I believed her. And looked at the paper: *Daniel Nam*.

Even as, year after year, we failed to find him, I believed her. This wasn't that unusual, sometimes it took us weeks, months, and even years to find someone's fated. People got plastic surgery, changed their names, moved suddenly. Some weren't even alive anymore. In those cases, we reimbursed our clients and told them we couldn't find a match. The rule of the agency was, unless we found their fated, we would not match our clients with anyone else. We were One & Only after all.

But I kept my faith, because I saw the successful matches day after day. Saw it in my family. I knew it would happen. I just had to keep looking and not waver.

And now it had happened.

I found him.

I'm on the road, my windows rolled down, sitting with Daniel's face imprinted in my brain, like a burn left on a device, the ghost of his face following every thought I've had since I left him and Ellis.

Once I realized who I was meeting, I was so flustered that I sped up our goodbye and turned my cheek ever so slightly when Ellis leaned in for another kiss. His eyes had pierced into mine wonderingly and I had driven off so fast that I probably left a trail of literal fire behind me. I can't believe Daniel is *Ellis's* boss.

But I shouldn't be baffled by the luck of it all. Because I've known my entire life that luck isn't real. That everything is meant to be.

That even having your mother die on your eighth birthday was already in the cards.

But the shock of it—his connection to Ellis—that's what I can't get over.

Siri tells me that I'm only four hundred feet away from my destination, and I snap out of it long enough to see the sign for the ranch. I drive between rough-hewn wood posts and dust is kicked up by my tires.

This year, I decided to screw roughing it and picked a high-end yurt hotel to stay in. I pull up to my yurt, located in the very back of the park, at the end of the dirt road. The other yurts are conspicuously empty but it's still early—just shy of noon, and a Monday. If there are other campers, they'll probably trickle in later when the workday ends.

The sky is white-blue and endless and there are low scrubby hills surrounding me. The horizon is dotted with Joshua trees—alien-like and twisted and completely original. My yurt is huge, with a bed and sofa, and there's a sink and barbecue grill outside. A picnic table and lounge chairs are arranged next to a firepit.

It's completely peaceful and solitary. Exactly what I need.

After I make quick work of unpacking, I pull out a bottle of chilled Sancerre and pop it open. I consider pouring it into a plastic tumbler for a second before I plop down onto an outdoor lounger and take a swig directly from the bottle. My legs are propped up on the chair and I stare out into the expanse of sky.

Daniel Nam. Found him at last. On my fortieth damn birthday, no less. The day after I slept with his employee. Not just once . . . but so many times I think I've lost count.

Oh, god.

The wine is ice-cold and I press the bottle to my forehead. I have to figure out how to untangle this mess. Luckily, it was just one weekend. Ellis is young, he'll bounce back from a random woman he spent a weekend with. Even if she starts dating his boss. Right?

Right.

But I need to give it a beat. Fling or not, Ellis deserves better than an unceremonious dumping for his boss.

His *boss*. I know where to find Daniel now. This is the first step. A buzz starts beneath my skin. This is the beginning of everything.

One of my rules during my birthday trips is to put my phone on silent and ignore it unless it's for practical purposes. But this year everything is different. I google Ellis to start and find the name of the firm he works for—Watson and Associates. *Watson*. It's missing the "Nam." This makes sense, why I never found him. I quickly read the "About" page on the company's website, which reveals that Daniel founded the landscape architecture firm eight years ago after working in the industry for a decade. Eighteen years of work. This means he's probably close to my age. He studied landscape architecture at Berkeley. He was born in England. As evident from his, frankly, hot accent.

Maybe, in addition to the name thing, that's why I had such a hard time finding him? Geographical blip? Maybe I wasn't meant to find him until now.

Either way, he's been under my nose for eight years.

I peruse his LinkedIn profile, the middle-aged equivalent of social media, but can't find any other online presence. Maybe he, like me, is stubborn about social media. It intrigues me. Everything about Daniel intrigues me. And now, I have to wait three nights before I can do anything about it. Soulmate be damned.

A text comes in as I stare at Daniel's résumé—Ellis.

> Hope you made it to JT ok. Proof of life desert pic appreciated ✌️

Ellis is conspiring to kill me one sweet gesture at a time. I do put my phone aside then. Birthday hermit mode initiated.

This is my day. My mom's day. I refuse to let romance get in the way of it.

My first afternoon is spent at a nearby hot spring, so for my second day I decide to go on a couple local trails and check out the wildflowers in bloom. By the time I return to camp, the sky is beginning to turn lavender. After a quick rinse in the outdoor shower, I'm starting to make dinner when cars roll into the other camps. Dust kicks up along the road and reaches me in a rolling mass as I'm making my bonfire.

I cover my eyes and cough. What the hell, did everyone in these camps decide to arrive at once? Like a big . . .

Group.

A big group coming to bond together over the week.

My back is so straight I can probably snap it in half as I peer out at the rest of the yurts. People start getting out—noticeably all adults and no children. They unpack between laughter and shouts at each other. My eyes skim the camp closest to mine. Two young women, both of them trying to get cell reception, holding their phones high in the air, wearing their Patagonia finery. I walk down the path to the next camp. Two men—one older white man with a bald spot and a younger Latino one wearing paint-splattered Dickies. This feels like the kind of motley crew that only an office or jury duty can create. The prick of dread grows into something heavy and leaden. And in the third camp, I spot him.

Ellis is grabbing something from the trunk of a black Jeep when he notices me. He stills—then grins. Oof, that smile. Gonna be hard to let go of that one.

"Are you for real?" he asks, walking over to me in quick strides, a backpack slung over his shoulder.

"Are *you* for real?" I ask, keeping my voice teasing but feeling every ounce of blood pump through the veins in my body.

"Wow, what are the chances?" He's so excited by the coincidence, but I know the truth. There are no chances.

"Which site are you in?" he asks, craning his neck.

"Ten, the very last one available."

His eyes are twinkling when they meet mine, his smile crooked—exuding intimacy and innuendo.

"El—no way you got your girlfriend to meet us here."

My eyes whip over to the sound of the voice. Daniel is walking toward us, his sunglasses hooked into the front of his half-zip. I finally get a good look at him, at his face.

He has what could only be called leading-man good looks. I suck in a breath at his jawline, the thick Clark Kent black hair, the well-managed physique. The devastating white smile with straight teeth that have no right being on a British person.

"I wish I was that slick," Ellis says with a laugh. "Cass booked this spot unknowingly."

I notice he doesn't correct "girlfriend."

"Sorry, you'll be stuck with us," Daniel says with another knockout smile.

"However will I manage?" The flirting is swift, instinctual. Every part of me is aware of this man. The connection is so real, so clear.

A pull on my overall strap. I look over to see Ellis's serious expression and I wonder if he senses my antenna tuned to Daniel. But he says, "Are you sure it's okay we're here? I know this trip is supposed to be private."

My antenna is going haywire. I soften and put my hand on his arm. "Don't worry about it. I'll be out hiking and doing my own thing."

"Okay, but seriously let us know if we're being obnoxious. Things can get rowdy."

"This lot is buttoned-up, but give it 'til sundown," Daniel says with a wink. "Cheers, Cassia." He walks off, his hiking boots crunching the sand. Hearing my name coming out of his mouth makes me legitimately speechless.

"I should probably . . ." Ellis waves at his yurt.

"Yeah, go!" I push him gently. "I'm just starting my fire."

"Can I come visit you?" he asks, a small smile hovering over his lips.

I clench my hands in my pockets. This is going to be painful. Every part of it. "Sure. Um, maybe after dinner?"

He nods, moves in as if he's going to kiss me on the cheek but thinks better of it. He looks apologetic. "Work people."

"I know." I smile, staving off the panic of the next couple days.

12

They *are* loud. Their voices carry in the arid desert air. Laughter and screams pierce the distance as I sit with my glass of wine and paperback copy of *The Secret Garden*. I always pick a childhood book for these trips—to transport me back to my old bedroom with the star reading light, a papier-mâché contraption that my mom made and hung over my bed for my late-night reading habits.

I read the same paragraph about Colin's hump for the third time when a glowing light catches my eye. It gets closer and I realize it's Ellis holding a lantern.

"Evenin'," he says in a funny little drawl.

"Evenin'." I watch as he approaches me, a little hop in his step. So excited to see me—and a part of me crumbles.

"Sorry to interrupt," he says. "Is this a good time?"

"Of course."

"We have so much booze and food and it's getting late so . . ." He waggles his eyebrows. "Would you like to join us?"

It feels surly to say no. And there's no denying that it's been near torture sitting here mere steps away from a man I have spent a decade waiting for.

"What kind of wine do you have?" But I'm already putting my book down and getting up.

He shrugs. "Sorry, I am the least helpful person about alcohol of any sort. I drink what is given to me. But I know we've got some fancy assholes in our office, and they would not be serving you sub-par stuff. Especially if Daniel's around."

I tuck that little bit of info away. *Fellow wine slut.*

A few minutes later, I'm bundled up in a fleece jacket I stole from an ex-boyfriend in Chile, and wearing a headlamp. The thing about fateds is that they will somehow fall in love with you despite your very unsexy outfit. I do, however, put on some tinted lip gloss and a swipe of blush. I'm not delusional.

We start the walk down to their camp together, and Ellis asks, "*The Secret Garden*, huh?"

"Mm-hmm."

"*Mary, Mary, quite contrary.*" He keeps the lantern held between us even though I can see perfectly fine with my headlamp. The desert is almost pitch-black, but the stars are scattered and give off a diffusion of light that reminds me of those stickers kids used to put on their ceilings.

A smile hitches on my lips. "Wow, you being familiar with the works of Frances Hodgson Burnett wasn't on my bingo card."

"I have an older sister, remember?" The lantern swings between us, our shadows long and entwined. "I know all the greatest hits. The BSC, *The Little Princess*, Margaret and her period, being Team Jacob, and knowing firmly that I, too, would be divergent."

"Did you actually read them, though?"

He stops walking, and his expression is one of mock indignation. "Did I *read* them? No, I just burned them in a fire as I popped wheelies around the raging flames."

I burst out laughing. "Okay, okay! You were 'not like all the other boys.'"

"Nah, I was. I was embarrassed about reading them so I did it in secret. But I was just a voracious reader in general. Still am, I guess."

I am not Rory Gilmore, and this kid is not going to seduce me with dog-eared copies of Bukowski. He will *not*. There is a grown man at the end of this path who enjoys good wine and is handsome in a way that makes me literally weak-kneed. The stars remind me to stay on course.

The camp is still rowdy. People are dancing, mostly swaying, to some Pearl Jam. A few are piled up on a blanket, like teenagers giggling at a slumber party, staring at the stars.

Daniel's sitting on a literal log playing a literal guitar.

Part of me wonders if, somehow, I got secondhand high. It's hard to explain, but this entire scene is just so *Fraggle Rock*. Daniel spots us first, and grins. "Ah, you managed to woo her back here."

This reminds me of his earlier, easy comment about me being Ellis's girlfriend. "No wooing necessary," I say. Also easily. My body moves just the slightest bit away from Ellis, and I snap off my headlamp.

"Welcome to day one of . . . this," Daniel says with a grimace. "We're usually a really proper bunch."

"This actually looks extremely peaceful for a drunk work retreat." There are two men attempting to balance lightweight tent poles in their palms.

Ellis and Daniel exchange glances.

"What?" I ask.

"I would say people are more—high. Than drunk." Daniel clears his throat.

"What, weed? Sir, I don't know if you're aware that marijuana has been legal here for quite some time," I say with mock gravity.

Ellis pulls something out of his pocket. "It's not weed."

Part of me fills with trepidation. Then I see what's inside.

"Oh, shrooms." There's relief in my voice which makes them both laugh. "Ah, I was scared you were going to hand me some kind of acid-laced wafer with a religious logo stamped into it."

Ellis shakes his head, laughing. "That is so specific."

We're smiling at each other for too long and I open the bag. "Shall I?"

"If you want," Ellis says. "Obviously no pressure. We're not a cult."

"The more times you say that the less I'm going to believe it." I take one piece. I've done this before in the desert, on a crafting retreat with Marcella and a couple of her college friends. At the time, I couldn't tell if the shrooms were there to make the crafting more interesting or if the crafting was just an excuse to take the shrooms. Either way, it was a good time and I could use a good time right about now—wedged between two men, one of whom I had lots of sex with, and the other of whom is my fated. Casual.

After I pop it in my mouth, Ellis hands me a cup of wine. I take it gratefully, the smooth red washing out the mild earthy flavor of the mushrooms. "Mm. This *is* good."

Daniel lights up. "Oh, I'm glad you like it. It's an organic red blend that always tastes better chilled."

"It's perfect and I want to have it come out of a tap in my home." I lift my glass to him. He lifts his, and that's when I get a nice long look at his left hand and notice that there is no wedding band. Something I hadn't even considered until this very moment, and a belated sense of relief rushes through me as I take another sip of wine.

Something passes between us—a low frisson of mystery. His eyes stay on mine for a moment, dark brown and thoughtful, before he puts his guitar down. "Take a seat and *please* drink the wine.

Some of the interns have been guzzling this like bloody juice and it makes me want to cry."

Before I can look for a chair, one is procured for me by Ellis. He's carrying two spindly yet efficient camp chairs under his arms. "Thanks." I sit down, facing the fire.

Daniel gets up and hollers, "Everyone, this is Ellis's friend Cassia. Be nice and be normal human beings, please and thank you."

Everyone hoots and hollers. A woman who looks to be around Ellis's age, with a cute French bob and perfectly slouched Kelly green sweatshirt, whoops, "Ooooh, *this* is Cassia."

The man next to her, the older one from the campsite I saw earlier, looks perplexed. "Wait, you invited her here? Already? After one date?"

Ellis is slouched low in his chair, taking a long pull from a beer bottle. "Please, everyone die right this instant."

It's endearing, if alarming. I wave with a small smile. "Hi. I just took a single mushroom."

Everyone laughs and cheers. "One of us!" some young person far away from me yells.

And within half an hour, I am so relaxed I can't remember how my birthday ever bothered me. Yes, my mother died. But Jesus Christ, woman, it happened thirty-two years ago! You've been in therapy for half your life, and you have the most loving family in the world. You have magical abilities that let you kinda time travel and help people find love. You have an *incredible* life.

And you are sitting between two very attractive men who seem to be giving off some very particular vibes.

End second-person mushroom narration.

"So, you are all, like, really into plants," I announce.

There's laughter and Ellis's is loudest. This guy makes me feel like John Mulaney.

"Some of us were into plants since childhood," a guy named Max says, pointing at himself. "And some of us are like this asshole who just showed a natural proficiency in plants and design." He's looking at Ellis.

"Really?" I look at him.

"Okay, he's exaggerating," Ellis says with a shake of his head, but his tone is good-natured. He is relaxed, stretched out in his seat with one of his arms lightly draped behind my chair. I feel his fingers brush against the back of my neck on occasion and it's all just very nice.

"When I found you on the streets of Los Angeles, you were canvassing for an MP who later got caught having not one, but *three* orgies with various staffers," Daniel says.

Everyone starts laughing, in this familiar way, as if this is not the first time this story has been discussed.

"Oh my god," Ellis says. "First of all, it's congressman, not *MP*, you British dork. Second, I didn't know that *at the time*. He supported universal childcare."

Fondness overcomes me and I find myself snuggling into Ellis. Even though Daniel is *right there*. Damn these fungi! "Did you want to go into politics?" I ask.

He shrugged. "Yeah. I was young and impassioned."

"As opposed to now—wrinkled and disaffected," I tease.

Daniel grins from across the fire. "But I literally did run into him outside of a grocery store one day, canvassing. He was so winning and persuasive, I actually donated money to the bloke's campaign. And then I asked El if he wanted to intern for me."

Green-sweatshirt girl rolls her eyes. "That's how the bromance started. These two are disgusting."

"I treat all my employees equally," Daniel protests.

"Yeah, but Ellis is your special best boy," Max says.

Everyone laughs but I look at Ellis with surprise. "Wait, so you didn't go to school to do this job?"

He shakes his head. "Nope. I barely knew the difference between a pine tree and a ficus when I started here. Daniel taught me everything I know." It's kind of said jokingly, but I can sense the earnestness behind it. "My major in college was Latin."

"What?" It almost sobers me, that revelation. "What in the hell? Who *are* you?"

Everyone laughs again but I'm kind of serious. This guy—he truly does go where the wind takes him.

"I wanted to go to college to learn shit," he says, in a lower voice, a conversation just between us now. "But when I started interning at Watson and Associates, something clicked. I knew this was a job I could love."

"And do you? Love it?" I ask.

"I really do. I owe Daniel a lot," he says with a fond glance over at him. "He's gone above and beyond for me."

Oh, god. I was going to now get in between two men who were pretty much in love with each other.

Again, that's a problem for Future Cassia. The night continues, the guitar strumming, the stars bright in the sky. At one point, someone asks me how I ended up in Joshua Tree, and I explain my birthday tradition.

Which then, of course, prompts a rousing and terrible rendition of "Happy Birthday." Ellis brings me a pot brownie with a candle stuck in it that I blow out. "Thank you," I say with a laugh, passing on the brownie. I don't need to be completely wrecked tonight.

"You do this *every* year?" Daniel asks as he strums lightly on his guitar. In my current state, I don't find this embarrassing. He holds the guitar like a natural part of his body. Like it's a hobby but one he's had as long as I've been in therapy. And it's nice to hear in the middle of nowhere, the air dry as bone and cold as hell. The fire crackles and almost everyone is huddled around it in various states of wellness.

I poke at the fire with a long stick. Earlier, I had stared at this stick for what felt like hours, marveling at the intricacies of *wood*. I almost called my grandfather to talk about it, but Ellis gently moved my phone out of reach. "Yeah, I've been doing this every year since I turned . . . twenty? So, a long time."

"Ten years, then?" Daniel says with a put-on innocence.

"Ha." I look up at him across the fire, feeling *merry*. "Nice try, fellow Asian. If I look thirty, I'm probably a retiree."

Ellis shakes his head. "Cass, you have no idea what you look like."

I catch the infatuation under the words and shoot a quick glance at him. Mm. Still cute. Probably still very good in bed.

Still very much twelve years younger than me. I think of a line from *Beautiful Girls*, one of my favorite movies. Noah Emmerich is making fun of Timothy Hutton's character for having weird vibes with teenage Natalie Portman (it was the nineties, okay?) and says, "The girl was a zygote when you were in the seventh grade."

Yikes.

But the uncomfortable moment passes, because I simply can't be negative right now while feeling so great. I feel like I am at the peak of a good wine buzz. Maybe it's the company. The desert sky. The sounds of other happy people around me.

"God, I would kill for a taco right now," someone grumbles nearby.

"You always want tacos," Daniel says with good humor.

"That's because tacos are the perfect food," the grumbler, I think his name is Parker, says.

"Name one item of food you can grab within five minutes that is as perfect as the carne asada taco," Ellis says boldly.

"Hear, hear!" someone shouts.

"Wait. A Filet-O-Fish," a man in his thirties says. He's wearing sunglasses in the dark and drinking what looks like a "hard kombucha."

"FILET. O. FISH?" green-sweatshirt girl screeches. "Get the fuck outta here."

It becomes a chaotic fast-food standoff, and I am laughing so hard. Ellis leans his head toward me and says, "Let's bail before they start a fight club."

Some fuzzy part of me knows that I shouldn't. That Daniel is *right there* and showing interest in me. But the part of me that is so happy and following every whim gets up with him, his hand gripping mine with assurance.

13

We leave the debate behind us and walk into the desert. The night sky is velvet-blue and feels like a weighted blanket for the soul.

"I'm glad you're here," Ellis says simply.

Our clasped hands swing between us with our slow, unhurried steps out into the abyss. "I'm glad, too."

"Glad to be here, or here with *me*?" He's teasing but it's also serious.

"Both." I look up at the stars. "I take this trip alone because I always tell myself it makes me feel closer to my mom. But if I'm being completely honest . . . it doesn't."

He squeezes my hand. I squeeze back and say, "She died on my birthday."

His step falters and he grips my hand again. "Oh, god." My little squeeze messages to him that it's okay but he is quiet as we keep walking.

I'm not someone who keeps my feelings bottled up inside, who avoids living in the hard emotions. But it's rare that I talk about my mom's death. If only because, with time, my childhood feels both far away and painfully oppressive. Mar knows about it; we've had a few drunken nights of emotional unburdening. But never with my aunts and grandparents. It's to protect them, but also myself. I don't know what will come out, and with how much velocity, and if it'll cause more damage than healing.

But Ellis feels so far removed from that fear. In fact, he feels safe. So I start talking.

"It was a school day, but she had made me birthday eggs. We didn't do shit like pancakes for breakfast because neither of us had a sweet tooth. Birthday eggs involved ketchup happy faces and hearts and eight candles. My mom was an artist—not in some abstract, looking-back-fondly-on-my-mother's-quirky-crafts kind of thing. She worked in animation. She designed some characters you probably know from your childhood. Maybe not, considering you're a zygote."

At this he doesn't even react, that's how deadly serious he's taking my monologue. I continue, "She took the day off from work because she always did that on my birthday. I often think about that because—well, we'll get to it. She dropped me off at school that morning, in her cool beat-up old Jeep—she never cared what anyone else thought. Anyway, she dropped me off and I really hate that I don't remember what her last words to me were. Probably 'Bye!' if I'm being real. She told me she loved me all the time, so that's a possibility, too. But maybe I deny myself that version because it's too brutal."

We are just walking, walking through the desert. And I can feel every star in the sky, and the love of the universe wrap me up. I keep going.

"My class sang 'Happy Birthday' to me that day and my best friend, Jennifer Rivera, made me a daisy-chain crown at recess. And then, sometime after lunch, the principal came into our classroom and looked straight at me. I don't remember a lot after that because, you know, traumatic. But I do remember my teacher, Ms. Lark, had tears in her eyes when she took me out of the class to tell me. Seeing your teacher cry . . . it's world-shifting to say the least."

I think Ellis might be crying, too, because I see him swipe at his eyes with the hand that isn't holding mine. I want to tell him it's okay, to stop crying, but whatever is happening in my body feels like it's okay, it's all okay. Crying about a stranger is fine! My tragic soliloquy continues.

"I found out later, from Sunny, who was the only possible person in my life with the strength to do it, that my mom had died swiftly around the time I would have been eating lunch. Brain aneurysm. She was discovered because of Betty. Betty was screaming bloody murder until a neighbor came by to see what was going on."

This gets a reaction from Ellis. *"Betty?"*

"Yeah. That's why I haven't put her in a pie yet."

"*How*? How is she still alive?" Ellis is seriously shocked, and it makes me laugh. A lot. This detail is what often stops people in their tracks. *Sorry, Mom, your brain aneurysm tragedy is always completely overshadowed by your Rip Van Winkle bird.*

"Cockatoos can live to be one hundred," I say. "It's the curse of my life."

But he doesn't laugh. "She's a terrible pet. But now I get it."

"Yeah. So now you know why I take these trips. I have to be far away from the family who misses her just as hard as I do."

Ellis stops completely and lets go of my hand, scrubbing his face with both his hands. "Cassia."

"Hey, I'm okay. Really."

But he doesn't believe me and wraps both arms around me, his tall, solid body completely engulfing me in a protective cove. And I don't know if it's the mushrooms or what, but I feel utterly at peace here. In Joshua Tree, but specifically with Ellis. He speaks into my hair. "I really hate that this happens to anyone, but I really hate that it happened to you."

Something in me cracks wide open, and I squeeze him harder.

"You know what the worst part is, though?" I say, ironic laughter spilling out from me. "I never think about my dad. But when I think about how my mom died, I do. I wonder if . . . if he had stuck around, if she wouldn't have died."

Ellis looks concerned and confused. "What do you mean? Wasn't it an aneurysm? You can't control that."

I wave my hand. "It's like, on a rational level I know that. But . . . aneurysms can also be caused by stress." My voice gets quiet, so quiet Ellis has to lean in to hear me. "Maybe, if she wasn't a single mom juggling a very emotional eight-year-old daughter, she wouldn't have—"

"Hey." Ellis tilts my chin up so I have to look at him. "The aneurysm had absolutely nothing to do with you."

I must not look like I believe that because he says it again, "It had nothing to do with you."

I nod and my eyes, horrifyingly, fill up with tears. "I don't want to end up like my mom. I need to start a family with the right person. The one."

Some big emotion comes over him, his features trying not to show whatever he's feeling. He presses his lips to my forehead and says, "You deserve that, Cass. You really do."

We stand like that for a few seconds. When enough time has passed, I feel sufficiently composed to say, "So, hey, this is where we unload our traumas. Tell me yours."

He's quiet. Too quiet. I swivel my head to him. "Did you have a perfect childhood?"

A rumble of laughter goes through him and because we're still pressed together, I feel it through my body. "I mean . . ."

"Wow, I hate you." I lean back and push him away, jokingly.

He starts heaving with laughter and I throw my arms around his waist, trying to tackle him to the ground. All six-feet-two of him.

It's impossible but he trips over something, and we both end up on the ground, rolling in silty desert grit. And I don't mind. It's not even the shrooms, it's him. Something about Ellis makes me feel like saying "Fuck it" to caring about sand in my hair, to caring about being high. He continues to unlock different layers of me, somehow.

We're both laughing hysterically, our hair and faces getting caked in sand, when he rolls me on my back, ending up on top, arms braced on either side of me.

Uh-oh. My laughter dies in my throat as we lock eyes and I feel the pressure of his hips against mine. And then, he says in a choked voice, "I've been married before."

"What?" I breathe out, the words not computing with the sensory overload of my body.

Not moving an inch, his eyes still on mine, he says, "I married my high school girlfriend after graduation. Then we got divorced before I turned twenty-two."

"Wow." I look at him with renewed interest. "What happened?"

"We were . . . twenty-two?" he says with a huff of laughter. It moves his body in a way that is seriously a problem for me. "It was mutual and we're still friends, but she moved out of the country. Probably for the best."

His eyes, normally light and multifaceted, are so dark in the darkness of the desert. I reach up and touch his cheek. "Why did you want to get married that young?"

Balancing impressively on one arm, he holds my hand, pressing a kiss into my palm. "Because we were in love, silly." I think about our conversation at dinner, and how defensive he got about romance and the future. Something is clicking into place. The sweetness of it all crashes over me and I bring him down so that our mouths can meet, letting the magic of the moment take over all logic and faith.

14

Joshua Tree National Park is unique from any national park I've ever been to. In place of towering trees are immense boulders in all shapes and sizes. I feel like I'm in an alien landscape, a tiny ant trundling through, attempting to scramble up the sides of these monstrosities.

It's eight a.m. and I'm feeling incredible despite the fact that I spent way too much time with Ellis last night. With mushrooms you get the best of a buzz without any of its lingering headaches, unless you continue to flirt with the twenty-eight-year-old when your fated is *right there.*

And especially when you unburden your deepest traumas to him. So, despite feeling great physically, I have a bit of an emotional hangover. Every few feet, I wince at the memory of the intimacy that I allowed on my indulgent mushroom trip.

I skirt past a family taking photos in front of a cluster of rocks the color of a sunset and think about how, if I'm being completely honest with myself, last night it moved a lot past a fling. And all along, I've sensed how all-in Ellis is in his approach with me. And if he sensed any currents between me and Daniel, he didn't show it.

There's a particularly large rock formation in front of me and I approach it with absolutely no plan. I just want to reach the top. To make my body struggle so my brain stops spiraling.

I start on the lower rocks—peach-colored and slightly bleached out by the sun. My hiking boots get an easy grip on those. Once I reach the tallest rock, though, a rust-red obelisk, I lose purchase. My hands can't find anything to hold on to, my feet the same.

"Shit," I mutter as I slide down and stare up at it, pushing my wide-brim straw hat back so it hangs from my neck.

"Need some help?"

I glance down and Daniel's standing at the base of the rocks. Oh.

He's wearing sunglasses, a Cal cap, and hiking shorts with a plain white tee. A backpack and good, well-worn hiking boots. I'm nervous at the sight of him.

"I am stupidly determined to make it to the top of this thing," I say with my hands on my hips. "Apparently I have a death wish for my fortieth birthday."

Daniel laughs, a low chuckle that brings to mind dim lighting and brown liquor. "On my fortieth, I went to New Orleans with the stomach flu. For Mardi Gras. So, yeah, I also had a death wish apparently."

Another fact nugget. He's at least forty. And an Aquarius.

"Hey, and sorry. El told me this was supposed to be a solo trip for you. I swear I don't mean to keep bumping into you like this."

It sounds genuine but also like he knows exactly what to say to put me at ease. I wave a hand, batting the apology away. "Where's the crew?"

"None of them wanted to go on a hike after last night." He winces. "Not the best planning on my part. I left them to nurse the hangovers and I'm going back with the promise that they'll have breakfast burritos ready for me."

"Great boss move," I say as I take a swig from my water bottle. I can't tell because of his sunglasses, but I sense his eyes on me and my bare legs beneath my cutoffs. I am immensely grateful for moisturizing my knees before the hike. And for my good sports bra and jaunty red socks above my hiking boots, which hopefully hint at an interesting personality.

He climbs up to me incredibly fast. This is a man who has spent his whole life doing athletic things effortlessly. When he reaches me, he assesses the large rock. "I'm guessing you don't have climbing equipment?"

"Uh, no."

We share a huffed exchange of laughter. Then he says, "Well, unless you have some superhuman upper-body strength or web shooters, I think you're going to need me to boost you up."

I don't answer right away. Do I want to climb up this thing that badly? Feels extremely awkward to let him help me do this. To have him touch my body?

But he is the one . . . the man who will soon know everything there is to know about me.

"Let's do it," I say, jogging in place and cracking my neck to make light of it.

He puts his backpack down. "Okay. And apologies, I wasn't able to shower this morning, because . . . well, yurt."

"I also live that yurt life. It's fine," I say, trying to keep the lightness up. *Buoyant, babyyyy.*

There's a brief moment of limbo where we're not quite sure where to begin but then Daniel gets into a lunge and pats his thigh. "Step on here."

I do. And once my foot is on there, he grabs ahold of my arm. "Okay, now's the time to hoist."

Maybe I wasn't expecting my fated to be funny, but he is. The delivery is absurd and I start laughing and have to step back down. After I gather myself, I step up again, and once he has me steady, he says, "Right, gonna lift you now, don't freak out."

And with that he does this little maneuver of holding me by the waist and lifting me above his head. "Step on my shoulder!"

I do it before I can think too hard about it, feeling his handprints burned into my waist long after I step onto his shoulder. Once I'm up there, it's a quick scramble to the top of the rock.

"Holy shit!" I cry out between pants. "Thank you!"

From below—"Yeah!" It's not like I climbed some huge mountainous peak, but it feels pretty breathtaking to be up on this small summit. I can see the entire desert stretched out around me. The twisty Joshua trees the only spots of dark green. The sky an impossibly bright blue.

Before I can relish in the view for too long, Daniel scrambles up right next to me. I'm so stunned I just step back. "What the hell?" I finally sputter, looking down.

He looks guilty. "I *do* climb . . ."

"Okay, okay, jock."

"Also, I'm a bit competitive," he says. "It's the most American thing about me."

I laugh. "Well, thanks for helping me up when you could have stomped over my head in one leap."

He grins widely. "You're welcome." We stand side by side, taking it all in. He eventually pulls out his phone to take a few photos. "Sending this to the work group chat so they can all feel inferior." Again, his deadpan delivery makes me laugh. Then he holds out his hand. "Fancy a photo of you for posterity?"

"Um, sure." I fumble for my phone. When I give it to him, our hands brush against each other. I point to the landscape behind me with a grin, going for a goofy over serious portrait, and he takes a few shots before handing the phone back to me.

"Well, thank you for that," I say as a warm breeze picks up around us. I pull my hat back on to shield myself from the sun.

"You're welcome. And happy birthday, again." He smiles then holds my gaze for a bit too long. He looks like he's about to say something then glances at his watch instead. "I should probably head back soon. We've got some trust-building exercises to get to."

"Like, falling into each other's arms and stuff?" I tease.

"No. Human centipede."

"Oh my *god*." I let out a hard, shocked laugh. "How do you say that with a straight face, you weirdo?"

He grins. "I was adopted by uptight British people, what can I say?"

That takes me aback. *Adopted*. Wait. "Your parents let you keep your Korean last name, then?"

"No," he says, shaking his head. "I actually found out who my birth mother was a few years ago, after my parents passed." A beat. "Car accident."

The blood drains from my face. "Both of them?"

He nods. "Yeah. It's okay. Well, no, it's not. But that's what you say. Anyway, had a big soul-searching thing and met my birth mother. Added her surname to mine since we've become closer."

"Oh, wow. That's incredible. And I'm so sorry about your parents." I hesitate before I say, "I've also lost both my parents. Kind of. My dad left and my mother died when I was a child."

Daniel's shoulders slump slightly. "Oh, Christ. I'm so sorry, love."

The "love" slips out of him so warmly, so full of sincerity, that it doesn't even catch me off guard. I know British people say it all the time, but the naturalness of it isn't lost on me. And the instant comfort I feel isn't lost on me, either. There's an understanding between us—a shared grief.

I squeeze his arm without thinking. "Thank you."

"Orphan club—not the best club," he says ruefully. And then he puts his hand over mine, a beat longer than expected.

"Maybe the worst club," I say, trying to cover up the intense beating of my heart with a smile. When our hands separate, mine is tingling and I can tell he's feeling something, too—he clears his throat and runs his hand through the back of his hair.

"Well, death talk. An amazing way for me to end a casual conversation, yeah?" He laughs. "It was great bumping into you here, Cassia. Shall I help you down?"

"Yes, thanks," I say, trying not to sound breathless like a goddamned damsel.

He clambers down first, sliding his body down, hanging on briefly with his hands, then hopping off.

"Ugh, you make it look so easy."

Looking up, he smiles. "I'm here, you got this."

The reassurance sends a zing into my spine. "Easier said than done, bucko."

"Just sit on the edge and I'll get you from there."

I scoot over to the edge, my legs dangling. Then, with no-nonsense swiftness, he grabs hold of my calves, his grip unyielding, and pulls me down so that I slide right into him—my ass resting on his forearms, his face almost pressed into my chest.

"Welp," I say with a nervous laugh.

He drops me quickly but gently. "Sorry, probably not the most graceful way." His cheeks are a little red.

"No, thank you, I would have been stuck up there forever otherwise." I also feel my own cheeks heat up. God, the desert is stupidly hot.

Daniel holds out his water bottle to me, reading my mind.

I take a sip, and when I move to close the cap, he takes it from me and puts his mouth where mine was seconds ago. And he keeps eye contact with me while he does it. My mouth goes dry, and I resist grabbing the bottle back from him.

"Well, enjoy the rest of your day, Cassia," he says, his voice cheerful, but something about his jaw looks tense. Ellis looms between us.

"Bye, Daniel. Nice seeing you again." I try not to watch him as he goes—and I can feel a silent willpower coming from his side as well—and he keeps walking with his gaze straight ahead.

15

"You have *got* to be kidding."

The group that I am having a sound bath with is—none other than Watson and Associates Landscape Architecture Firm.

"Nooo," Ellis says with a groan. "Shit, I'm sorry."

I can't even be surprised at this point. "Joshua Tree is apparently the tiniest desert in the entire world."

Everyone's taking off their shoes in the giant dome we're sitting in. When Marcella told me to book a sound bath, I almost dumped her as my best friend. Born and raised in L.A., with magical powers to matchmake people, I hate all this woo-woo stuff. But she said it was like taking the most relaxing nap of your life. *With strangers?* I had asked.

What if it *isn't* strangers, though? Is it relaxing then? *IS IT?*

There are mats placed at the perimeter of the dome with various-sized quartz bowls placed in the center. They'll be "played" by people holding drumsticks with padded ends. Think of running your finger along the rim of a glass and the sound that it creates—sound baths kind of feel like this concept at heart. We're directed to pick a mat and then lie down.

The only mats available for me and Ellis are next to Daniel. Oh my god.

And, of course, I end up sandwiched between them.

Daniel shoots me an inscrutable look before he plops onto his back. Ellis winks at me before he lies down.

I stare up at the ceiling wondering what the hell my matchmaking gods are thinking. Soon, the sound bath begins. This entails all of us being encouraged to close our eyes and just let the sounds and vibrations of the bowls wash over us.

For the first few minutes, you can hear and feel everyone's shifting bodies. Some giggling here and there. I am so aware of the two men beside me that I'm surprised I'm not spontaneously combusting from the pressure of it.

But then something clicks—I feel a lull take over me. There's this feeling I love, that I've had since I was a little kid. Lying so still, in such a comfortable position, that you no longer have any awareness of where your limbs are. It's like you become a bit of a ghost.

I feel my surroundings disappear. The din of the drums fills my ears, the vibrations are in my bones. And in this state, I can imagine my blood is slowing down, that I am becoming a ghost.

It's not dissimilar to when I see someone's past life. I'm here but I'm not, and I'm not somewhere else, either.

But then I sense the two men next to me. On my left, the warmth coming from Ellis, the pureness of it. It electrifies me. On my right, the heat coming from Daniel. The mystery of it, the allure. It makes me curious.

I exist between these two states of being for a second and forever.

And then, suddenly—I feel a familiar tug. I open my eyes and I'm in a quiet, candlelit room. I peer around and it looks like an old

Korean house, with wood-framed paper doors and wood furniture low to the ground. *What the hell, am I in a past life? Whose?*

Then one of the doors opens, and a man steps in.

The air is sucked out of my lungs. It's Daniel. His warm brown eyes look into mine and he says, in Korean, "There you are, wife."

And I feel it then—the history, the love between us. The easy intimacy. The protection and safety I feel near this man.

He brings in a tray of tea, the porcelain clinking gently as he lays the lacquer wood tray down between us. The scent of barley wafts up and its familiarity makes my eyes sting. Halmoni has made this tea for me countless times in my childhood, bringing it up to my room with cut fruit while I did homework.

An easy silence settles between us as he pours the tea into our cups, elegantly and with practiced precision. The soft clinking and liquid sounds are hypnotic. Am I here, can he see me? This isn't like any past life I've been in before and I can't tell if I'm dreaming. Just as Daniel lifts my cup to me, I can hear a baby cry out, and when Daniel's eyes dart to the door, I am thrown out of the vision. I snap my eyes open. Everyone is stirring around me.

"Best nap *ever*," someone says with a yawn. Scattered laughter.

Holy shit. Did I just see my own past life? My heart is thumping, and I am trying to act normal when I turn my head to the left and see Ellis watching me with a softness in his eyes. "You look cute when you sleep," he says in a whisper.

"I wasn't asleep," I say, trying to sound normal even though I kind of want to scream and run out of here. He looks a little concerned by the tone of my voice, so I say, "But, hey, why were you watching me? You were supposed to be in the sound-bath zone."

"Honestly, that was just intensely weird," he says, still lying down. "I had to open my eyes before I astral projected or something."

Bro, you have no idea. I push myself up to a sitting position and look over at Daniel. Surreptitiously. Something about him seems agitated. Did he have a similar vision? No, it's impossible.

I must have been dreaming. I've had these two guys on my mind nonstop for the past twenty-four hours. But then I remember the sound of the baby's cry, and I feel lightheaded again. Did we have children together? What did this all mean?

When we leave the sound bath, I wave goodbye to the crew. "See you guys in five minutes at wherever we all end up somehow," I say and everyone laughs. Ellis walks me to my car, and for the first time, I feel burdened by his attentiveness. How long will I drag this out?

"Hey, sorry if I made fun of the sound bath," he says when I get into my wagon. "I wasn't trying to be a jerk."

"Ellis, you are never a jerk." I put my seat belt on.

"Absolutely not true," he says, his arm draped over the car door, his body stooped to talk to me. His hair falls into his eyes. "We're totally crashing your birthday trip in every way possible. You need a vacation from your vacation."

"See you later," I say, sitting back in my seat to look up at him. Already saying my goodbyes.

He leans in and kisses me, softly, softly. "Drive safe." Then he shuts the door and watches me as I drive away. The pull in my ribs—it stretches the farther I drive away from him, the connection between us fighting what I have to do. It feels wrong. But that's my own fault for letting this whole thing with Ellis happen in the first place. I only have myself to blame as I swipe at the tears on my face.

I spend the rest of the day alone, wandering some vintage shops and visiting an outdoor art museum by an artist named Noah Purifoy. Each art installment is left out to face the elements of the desert, and the rust and decay become a part of the story. It's weird and fascinating and exactly the right way to spend this birthday time, which often passes in surreal swathes mixed with reality.

I grab a burrito for dinner and eat it sitting in the trunk of my wagon, parked on a scrubby slope where I have a spectacular view of the sunset. The sky is a blush pink for a few minutes, and I enjoy my food with a cold beer, a lime squeezed into the neck of the bottle.

Before the night is over, I'll need to end things with Ellis. This is clear. It's unfair to keep this going just because I enjoy it.

And whatever happened in that sound bath—past life or no—it was telling me something. Pushing me toward my fated. Enough is enough.

I have big, *big* regrets about burdening Ellis with my tragic backstory. It was a step in the wrong direction. Even if, at the time, it felt so right.

A bean drops into my lap and I stare at it, feeling sorry for myself.

My dread of this interaction feels new. My entire life—I've known I'd end up with the right person. I just had to be patient. I don't stress about the big questions because in a way I've always known the answer. The universe has a plan.

A breakup was a breakup because I was over it. The romance had died.

So *this*, this dread is different. I don't feel over it, even in the face of my fated. The romance with Ellis isn't dead. It's a baby spark that I need to snuff out. And I have to ignore the terrible feeling that accompanies this shitty task ahead. The feeling will be temporary, I remind myself. Because me and Daniel? It's the real thing. The table has been set for us.

16

It's night by the time I get back to my yurt. I turn on my lantern and open the flaps that serve as doors. I'm taking off my shoes when I notice the mason jar full of blooming purple sage sitting on the nightstand next to my bed.

The sage is fragrant and fills the small space with its perfume. I pick up the folded piece of paper laid next to it.

> *Happy birthday. I'm glad to know you and wish you everything good this year.*
>
> *Love,*
> *Ellis*

My gaze stays on the "love"—written so easily. His handwriting is slanted at an assured angle, precise with strong strokes. The confidence with which he's written "love" to me is instantly clarifying. I take a deep breath because it's really time.

There's a light on in Ellis's yurt, and it glows yellow in the dark.

I can hear the sounds of revelry happening down at the first camp, again.

I knock on the frame of the yurt, even though the flaps are tied back so that I can walk right in. “Hi, you decent?”

He’s not. Ellis walks up to me shirtless, just wearing hiking pants. *Thank you, universe, you complete asshole.* His hair is mussed, his pants covered in dust, and he’s holding a shirt in his hands.

“Hi.” No one else is in the yurt and he pulls me in by the arm. “Get in here.”

“Sorry if I’m interrupting,” I say, already much too used to his casual touch. “I just got back and saw your note. And flowers. Thank you, they’re lovely.”

“You’re welcome. And you’re lovely.” He’s still holding my wrist and steps in closer to me. I feel where this is going and step back.

“Ellis, I have to talk to you.”

“Okay.” He steps back immediately, too, but is still looking at me with his expression lit up and glad to see me. The silver chain resting on his collarbone glints at me, a little “RIP, you” wink.

Everything about this feels wrong even when I know it’s right. My hands feel like curled up little claws, my body slowly petrifying with the absolute hatred of what I have to say. At how, as soon as I say it, his expression will completely change, and I’ll have ruined someone’s day.

“So, I’ve had such a good time with you,” I begin, having practiced this, but still feeling clumsy. “It really was a nice surprise seeing you here.”

Ellis registers something happening. He puts on his shirt hastily. “I’m glad.”

“But the thing is, I *didn’t* plan on it. And I thought that the other night, um, at my house, was a one-time deal. Until, it was a lot of deals. Ha.”

Something shutters in Ellis's eyes. "Okay."

I need to keep going or I'm going to cry. "I'm sorry. I just get the feeling that maybe you're looking for something more . . ."

"Don't be sorry," he says, and it's not with bitterness or resentment. It's genuine. "Hey, you made it clear from day one. I was just hoping I could win you over, I guess."

My chest hurts, actually *hurts*, and this ridiculous yurt feels like it's closing in on me. "In different circumstances, I'd be won. Completely."

He looks down, the sadness on his face clear for the second I see it. "But the age thing, huh?"

"Yeah. The age thing." *The Daniel thing.* But that I will handle later.

"Thanks for being wonderful company," I say softly, reaching out and touching his arm, and I feel goose bumps rise on his skin immediately. "I'll probably be leaving early in the morning."

With his head still bent down, he nods. Then, after a second, he looks up, a small smile on his life-ruining handsome face. "Have a safe trip back, okay?"

"Yeah. You guys, too. Good night." And with that I rush out before I can drag it out any longer, practically sprinting back to my yurt.

17

Mar's waiting for me on my front doorstep when I get home. I'd texted her for an emergency download session and she's sitting outside with two bottles of wine and a greasy bag of smashburgers and fries.

"You could have let yourself in," I say as I give her a hug, dusty and exhausted. Mar has the front door code—it's her birthday so she'll remember it.

She gets up. "Not on your life. Betty sees me coming in alone? I'll leave with no eyeballs."

I laugh a little as I let us in, leaving all my stuff in the car. I'll have to deal with reality later.

"That was a pity laugh," Mar says as we step inside.

"Sorry, a lot's on my mind," I say as I start opening curtains and windows. I can't do anything until my house is aired out first. "Can I please have some of that rosé I see in your grubby little mitts?"

A few minutes later I'm in sweats and lying on my rug with a glass of wine after having annihilated my burger. Mar sits on the sofa like my therapist, picking at the fries, and Betty is flying around, indignant that we dare have a guest right when I get home.

"I can't even believe it," she says, staring out the window, munching a fry. "How in the world does this happen?"

"Magic is real, son," I say, already drunk obviously.

"Can *I* be real for a second?"

"When are you not real?"

"Well. I mean, I don't know if I believed in this fated stuff until now."

I flop my arms around. "What? You mean my family's life work?"

"No offense, Cass, but I thought you guys were just *really* good at matchmaking. I grew up Catholic! All the stuff you guys do seems straight pagan."

"A lot of cultural customs are pagan," I say, my finger up in lecture mode. "Doesn't mean it's not rooted in something real."

"Listen, I'm not going to argue with you about this because I am white and uncomfortable with your culture."

I laugh. "Shut up."

"Anyway, I feel bad for Ellis."

"Stop."

"I *do*! Couldn't you have had a few more nights with him before calling it quits?"

"No, you freak!" I sit up and level an attempt at a serious gaze at her. "What's with married people forcing their single friends to make dubious dating choices so they can live vicariously through them? This is my *life*."

"Because we haven't felt the fear of dying alone in too long and have grown reckless in our sordid daydreams," she says with a laugh, sloshing her wine around her glass. I love her.

Her phone buzzes with a text, and she holds it up away from her face.

"You know, I don't mind aging that much but having to squint to read is a real motherfucker."

"Really looking forward to it," I say. While Mar types out a text, my mind wanders. "I actually think I feel chill about aging because my mom never had the chance to do it."

Mar looks up at me, her expression surprised. I don't bring up my mom that often. But I just had my birthday and, of course, she's been on my mind.

I take a sip of wine. "I'm not scolding you for complaining, I complain, too. I hate how I have to do ten squats in the morning in order for my back to *not* feel like a piece of petrified wood. And RIP to raw garlic. It's just that, when I think about how young my mom was when she died—it seems so completely . . ."

"Tragic?" Mar finishes for me quietly. "It was awful, Cass."

I nod. "Yeah. It was. She was thirty-two." Mar knows this but it bears repeating. I'm lying on a rug my mom picked out on a trip she took to Morocco when she was in college. We used to lie on it together and watch the shadows cross the ceiling as the day passed through the windows.

"Cass?" she said one of those afternoons. "Did you see that?"

My eyes searched the ceiling. "What?"

"The shadow fairy."

"Huh? Where?" I kept looking.

She pointed, her fingers stacked with rings—all different kinds of metal and colors. "There. You just have to look, Bean. Look for the shape."

And I saw it then—a tiny darting figure. "Is that really a fairy?"

"Sure."

"When you say 'sure' it means 'maybe.'"

She laughed and looked over at me. "Smarty-pants." Then she paused. "You're smart but that's not the most important thing, okay? I want you to always see the magical things—like shadow fairies." Even then my mom saw my nascent type A side. As an artist, she was always trying to nurture my imagination. To make sure I remembered to have fun.

"Okay, Mama." I reached over and grabbed her hand. She squeezed it tight, lacing each finger through my small ones. I loved the feel of her cool rings on my skin. Sometimes I felt them like a phantom on my hands.

I feel them now, her presence everywhere. "You know what's wild?" I say to Mar. "I ended up spilling my guts to Ellis about my mom."

"Was this before or after you fornicated on every surface of this house?"

"After, you perv," I say with a laugh. "It was in the desert, when I was high."

"Ah, yes. The shroom musings. Remember how I came up with that genius movie idea on our retreat?"

"How could I forget *Ejaculation Inoculation*?"

Mar shrugs. "I stand by its brilliance."

"I should have remembered that before I got high with my fated and his employee. I ended up crying about my mom. About how, well, how I thought she wouldn't have had the aneurysm if my dad hadn't left her." Mar just looks at me quietly, and I continue, "In the back of my mind, I believe that having to raise me alone made her so stressed that she had an aneurysm."

"What?" Mar is instantly defensive for me, like I knew she would be. "I can't even begin—"

"I know, I know. But the thing is, I also told him I wanted to have children one day."

At this, Mar looks shocked. "Wait, what?"

"Yeah. I didn't even really know I felt so *decided* about it until I said it?" I lean toward her, my voice low. "I can't risk it, Mar. I can't risk ending up like my mom. The only person I want children with is my fated."

"Oh, Cass," she says softly. "But you know that's not the reason why she died."

"*Do* I know that?"

"Yes," she says firmly. "Because people die for all sorts of reasons. It's unfair, indiscriminating, and completely out of our control."

I shake my head. "But we can control who we end up with. *I* can control that."

"So, what's the problem?" she finally asks.

"What do you mean?"

"What's holding you back from throwing yourself into this future with Daniel?" Mar dodges Betty coming for her.

Extremely good question. "I don't know. I guess I thought once I met Daniel I would just feel this huge relief. Euphoric, even. But instead I feel . . . I don't know, it feels complicated because of Ellis."

Mar drops onto the floor and crawls over to me until we're eye to eye. "Was it that good?"

"Come on!" I push her shoulder.

She pushes me back. "No, *you*! You've been searching for your fated for eons. And now that you've found him, suddenly you're indecisive because of this guy Ellis? He had to have been *good*." And she must see it on my face because she howls and rolls onto her back. "My god, I thought all young men lately were bad because all they did was watch chokey-chokey porn."

I fall back next to her, our hair mingling and becoming one. We both stare up at the ceiling, the evening light creating bouncy shapes. "Dude. He was good. It was unreal."

"Now you're just trying to rile me up."

"No, I swear. I haven't had sex that good since . . . I don't know. Ever."

"Not even with that one Brazilian DJ?"

"Not even him."

"Wow."

"Yeah."

We're quiet for a second, showing reverence for Ellis's god-tier sex status. Then Mar rolls over to her side and props her head up as she looks at me. "But, you know. What does that matter with Daniel in the picture? For all you know sex with him will like, heal the world."

"True." I turn on my side, too, so we're facing each other. "Let me read your face, Mar."

She rolls over and does a weird army crawl away from me. "For the last time, no!"

"Come on, please? I can just confirm what you already know, right? That Logan's the one." I don't know why I'm pushing this all of a sudden. I know that Mar and Logan have a great marriage, and I would never ever want them to split up. But sometimes . . . just sometimes I worry that because I'm not sure of Logan being her fated, their relationship could be jeopardized. She's always resisted, but today I can't help asking again. I need some kind of validation. That, *of course* Mar and Logan are fated. That's why they work so well.

That breaking up with Ellis was the right move.

Mar is standing now and her hands are on her hips. She has the expression she uses on her kids. "No, Cassia." Oh, she used my real name. She's not pleased. "You know how I feel about it. If I was single, I'd do it in a heartbeat. But I already made my choice. And I love him more than anything."

The words make me smile. Underneath it all, Mar is just as romantic as me. "You're right. Sorry. I'm just . . ." I wave my hand in the air, helpless to it. "I'm just emotionally all over the place. I've got to sit with this for a while."

"What did Halmoni say? I bet she was over the moon."

"Actually . . . I haven't told them yet." It's something I thought about my entire drive home. When to tell them and how to share this news. I know I should be bursting at the seams to tell them I've finally found Daniel.

"What? Why not?"

"I don't know. Like I said, I need to sit with it. It's just so much expectation."

"A decade's worth," Mar says. She gets it. She always does. When she goes home, I wash my sheets. The scent of Ellis lingers.

18

A week later, I choose one of my favorite lunch spots for the big reveal—a swanky yet understated restaurant tucked into the back of a West Hollywood hotel that is so full of covert celebrities, the entire restaurant is made up of dark booths so people can remain incognito.

The Park women all turn on their phone flashlights to read the menu. I start by ordering French fries and a bottle of champagne for all of us and Sunny raises an eyebrow. "Cause for celebration?"

"I think so." Even though I've had a week to process this, I'm still feeling nervous. Once I tell them, there's no turning back. The Park women are just as—if not more—invested in this as I am. And even though this is what I've wanted, now that it's here, the no-turning-back part feels daunting.

They all stare at me expectantly. Halmoni has her hands folded on the table in front of her, nails perfectly manicured a shell-pink. I look at each of them a second, feeling the bigness of the moment.

"I found Daniel."

Emoni bursts into tears immediately. Sunny slouches back with relief, and Halmoni stays exactly where she is, not moving a muscle.

This is when our fries and champagne arrive, of course, and the server reads the mood immediately and disappears as soon as the last fizzy glass is poured.

"Tell us everything right this instant," Sunny says as she picks up her champagne flute.

I take a sip of the bone-dry drink, not even bothering with a "cheers." The glass is cold and my lip sticks to the edge for a brief second before I speak. "Well, in a weird twist of, er, *fate*, he's actually Ellis's boss."

Halmoni finally speaks. "How did you meet his *boss*?" She is so damn sharp. I have never been able to get away with anything.

"I dropped him off at work one morning." I let that hang there, making Halmoni sit in the discomfort of the revelation. Looking at her with a slight challenge.

Emoni clutches her chest. "Omo. Uh-oh."

"I need more than one drink to get through this," Sunny mutters.

"Okay, that's not important," Emoni barks, waving her hand. "Tell us about him!"

I take a golden fry and swirl it in the ramekin of ketchup. "He's around my age or older, and he owns a landscape architecture firm. He's adopted and grew up in England. He's very attractive and athletic and, so far, exactly the kind of guy I have imagined myself being with."

"Wait, how do you know all this about him already?" Sunny asks, also not one to miss anything.

"Because I happened to bump into their entire firm while they were on a work retreat. They stayed in the same exact location as me in Joshua Tree last week."

"*Last* week?" Sunny asks. "You've been sitting on this information for one week?"

"Also, interesting how you *happened* to go to the exact same location," Halmoni murmurs. "Nothing is a coincidence."

"I am aware," I say, eating another handful of fries. They are salty and delicious. "Anyway, I haven't seen him again, but I thought I should let you all know."

"What about Ellis?" Emoni asks. "Was he on that retreat, too?"

Being raised in a complete matriarchy humbles a person. "Yes. I made it clear that there was no future for us."

Emoni nods her head. "Poor guy. But necessary."

"Very necessary," Halmoni says, finally eating a French fry. "You did the right thing."

I know it, but it hasn't felt right all week. "I'm just not sure how to approach Daniel in a way that isn't going to be heartless to Ellis."

Emoni rests her small hand on mine. "You're a good girl, Cassia. You always were."

"Yes. But you barely know Ellis, you don't have to be this careful about his feelings," Sunny says. "He's a twenty-eight-year-old hunk, he'll be fine."

Something about that stings and I'm glad when the server returns to take our lunch orders.

After the orders are put in, Emoni then holds up her glass and says, "Cheers to Cassia, here's to the start of a beautiful love story."

"Our most important match yet," Sunny says with a smile.

We drink to that.

Halmoni smiles, too, her eyes shining. "You're in for a wonderful journey, my Cassia. And I have some ideas about how to approach Daniel."

"You do?"

She takes a sip of champagne. "Of course. I do run a matchmaking agency after all."

"We've got to make it seem natural," Sunny says, tapping her fingers on the table, deep in thought. "A meet-cute."

"A what?" Emoni asks, her face scrunching up.

"You know, the cute way that people meet in romantic comedies," Sunny says. "Like, how J.Lo meets a man while getting her shoe stuck in a grate."

Emoni is so confused. "What? Why not just the regular way, like a date?"

"No, no," Halmoni says. "This is a more delicate situation because of Ellis. We have to make it seem like an accident."

"Like a real accident?" Emoni says. "How many times can we make Cass get hurt?"

I wince. Yes, I did actually already have a movie meet-cute with Ellis. "No, we're not gonna go that far, guys."

"No physical injuries necessary," Sunny says through a mouthful of fries. "Maybe something related to plants. These men seem to love their plants."

"Oh, maybe they can meet in the Huntington Gardens!" Emoni says with starry eyes. I suddenly get this nightmare image of Daniel and me bumping into each other at the Japanese Gardens, an Asian couple farce.

I wave my arms. "No, no weird meet-cute setups."

"But you have to do *something*," Emoni says, the stars in her eyes replaced by something more cunning. This is the Emoni who haggles at both the farmers market and Neiman's. The Emoni who once, while getting mugged in New York City, took off her sandal and whaled on the mugger on the head so many times that pedestrians had to stop her. Basically: This look terrifies me and I glance at Halmoni imploringly.

She gets the hint. "You are all thinking less simply about this. What do we do? We are a matchmaking agency. How do we match people? At our events. When is our next event?" She looks straight at me.

I smile. "The summer event at LACMA."

“There you go.” Halmoni sits back and eats a second fry, the matter settled.

Sunny nods. “Okay, now all we have to figure out is how to invite him in a way that seems natural.”

“This is not a group project,” I say, swiping some fries. “I’ll figure that part out on my own, thanks.” Our food arrives and everyone blessedly tucks into their lunches, the Eye of Sauron off of me briefly.

19

It's a gloomy Saturday, a dull haze over everything, but it feels amazing to shoot the shit with Mar again as we feel the wind in our hair.

After the ride we park our bikes at our coffee spot and grab a couple stools that overlook the river. "So tell me the latest and greatest Ozzie-ism," I say.

"Oh, this one's a doozy," she says, with a dark chuckle. Then she pushes up her sunglasses and her eyes go wide as she looks over my shoulder. "Holy . . . I shit you not," she breathes. "Ellis is here."

Of course he is. I turn, and my gaze lands on him immediately—standing in line. With Daniel. Both are in dirty carpenter pants, T-shirts, and baseball caps. They look sweaty. And handsome.

Nothing about this is going to be easy, I guess. "He's with Daniel." My voice is equally low. Pained.

Marcella gasps and turns so dramatically that other people look where she's looking. There is absolutely no way I am leaving this interaction with even a scrap of dignity intact.

"Holyyyyy *shit*. That's him?" Her voice is no longer quiet, her jaw practically scraping the floor. "Happy birthday to *you*."

"An embarrassment of riches, I am aware," I say with a suppressed laugh at her expression.

Daniel glances over then does a double take. He waves.

Shit. I wave back with a smile and try to look relaxed when Ellis turns as well. Our eyes meet and his smile is tight. After they order, they walk over to us.

"Hey," Daniel says with a grin.

"Hi, guys," I say, trying to avoid looking at Ellis again.

"Hey, Cassia. Marcella," Ellis says, comfortable like he always is.

"Hi, Ellis," she says with so much chipperness that I try not to wince. "Lovely day for rolling around in the dirt, it seems?"

They laugh. Daniel says, "We're doing a site visit because a bunch of our plants and trees were just installed. Helping out a bit with watering and all that."

"How's it going?" I ask, trying my damnedest to act normal.

"Good, good," Daniel says, quickly. He throws a little glance between me and Ellis, and I know that he knows. Then he holds his hand out to Marcella. "Hello, I'm Daniel."

"Marcella, nice to meet you." She smiles at him like he's handed her a million dollars.

Ellis does a quick visual sweep over me—head to toe. I'm in very utilitarian yellow Patagonia baggy shorts and a white ribbed tank, but I flush under his gaze. Then he says, "Not too traumatized for this ride, again?"

I can't help but smile. "Still traumatized but somehow back in the saddle."

He nods, not following my playful tone. "Great. I'm glad you're healed."

Marcella makes a sound next to me that sounds too much like an "aw," and I resist elbowing her. Daniel looks at me curiously. "Were you hurt?"

"Yeah, a few weeks ago I had a fall off my bike. That's how I met Ellis, actually." My eyes flit over to him and he's suddenly busy looking at the menu on the board. "He called for help and kept me calm."

There's an awkward pause and then their drinks are called out, thank god. Marcella gives me a *look,* and I have no idea what she's trying to relay to me. When they're both out of earshot, she leans over and whispers, "Hey, shouldn't you do the thing?"

"What thing?" I whisper back, so flustered by this entire situation that I've shredded my napkin into smithereens.

"Halmoni told me about Operation Meet-Cute. You need to ask Daniel—"

But they're walking back and she slams her mouth shut with a panicked smile.

"There's the restoration section we're in charge of," Daniel says, pointing to the river where orange cones and tape set off a large patch of concrete and greenery. "Hopefully, in a few weeks, there will be a nice walkable path and park that you can hang out in after popping in here for a coffee."

"That'll be so nice," Marcella says. "The L.A. River has always been depressing af. When I first moved here, I couldn't believe that trickle was considered a river."

"Where are you from?" Ellis asks.

"Minnesota," Marcella answers. "Land of a billion lakes."

"I quite like Minnesota," says Daniel, his eyes still on the restoration site. "The nicest people on earth."

"Yeah, you have to be nice to live there so I was booted out," Marcella says with a devilish grin. "Snagged myself a guy first, though. What the Midwest lacks in warm weather it makes up in good husbands."

Daniel chuckles. "That should be on the travel brochures."

I laugh then and he looks at me quizzically. "What?"

"Travel brochures. Do you read a lot of those?"

We hold an amused glance for a bit before Marcella says, "This restoration project is huge. A pretty big coup for your firm, yeah?"

Daniel nods. "It really is. Especially for one so young like ours."

"Dan's being incredibly modest," Ellis says with a grin. "It's really unusual for a firm like ours to get the project. But Daniel's a star."

I look at Daniel curiously and can see it. He's charming and a bit dazzling—but there's steeliness under the slick exterior. This man gets it done.

He shakes his head, embarrassed. "Let's not exaggerate. I have great employees, too." Then he glances down at his watch. "We've got to head back. Enjoy your Saturday, ladies," Daniel says, putting his sunglasses on, his teeth white and straighter than anything.

Ellis nods and pulls his cap down lower onto his head. "Good seeing you."

"You, too," I say, holding up my coffee. "Good work. Lads."

I turn and mutter, "Shut up, don't say anything," to Marcella before she can.

"Okay, I won't." A pause and then, "You're so fucked, my friend."

I'm about to agree when Daniel jogs back up to us. "Forgot to ask for a sleeve," he says, sheepishly holding up his paper cup. "I'm a bit precious about holding hot coffee cups."

The confession knocks something inside my chest. I can't help but say, "Don't want to mess up those hands of yours." An awkward silence passes in which I swear to god Marcella is about to pass out from holding in her laughter. "Since, you . . . draw for a living?"

"Oh, yes, that," he says, in this level tone that I can't quite read.

When he goes up to the counter for his sleeve, Marcella pushes me forward.

"What—!"

"Go," she says. "Ask him to the event. When else will you see him?"

Damn it. I was hoping to wait but she's right, this is actually the perfect time. Fate is, yet again, forcing my hand.

I stand next to Daniel at the counter, pretending to grab some napkins. "For my runny nose," I say before I can think. *Real hot-girl behavior, Cass.*

"Ah," he says. "It's nippy out today."

"Mm-hmm. Nippy." I keep taking napkins. Please dear god, someone stop me. I can practically see Halmoni's furious face. "So, Daniel. Are you single?"

He almost drops his coffee. "Yes? That is, *yes*."

"Great! I mean, great-ish. My matchmaking agency is actually having a really big event next weekend. It's going to be at LACMA, our big mingling event all wrapped up in art gala packaging. If you're interested, I can send you an invite."

He's concentrating on putting the sleeve over his paper cup, as if it's a task that requires surgical precision. Then, he says, "Yeah, that sounds killer. Should I . . . extend the invitation to other single people I know?" With that pointed question, he looks at me.

I shake my head. "Sorry, it's a pretty exclusive event."

"How did I make the cut?" His mouth hitches up at the side.

I hold up my hand and wiggle my fingers. "You're a normal single man over the age of thirty. A unicorn, check." I fold down my thumb. "You work in the arts. Check. You . . ." I pause. "You're easy on the eyes." I hold eye contact with him. "Check."

He goes still then holds his available hand out. "Let me give you my contact info, then." Smooth and unbothered.

After he taps his number into my phone, he slips it back into my shorts pocket for me. It's a little too familiar but also . . . it's good. "Looking forward, Cassia."

Things have officially been set into motion.

20

All the women of my family are at my house and Betty is about to punch a hole through the roof to escape them.

"Someone put this bird out of its misery," Sunny says, covering her head when Betty swoops over her—purposely low, may I add.

It's the day of the LACMA matchmaking event and everyone wants to make sure every part of my outfit, makeup, and hair is exactly right lest I show up looking like a bog woman and lose the love of my life before the romance has a chance to get started.

I've put on a Fleetwood Mac record to create the proper vibes for these boomers, and as usual Sunny makes fun of me for owning vinyl. I imagine it's like when I make fun of a teenager for wearing a Nirvana T-shirt.

Several outfits are laid out on my bed, and my hair is in a towel turban, still wet from my shower. Emoni is in my bathroom getting my curling iron heated up so she can help me with my hair while Sunny and Halmoni survey my clothes and shoes.

"It's not quite warm enough for this, but I *love* it." Sunny holds up a black crotchet number with suede fringe.

"Too hippie," Halmoni says dismissively. "What about this?" She's pointing at a deep-blue knee-length dress that slips off the shoulders prettily and is cut on the bias.

I consider it. "It's really nice but will make me think about how much I'm eating all night."

"You don't want that, you need to feel comfortable!" Emoni calls out from the bathroom.

"I agree," I say. "Should I wear something looser?"

Both Sunny and Halmoni make disgusted sounds. "This is not the time to be avant-garde and all quirky Japanese street-style," Sunny says. "You need to knock this man's socks off. He has to know about this body." She sweeps her arm over my general body.

"Yes, one look and *done*," says Halmoni.

Nothing like being decades younger than people to feel like a desirable little snack. "Let me see what I might be overlooking," I say as I pull out my phone.

Sunny comes over to see what I'm doing. "Don't tell me you have an *app* for your clothes."

"Of course I do," I say. "Every single item of clothing I own is cataloged in here."

"You have a disease," Sunny says with a laugh. But then she stops as she sees the dresses populate on my screen. "Wait, that is amazing."

"I know," I say smugly. The app reminds me of a few dresses I have in a different closet. After a few more minutes of me hauling things out of garment bags, I lay out as many eligible pieces as I can on my bed.

Halmoni sits on the edge and runs her hand over the lacy sleeve of a butter-yellow dress. "Was this your mother's? It looks familiar."

"Yeah," I say fondly. "I still have a few of her things, even if they're all a bit too small for me."

Halmoni nods but I see that her mind is somewhere else, somewhere in the past. It's often painful for her to come to this house, the house her daughter made a home. And, critically, the home where she died. I feel the opposite. This house gives me comfort. The memories aren't sad for me, because they're all I have.

"I was so relieved that Daniel wasn't already married with kids," Sunny says as she pulls out a stretchy, acid-green dress. I make a face and a note to self to add that to my resale box.

"I knew he wouldn't be," Halmoni says firmly.

"How did you know that?" I ask with a laugh, shaking my hair out of my towel. "It happens."

"Rarely," Halmoni says. It's true—in some cases, with older clients, their fateds have already moved on, or picked different paths. In those cases, we put them in the pool of candidates who are in similar boats: ineligible or dead fateds.

Sunny picks up another dress. "Oh, how about *this*?"

It's a long, silk fuchsia number that I wore to a friend's movie premiere once. It's got a high Katharine Hepburn–esque boatneck with loose, dolman sleeves. It cinches in neatly at the waist before flowing all the way down to ankle length. The back opens with a deep V, and when I wear it, I look ten feet tall.

"Hmm, it's not too much?" I ask, already feeling swayed.

"No, it's just right." Halmoni shoves it at me. "Try it on. Do you need the Spanx?"

I want to say no but wordlessly hold out my hand. I shut myself in my walk-in closet to give myself a shred of dignity while I maneuver into the Spanx and then the dress. It fits exactly how I remembered—perfectly without any real constraint.

When I step out into my room, everyone's sitting on the edge of my bed.

"*Oh*, Cass," Emoni breathes. "You look like an angel."

"No, you look like a hottie," Sunny says.

"Really, Sunny? *Hottie*?" I tease, but am pleased. Sunny still gets physical issues of *Vogue* delivered to her house and she doesn't dole out compliments easily.

"It's perfect," Halmoni says with finality. "I can already see my future great-grandchildren."

I almost trip on the hem of the dress. "Halmoni!"

"What?"

"Let's just . . . take a beat," I say, feeling my chest tighten. Suddenly this night feels so high stakes. Having this not work out with Daniel wouldn't just mean failing Halmoni and all her hopes and dreams. It could mean ending the line of the family gift. I've known this, but it hits me hard at this moment.

Sunny comes over to me to adjust the neckline, and the cool touch of her fingers instantly calms me. She squeezes my shoulder. "Umma, let's not get into baby talk."

"Just because you didn't want any doesn't mean that's how Cassia feels!"

Emoni shakes her head. "Of course, Cassia wants children. The gift runs strongly through her. She's just been waiting for her fated."

Sunny closes her eyes. "Everyone. Stop. Let's not ruin this for Cass before it even begins."

I look at her gratefully. "We have bigger fish to fry. Which shoes?"

We pick out some strappy silver heels to go with my little jeweled clutch (vintage Dior that Sunny brought from home, thank you very much). In the bathroom, Emoni and I nix the idea of waves and just blow out my hair so that I feel like a nineties supermodel. I'm not always comfortable in a lot of makeup, but I agree with Emoni that this time I need to be a bit more dramatic. She gives me a smoky eye and a bronzy highlight on my cheekbones and I'm done.

"Are you ready for the beginning of everything?" Sunny asks me, her tone only half teasing.

"I've *been* ready," I say, but the conviction only runs through part of my body. The other part—well, it's nervous. I know things will go well—it's been predetermined—but I don't know how the details will fill in yet.

Emoni tucks a strand of hair behind my ear. "You look a lot like your mom tonight, more than usual."

There's a moment of quiet as they all look at me, and I can feel that they are not just looking at me but the ghost of my mother. It's both a gift and a burden to be able to give that to them. I've now lived eight years longer than she did—everyone in this room has known me longer than they knew my mother.

Later, I catch Halmoni looking at a painting in the kitchen, a small oil painting of a K-Town strip mall. My mom's, of course. It's the first One & Only office. There's a neon sign, the sky blue-gray, and a red sedan is parked in front of the office. Halmoni's hand covers her mouth. "Oh. That's my car."

"Really?" I peer at it. "I always wondered why there was only one in the entire parking lot."

She nods, her lips tightly sealed in a line. "It barely fit our whole family. But it was the first car we were able to buy, and I was so proud of it." Her expression is faraway. "Your mom and Sunny fought endlessly in the back seat. One time so viciously that Halabuji had to whip his arm back to separate them and he dislocated his shoulder."

"Oh my god," I say with a laugh. "Bet they behaved after *that*."

"You would think," she says dryly. "But your mom never let anyone have the last word. She kept all of us on our toes."

The unspoken words hang over us as we stare at the painting. That she brought chaos into both of our lives because her death was so utterly shocking. We look at her paint strokes, so effortless and wild. But when you step back, the painting is totally in control. All the loose and breezy daubs of paint end up creating a feeling, a place. A memory that has the ability to make you time travel. Mom surprised you like that. Halmoni reaches for my hand and I hold it tight. I don't want to let her down, I don't want to fill her life with any more pain. And I won't. That familiar steadiness comes over me. A lifetime of happiness will start tonight.

My family heads back home to get ready themselves since I'll be going to the museum early to oversee everything. I thank them, and before Halmoni shuts the door behind her she says, "Was this a good idea, or what?"

I brush my lips on her powdered cheek. "We won't know until the end of the night. So, save your gloating."

She doesn't even try and hide her smug smile. "I'm already planning the wedding."

21

Located in the center of the city, LACMA is iconic and the perfect spot for this year's biggest matchmaking event. It's being held in an airy courtyard at the sprawling art museum. With Chris Burden's *Urban Light* sculptures as the backdrop, we've set up a bar and there are high-top tables scattered through the rest of the space. Napkins with our logo are spread on the tables, along with little conversation-starter cards. The string lights lend a magical glow to the evening.

Everything is ready to go when the guests start trickling in. They check in at the entrance with the interns, receiving brass-plated pins with their names etched onto them. Much cuter than name stickers. Have to give Shreya props for that idea. Everyone also has a QR code etched into their nameplates, with the codes leading to their public profiles on the One & Only database. That contribution was mine. It earned me "snaps" from the interns when I suggested it.

I meet our VIP guest at a discreet back entrance.

Gemma Flores is low-key but stunning in a simple black slip dress with a blazer thrown over her shoulders. She's wearing dark sunglasses until she steps inside.

"Nervous?" I ask as I give her a hug.

She tugs on her rings. "Very much so."

I guide her through the halls that lead to the courtyard. "Everyone who comes to our events signs an NDA," I say. "And in the past, when we've had public figures at our events, we've found that most people are too wrapped up in their own connections to be too starry-eyed."

When we step outside, Gemma tenses slightly. I look at her with reassurance. "That said, if anyone bothers you, my great-aunt will drop-kick them to the curb."

This gets a laugh out of her and she nods. "I trust you guys."

"And I'm not kidding, if you have any problems at all, come straight to me, okay?" She nods and I squeeze her arm before handing her a name pin, which feels silly but I do it nonetheless.

I'm overseeing the jazz band setting up in a corner when my phone buzzes with a text:

> Would it be too much to wear an actual tuxedo?

It's Daniel, and he's sent me a photo of a fucking corgi in a mini tux. And bow tie. Oh my god. It's so corny but endearing.

> Do you turn into a corgi when the sun goes down? If yes then, yes, only a tux will be appropriate.

I'm not even thinking about how quickly I'm responding, at how available I am when I'm in the middle of preparing for a huge work event.

He texts me back:

You've caught me.

A pause as he types something else.

See you soon. In normal fancy clothes.

I'm smiling when I rapidly text back:

Looking forward to it.

It's a little risky when we set these events up—sometimes people hit it off with the wrong person. But we usually manage to maneuver things, and our success rate is maintained. Because it's just a fact: When we get the past loves right, the connection is undeniable. I think about Daniel's eyes catching mine over and over again at the bonfire in Joshua Tree. At how he bumped into me hiking. What it feels like when our hands touch.

There is obviously the small chance that Daniel might be interested in someone else tonight, but it'll be pretty hard when I'm masterminding this entire thing.

Halmoni, Sunny, and Emoni show up all looking lovely in their dresses and St. John suits.

"Everything looks wonderful," Halmoni says approvingly, eyeing the tastefully lit courtyard. "Great job, Cassia."

"Thanks." I signal to the head caterer that they should start serving the appetizers.

"How's Gemma?" Sunny asks in a low voice.

"Good, so far." I see her in a corner, talking to a man who is not Peter Cruz. But she looks relaxed, smiling, and the man looks happy but not *too* happy. I happen to know for a fact that his fated is a dental hygienist who likes playing pickleball on the weekends. "Peter just got here, so we simply have to make sure they chat."

We disperse, each of us assigned to specific couples. I'm talking to two women who used to be lovers in 1879 Kansas, when I feel a ripple go through the night air. Like the heat and force you feel with the first Santa Ana winds in L.A. My hair swirls into my face and when I push it aside, I see Daniel walking into the courtyard.

He's wearing a gray suit that fits him like birds spun it around him while he stood perfectly still and sang. It's shot with black thread that matches his perfectly crisp black shirt visible under the open jacket. He is a tumbler of whiskey on a cold night—warm and exactly what you need.

When he spots me, a slow smile stretches across his face. Then he makes his way to me, dodging people in a graceful dance. I notice more than a few heads turn as he walks by. Something about Daniel commands your attention, he gives off that strength and confidence that all leaders do. Plus, he's really good-looking.

My heart is thumping because everything about this feels exactly like how it's supposed to when you meet your fated.

He finally reaches me. "Hello there."

"Hello back," I say with an easy smile. "Thank you for coming."

"Thank you for having me," he says. Then he takes me in. "You look stunning."

I flush. There aren't many men who could get away with that, but I guess if you're Daniel, you do. "Thanks, so do you."

We both seem to understand that we have just told each other that we find the other hot, so we look anywhere else. I spot a server carrying a tray of champagne and wave him over. "Thank you," I say as a I take two flutes. Daniel takes one and we clink our glasses together.

"So, please, I am dying to know everything about this," Daniel says after a sip. "I admit I googled the agency after you gave me the invite and I am quite intrigued."

"I'm *sure*," I say with a laugh. "We're not your average matchmaking agency."

He sweeps an arm across the courtyard. "No, this is not your typical Tinder date."

"Tinder," I say with a growl.

He laughs. "Your competition, yeah?"

I shrug. "Actually, no. If you look around, our demographic's a little different." He does look around then, noticing that most of the people are in their thirties and older. "Everyone can get a hookup or a shitty first date at a bar in Silver Lake on the apps. We only take serious people who don't want to fuck around. Or, as your people would say, faff about."

His laughter makes champagne go up his nose and we take a few seconds to handle it with some napkins. "You okay there?" I ask with a grin. He nods and I love catching this slick guy in a silly, vulnerable moment. It reminds me of seeing Stu trip on that infamous first date.

"Anyway, yes, we have events like this and we also meet everyone in person before we decide to take them on as clients."

"Face-reading, right?" Good-humored skepticism underscores his words.

I remember Ellis's reaction—his absolute belief that it must be real if it was my line of work. I know this comparison isn't fair, so I push that memory aside. "Yes. It's an old Korean tradition that goes back for centuries. It's run in my family for just as long."

"Centuries? Wow, that's amazing. To be able to trace your family history like that," he says.

I remember he's adopted and soften. Growing up Korean American, I had my fair share of skepticism about the dozens of little traditions and beliefs that were passed down to me from my grandparents and aunts. It's probably that much more dubious to someone who didn't grow up with it. Or maybe it's more intriguing?

"Yeah, my mother's side has a meticulous record of everything," I say. "Including the secrets of face-reading. We read your 'fortune,' and essentially learn how to find you the perfect match."

He covers his face with the hand not holding champagne. "Do I need to sign another waiver?"

I push his hand aside and laugh. "We don't read anyone's face without explicit permission."

He keeps my hand in his for a second before dropping it. The sizzle of it moves up my arm.

"I realize that I was very presumptuous inviting you here tonight," I say.

"Oh?"

"Yes. I know you're single, but are you actually looking to get serious with someone?" It's one of those loaded questions that women never ask men because they're worried it'll "scare" them off, but I can ask it since we're not technically on a date. More than that, with my line of work, being certain and straightforward is the key to everything. Like I said, we don't fuck around. The finiteness of our time on Earth is what keeps the agency in business. That urgency never goes away, no matter where we are in time.

Daniel takes another sip of champagne. "Is that a nice way of asking why I'm still single at my age?" His tone is teasing.

"Absolutely not," I say with a laugh. "I'm single, too."

There's some weighted silence. God, we're both being incredibly awkward about all this. He finally says, "Sorry. I mean, yes, I am looking for someone serious? I'm forty-two, so I'm not faffing about, either."

"Mm, yes. Don't want to faff."

Our eyes meet and his are twinkling. In a way that makes me feel like we're the only two people who exist in that moment. "So, yes. I have been incredibly picky. Which, of course, my friends give me shit for. They think I'm some forever-bachelor type. But it's really because my parents didn't have a great marriage."

"I'm sorry to hear that." And I am, a little pang of heartbreak for little Daniel.

A shrug. "It's not a unique experience. But it's made me less focused on the 'marriage' bit and more focused on the 'finding the right person' bit. I think I'll know it when I see it."

"I know exactly what you mean," I say, my heart starting to thump. It's really happening, this thing with Daniel. We are on the same wavelength, everything has been leading up to this.

The music switches up to something sultry and I suddenly feel hot in my silk dress. A weighted silence passes while the music basically takes off our clothes for us and I'm about to slide an ice cube down my dress when I see Sunny waving at me.

"Shoot, I'm needed elsewhere." A genuine pang of regret shoots through me. I feel like we'd just begun. "But, please, enjoy the drinks and food. I'll see you soon?"

Daniel nods. "Of course. Go do your thing." It's confident and assured, the way he says it, but as I walk away, I can feel his eyes on my back, and I resist turning to look at him, too.

22

"This is Peter Cruz."

I watch Gemma's eyes turn luminous as the handsome man from her past life approaches her. Earlier, I'd introduced her to two other men, and while the interactions between them were warm—this immediately feels different.

Peter has the same look in his eye, taken aback and curious, as if he's meeting someone he's met before. And not just because she's famous. It runs deeper than that.

I love this part so much.

The moment when two souls who have spent centuries in different love stories recognize each other in this lifetime. I feel it deep in my chest, the rightness of it. I turn and find myself looking for Daniel.

But I don't see him and duty calls. So, I mingle with a few more clients and make sure everything's going well. So far, I've counted three matches of just my own clients: Taylor the improv comic and Jason the baker. Lauren the jewelry designer and Nicholas the hotelier (so obvious and easy I almost feel like I can't take any credit for it). Meghan the writer and Jon the finance bro.

Check, check, check.

Daniel's talking to a petite woman with a chic blond pixie cut when I finally find him. "Sorry to interrupt"—I glance at her pin—"Daniel and Brooke. But just wanted to let you both know that some of the galleries will be opening up shortly if you'd be interested in exploring."

"Oh, I didn't know that was happening tonight," Daniel says, genuinely excited. "I'd love to go view."

Brooke glances across the way, and I see her eyeing a man with sandy hair and wire-rimmed glasses. These two were lovers during the Spanish-American War. "I think I'll grab another drink before heading over there. So great to meet you, Daniel."

Daniel gives her his full attention with a warm smile. "Very much the same, Brooke."

When she leaves, I look at him with a clear question on my face. He grins. "She was nice."

"I know what that means," I say, hiding my relief. "Are you having a good time, then?"

"Yes, of course," he says. "This is such a thoughtful, beautiful event."

It's gratifying—even if it's because this guy is maybe trying to get into my pants. "I'm glad to hear it."

"So, do you want to show me these galleries?" he asks, holding out his arm like a Regency-era gentleman or an undercover spy.

I take it. "Sure." We head to BCAM, the Broad Contemporary Art Museum, within the museum—a large modern structure made up of limestone and red steel beams. The tall palms lining the path to the entrance make the walk feel dramatic.

"Ooh, they opened up BCAM for us?" Daniel asks, his pace getting quicker as he realizes where we're headed.

"I thought this might be up your alley." I push the doors open and we're greeted by a security guard. We're the first ones here, and our footsteps make satisfying echoing *clack*s as we walk through in our fancy footwear. We take the elevators, which are filled with large Barbara Kruger murals—giant advertising text in stark black, white, and red.

"These always feel like an attack," I say with a laugh.

"An interesting choice for an entrance into the place, right?" Daniel says. "She's yelling at us about consumerism and consumption, but in this rarified space."

I'm struck, yet again, by how earnest Daniel is about things that, on a Tinder profile, would have me rolling my eyes: travel, food, music, art. But Daniel knows his stuff, he walks the walk.

When we step off the elevator, we run straight into Halmoni. "Cassia," she says with a smile. She glances at Daniel, as if wondering who he is. But she knows. I see the quicksilver moment when her eyes flash in recognition.

"Halmoni, this is Daniel. Daniel, this is my grandmother, the founder of the agency."

He seems to lose his composed veneer for about two seconds as he says, "Oh! Hello, lovely to meet you. Thank you for the invitation."

I have to give Halmoni credit for not looking more curious. In fact, she acts almost indifferent to him. "Hello." She looks down at her phone. Then she glances up and gives him a cursory smile. "I hope you have a good evening and meet some interesting people." Then a look at me. "See you later?"

I nod and ignore the bead of sweat making its way down my back. With Halmoni meeting him—it all feels incredibly real suddenly.

Daniel must sense something because he raises an eyebrow. "Scary Halmoni?" His British accent speaking in Korean is *delightful.*

I laugh. "Yes, but also no. My grandmother has high standards for these events. Just wants everything to go smoothly."

"Does she mind you mingling with the clients?" Teasing and aware.

"No, she wants us to get to know all of you." It's not a lie. "We do our jobs best when we truly know our clients."

We walk into a gallery filled with modern art from the 1900s when Daniel says, "So, I have to address the elephant in the room."

"What's that?" But I have a feeling I know what he's about to say.

"Ellis."

I give him my full attention, keeping my features very, very neutral. "What about him?"

Daniel tilts his head as he looks at me. "He's my employee but also a friend."

"Mm-hmm."

"Are you two . . ." He falters a bit, looking less assured of himself. "I know it's really none of my business, but I just want to be super clear about where you two left things?"

I remember the yurt, the light glowing off of Ellis as he rushed to put on his shirt. "I ended things."

Something indecipherable flickers across his face. "Oh, okay."

We walk in silence through a room full of bronze cast statues by Alberto Giacometti—intricate and grotesque shapes that seem to stretch toward the ceiling.

Finally, I speak. "I just . . . he's really wonderful. But the age gap was . . . it felt insurmountable to me." All I can be is honest about this. I don't care if it makes me feel like I'm aging myself, making myself less desirable.

"Ah, okay, that explains it." Daniel has stopped, looking at a huge David Hockney painting of Mulholland Drive, his shoulders a little more relaxed now. "He seemed a bit . . ."

We stare at the Hockney together, with its vivid blues and imprecise grids, and I realize I am tense waiting for the rest.

". . . subdued."

My head turns to his too quickly. "Subdued?"

"Yeah. Ellis is like this glowing ball of energy, you know? He just kind of lights a place up. But the last couple weeks he's been . . . subdued."

This feels crushing to me and Daniel senses the mood has dampened. "Sorry, I'm not saying this to make you feel guilty." I nod and he rubs his cheek in agitation. "Ah, bloody hell, I shouldn't have said it."

"No, no, really it's fine," I say. "I feel a little bad about it, but let's be real. That kid will be *fine*. We went out a couple times and he is . . . well, the way he is."

"Yes," he says, and it sounds like he wants to say more but doesn't. "Just wanted to make sure."

"Sure," I echo. And then we both laugh from the awkwardness of it all.

Voices reach us as more people fill into the museum. I decide to be bold while I can. "Did you want me to introduce you to more people?"

He seems to understand the other part to this question. "To be perfectly honest, I'm having a good time with you."

Pleasure fills me and it wars with the vestiges of guilt about Ellis. "Okay."

"Do you have other people to tend to?"

I glance at my watch. "I think I'm good for a bit."

"Brilliant," he says. We walk through the galleries—passing by an incredible chrome sculpture by Man Ray, a painting by Joan Mitchell that stops me in my tracks, and a walk-in installation that meticulously replicates a nostalgic garage from the 1950s. We leave the installation with goose bumps—the empty museum adding to the time-trapped feeling. Daniel knows so much about art that I stop reading the placards. And he's not lecturing me tediously—he's sharing a genuine passion of his and it's refreshing to be in someone's area of expertise.

"Did you always want to do landscape architecture? Seems like you have a real interest in fine art," I say.

He peers closely at a piece by Ellsworth Kelly before answering me. "Hm, yes and no? There's this thing about being adopted. Sometimes, you kind of feel like you have to be the gold standard of children?"

I look at him, feeling sad. "Oh, but—"

"I know, I know. I've years to process this in therapy," he says with a self-deprecating laugh. "And really, I shouldn't speak for all adopted children so maybe it was just a *me* thing. Regardless, it was there for a long time. My parents encouraged me to do whatever I wanted, but they were right proper, pragmatic people. My father was an accountant and my mum was a sales rep for a food supplier. I voluntarily squashed all love of fine art and directed my love of design into landscape architecture."

"Do you like your job, then?"

"Yes," he says without hesitation. "It's really interesting, but also feels purposeful. You're creating work that endures beyond your own lifetime. And I love the outdoors."

"But?"

He smiles. "There's no 'but.'"

"Okay," I say easily. I'm noting a few things—this man is purposeful. Goal-oriented. I think about the way his life has unfolded; he's created all this for himself. I admire him for it. I wonder if this is why Daniel and I are fated, and why we might be drawn to each other life after life. I appreciate his steadiness, his clear-eyed view of what he wants. We're similar, and maybe that's the trick to making relationships work: an ease, a lack of friction in desires. I remember Ellis—going where the wind takes him.

We go downstairs to the first floor and walk out into a long corridor that is dark and cool and lit by a wall of fluorescent tubes by Robert Irwin. We're the only ones in here.

"Do you have a 'but' with your line of work?" he asks, his voice quieter in the quiet space.

The lights range from cool blue to a fiery neon orange. The glow makes everything in the room warmer, more intimate. "Not really, I love my job," I say simply. "It's *literally* hope in action."

"That's a very poetic way to look at it." Something about the way he says it, I wonder if despite his love of art, he's pragmatic at heart.

"I get to believe in love as my job."

The word "love" feels outsized and overwhelming in this space. He asks, "So, you're planning on it for yourself? A match?" I feel his eyes on me, his unconscious sway closer.

"I am," I say. "I know I'm forty so, like, what's taking so long when it's my specialty?"

"Is it a case of the cobbler's family not having any shoes?" he teases.

"No, nothing like that," I say. And when I look at him, his expression is completely absorbed, so fixed on mine that I feel breathless for a second. "I just know exactly who I'm looking for, too."

When we leave the room, everything shifts into bright white, illuminating everything. We don't say anything else as we step out into the L.A. night.

23

The office is a little quiet on the Monday after our event. This is normal—everyone needs to decompress after big events. The young people have partied hard and are unusually taciturn as they drink their giant beverages.

I'm exhausted, too. The Park women barged over last night and demanded all the Daniel deets.

"May I help you?" I asked when they stampeded inside.

"Don't pretend like you don't know why we're here," Sunny said with a *tsk*. "Give us the dirt."

Emoni rolled her eyes. "You are too much, Sunny."

"What? Like you're not thinking the same!"

Both of them had also met Daniel at the mixer and had been way less cool about it than Halmoni. Emoni literally stroked his arm and said, "So exquisite." Nonetheless, I don't think he suspected anything, nor did he find it annoying. He, in fact, seemed charmed by my family. They were, of course, utterly charmed by him.

"You two just look *so right* together," Emoni said dreamily. "Very good-looking couple."

"Yes, and in a less-superficial observation, you seemed so comfortable around each other already," Sunny added. "It was like you've known each other forever." She paused. "Which I guess you have, in a way."

It *did* feel comfortable with Daniel. There seems to be this shorthand for us getting to know each other. Maybe it's just because we're around the same age—we cut through the bullshit. We also have many of the same pop culture references—I discovered that as we walked through the gallery and both made *Friends* jokes when we overheard security tell someone to "pivot away from the art." And even though we hadn't met under romantic circumstances originally, I know we're on the same page about this. Other than Brooke, Daniel didn't speak to any other women that night, and when I had to go back to work, he left the event.

"We had a nice time," I said, aware that I was being annoying and cryptic. But the entire situation was so heavy with expectation that I found myself treating it with care. At the moment, anyway. "I think it's clear that he came to the event for me and is interested."

"*Of course* he's interested," Emoni said heatedly. "Look at you! Our perfect girl."

"Oh my god," I said with a laugh. "Please refrain from that kind of sweet but delusional talk around Daniel."

Halmoni waved a hand in the air. "This is all going well. Did you make plans to see each other again?"

I hesitated. "Well, kind of? It was implied . . ."

Everyone groaned and I stood up. "Okay! That's enough girl talk, ladies! I have to go to sleep—good night you pushy broads!" They left, but Halmoni gave me one final death stare to make it clear to me that I needed to follow up with Daniel.

And I will. After work.

My first appointment today is with a man in his fifties who lost his husband two years ago, Lawrence. He's got thinning red hair and a beard. His nose is strong and high-bridged, and his eyes are deep-set and sorrowful.

Hairline: *A thinker. Intelligent.*

Eyes: *An emotional open book. It makes you both vulnerable and open to good fortune, as well.*

Nose: *Ambition and generosity.*

I like Lawrence. I want to find Lawrence's fated. "Look over my shoulder at the bird charm, please." His eyes shift and I concentrate my entire being into finding his fated.

In a few seconds I am in one of his past lives—a rural village. The hills are verdant and rolling, sheep dotting the landscape. Two men walk by, wearing furs and wool, heavily bearded. *Northern Europe?* I catch an exchange of words and the region is confirmed, although I can't make out the language. I've done this hundreds of times and it's still not enough to place European countries fast enough. I look closely at their clothing, too. Maybe medieval? Early Enlightenment?

Honestly, who cares. I'm here to find Lawrence. As the men reach a dwelling with a thatched roof and simple wood structure, the front door flies open and a man's standing there, cheeks ruddy with a huge grin. I can smell woodsmoke and meat. Feel the warmth of the building through the crisp air.

Lawrence. Perfect. Which one of these men is the one? Within seconds, the red thread unspools from him to one of the men carrying fur—a tall one with a blond beard and sparkling green eyes. The two exchange a secret smile and I see the longing in the blond man's face before I'm brought back to present day.

After I set the name of Lawrence's match in his drawer, I go to Halmoni's office, where she's writing something down in a notebook. She looks up with a smile. "Did you want to have lunch today?"

I sit down in a chair. "Oh, actually I'm meeting Mar today. I came in to talk to you about something else."

She puts her pen down. "Okay, what?"

I'm nervous about this talk, but I know what makes Halmoni happy, when to approach her with big asks. And now that I've found Daniel, she should be the happiest she's been in a long time. "So, while we did great for the summer event, we still need to drum up more interest so that we can increase our prices. I think we need to seriously expand our reach."

"I don't know, Cassia."

I pull out my phone. "Look. I told Matteo and Lila to create an Instagram account to start. We already have one thousand followers from them doing a couple weeks' work."

"Really?" She puts on her readers to look. Her eyes skim the screen and then she takes off her glasses, looking weary. "I just worry that this will put us at risk."

"Halmoni, no one in the whole wide world would believe us even if we told them!" I wave at the cupboard. "'We see past lives and a magical thread spells out your past love's name'? We'd be laughed off the internet."

She rests her chin on her clasped hands. "You're probably right. It's just . . . a lifetime of habit."

"I know," I say, and I mean it. It's been drilled into our family—a trauma that's been passed down since the days women in our families were persecuted for their practices. "But maybe change will help us create more love stories, and isn't that ultimately what we're here for?"

She eventually nods and says, "You're right. I just hope it doesn't change what we've worked so hard to build."

I reassure her it won't, but I feel a bit uneasy making promises I'm not sure I can keep.

Marcella meets me later at one of our favorite lunch spots—Little Dom's. We grab a table on the sidewalk under a striped awning, the best spot for people watching. You're always guaranteed good celeb spotting here, and not B-list reality-TV-show types—for-real movie stars. I once saw all the hobbits gathered in a booth together.

She digs for every detail about hanging out with Daniel while we start on our deep-fried rice balls.

"So, did you guys kiss?" she asks after I give her a literal beat-by-beat breakdown of the night.

Our arugula salad arrives and I heap some onto my plate. "Bro. No! Way too soon and it wasn't even officially a date. It felt like we were dipping a toe into the water, feeling things out. Not saying *the thing* out loud."

"Probably because of Ellis," she says with a mouthful of greens. "My poor little cutie."

I roll my eyes. "Poor little guy will forever mourn the loss of the middle-aged lady who fell off her bike."

"To him, the story is: This babe he was into dumped him. And then he discovered that his older, polished, successful boss stole her from under his nose." She shakes her head. "God, I love this, let's be honest."

I laugh as I pour more sparkling water into both our glasses. "Get out. Listen, I don't feel great about it. But I feel confident knowing he'll be just fine."

"I'm kidding." Marcella puts her hand on mine across the table. "He's probably fucking someone against a loft wall right now."

The couple next to us hears and their conversation comes to a complete halt. I bite back my laughter. "Hey, so how's the construction going?" I need to switch topics before we get kicked out of here.

And I really don't want to imagine Ellis doing anything with anyone. It hits me in a way I won't examine.

She groans and her aviators reflect the sunshine. "A nightmare. Ninety-two percent of being an adult is complaining about contractors," she says. "My memoir will be called: *Don't Even Get Me Started on Reliable Contractors*."

"It's going to be a hit."

Marcella grins briefly. "Yeah, it's going terribly terrible and probably going to push back the opening by a couple months."

"I'm sorry, dude," I say. "But no one in L.A. will expect a new restaurant to actually open when they say it will. It's like traffic. You need to pad on timing for reality."

"I know. But I'd love to get this done before winter when the kids will be home half the time because of some plague or another."

"Remember my evergreen babysitting offer."

"Ooh, yes!" Mar gets animated. "Speaking of. Very last minute, but can you take them this weekend? Logan and I were taken off the waitlist at our fave hotel in Los Alamos, after we couldn't get in for our anniversary." Los Alamos is just a couple hours north of us and is wine country for Southern California. It's gorgeous this time of year, everything green and lush.

"Sure," I say, taking a bite of salad. "And since it's not the season of hellish cold and flu, hopefully I won't get norovirus from them again." I have been babysitting these kids since they were born, and I have yet to have a winter without projectile vomiting since Mica started preschool.

"God, every year we come out of it alive I'm shocked. Luckily, they're old enough to just turn into TV zombies on sick days," she says. "I just wish I could plan ahead, know *exactly* which days they'll be sick."

"You'd just get a monthly email from the future telling you

which days to plan for, right?" I say as our pizza arrives—a Margherita piled high with prosciutto and fat dollops of ricotta. "*Dear Marcella, Please plan to be entirely fucked from the twelfth through fifteenth. Sincerely, Future.*"

She pushes her sunglasses up. "You kid, but that's because you know the future."

"I do not." I pull a slice and the cheese stretches enticingly. I motion for Mar to give me her plate and place the slice on there. "I know how to find your fated."

"Isn't that knowing the future?" she asks. "You are the most laid-back person I know because of this. What's it like not to be haunted by the specter of anxiety?"

"I get anxiety!"

She makes a *pfft* sound. "Being controlling and type A doesn't mean you have anxiety."

"Rude. What about my insomnia?"

"You drink espressos after dinner. Your fault."

The cheese on my pizza burns the roof of my mouth. But it's worth it—salty and hot, delicious. "You know I've been worried about finding Daniel for a long time."

"Of course. But you knew the ending ahead of time. What a gift." Marcella seems to catch herself. "Not a gift, sorry. I know it's been stressful. Like, you can't even bone a hot guy before your fated shows up ruining the whole thing."

"*That* is real," I say holding up my water. "Rest in peace, careless banging."

"God, I might cry," she says.

"But in all seriousness," I say. "I think now the stress has moved from *where is he* to *am I really doing the right thing here?*"

"Versus what? Dating Ellis?" The skepticism is high; I see Mar struggle not to sound judgmental.

"Not Ellis, necessarily, although yeah. More like . . . I don't know. Now that he's here I guess I might be having second thoughts?"

She nods. "I hear you. That's normal. It's like, once Logan and I got engaged, suddenly I was like, *Wait—for real*? The choice feels like it's taken away from you."

"Yes, that!"

Her red lips scrunch to the side, thinking for a beat before saying, "The thing is, that *is* the choice. You made the ultimate choice. Nothing is taken away; the world has actually opened up."

I'm silent for a second. "Wow, bitch, that got deep."

She laughs and throws a piece of bread at me. "Shut up."

When I get back to the office after lunch, I see a message waiting for me on my desk:

Daniel Nam called.

The ball is now firmly in my court. I don't bother figuring out how long to wait until I text him. I type it out before I can think:

Hi, it's Cassia.

Immediately:

Ooh, a text message in response to a phone call. You ARE younger than me.

I smile.

I work in an office with my family. It's like calling a boy on your family landline in the kitchen.

A boy, huh?

There's a goofy smile on my face as I type back:

I could pretend you're my best friend calling about math homework

Wow, intense flashback to algebra right now.

I'm sorry. Unless you liked math?

I hated it but joke's on me—architecture requires maths.

Sad.

There's a brief pause. He types back:

I called because I wanted to ask you out.

My hands hover over my keyboard, heart pounding. When I say yes, this will be real. I push back feelings about Ellis, about his enthusiastic and awed touch when we slept together. His face when I told him my mom died on my eighth birthday.

This is my future opening up for me, like Mar said. I type quickly:

Do it, then.

Another pause, and I wonder if I was being a bit too much. But he responds:

Dinner this weekend?

I'm babysitting my friends' kids all weekend. Maybe Sunday night?

Or I can help?

It's very sweet but I'm not sure that's a great idea.

Very unromantic first date. Let's keep to Sunday?

Sure. Should I steer us or do you have a spot you want to try?

There is just something so incredibly nice about a man who just makes a plan and follows through.

I love all food. You pick.

Okay. Will send you details EOD. Looking forward to it.

I heart the message and leave it at that.

24

The weather is perfect that weekend, so I take Ozzie and Mica to Echo Park Lake to ride the swan paddleboats. The sky is a pale blue, the clouds are gauzy, and the lake and surrounding park are filled with couples and families enjoying the day. The small man-made lake gleams dark blue, and a breeze kicks up the mist off the giant fountain set into the middle of it all.

We're in line, both of the kids eating paletas like they've never had sugar before—Ozzie's strawberry one staining her mouth red already. I'm slowly working on my mango one dipped in Tajín, enjoying the warm sun mixed with the cool breeze. I always relish the days leading up to our endless summer, making the most of lightweight jackets and closed-toe shoes before I have to wear linen for months.

"I don't want to wear a hat," Ozzie complains in her little lavender bucket hat embroidered with a sloth.

She makes a move to take it off with a grubby, red-stained hand, but I grasp it just in time. "Hey, hey, your mom will never let me near you again if you come back with a sunburn on your perfect little nose," I say as I bop it for good measure. She giggles. The routine for leaving Marcella's house is insane. Everyone slathers on sunscreen over every inch of their skin no matter what the activity, and no one leaves the house without grabbing a hat. I don't think kids today have had the sun touch their uncovered skin since birth.

Mica jumps from foot to foot. "Can I be the one to pedal?" The sugar's hitting this one hard.

"You can definitely be *one* of them," I say diplomatically. "It takes two to party."

"Will Mama and Daddy be sad they couldn't pedal?" Ozzie asks, dark brown eyes big and imploring.

"No, they will be quite happy for us." *Mama and Daddy are currently day-drinking their way through the central coast.* Just then, a plop of Tajín lands on my white jeans somehow. "Oh, crap." When I bend over to wipe it off, a small dog comes bounding at me—salt-and-pepper fur with floppy black ears, lolling tongue, and trailing leash—and literally licks it off my leg. "What is even—!"

"Pickle!"

The dog looks behind itself with a naughty little wiggle. When I look up to see the dog's owner, I almost fall over.

It's Ellis. He's running toward us, a pretty girl keeping up with him. His eyes are on the dog, and he doesn't realize I'm there until he's gotten ahold of the dog's leash.

My insides churn at the sight of him. It's like being dropped into a roller coaster seeing him this way. He looks so good—the breeze ruffling that head of hair, his black sunglasses perched on the strong bridge of his nose. When his head tilts toward me, all the angles of his face feel like a physical attack.

"Cass?" He's shocked when he notices me.

I try and hide my utter devastation at his mere presence. "Is this your dog?"

"Yeah." He reaches down and scoops the wriggly gray-and-white fluff in his arms. "Sorry, Pickle's new. Still trying to train him."

"He's an escape artist," the girl with Ellis says, her smile big and effervescent.

I look at her with a questioning smile and Ellis says, "Um, Cass, this is Avery. She's actually training Pickle." Avery's got that dog-person vibe—wearing cutoffs, a vintage sweatshirt, her dark hair in a low braid that manages to be messy and cute. She's beautiful in that freshly scrubbed way that you can be in your twenties. And she's got an ass that even I can't stop looking at. She's scratching Pickle under the chin and looking at him with big heart-eyes. "Avery, this is Cass. Cassia."

"Hi." I look at the dog. "And hi to you, Pickle." He wiggles his butt some more.

Ozzie and Mica are next to us in an instant, squealing over the dog. Ellis looks down at them, then at me. "Marcella's kids—Ozzie and Mica," I clarify. They ignore me as they are consumed by puppy love. Avery takes the dog from Ellis and crouches down so they can pet him.

"He's very friendly," Avery says to the kids, and they are enamored.

"Babysitting?" Ellis asks me.

I nod. "We're starting our weekend of utter chaos with the swan boats." I am very nervous suddenly. Has Daniel mentioned any interest in me to Ellis? Are there hard feelings? Of all the parks in the city . . . L.A. can be such a small town, sometimes.

"Good call," he says. "Tire them out with manual labor."

"Exactly," I say with a smile. And then I notice Avery noticing us and I wonder if they're dating. I'm sure that, at first glance, I just look like some woman he knows. But Ellis . . . the way he looks at me would make anyone look twice.

"Who are you?" Ozzie is suddenly between us, staring up at Ellis.

"Hey, I'm Ellis," he says, as if he's talking to a random adult at a party. "Do you like dogs?"

"I LOVE dogs!" she cries out. "But my dad is 'lergic."

He frowns. "'Lergies suck."

"They suck!" she relishes that word. He laughs, so incredibly charmed. Watching this interaction makes me feel turned inside-out. "Well, we have to get on the boat," I say loudly. "Come on, guys. Say bye to Pickle."

There are protests but I bulldoze over them, and we say goodbye. After tossing our popsicle sticks, we board our boat, and I try my damnedest not to look at Ellis, to keep my eyes on the kids and not have my gaze magnetically drawn to where he might be.

The boats are spacious, like little golf carts on water, and I sit next to Ozzie and pedal with her. I handle the steering so that we don't accidentally bump into other boats, or the fountain. The kids are loving it, and I bask in their pleasure. I've been a part of these kids' lives since they were in utero, and I relish being their source of fun.

While we float along the perimeter of the lake, I spot Ellis. He and Avery are standing far apart, clapping and urging Pickle to run between them. I guess it could be dog training, but they also look like a couple playing with their dog in the park. I shouldn't be bothered by it—I have *zero right* to be bothered by it. But I am.

"Can I pedal now?" Mica asks, already standing and shoving his head between us.

"Sure, bud," I say. "Let's pull over to the side to switch it up. You ready, Oz?"

She nods. "Okaayyy," she drags out.

I squeeze her shoulder. "Thank you, big generous girl."

We get the boat over to an uncrowded spot near the docking area and I risk one more glance at Ellis. He and Avery are standing close, the dog between them. Their heads are almost touching. It's intimate. Good. Good, she seems incredibly lovely and that's exactly what he deserves.

Then I hear a splash and my head whips back to the kids just in time to see Mica's head dip under the water.

"Mica!" I yell. Ozzie starts screaming and I say, *"Oz, do not move!"* and jump into the water. The water isn't deep—maybe five feet, but Mica cannot swim. I know this because I've heard Marcella complaining about this over the years, and how stressful going to the beach is because of it.

The water is ice cold and probably full of unspeakable things, but I do not think about it as I reach him quickly, and he hasn't drifted far. But he's panicking, flailing his limbs, and he pulls on me like a deadweight.

"Mica, please calm down. I'm here, you're fine," I say as I try and get ahold of him.

"I can't swim, I can't swim!" he screams in my face, his hands grabbing at my hair.

"Babe, I know. It's okay, I've got you," I say calmly, trying desperately to keep us both above water. Because I'm trying so hard to get a grasp on him, I don't realize how close we've gotten to the boat and one of his flailing arms hits the side. Hard. He screams out in agony, and this is when I start to panic.

Ozzie is now screaming her brother's name and sobbing and I am trying to get him on the boat when I see blood streaming from his arm. *Oh, fuck.*

And then a pair of arms is hoisting Mica up onto the boat. When I turn to see who it is, it's Ellis, of course, beside me in the water. Then, without saying a single thing, he puts his hands on my hips and pushes me up, too. I grab hold of the railing and get up onto the boat. I scramble over to Mica immediately, both of us soaked from head to toe.

"Let me see," I say, trying to keep the worry out of my voice. He's wailing and clutching his arm close to him. He shakes his head and just keeps wailing, pushing his body farther into the boat so I can't reach him. "Mica, sweetie, let's look."

I notice then that the boat is moving—Ellis has gotten on and is steering us back to the dock, where a crowd has formed. He's steering with one hand, his other arm looped around a crying Ozzie, keeping her tucked into him. His clothes are soaking wet.

After an inspection of Mica's entire body, I see nothing else injured on him but the long scratch on his arm. It's still bleeding and I take my sweatshirt off and wrap it around his arm before I carry him off the boat, and Ellis helps Ozzie off. One of the workers, a frazzled teenage girl, asks me, "Is everyone okay? Should I call an ambulance?"

I shake my head. "I think we can drive ourselves to the hospital. Thank you."

Ellis is now carrying Ozzie, who is clutching onto him for dear life. "Hey, let me take you guys," he says.

"Okay, thank you." My voice is shaky, and I know I shouldn't drive. I am so horrified by everything that I can't even be embarrassed that Ellis has managed to save me—yet again.

25

At the hospital, Mica is given a couple stitches and a sling so that he can take care of his arm for a few days. Ozzie is given a lollipop. Ellis watches the kids when I step out to call Marcella.

She answers immediately. "What happened?" she says as a greeting.

Normally I would make fun of her for that. But I burst into tears instead.

"Cass?? *Cass*. What happened?" There's an edge of hysteria to her voice and it immediately sobers me.

"Sorry, nothing big, don't worry." I take a breath. "Um, so you know how I always make fun of you for giving me that handwritten medical consent note when I babysit the kids?"

I hear her suck in a breath. I hurry and say, "Mica fell off the swan boat and hurt his arm, so he got stitches and a little sling. He'll be fine but I am *so fucking sorry*, Mar."

I hear her giant sigh of relief as if she's right next to me. "Oh my god, that's it? I almost fucking walked into the sea right now!"

"I know, I'm sorry. I think I'm wound up from it all and should have waited a beat before calling you. Sorry I worried you. I'm just . . . sorry."

"Hey, it's fine." Her voice is gentler now. "He's a kid, he's going to get hurt on my watch or your watch. Don't beat yourself up about it. But can I speak to him?"

"Yes, of course, let me go over there." I change the call to FaceTime and walk back into the curtained-off area where Ellis is sitting with the kids. I turn the phone to Mica.

"Ellis?" I hear Marcella's voice ask incredulously and I wince. Right, forgot to mention him.

"Oh, he happened to be at the park," I say with a *Can you fucking believe it* tone. "And yet again, saved the day."

Ellis turns red. "It wasn't a big deal."

"You saved *my child*." Marcella's voice echoes in the room. "It's a big fucking deal! Now, where's my baby?"

I hand Mica the phone and he FaceTimes with his mom, cheerfully showing her his stitches and sling. Ozzie, sitting beside her brother on the bed, clambers over to him.

I gesture for Ellis to follow me outside the curtain. He does, and it's only when we're alone that I finally feel my adrenaline go back to normal human levels. "I don't even know how to thank you," I say.

"You just did," he says with a smile. "It's okay. Please, stop thanking me." And there's something on the edge of his voice that makes me pause.

"I feel so awful," I say. "I knew Mica couldn't swim. Why did I pick this stupid activity? It was so irresponsible." The weight of it suddenly pushes down on my shoulders and I wish I could sit down.

"The odds of him falling off a goddamn *swan boat* were pretty low," he says. "And the lake is five feet deep. He wasn't really in danger."

"Except he tore up his arm and is probably traumatized for life!"

"Yes, I'm sure every time he sees a giant swan boat, he'll have a panic attack from here on out."

Laughter comes out of me in an ugly honk. "You kid, but . . ."

And then Ellis reaches out and squeezes my arm. "You did nothing wrong. Everyone's fine."

I nod. "Thank you for being there." His touch is instantly comforting, and I resist curling into him to exhale out the entire afternoon. "I wonder what our next run-in will be. Maybe involving some kind of embarrassing animal chasing me in a public square. What's an embarrassing animal? One of those baboons with the red butt, maybe?"

He throws his head back and laughs, so full-bodied and genuine. It makes me feel like I could fly and punch the clouds. Then he says, "It has to be one that's weirdly fast, so you have to *scurry*."

I snort-laugh. "Yes. Scurrying would be the only option. You've already seen me roll down a hill and wrestle a small child in a body of water." I am smiling so big, I feel it in my bones. "Small Chihuahua?"

"No, that's too cute. Maybe a mole rat?"

"Or what about, something large and weird? An ostrich."

We catch each other's eyes and start laughing, and suddenly it feels like we are standing very close. I take a step back. "You should head out," I say. "You left your dog and girl behind."

He makes a funny face. "Avery's not my girl."

"Oh, okay." I try and be cool about it, like hearing that isn't some sort of relief.

"There's no rush, Pickle loves Avery way more than me and she's happy to watch him."

I want to take him up on this offer so badly. Even though Mica is fine and Marcella isn't upset, I still feel shaky from the whole experience. But it's completely inappropriate.

He must see the indecision on my face because he says, "Happy to leave you all to it, too."

Really wish he wasn't being so incredibly perceptive right now. Making everything so much damn harder.

"Cassie!" I hear Ozzie's voice call out. I shoot Ellis an apologetic look and duck back in.

"Mom wants to talk to you," Mica says, holding out the phone. I brush his mop of curly brown hair out of his eyes before taking it.

Marcella's wearing a hat and is outdoors in some lovely location. Her cheeks are a bit flushed—from the sun or wine, I don't know. She says, "Just wanted to tell you that you better not beat yourself up about this for the rest of the weekend."

I nod, my throat closing up. "I'm sorry if this ruined your trip."

"What did I *just* say?" she says. "Also, you didn't ruin anything. It will take more than a few stitches on my firstborn to pry me out of wine country."

We hang up right as the doctor comes in and gives us the green light to head out. The doctor, an older woman with warm brown eyes and a kid-friendly disposition, gives us instructions on stitches care and hands me a prescription for some pain meds. Ellis comes in and Mica instantly holds his hand, which is so sweet I almost burst into tears, again.

It's already getting dark when we head out to the parking lot. "Should we get some food on the way home?" I ask the kids as we pile into the car. "Maybe some soup dumplings?"

Mica and Ozzie can't believe their luck. I look at Ellis as I secure Ozzie into her car seat. "Should I drop you off at home?"

"Only if you really don't need the help."

"Eat xiao long bao with us!" Ozzie's little voice is laced with a plea. Foodie toddler is hard to resist.

Mica is trying to play it cool, but I can tell he wants Ellis to stay, too. He hasn't left Ellis's side since the lake. "Want to have dinner with us?" I ask, trying to keep my voice, my face, every molecule of me, neutral.

"Sure," he says, getting into the passenger side.

The four of us head out, Mica and Ozzie chattering about all the dumplings they're going to eat, Ellis and I silent in the front, avoiding eye contact.

26

You guys really know your stuff," Ellis is saying as we sit around my dining table surrounded by the compact and wonder-filled boxes of Din Tai Fung. He's talking to the kids, who are expertly balancing their soup dumplings on their spoons, then biting off the tops before slurping out the soup in them.

"I've trained them well," I say. We all have damp hair from the showers that I immediately made us take once we got home. I started babbling to the kids nonstop while Ellis took his—trying not to imagine him naked in my shower, using my products and having them wash off in a sudsy glide down his body.

Jesus.

Suddenly, Mica pushes out of his chair. "Can I play a record please, Aunt Cassie?"

"Sure, baby," I say. "Just wipe your hands before touching."

He hastily wipes his hands on a napkin then rushes to my living room shelf of records. Mica loves my records. I'm sure they're the most novel thing in the world to a kid growing up today. He's flipping through them when Ellis looks at me. "You're such a hipster."

"Ugh, how offensive. I just used to date musicians a lot and the best thing to come out of that was my love of listening to music this way."

"With intention and focus," he says. "I get it. Sometimes I don't even know the titles to songs I listen to all day." Then he pauses. "You dated a lot of musicians, huh?" His eyebrow is cocked, challenging me.

Before I can answer, Mica finds something and places it on the record player. Slow and careful like we've practiced hundreds of times before. And then the first few notes of Pavement's "Cut Your Hair" starts playing.

"Good choice," I say as Mica comes back to the table, ignoring Ellis's question. "Did your dad introduce you to Pavement?" This is where Logan and I have shared interests—what Marcella disdainfully calls our love of sad-white-guy music. Which she says is doubly shameful since neither of us is white.

"Yeah! This song is funny because the guy doesn't want to cut his hair, like me!" Mica's perfect curls haven't been touched in years.

"Yeah, you and Stephen Malkmus are soulmates," I say.

Ellis looks amused. "You get dumplings *and* an indie rock education at Cassia's house? *Luuuucky.*"

Ozzie giggles. "We love Aunt Cassie's house."

At that Betty screeches. "Ooh can I feed her?" Ozzie begs.

"Sure, but after dinner. She knows she can't just demand treats," I say, which is punctuated by another vicious cry.

"You guys aren't scared of Betty?" Ellis asks.

"No!" both kids cry out. Ellis widens his eyes in surprise, and they giggle.

"She's nice to little ones," I tell him. "She can sense her dominance."

"Does that mean she actually accepts you as her alpha?" he asks me.

"Hardly. I'm her handmaiden."

He laughs. "She's a powerful bird."

I remember her behavior with him when he was over. "And she likes *you*, too. Literally the only human beings she tolerates are all in this room right now."

After we're done, the kids run into the living room to play with Betty while Ellis and I clean up the kitchen together. The sounds of the kids' squeals and laughter are a welcome backdrop so that standing side by side with Ellis at the kitchen sink doesn't feel too awkward.

The everydayness of this moment suddenly hits me in the chest. The possibility of it. A family eating dumplings, a mom sharing her favorite music with her son. The kids running around while Mom and Dad do the dishes in comfortable, companionable silence.

This is what I want. A family. Not out of obligation to my family business, but because I want to build a world around a child—make it as magical and wonderful for them as my mother made life for me.

The realization shakes me, and I switch my focus to Ellis. I watch as he makes neat piles for recycling, rinsing out containers before placing them in a paper bag. He turns off the faucet between washes and uses only a trickle of water.

"Environmentalism runs deep in you, it does," I say in a bad attempt at Yoda's voice.

He looks startled for a second then starts laughing. "Oh, that's so bad."

"I know. Erase it from your memory." My face feels hot and I'm truly shocked at such a dorky fumble in front of a guy. This is the uncool side of me I usually save for Mar. I blame it on my sudden family epiphany.

But he won't let it go. "Forget it, I won't," he says in an *excellent* Yoda voice.

"I hate you." I flick water at him from the sink, but he dodges it artfully. "Look, I'm wasting water. Arrest me."

"That is so . . . mature," he says. "And listen, I have no choice but to save water. My retirement is going to be spent in line for water rations."

"Bleak."

"Yeah. I'm really going to miss trees."

I lean against the counter, drying my hands off with a kitchen towel. "You really believe that, though? No trees in your lifetime?"

He shrugs. "I mean, no. We'll probably have trees for a while. But it's part of the appeal of my job, you know? Creating landscapes that are equipped for whatever the future may hold. It's hopeful."

Something softens in me, and he must see it in my face because he looks at me intensely before clearing his throat and turning away.

It's like being doused with water. I'm going on a date with Daniel *tomorrow*.

The kids want to show Ellis the tricks they've taught Betty, so he sticks around for a little longer and I feel myself fidgeting with restlessness. He's so good with them, so fully present and into whatever funny things they are sharing with him. I try not to read too much into it—it's easy for twentysomething men to be good with kids. There are no stakes, they are here to be fun for a couple hours, then they can seamlessly go back to their regular lives of sleeping in and leisurely dinners.

Wow, okay, really convincing yourself there, Cass. But I do have to remind myself of reality. Just because I am having big baby family feelings today doesn't mean that Ellis is the solution for it.

It's hard for me to cut it short, but I have to. If only because Mica really needs to get some rest.

"Last Betty trick," I say once they show her hanging upside down from Mica's index finger.

They groan and Ellis says, "It's getting late. I need to get my beauty sleep."

Mica giggles. "Boys don't need beauty sleep."

"Pardon me?" Ellis says, playing affronted. "You think I just wake up this way?"

The kids are still laughing when he gets up to leave. He gives Mica a high five and spins Ozzie in the air before he steps out. I tell the kids to go brush their teeth while I step outside with him.

It's cold out, and I rub my arms for warmth. The porch light flickers overhead. "Thanks so much, again. Really."

"Hey, what did I say? No more thank-yous." Again, that little edge to his voice.

I refuse to keep making bad decisions so I say, "I have to tell you something." It comes out urgent and he instantly steps back.

"Okay." He crosses his arms.

"This is . . . I really don't know how to say this without it being kind of shitty." I run my hands through my hair, long and tangled. Then I look him in the eyes, because he deserves that. "I'm going to have dinner with Daniel tomorrow night."

He looks confused for a second. "Daniel?" Then it registers. "Daniel . . . my *boss*."

I nod and tense up all over. I don't know what I'm expecting but my body is bracing itself for it.

Ellis just stares down at the ground between us, then takes a deep breath. "Okay. Wow." His voice is even, not revealing a single thing.

I want to give him more space to digest but instead I keep talking. "I'm sorry. He came to one of our matchmaking events and well, we ended up talking. So . . ."

"I should go." He won't even look at me as he turns and heads down the stairs.

And before I can help it, I say, "I'm so sorry, Ellis."

He doesn't say anything as he walks away.

That night, as I'm in bed, tossing and turning, I realize that I drove him to my house. He probably had to take an Uber home. I don't know why, but this is the thing that gets to me most, and I stay up for another couple hours feeling like a piece of shit.

27

For the first time in weeks, I have a dream that night.

There's rushing water, I can hear it but I can't see it. I am surrounded by water and it's overwhelming. A voice calls out to me, and when I turn to look for who's behind it, I spot a creature through a cloak of fog. It's white—but I can't tell what it is. A horse? Someone is calling me, but it's not my name. I just know they are calling out for me.

I wake up tangled in my sheets. I don't have time to process the dream because both Mica and Ozzie discover that I'm awake and jump into bed with me—elbows jabbing into my sides, little bare feet bouncing off my pillow.

"Wake up, Auntie Cassie!" Ozzie screeches, getting me into a chokehold. Who needs caffeine with these two, honestly.

We're on the deck repotting some houseplants (well, Mica's watering mostly himself and his sister) when Mar and Logan arrive. After all hugs are had and bags are packed, Mar hands me a crate of wine.

"Oh my god," I say, almost falling over when I take it. "This is too much."

"No, it's not," she says firmly. "You had to go to the hospital and hang out with a kind-of ex for me."

"Because I'm the world's worst babysitter!"

"Shut up already. Show me what you're wearing tonight for the date?"

After they all leave, Daniel sends me a text asking for my address. We make plans and I spend the rest of the day prepping my bod for this very-big-deal first date. And at seven on the dot, the doorbell rings.

He's right on time. Tonight, anyway. In life, he's a little late.

I open the door and Daniel's standing there holding a bouquet of dark purple calla lilies wrapped in butcher paper, tied with a dark-green velvet ribbon. The sight of them fills me with intense pleasure.

"Hello," he says, the corners of his eyes crinkling in a smile as he takes in my loose gray trousers and clingy powder-blue cardigan with only two buttons fastened. My wavy hair tumbles over my shoulders, having been air-dried and artfully "undone."

"Hello," I say back, opening the door wider. He hands me the flowers.

"Beautiful," I say, taking them gingerly, not wanting to crush a single stem. "Come in, I just have to grab a jacket."

He's looking around my place, staying in his spot in the entryway, when I come back from my room with a suede jacket. When I look at him quizzically, he points to his black oxfords. "Don't want to move beyond here."

"Ah, your British parents taught you well," I say solemnly.

He laughs. "Actually, it was my flatmate out of uni. A Chinese American bloke who nearly murdered me when I wore shoes into our flat the first day."

"Good man. Or bloke," I say. "Oh, and one second." I duck to the corner of the dining room where Betty is currently hidden from view. I pop in some treats and she makes a loud squawk, furious that my movements are so rushed. And pecks my hand for good measure.

"Is that a bird?" I hear him ask from the other room.

I close the cage and walk back to him, nursing the attacked finger. "Define 'bird,'" I say dryly.

"Did it *bite* you?" he says, stepping over instinctively, forgetting about his shoes. He gently takes my hand to look at it.

"Oh, yeah. Betty shows all feelings by biting," I say, letting him cradle my hand in his for a second before pulling it away. "I'm fine, she didn't even break skin this time. Downright mild!"

"Wow," he says. "Living on the edge, here."

I'm slipping on some kitten-heeled mules when he says, "Your house is a perfect little dream. The structure, your furniture, all the details like those cupboard handles . . . just really gorgeous."

I soak in the words. "Thanks. I grew up in this house and it took me a few years to make it really feel like my own."

"You grew up here?"

"Yeah, long story," I say. "I'll tell you over dinner."

On our drive, Daniel fiddles with the music so much that I take over, picking Caribou.

Some light chitchat about our weeks is exchanged before I bring up what happened yesterday with Ellis. I want to get it over with.

"So, he knows?" Daniel finally says when I'm done explaining.

"Yeah. And sorry if you didn't want him to know, but I did. I just didn't want this to feel all covert and *bad*."

"You don't have to be sorry. He would have found out, you're right." But something seems to be bothering him. After a few seconds he says, "How does Ellis always seem to be there when you need him?" His tone is genuinely perplexed, not bitter or insinuating.

"I don't know."

"Actually, I don't even know why I'm acting surprised," he says. "There's a joke around our office that Ellis is, like, psychic."

"What?" I try not to sound as alarmed as I feel.

"He just . . . seems to *know*. When you need help with something, when you're going through a bad time—he's that guy. You can rely on him."

Well, this is distressing. Daniel seems to sense the slight shift in my mood because he says, "Maybe we can *not* talk about Ellis on our first date?" with a grin shot my way. It goes straight through me, landing firmly low in my belly. It is just a fact of nature that Daniel is incredibly attractive. His eyes burn over me before facing the windshield again. "You look beautiful, in case I didn't say it already."

My jacket feels warm. "Thank you." I take a surreptitious glance at his camel crewneck sweater and navy trousers. His sleeves are pushed up and long white shirtsleeves peep through. Impeccable. "You look . . . like a Frenchman. In an ad. About nice watches."

We both start laughing. "Wow," he finally says. "I've peaked."

I ask Daniel to tell me "fun architectural facts" about L.A. as we drive down the 110, twisting through the Arroyo full of oak trees and ancient bridges. "Did you know this was the first highway in America?"

"I did, and it makes sense given that it has literal ninety-degree-angle off-ramps."

"It's dangerous but exciting, right?" His enthusiasm for L.A. is contagious.

"You're truly gambling with your life every time you get on it," I agree cheerfully.

"What was it like for you to grow up here? I can't imagine."

Cars are stopped ahead of us, so Daniel slows down. He knows my mom died but not the full extent of the tragic details. "I always thought L.A. was actually really normal and not that glamorous. I mean, I went to school and hung out with friends at the mall. But when I traveled after I graduated high school, I realized how unique L.A. was. How integral sunshine was to keeping me sane. How I was so blessedly invisible here."

"Really?" he says. "I always imagined growing up in L.A. was like, you studied at the beach and partied with celebrities at night."

"Okay, I think you watched too much *90210*."

"Oh, I had *such* a crush on Jennie Garth."

"You would!"

"Please, you were a Dylan girl."

"Literally I'd be a psychopath if I was a Brandon girl."

There's our shorthand again. It's almost like the getting-to-know-each-other has been bypassed, and we're in a super comfortable space already. In that way, this doesn't feel like a first date at all—it feels like one in a string of many we've had over the years. We drop the car off with a valet and walk into the unassuming but immaculately designed space. It's an upscale Korean restaurant that has been buzzy ever since its opening and we get seated in a cozy corner table. The hostess seems to know Daniel and the two exchange pleasantries.

"Are you like the Mister Rogers of the L.A. restaurant scene?" I ask as he pours me a glass of water from the carafe placed on the table.

"Maybe? Sexy, huh?" His hands are steady as he fills my squat glass. The word "sexy" vibrates in the air for a second.

"Nothing hotter than a man in a cardigan," I say.

"I've got a wardrobe full of them," he says quickly, winking. I laugh and am still laughing when the server comes to take our order. I wave at Daniel, giving him permission to order for us. He does, with care, but zero pretension somehow. I realize, then, that I've been secretly waiting for him to be an asshole of some kind. Some very smooth, urbane, bachelor type that is single for a reason. So far, I've got nothing. He's smooth, yes, but just because he's comfortable with himself. It's not practiced, it's natural. And I suppose that the whole British factor might be a part of it. We American women are so utterly incapacitated by a British accent.

"Tell me about your dating history," I say after the server leaves. It's time to cut to the chase.

"Pardon?" he says, only half joking.

The soft lighting in the restaurant makes him look dreamy and soft, but I will not be deterred. "I'll give you mine. I've had a few serious partners, but I've never had one serious enough to live with or contemplate marriage with. And my last serious relationship was a whopping five years ago."

"Okay," he says slowly, smiling. "Well, I have had only two serious girlfriends, and one of them I *did* live with."

Something jealous and spiky pushes into my chest. "Oh yeah? How recent?"

"We broke up seven years ago. I beat you. Anyway, we broke up because I worked too much," he said. Then he shakes his head. "Actually I don't know why I said that. It was because . . . I didn't let her in. That's what she said, anyway. And she was probably right, although I felt like I was letting her in as much as I could."

Our drinks arrive and he thanks the server before continuing. "My parents died. And I shut her out because I didn't want to talk to anyone about it unless they truly understood grief. And Elenore, bless her, she didn't."

I take a sip of the bracing ginger cocktail in front of me. "Unfortunately, I know what you mean." His eyes meet mine in understanding, and then I tell him an abbreviated version of my sad Mom story.

"Cassia. I'm so sorry," he says when I'm done. His voice is low, feeling every one of the words.

I meet his eyes. "Thank you."

"But it's quite beautiful," he says, not eating, his chopsticks held in his hand, his elbows on the table. "How your grandparents kept the house for you."

They kept the house because for the entire first year of my life in Hancock Park, I cried every night, asking to go back home. Halabuji eventually turned my bedroom at their house into a carbon copy of the one in Mount Washington: replicating my little built-in desk, even adding a window so that it looked out onto a tree the same way the one at home did. Painting the walls a sage green and putting up all the same art and trinkets my mother had placed in my room over the years. They felt guilty for not moving into the Mount Washington house for me, but I knew it was too painful for them. Not to mention so totally not my grandmother's vibe.

"It was the best gift I could have ever received," I say simply.

"It's really very special," he says quietly. "I can see why you'd want to hold on to that connection to your mother."

Daniel's right. There is something so comforting about knowing that the person you're with gets it. The grief that takes different forms every hour of the day. Sometimes it's monstrous and suffocating. Sometimes it's a fixture as mundane as a persistent backache.

"Tell me more about you," I say after most of our food arrives. "I want to know all about how it is to grow up as an Asian dude in England."

He laughs. "Oh, it was a fantastic time."

"Really?"

"Actually, I don't know why I said that in a sarcastic tone," he says. "It wasn't that terrible. In fact, it wasn't terrible at all. I grew up in Woodford, which is kind of a suburb of London, or the equivalent. I went to normal schools, nothing too elite or posh to make me feel inferior. But I just—I never felt right there. And not just because of being adopted. The age, the history that's entrenched in every part of England—it felt stifling. When I came to California for graduate school, it was the first time I felt like I was home."

I let the zippy flavors of vinegar and pepper in a scallop hit my tongue before responding. "I know I'm biased, but there's nowhere like California. And Los Angeles is the best city in the world."

"Absolutely no bias there," he says, eyes twinkling in the warm lighting of the restaurant. "But also, you are correct."

We laugh and before we move apart, he reaches over and brushes my hair away from my eyes. There's something very familiar about it and he seems surprised, too, pulling his hand back quickly. And suddenly I feel like we've known each other for years. I've never felt this with anyone before, and I know it's because the connection of our past lives is getting stronger with every second I spend with him. The relief of it floods me. *I've found him.* At last, at last.

Dinner lasts for hours, and we never run out of things to talk about. Our families, childhoods, movies, music—all of it. And when we leave, he holds my hand, his grip firm and warm. The car ride is quieter. We open the windows a little and let the sounds of the freeway, of the city whooshing by, fill the spaces between us.

When we get to my house, Daniel walks me up to my door. We stand under the porch light, facing each other as the fragrant evening air surrounds us. My jasmine is bursting with perfume, like it knows this is its moment to shine.

"Thank you for dinner," I say. Because, of course, Daniel nabbed the check at some mysterious point in the evening.

"You're so welcome," he says, his voice gravelly and proper. "Thank you for the brilliant company."

It feels like we're in a play and I start laughing. "Sorry," I say when I catch my breath. "This is just so—*how do adults end a date?*"

He gets in close, his hand catching mine again, his fingers entwining with mine. "How *do* adults end a date?"

My breath hitches as he lifts my hand up to his mouth and brushes his lips against it. I feel it in my cells. I pull him to me until my head is tilted back, my eyes meeting his. "They make jokes about how to end a date," I murmur.

When he kisses me, it's questioning, his lips brushing against mine like a whisper. I respond by parting my lips, telling him *yes, yes, yes*. And the kiss gets real then, his tongue touches mine and both of us kind of melt into each other. He lets go of my hand to wrap an arm around my back, his other hand cupping my jaw, his thumb stroking the soft skin beneath my ear. I make a noise against him as I grab hold of his arm. The kiss is searching, unearthing things. It feels like the *beginning*.

I have no idea how long it goes when he makes the first move to part. When we do, I feel dazed, slightly drugged. The jasmine envelops me. He looks as taken aback as I do, and he runs a hand down my arm. "Well."

I nod. "Mm-hmm." My lips are tingling, they feel burned.

"I should go," he says.

"You should?"

He laughs. "Yes. I want to . . . do this properly."

I know what he means. And how it feels contrasted against that weekend with Ellis. "Okay. Thanks, again, for dinner."

He brushes his lips on my forehead. "The pleasure was mine." And then he waits on the porch until I get inside. I wave at him before closing the door, and from my window I watch as he walks back to his car. He takes his time, looking at my yard on the way. The flowers bloom in the night for him.

28

I balance a takeout tray of various caffeinated beverages to my grandparents', dodging small dogs and strollers through Larchmont Village.

When I make it to the house, I find the Park women out on the back terrace. The roses are fragrant, and the magnolia trees are thick with glossy green leaves.

"Thank goodness," Emoni says when she spots me. "I can't believe you ran out of coffee, Unni."

Halmoni makes a grunt-like noise. "Costco stopped carrying my favorite one. I have to figure out my next plan."

I set the tray down and pass everyone their drinks. "You know, you can just buy it at normal price somewhere else."

"Please," she says. You could never take the Korean War out of Halmoni. She has entire drawers in her kitchen dedicated to unused takeout utensils and napkins.

Halmoni called a meeting for us at the house today, saying she had too many errands to run to stop by the office. After a sip of coffee she says, "I called you all here to talk about my retirement."

My eyes widen. "Really?" It's not the biggest surprise in the world. Halmoni is in her eighties, and this topic has certainly been discussed. But never officially.

"I'm not dead yet," Halmoni barks. "It makes sense to make the plans now."

I sit back in my chair. "Wow, okay. I'm ready. What are you thinking?"

"I'd like to retire by the end of the year."

Emoni makes a small noise and I look at her. "I'll also be retiring," she says, almost apologetically.

My head immediately snaps to Sunny, who says, dryly, "Don't look at me. I'm here for a while."

I sag with relief. "Christ. I was about to have a heart attack."

"We would never leave you alone, anyway, Cassia," Halmoni says, softening. "But it's time for me and your Emoni to get our rest."

"Of course." I reach both my hands out to touch theirs. "I'm really glad, for you both. You've worked so hard."

"And so have you," Emoni says, squeezing my hand.

Halmoni nods. "Yes, you have. So, we have some more news for you."

My scalp tingles, and I have a feeling I know what they're about to say.

Sunny says, "Can I tell her?"

Halmoni nods and Sunny shoots me a huge smile when she says, "You're going to succeed Halmoni as president."

Emoni claps her hands ecstatically while Halmoni and Sunny both beam at me. Suddenly, Halabuji rushes out of the workshop in the garage. "Did you tell her?" he hollers, holding up a ruler and wearing safety goggles.

"Yes!" Halmoni hollers back.

"Congratulations, Cassia!" he says, waving the ruler at me.

It's like *Succession* but only one episode and very cute. I start laughing. "Oh wow, are you sure?" I look at Sunny. "What about . . ."

She shakes her head. "Sorry but I have zero interest in taking on that responsibility in my golden years. I'll be helping with readings but that's it."

"Wow, okay," I say, taking it all in. "Maybe it's time to let the interns loose on TikTok?" I joke.

Halmoni doesn't laugh but she smiles. "I trust you, Cassia. Go do your social media thing."

"Okay, okay," I say under my breath, still taking it in. "I mean, I knew that this would happen but I guess it's still somehow surprising."

"Like everything," Halmoni says with fondness in her voice. "I am so proud of you. And I know that the company will continue to thrive under you."

"Especially now that you've found Daniel!" Emoni says as she wraps me in a tight squeeze.

I feel myself tense under her touch. Suddenly the timing of all of this feels strangely fortuitous. "What does the company's future have to do with Daniel?" I ask, pulling away.

Sunny drops her head into her hands. "Emo, Jesus."

Emoni flushes. "What! It's not anything *bad*."

A foreboding lodges itself in the pit of my stomach and I look to Halmoni, whose expression is stoic as always. "Were you guys . . . were you waiting on me to find Daniel before naming me the successor?"

"No!" Sunny exclaims. "It wasn't that."

"Well," Emoni says, dragging the word out. She catches my expression and says, "Cassia, it was only practical. We wanted to make

sure everything was stable and on course for your future and your future daughter."

My head swims at those words. "Pardon. Me?"

"You've gone and done it now," Sunny says as she plops back in her chair. "Shit."

Halmoni claps her hands loudly. "Everyone, stop being so dramatic. My goodness." Before I can even open my mouth, she points to the chair near me. "Please, sit down."

I remain standing. "No! Do not talk to me like I'm ten years old."

"If you were ten, you would listen."

Normally, a sharp comment like that from Halmoni would make me yield. But I surprise myself by remaining standing, staring her down. It's a silent standoff in the splendor of this yard, the scent of roses wafting over us.

She takes a deep breath and places her hands on the chair in front of her. It's a tiny, almost imperceptible waver. "Cassia, you know we always wanted you to find Daniel. And we're so happy you have. And we never wanted to put this pressure on you."

I continue to stare silently.

"But it's true—we weren't sure if giving you the company would distract you from finding your fated. And more than the company, more than anything, we want you to start your life. Your family," Halmoni's voice gives way here, to a tenderness.

Tears well up and I blink them away. "I know. But, what if I didn't? Would I have lost my value then?"

"Of course not," Sunny says vehemently. "I, more than anyone, understand the value of a life on your own terms." There's a moment between her and Halmoni here—a reckoning that I know will never really be reckoned, but that had been buried under the passage of time, as everyone's focus moved to me and finding Daniel.

I never felt like my gift was a burden until right this very second. That feeling low in my belly—it's radiating through my body. A dread poison.

"Yes, but you had that choice because of *me*," I say. "Mom had a daughter, I have the gift. Pressure's off." The bitterness slips off my tongue and I see it land on everyone. Sunny, particularly, looks stung.

"It was never supposed to be a burden," Emoni says, her voice sad. "We're sorry if that's how you feel."

My anger starts to plateau as I take in the misery of my family. Halmoni looks pale when she says, "I am always thinking of you first, Cassia." In that raw confession, I see all the nights of Halmoni helping me with homework. Of Emoni teaching me how to play Go-Stop. Of Sunny chaperoning school field trips, sanitizing her hands every five minutes. All the trips to the dentist, the back-to-school shopping, the sleepovers hosted in this very house.

These women raised me and I have never second-guessed my place in this family until right this minute. I feel myself deflate, the anger leaving me as quickly as it came. "I know that, of course. I appreciate you all. But, the Daniel thing—I want it to feel happy and real. Not . . . a duty."

Emoni's face is soft when she says, "Love is never a duty."

I want to smile and be done with it but something about this is still making me uneasy. Love is never a duty, but for my family it kind of is. There's expectation there—it might be tied to the idea of me finding happiness, but my family's business relies on that happiness.

And when my mother rejected her fated—her relationship with her parents fractured. With Halmoni.

So, love isn't an easy concept, a given, in my family. It's way more complicated and for the first time, maybe ever, I wish that we were just normal.

29

When wedding season hits, work is beyond busy. People get marriage and true love on the brain when they're forced to spend every weekend from May through September witnessing love over and over again. A fun perk during wedding season is that we get the occasional engagement announcement of successful matches. It's a hectic but fulfilling time.

Despite working a ton, I find time for Daniel because guess who loves digital organization more than me? I'm responding to an email at my desk when Daniel texts me with a link to a shared calendar called "Daniel and Cassia Date." It's hard not to smile as I open it and find that he's input all his availabilities for the next month. I add mine, and within minutes, I get a calendar invite for a hike that weekend.

"You are a very outdoorsy Brit," I say between huffs as we walk up a steep trail in Griffith Park. The sun is out and I am sweating profusely in my tank and shorts. I have the world's biggest straw hat on because all headwear pride goes out the window after a certain age.

Daniel stops under the blessed shade of an oak tree, letting me catch up. "Excuse you, but Brits aren't all dandies sitting around parlors. I'll have you know some of us spent our childhood summers in the woods."

"Did you?" I ask as I take advantage of our break to take a swig from my water bottle.

"I did," he said. "My grandparents lived in Kent and I spent weeks tramping through the forest nearby."

"Aw, like Christopher Robin," I say and he sprays a little water on me from his bottle. But I gather all these little facts about him like a magpie.

We reach a peak overlooking all of Los Angeles, the sky a pale blue with a layer of gray hovering over the city. "This is one of my favorite spots in the entire city," he says. "When I first came here I couldn't believe everyone had access to all this nature."

I take it in—the clear grid of streets, downtown a clump of buildings in the distance, the palm trees that outline this city like topographic borders. Everyone in L.A. loves hiking, but it's never really been my thing. I didn't grow up in a "nature" family—the trips I take on my birthday are usually my only jaunts into the wild for the most part.

"Thanks for sharing this with me," I say. "I feel like it's always the transplants that show me new stuff in my own city."

Daniel comes closer and fans me with his hands. "Even if I make you hike in the middle of the day?"

"I won't hold that against you. I know people who didn't grow up here actually like the heat." When I say it, he reaches down and kisses me. The temperature goes up a few degrees.

A few days later, I've scheduled a date for us—at a K-Town spa. On my way there, Mar texts, asking if I want to meet her at a bookstore for browsing and a coffee. I tell her I'm on my way to see Daniel.

Again? You guys have been hanging out like a lot a lot.

Yeah—fast forward courtship, baby!

No more communication with Ellis, then, huh?

I get annoyed and put my phone on Do Not Disturb. Ever since the Echo Park Lake rescue, Mar has brought up Ellis a couple times and while I understand that he endeared himself to her by saving her child, I need her to stop bringing him up. I'm in this with Daniel, and we've already been dating for a couple weeks, and I really wish she could just be one hundred percent behind me on this.

Daniel somehow manages to look good in the cotton T-shirt and shorts they provide for us at the spa. "It's offensive how handsome you are," I say.

He grins, comfortable with compliments in a way that makes him more attractive somehow. "Well, I *am* going to be judged by a bunch of halmonis, you know."

"You will, and probably the halabujis, too," I say as I lead us to the salt room.

"Oh, I *know*," he says. "I just showered and sat naked in soaking tubs surrounded by very curious farsighted eyeballs."

While I laugh, I wonder if there was something very worth looking at. We haven't slept together yet and while I'm not in a huge rush for it, I am starting to feel the embers of impatience whenever we touch, when our bodies hover near each other's—the desire thick between us. I have faith in our compatibility but . . . it would be nice to have confirmation.

The salt room is empty when we walk in—a dimly lit space full of pink salt and bamboo mats. We lie down on the mats, resting our heads on contoured wood blocks. The sound of woodwinds wafts over us. "According to my grandmother, the salt in this room is thousands of years old and when it's infused into our bodies, it fixes an array of ailments."

Eyes closed, Daniel murmurs, "Hm. Sure, it's also very relaxing."

"That too." I glance over at him and get a good look while he can't see me. His strong profile and relaxed posture communicates so much to me: steadiness and strength. Confidence. Is that what has drawn me to him life after life? It does appeal to me, obviously. We're an Excel-sheet power couple.

Later we grab lunch in the spa, sitting on the heated floors with a low wood table between us. The setting reminds me of the weird dream/vision I had at the sound baths. I can't believe it's been more than a month since my birthday. Ellis feels like both yesterday and a lifetime ago.

We immediately start sharing our meal, as though we've done it before. Daniel takes some soy sauce and scallion–covered tofu and puts it in my bowl of rice. I push the kimchi closer to him when I can tell he needs it. Everything is well-orchestrated despite us having had no practice.

Well, in this life anyway.

"So, how's your first K spa experience?" I ask him.

"Other than being ogled by old men—great," he says.

"You mean *because* of the ogling," I say. When he laughs I reach for the soybeans and am reminded of Ellis's love for the bland banchan. *Cass?* I say this with the utmost, gentle kindness to myself: *Stop fucking thinking about Ellis!*

"No, but honestly, I love it," he says, dipping his spoon in the kimchi jjigae. "I haven't had many Korean friends, even in Los Angeles, weirdly enough. I love having you as my tour guide to all the most Korean spots."

It warms me, this vulnerability. "Well, I have yet to take you to the most Korean spot yet."

"Really, and where's that?"

"Costco."

He throws his head back with laughter, the sound attracting everyone's attention around us.

A few days later, we're driving back from watching *Reality Bites* at a revival theater. "That movie *is* the right movie to lose your virginity to. Smooth move," I say.

"Thank you," Daniel says with a laugh, his hand on the steering wheel. "I owe Ethan Hawke some credit, I think."

I pick music from my phone. What I've learned is that Daniel has no opinions on music and it is now my life's mission to educate him. Otis Redding starts playing and I look at him. "Ethan Hawke in that movie almost ruined all men for me."

"Understandably," he says. "But we all know she should have ended up with Ben Stiller in the end."

"My god!" My body does a full-body shudder. "He was a walking, talking boner kill."

"He was just an adult!" Daniel protests. "Sue the man for having a job!"

"Touchy, touchy," I say with a laugh.

He shoots me a look, still grinning. "I'm going to choose to ignore that because you're so pretty."

We pull up to his house where I've left my car. Daniel lives in a beautiful little Spanish cottage in Los Feliz, covered in hot-pink bougainvillea and shaded by olive and cypress trees. "Not native," he had pointed out to me with chagrin when we met there earlier.

In the parked car, he leans back in his seat and looks at me. There's a little something in his heated gaze, his face lit by the warm yellow of the streetlamp. "Would you like to come in?"

"Yes, please." I've been dying to see the inside of his house. There is a bit of formality with Daniel in this way: He is a gentleman to the nth degree—always taking me out, paying, and driving. I sense it's his old-fashionedness, about doing this "the right way."

Everything feels oh so very right as we walk through his door, his house smelling like wood and expensive candles. I have every intention of looking at his sure-to-be-immaculately designed home, but as soon as he hangs my jacket, I'm pulling him in for a kiss. He's surprised, and smiles against my lips. "Well, okay." His arms wrap around me tight, one hand spanning my back and the other gently gripping the back of my neck. Our bodies are practically sealed together as the kiss gets deeper. He walks me backward as we kiss, and I slip my hands under his navy sweater, his skin so incredibly warm and firm. When my legs hit the back of his sofa, we disentangle long enough for me to pull the sweater off of him.

His eyes are hazy when he stops my hands and says, "Let's go to my room."

I'm sure his sheets are perfect and his mattress feels like heaven, but for once, I don't want all that perfection. I get flashes of sleeping with Ellis—laughing as we awkwardly figured out each other's bodies. The memories buzz in my brain and I need to shut them off. I start unbuttoning my top—a silky blouse that puddles to the ground when I take it off. "I like your living room."

He bends his head close, his lips hovering near mine. "Oh, do you? What color is the rug?"

"Mm, ecru," I say as he finds a sensitive spot on my neck.

His laughter is warm on my skin. "Ecru? Such a specific color choice."

Daniel keeps his eyes on my face, a gentleman until the end. I unsnap my bra and his jaw clenches as he keeps his gaze fixed on my eyes.

"You seem like an ecru kinda guy," I say as I slide my bra off.

He swallows. Hard. "Yes, one of the finer, ah, off-white shades."

My belt drops to the floor. Then my jeans. "Keep talkin' color theory to me."

His resolve breaks and he's on me in an instant, his bare chest on mine as I wrap my legs around him. When he traces my shoulder with a fingertip, his mouth is by my ear when he asks, "Is this okay?"

I answer with my mouth on his, and when his hands roam over my body, a feeling of intense déjà vu washes over me. We've done this before. I've felt this skin before. When we touch, skin to skin, it feels like a homecoming. And I know Daniel feels it, too, because when he looks at me, it's with an intensity that seems to overwhelm him. "Cassia," he whispers.

He takes me on the living room rug, which, I later find out, is actually a pattern of deep blues.

30

I move through the next few weeks as if in a dream. Everything is falling into place, everything feels so right. Our date calendar is on fire, constantly updated. There is such an ease in folding Daniel into my daily life. On the days we start together—whether at his house or mine—we brush our teeth at the same time, our electric toothbrushes whirring while the kettle is heating up water for coffee.

I shower at night, him in the morning. Sometimes together.

Daniel and I are on the same page about our eggs-and-toast breakfast—especially on the days he's made bread. The first time he made me a loaf of sourdough, I almost got pregnant from my first bite.

And we *excel* at evenings. Between Daniel and me, we have the entirety of the L.A. restaurant scene covered. Some nights it's Szechuan in the San Gabriel Valley. Other times it's old-school steak houses in Beverly Hills, sometimes tacos grabbed from a truck and eaten on the hood of our cars. Sushi in the Valley and handmade pasta in the arts district. We catch movies, comedy shows, and concerts at the Hollywood Bowl and the Greek. Daniel always scores the best seats—whether it's front row or in a box. I feel taken care of, shepherded from one lovely activity to the next without effort. But I can't fully relax—Daniel is my fated and that comes with a heaviness inherent in the promise of it. This isn't casual dating, even if it feels like it to him. But I hide that pressure, bury it to try and just be present with Daniel as we get to know each other.

If weekday evenings are packed, weekends are lazier. When we're feeling up for it and Daniel wants to cook something good, we might hit up a farmers market. If there's a particularly exciting exhibit, we might stop by a museum as well. But most days we do what we love to do best: work. Next to each other either on his giant dining room table or side by side on my kitchen counter.

Turns out, dating a guy who runs his own business can help you with your own. "Hm, I think you can raise prices. You guys are pretty affordable considering your clientele," Daniel says as he scrolls a financial report.

"Just a matter of convincing my grandmother," I say with a sigh. "I'm taking over at the end of the year, but I still feel like she doesn't fully trust me with the big decisions."

He kisses my forehead. "It's just because you're her granddaughter. She'll get over it."

I barely get to see Mar in all this dating frenzy, and a cloud of guilt hovers over me. At one point, I send over a dozen bagels to her new restaurant and that evening she calls me as I'm doing a load of laundry.

"Oh my god, I was about to leave a message," she says when I answer. "Your voicemail greeting is my new best friend."

"Ha," I say as I throw some towels into the washer. Betty roosts on the dryer, basking in the vibrating warmth as it runs. Weirdo. "Sorry, it's just been nonstop. How are you?"

"Me? I'm great now because of those bagels. Thanks for that. It kept the electrician jazzed a couple hours longer. But yeah, same ol' new-restaurant stress. Oh, and Mica's teeth are falling out all at once."

"Ew, what? Is he okay?" I start the washer and head to the kitchen.

"Yeah, yeah. Just, three teeth got loose. At the same time? No one told me about this in my parenting orientation."

"Poor guy. Can I take him out for ice cream this week?" I put the call on speakerphone as I pull on rubber gloves to start scrubbing the hell out of my sink. It's the third Tuesday of the month, which means it's Kitchen Deep Clean Frenzy night. I set my egg timer for fifteen minutes so I know when to move onto the fridge.

"Ah, this week might be hard because of some dumb stuff," she says, her voice sounding hollowed out.

I pause my scrubbing. "You okay?"

"Yeah. Just overwhelmed."

Her faraway voice reminds me of the days when Mica was a toddler and Ozzie was a newborn. Drained and hanging on by a thread. "Mar, do you need some help?"

A pause. "No, it's fine. I just . . . I miss you."

My throat tightens. "I'm sorry. I know I've been really busy with Daniel and work."

"Hey, don't feel bad! That's not why I called. This helps, I just wanted to talk."

But I still feel terrible. "I'll come by this week with dinner for you guys. I'll bring soup dumplings, Mica and Ozzie's favorite."

"Really?" Her voice perks up and it makes me feel doubly bad.

"Of course, bro."

I do manage to swing by with boxes of dumplings and noodles later in the week and am treated to a live demonstration of all of Mica's loose teeth.

Later in the week, I tell Daniel all about Mica's teeth woes while he's roasting me a chicken at his house, something jazzy and inoffensive playing on his fancy speakers, and I'm watching him from the marble counter, drinking an ice-cold gin and tonic.

"So when will I be properly introduced to them? And your family?" he asks as he rubs olive oil over the chicken.

There is just *one* little thing I haven't shared with him yet.

"I don't know," I say, keeping my voice light. "I'm kind of being greedy keeping you to myself for now. Once we open those doors—we shall never be able to close them again." I'm trying to be funny, but he frowns slightly.

"Well, I don't really plan on closing those doors, do you?" He has his hands held up in front of him, not wanting to contaminate anything with his raw-chicken-juice fingers.

"No, it's not that," I say, feeling like I messed this up somehow. "It's just . . . I like *this*. And my family, I love them, but they're a lot."

He washes his hands and dries them on the checked towel tossed over his shoulder. Then he walks over to me, bracing his hands on either side of me on the counter. He ducks down to look directly at me with those serious brown eyes of his. "I grew up with a tiny family and have always wanted to know what it was like to be in one like yours—spanning generations and cultures. I'm not scared."

It melts me from the inside out. "Of course. I'll plan it, okay?"

He kisses the tip of my nose. "I'm looking forward to it."

As I set the table, my phone blows up. A string of texts. It's the interns.

> omfg Gemma Flores posted about O&O!!!

I immediately tap the link to the post. It's a video of Gemma and Peter walking on a sidewalk, his arm around her shoulders as she smiles radiantly at the camera. There's dreamy music playing and the text over the video says, "POV: You find your true love via ancient matchmaking methods." In the caption, she tags the One & Only account.

The post already has more than twenty thousand likes and hundreds of comments:

> **@friendor** imagine being matched with gemma fucking flores?????
>
> **@spideydaddy** brb going to one & only
>
> **@tcmc** YOU need a matchmaker?? Not me dying alone
>
> **@wednesdaycake** DROP THE MATCHMAKING DEETS

I check One & Only's account and find that we've more than quadrupled our 1,900 followers in the half hour since Gemma posted. We now have nearly *eight thousand* followers. In thirty minutes.

"Holy shit."

Daniel comes over to see what I'm looking at. "What?"

I hold the phone out to him. "Gemma posted about us, and we've gone viral."

He scrolls through, his eyebrows shooting up. "This is incredible!"

"Right?" I can't stop smiling. "Oh, I'm so happy for her."

"Happy for her? Happy for *you*!" Daniel exclaims. "Cass, you've gotta capitalize on this ASAP. This is great for your company!"

He's right, but in the moment I can't absorb it. "Okay, but how?"

Dinner's forgotten as Daniel clears the table and brings his laptop out to help me brainstorm leveraging this viral moment into a new marketing campaign. He's a machine, and I'm impressed by how quickly his brain works. By the end of the night, the chicken is left cold, but we've come up with some ideas for social media posts and advertisements based on Gemma's endorsements.

And then, on a late-July afternoon, Daniel asks if I will attend a wedding with him—a wedding for one of his employees. We haven't talked about Ellis in weeks, since our first date, actually. But that doesn't mean I haven't thought about him. And so, I pause when I get the email from Daniel. It has a link to a wedding website for Max, the young Latino guy with the paint-splattered pants who I remember from Joshua Tree. He's marrying a man named Curtis at the Madonna Inn—a wonderfully kitschy hotel up the central coast. We've had a couple of our clients marry there in the past, so I am very familiar with it.

In the email, he apologizes for the last-minute ask—it's in two weeks—but he says he forgot it was on his calendar for months until today and he'd love for me to go with him.

So, not only is this going to be our first weekend trip together, it will be with Ellis. I assume he's going, anyway. I feel the pressure of it bubble inside of me before I twist my jade bracelet around my wrist. My anxiety dissipates with the assurance of the cold band on my skin. It reminds me of my gift, of who Daniel is to me.

Sounds great, I reply. Should I get Betty stuffed and take her as a purse? Daniel and I have a running joke that we're going to hire a hit on her, since the first night he slept over she shat on his Wales Bonner sneakers.

I try not to remember how much Betty liked Ellis. I need to give him a heads-up before the wedding. It's the right thing to do. It'll also give him an opportunity to duck out of it if he wants to, although that makes me feel shitty. My phone still in my hands, I start texting him: Hey Ellis. Daniel asked me to go to Max's wedding. I wanted to make sure that was okay with you first?

I stare at the text and feel lightheaded at the thought of sending it. It also feels weirdly passive-aggressive. I delete and try a new one: Sorry for the rando text lol but just thought you should know I'll be at Max's wedding. I can hear the interns' "cringe." Delete, delete. Hi Ellis, I hope you're doing well—

Omg delete. Finally I draft: Hey, just wanted to give you fair warning that I'll be at Max's wedding. It's the right text but I just can't hit send.

Someone knocks on my doorframe—it's Shreya, smiling. "Gemma Flores posted about us again."

I put my phone down, relieved. "Oh, a good post, right?"

She nods as she walks in. "Very good. She's all in with Peter."

We sit at my desk as she shows me the latest video Gemma posted—this time with both of them holding hands walking along the beach. She shouts out One & Only and tags us as well.

They look genuinely head over heels in the video and it makes me smile. "Bye to all the fuckboys, am I right?"

Shreya shakes her head. "Please don't, Cassia."

"Got it, got it. Did we get a ton more followers?" Our follower count topped out at twenty-two thousand after her first post.

"Beyond. And now we're booked until the end of summer. The Instagram ads seem to be working well, too. So much traffic is directed from there." She's hesitant before she says, "Maybe it's time to pull the trigger on higher pricing?"

I nod slowly, thinking about it. "Yeah, I think you're right."

We high-five when there's another rap on the door and a giant flower arrangement appears, held by Matteo. His face is obscured and his disembodied voice says, "A delivery for you, Cass."

They both look at me with undisguised curiosity as I pluck out the card tucked into the flowers, taking in a heady whiff of the garden roses and peonies. The loopy cursive on it reads: *See you at the Madonna Inn xx DNW*

This little acknowledgment from Daniel—that the wedding won't be easy for me—takes the tension out of my shoulders. His thoughtfulness steadies me.

"Send in the next client," I say to Shreya.

"Where should I put the flowers?" Matteo complains, still staggering under the weight. I put them on my desk so that I can be reminded of Daniel all day as I find love for other people.

31

After a productive morning of clients and talking new price structures with the Park women, I feel I've earned myself an afternoon ride. It rained yesterday so today is basically the perfect L.A. day: crystal clear skies and sunshine for miles. I grab my stuff and try and duck out but Lila spots me first. "Do you have a doctor's appointment?" She's mentally going through our work calendar, trying to see if she missed something.

"Oh, no, just taking the afternoon off," I say as I open the door.

"Huh? Why?" she asks. Matteo sidles up, sensing something mildly dramatic in the air.

I put on my sunglasses with a groan. "Can't a bitch just leave work early one day?"

"Yes, but not *this* bitch," Matteo says pointing at me.

"I know I'm a cool boss but watch it!" I say as I leave them in the dust. It's true, I rarely ever duck out of work for any reason other than illness, and I'm sure everyone thinks I'm dying now. I dodge texts from my family and drive home. Between work, Daniel, and this upcoming wedding, I need to clear my head.

As soon as I get inside, I change into shorts and a tank and head to the garage.

The bike ride down the hill is invigorating and does the mental health work it needs to do. In this state, all that exists is me, the wind, the bike beneath me, and my legs moving my body through the world.

Ever since the wedding invite email a few days ago, I've been feeling unsettled and worried about seeing Ellis again. In that setting, surrounded by coworkers who last saw me when I was dating Ellis. And I never did send that text.

The best thing about getting older as a woman is that you truly stop caring so much about what other people think about you. My sense of self is pretty crystalized, but it's not invincible. The idea of everyone thinking I'm some landscape-architect groupie picking through Watson and Associates makes me feel slightly ill.

I decide to ride to Highland Park, a neighborhood at the bottom of my hill where taco trucks bump up against tattoo parlors and fancy bagel shops. I park my bike outside a soft-serve spot, making sure I put a lock on it (learned that lesson the hard way) and feel a blast of air-conditioning as I step into the shop. I order a malt chocolate and vanilla twist with a heaping of rainbow sprinkles. While I watch the teenage girl behind the counter meticulously scoop my sprinkles, a gust of cold air hits the back of my neck as someone walks in.

Before I even see him, I can feel who it is.

Ellis looks at me with sweat dripping off his brow. He's wearing running shorts and a sweat-soaked T-shirt.

"L.A. is the smallest big town in the world," I say weakly.

He gives me this little grimace of a smile. "It's really too much. But also, I live around here."

Did I know that? I try and remember if we went over where *he* lived in between . . . everything. "Oh, right." I take my soft serve and turn to him. "Running?"

"Yeah," he says, still catching his breath. "And then the soft serve beckoned. Also, I saw your bike."

"Oh." I digest that. Ellis always shows up in ways both serendipitous and intentional.

"Hey, congrats on the Gemma Flores stuff," he says, as if he'd been meaning to tell me for ages. "Your social media is blowing up."

He's still following O&O? Oof. I smile through the pang. "Thanks, we're blown away by the response."

"It's awesome," he says.

I'm basking in that when I realize something. "Why aren't you at work?"

"I took a personal day. The weather was too nice to be chained to my computer."

I go where the wind takes me. And of course the wind pushed him toward me, the one day I decide to break out of my work calendar.

"It's really gorgeous out," I say. And then I'm self-conscious about talking about the damn weather, as if I've never been naked with this man before. After he puts in his order, I ask, "Uh, would you want to sit with me outside?"

I expect him to say he has to be on his way, but obviously neither of us are going anywhere with ice cream in our hands so he says sure.

We sit outside at the table and chairs set up on the sidewalk. The sun feels good while I take cold bites of soft serve.

"How have you been?" I ask, trying to sound casual.

He nods. "Good." Monosyllabic and even. Giving away absolutely nothing.

"Great," I say, painfully aware of how trapped we feel right now. "It's good to see you."

Ellis puts on his sunglasses, which feels like a self-defense move. "Yeah. Is, uh, is Mica's arm okay?"

Right. That was the last time we saw each other. "Yes! Healed great, superstar at school. Remember how cool it was to have stitches when you were little? Or like a cast?"

"I never had them," he says.

"What! How is that possible? You're a"—I wave my spoon in his general vicinity—"a boy!"

Finally, he cracks a smile. "Yeah, I am a boy. But somehow I managed to avoid big injuries."

"I'm a type A perfectionist who was raised by a billion Korean women and somehow still managed a couple broken bones and some stitches."

His eyebrows raise. "That's because you're not really."

"Not really what?" I say with a laugh.

"Type A. Perfectionist."

It's so matter-of-fact that I almost just accept it. But then I straighten in my seat. "Wait a second. Yes, I am."

He crosses his arms. "You think you are. That's what you aspire to. But deep down, you're chaotic, too."

Something about the way he says it gets under my skin. It's too assured. "Literally no one has ever called me chaotic."

He shrugs. "Okay."

That shrug bothers me. "Every personality test in the world pegs me as type A!"

"You're . . . a Gemini, correct?"

The stare is so accusing that I start cracking up. "Damn you!" There's that smile again, his dimples popping up, and my body immediately relaxes. I know it's selfish of me, but I want to thaw him from this cold mood. "Geminis get a bad rep, okay? We can still be organized and uptight."

"Yeah, because you're working against your true quixotic nature."

It's actually startling how right he is. But Ellis has always done that—surprised me with his perceptiveness. With his quiet observations of me and the world around him. I try to cover up my big feelings. "Wow, damn, didn't know you were an astrologist on the side."

He laughs and I want to keep him in a better mood forever, but I know I have to bring up something that will put him back into deep freeze. Teenagers on skateboards, sporting jeans I used to wear in middle school, zoom by us. It gives me a moment to brace myself to ask, "Hey, so . . . are you going to Max's wedding?"

He goes absolutely still for a second. Then, "Yeah."

"Oh, okay. Well, the thing is . . . uh, Daniel asked me to go with him," I rush it out. "And I wanted to, I don't know, give you a heads-up? I meant to text you, but . . ." My bottom lip is being chewed to bits and I avoid looking at him. "Anyway I was hoping to give you the option to tell me you'd rather not see me there?"

The chair scrapes as Ellis pushes it back in agitation. "Cass, it's really not fair of you to ask me that."

Cass—the intimacy of it hits. "I—sorry? I'm actually trying to be fair here."

He takes off his sunglasses and really looks at me then. And I see that his eyes are wide, incredulous. "Here's the thing: I want to be okay with this. Because I respect you and want to respect your decision not to date me and date Daniel instead. Because I think Daniel is the best guy I know. He's the older brother I never had. But I just . . . it's hard, okay?" He looks down at his soft serve melting in the sun.

A bus whooshes by us, giving me a moment before I say, "I'm sorry." My voice is small. "But I'd like to go to the wedding because it seems to be important to Daniel. And I just . . . I wanted you to know, I guess." It's hard to breathe, and the air feels so thick suddenly. The sunshine a curse instead of a gift.

He gets up and throws his cup into the trash. "I appreciate it. And hey, don't worry about me. This is awkward as hell, but we're grown-ups right?" Something about his tone makes me look at him sharply. "See you soon, Cassia," he says, taking off down the street. Not looking behind him, his sneakers pounding the pavement with a vengeance. And I don't know if I feel better or worse.

That night, Daniel's over at my place, both of us reading our respective books in bed. He's deep into a nonfiction hardcover about the bubonic plague and I'm deep into a mystery set in a British village. But I've read the same paragraph a hundred times and finally I put the book down and look at Daniel. "So, this wedding."

Through his slutty little reading glasses—"Yes?"

"Do you . . . do you really want me to go with you?"

He places his bookmark neatly into his book and closes it as he puts it down. "Of course. Why?"

I decide not to tell him about my Ellis run-in. "I just . . . I'm getting second thoughts. It feels like a potentially awkward weekend, don't you think?"

Concern creases the corner of his eyes as he reaches out and strokes my arm. "Everyone's an adult. They'll just have to deal with my beautiful date."

It's sweet but not quite reassuring enough. "I feel kind of shitty about it all."

He takes off his glasses then and rubs his eyes. "You know, that's not great to hear. I don't want our relationship to feel shitty to you."

Guilt immediately curdles inside of me. "I don't feel shitty about us! Just . . . the whole Ellis situation."

"It's been over a month," he says firmly. It's the first time he's ever sounded annoyed with me, and I pay attention. "We can't avoid him forever. He works for me."

"You're right," I say, instantly trying to lighten the mood. I regret bringing this up. "I'm sure it'll be fine once we're there. It's just . . ."

"A bit of nerves?" he asks, his voice back to normal Daniel levels.

I nod and he reaches over to kiss me, his hand stroking my jawline. "Let's calm them, shall we?"

32

Are we really at the point of 'listening to podcasts' instead of talking in our relationship?"

Daniel laughs, the wind whipping through his hair. The windows in his car are rolled down, the sunroof wide open. It's Friday afternoon and we're headed to San Luis Obispo, the site of the wedding. After an obligatory In-N-Out pit stop, we have two hours left on the trip and Daniel just asked if I want to listen to a podcast.

"I'll be DJ instead," I say. We hold our hands between us and the music and California air instantly signal vacation. I focus on that and try not to relive my pretty awful conversation with Ellis.

The Madonna Inn greets us right off the 101 with a retro hot-pink sign soaring over the sprawling property. Nestled between the hills is this oddity—a group of buildings with zero architectural cohesion. It's a little Thomas Kinkade English village, a little Vegas pizazz, and a lot of pink. We park the car at the valet and they help us with our bags. Inside the lobby, it's more of the same clash of aesthetics—floral-red carpet, river rock walls, and gilded furnishings.

"So, we have you booked in our Pioneer America room," the man at the front desk tells us, handing over our key cards. I pull a face at Daniel, who shrugs. "Hey, I was going solo at the time." We get to our room, which is hilariously unromantic with dark-green carpet, brown leather furnishing, and a giant hand-drawn map of the American West above the bed. We decide that we still have enough time to hit the pool before the rehearsal dinner. So, before we unpack a thing, we pull on our swimsuits and head to the pool.

It's set on a hilltop with gorgeous views of the surrounding hills and valleys, and we get there right at golden hour. It's pretty empty and we set our things on a couple of lounge chairs. I'm wearing a simple black one-piece suit but it's backless and gives my ass the perfect boost. I feel good in it, and I can tell Daniel agrees I should feel good in it with the way his eyes light up when I shed my cotton cover-up.

The pool has a beach entry so we walk into it easily, the water heated and delicious. After the chaotic past few weeks of work, this feels perfect. I dip my head back, letting the long ends of my hair submerge in the water. "So, are you one of those weirdos who has to start doing laps when you're in a pool?"

Daniel's guilt-ridden silence makes me laugh. He grabs ahold of my wrist underwater and pulls me to him, my body buoyant and light as it drifts toward him. "I'll hold back on the butterfly stroke today." His killer smile dims suddenly. I follow his gaze over my shoulder.

A group of people have entered the pool—Daniel's employees who I recognize, and some others who I don't. They all have drinks in hand and that "It's Fridaaay" vibes. But standing a head taller than most of them is Ellis.

Suddenly I am so glad we ran into each other, that this isn't shocking for him.

"Jefe!" cries out a redheaded woman who I know is named Mary. "You got an early start on the pool, huh?"

"Of course," Daniel says, his voice even, his expression neutral. Then he tilts his head to me and whispers, "Sorry!"

I hear someone say, "Wait, isn't that Cassia?" Then someone shushes them and there is an awkward passing of information. I wasn't sure who would know that Daniel and I were dating now and the idea of breaking that news to his employees at a wedding, in person, felt a little dramatic, but at the same time it's painful and quick.

I hear Marcella's voice telling me that being forty means giving zero fucks and I cling to that as I smile at everyone and say, "Hey."

Ellis is the first to say, "Hey, guys. How's the water?" It instantly puts everyone at ease, and I feel a pang, recognizing and appreciating this small mercy.

"Aces. Ten-out-of-ten pool temperature," Daniel says.

And everyone makes their way in, with the Madonna Inn's signature colorful glass goblets in hand. When Ellis gets in, I try so hard not to look at him more than anyone else. It's hard, and not just because he's in swim trunks. I am hyperaware of him, my body always in tune with where he is. I chalk it up to having slept together, at how irresistible he is as a human being. That the connection is no deeper than that.

Introductions to dates and spouses are made and I notice that Ellis doesn't have anyone to introduce. I try not to read into that even though the guilt and relief are undeniable.

We stay a little separate from the group, but the intimacy of a sunset swim has definitely been dampened. Daniel looks at me with an amused but slightly concerned expression.

I don't want him to feel bad about this. "It's okay. This will be the worst part. And if the worst part is being in a swimming pool at sunset with you in those tight little trunks, then I think I'll be able to handle the rest."

Underwater, he brushes my hip, then keeps his hand there, keeping me within arm's reach. "Glad to hear it."

After a few minutes of boozing in the pool, someone starts a game of chicken. This is probably the worst idea ever but after a few rounds of people screaming with delight, it's actually pretty fun. In the middle of a bout with me on Daniel's shoulders, trying to knock over a buff guy named Zachary who's sitting on the shoulders of the firm's accountant—the gate to the pool opens and in walks Avery. Avery from the park. She's wearing two tiny scraps of white crotchet, with an open oversized man's shirt thrown over it.

She smiles and says, "Who's winning?" before tossing the shirt on a chair and jumping into the water—straight into Ellis's arms. I ignore the clench in my chest and smile back at her. "Us!" Then I push Zachary off with a splash. Daniel pulls me off his shoulders with a slide down the front of his body and turns me for a celebratory hug.

"I'll take that challenge," Avery says as she starts climbing up a surprised Ellis's back. He makes eye contact with me for the briefest of seconds before he grips her toned dancer legs, which are now thrown over his shoulders.

All right. Okay, bitch.

I climb back up on Daniel and we face Avery and Ellis. Someone starts laughing hysterically. "Oh *shit*," someone else says. Yes, folks, welcome to the fucking show.

"You've got this," Daniel says. His grip on my legs is tight and I can feel that he wants to win this, too. It's stupid and macho because he's *already* won this. But my own competitive streak roars to the surface, too. I am not going to let us lose to these unfairly built kids.

Someone does a countdown and when they shout, "Go!" Daniel

charges ahead and I have to grab hold of his shoulders to keep myself from falling off.

Avery is all smiles when we rush them, but I catch a glimpse of Ellis's grimace before I reach for Avery's arms. She instantly pulls out of my grip, surprisingly strong for such a slip of a girl. She laughs. I hear the *Kill Bill* sirens in my head.

All right. Level up.

Daniel seems to understand and lunges forward again just in time for me to dig my shoulder into hers. She makes a surprised "oof" sound but stays on. Our audience starts making wild cheering noises.

"Go Avery and Ellis!" someone yells. Others join in. Okay, we're the bad guys here, clearly. The expression on Avery's face is a little more determined now. She reaches for me first next, gripping my upper arm with one hand, and I feel myself get slightly off-balance. But Daniel shifts so that I'm steadied again, and I grab ahold of *her* arm with my left hand. We're stuck in this mutual grappling hold for a second, both of our jaws clenched as we try to hold on. Then I see Ellis move forward and Avery gracefully twists her upper body so that I lose my grip and she tightens hers. Then she gets ahold of my other bicep so that I'm trapped. The cheers get louder.

"Inside, get inside!" Daniel shouts over the cheers. I know what he means. I twist my arms in an outward motion so that she is forced to let go of both my arms and I instantly get my hands on her upper arms, my arms braced inside of hers. I feel the strength of that position and *push*.

She topples off Ellis's shoulders, but he catches her before she can fully crash in the water.

We've won and Daniel whoops while hoisting me up higher in the air. I try and smile as everyone groans, and someone even boos. I don't care what they think, but I see Ellis's expression as he handles

Avery with care, setting her in the pool and examining her upper arms where my hands had been holding on with a death grip. They are red and you can see little crescent-moon imprints where my nails had dug in.

She laughs it off and says, "Good game, Cass!"

The use of *Cass* grates on me, as does her gracious losing attitude. I try and smile when I say, "Nice effort." It sounds stiff and arrogant, and Ellis shoots me a disappointed look. It hits me in the chest.

Someone's phone alarm goes off. "Rehearsal dinner in an hour!" Zachary shouts as he towels himself off at the side of the pool. Everyone disperses quickly.

When we get out of the pool, Daniel drapes a towel around me and pulls it tight under my chin. "Good job, champ."

I shiver when a breeze hits me. "Likewise."

"Did you play water polo or something in school?" he asks.

"No!" I laugh as I towel off. "Why?"

"You were *mental* out there," he says with a grin. "Real hot-jock energy."

I know he means it as a compliment, but Ellis's expression plays back in my mind and I feel low. It's not like I *really* hurt Avery, but there was something in there that was spiteful and I know Ellis sensed it. The way he senses everything. The first embers of resentment start burning in me—at having been pressured to come to this wedding when it's probably a very bad idea. And we have the entire weekend ahead of us.

33

The rehearsal dinner is at a cute Mexican restaurant in town. We sit in a courtyard filled with lights and flowering orange azaleas as the grooms, Max and Curtis, thank us for joining them for their special weekend. The margaritas and sangria flow generously, and a few hilarious toasts are made by friends and family.

Daniel and I are seated with coworkers; it's relaxed and fun despite the tension from the pool. Maybe it's only tension between me and Ellis, though, because everyone—including Daniel and Avery—are having a grand ol' time.

I'm waiting outside the restroom for it to be vacated, when I notice a slew of missed text messages from the Park women group chat.

When are we really meeting Daniel?

Yeah, he hasn't had Emoni approval yet!

We will plan a dinner when you are both back from the wedding. No more excuses.

Halmoni's bossy last text doesn't leave room for arguments. I've been putting off this dinner for some reason, even after promising Daniel I would plan it. It makes me feel guilty, this foot-dragging; I'm not even sure why I'm doing it. But I know I've got to rip the Band-Aid off sooner or later. I'm about to respond to them when Avery sidles up to me. She's in a lime-green two-piece that barely covers her butt, and it looks amazing. I smile at her and make the gesture of conciliation that all women understand: "I love that outfit."

"Thank you!" she says genuinely. "I *love* what you're wearing. So chic."

I'm in a sheer black maxi skirt, black boy shorts, and white tank. I've pulled my hair back into a low knot, which shows off the sapphire hoops in my ears. "Thanks. Nothing like being in your twenties as the ultimate accessory, though," I say.

"I can't wait for my twenties to be over, actually," she says with a sigh. "I feel like, maybe when I turn thirty, I'll know what the hell I'm doing with my life." She pulls out a vape pen from her tiny glittery purse.

"At no age do you know what the hell you're doing," I say. "But at least when you're twenty you can have less steps in your skincare routine."

She giggles. "You're hilarious." She takes a drag from her pen then looks at me. "Ellis talks a lot about you."

I try and keep my expression neutral. "Oh, yeah?"

"Yeah. He was pretty bummed when you started dating Daniel," she says frankly. "But he gets it, don't worry. Ellis doesn't hold grudges."

"Well, and now he has you," I say lightly, praying for the bathroom to open up already.

She looks at me oddly. "We're just friends."

"Oh, sorry. Didn't mean to assume . . ."

"It's okay." She tucks the pen back into her bag and pushes her hair behind her ears. "I'm into him but . . ." She shrugs and looks sad for a moment. The bathroom door does open then, and a sheepish man ducks out.

I shoot Avery a little smile before going in, feeling discomfited by what she's just told me.

That night, Daniel and I fall asleep with the windows open to let in that central-coast breeze.

While I sleep, I have a vivid dream. There are rolling green hills. Fog settling in. I hear the rush of water, again, like in my last dream. And then I see them—a herd of wild horses. Dappled gray and white. Brown with black manes. There are at least ten of them, and they are beautiful.

I'm drawn to them and as I get closer, the fog lifts. The sun illuminates them. I hold my hands out to touch them, but just as I get close enough their heads lift, their ears prick. A wind sweeps through the valley, and they start running.

I wake up with a start, my entire body scrambling for purchase. After a second, I realize I'm safe in bed with Daniel, his arm flung across my waist. The nightstand clock glows 3:14. I gingerly move Daniel's arm off of me and go to the bathroom. After I flush the toilet, I look at myself in the mirror. I am so awake.

What the hell was that dream? It's my second dream with a

horse in it. Both left me with a weird sense of disorientation and longing upon waking. I have to remind myself not to put too much stock in dreams.

I pull on some gray sweats then throw my coat on. Before I leave the hotel room, I grab my phone and room key.

It's completely silent as I walk across the mist-shrouded grounds, no destination in mind. Then, the bright lights of the tennis court beckon me. The court is painted, delightfully, hot pink. I open the gate to enter, my footsteps echoing, then sit down at the baseline. After a few seconds, I can hear the sound of crickets and the mist thickens.

I think about the big family dinner ahead. How everyone will be there to grill Daniel, to initiate him into the family. After a decade of waiting for things to fall in place, everything feels sped-up—fast-forwarded to the future at supersonic speed.

But maybe that's just how it is. That's how it feels when everything is right. I can't shake this slight panic, though. I remember how eager I was to find my fated by the time I turned forty and it feels like a billion miles away. The relationship suddenly feels like a runaway train.

A metallic *clang* interrupts my thoughts and I startle when I turn to the gate. It's Ellis.

My breath comes out in puffs in the cold night air. Of course he's here.

"Hey," I call out.

"Cassia?" he asks. "I thought that was you." He has Pickle on a leash. "This guy had to pee," he explains. Pickle yanks on his harness, yelping in excitement at seeing me, and Ellis unclips him.

Pickle makes a beeline for me, licking every exposed patch of skin—my face, my wrists, and peek of ankle. I give him pets around his scruff. "Hey, you weirdo."

"What are you doing here?" Ellis asks, concern etched on his face. He's wearing a light puffer jacket over pajama pants. Something about those pajama pants comforts me. How sexy could his night be in those pajama pants?

I have no claim to this relief and I bat it away. "I had a dream and couldn't go back to sleep. And then I found this incredibly strange tennis court."

Ellis looks around. "Yeah, this entire place is a trip. Perfect wedding spot for Max, though."

"It's like Disneyland for adults," I say as Pickle decides to lie down next to me. I pet his soft fur, moving my hand slowly from his head to his tail. "A nice break from reality," I say before I can stop myself.

Ellis joins me on the court, sitting down on the other side of Pickle. He looks straight ahead at the net when he asks, "Everything okay?" It comes out casually, but I can feel the effort behind it.

I look at him in profile. His mop of dark hair, his strong nose, his clean jawline. The bob of his Adam's apple. "Yeah, everything's fine. Great. I just—it's our busiest season at work, especially with Gemma's posts. It's been a lot. But other than that, nothing to complain about."

"Gotcha." He's quiet for a second, and still not looking at me. Then he puts a hand on Pickle, letting his hand rise and fall with Pickle's little panty breaths. "You and Daniel seem good."

The crickets are deafening and I let them fill in the space before I say, "Yeah. Things are good."

"I'm glad." And he sounds like he means it. "I'm sorry if I was kind of a jerk the last time we saw each other. I was just . . . processing in real time. But Daniel seems really happy. I like seeing him this way."

A lump forms in my throat. "That's . . . that's really kind of you."

I think about their fondness for each other, that night at Joshua Tree when everyone at the firm teased them for their bromance.

This suddenly all feels really horrible. Because being with Daniel will always mean proximity to Ellis, too. And the part that is most confusing is whether or not I want Ellis to just . . . not be a part of my life.

Because here he is—finding me when I'm feeling lost. I remember what Daniel said about him—*he's a little psychic*—and I wonder if there's a warring between magics here. If his is pushing back against mine.

"I like all your coworkers," I say, changing the subject slightly. "Rare to invite your entire company to your wedding."

He laughs and the sound rings through the cold night air. "We are a big, dysfunctional family that can't stop hanging out with each other."

"As someone in the family business, I understand," I say. "But it's really nice to see. Everyone is great."

"They are. And we're all so happy for Max and Curtis. It's been a torturous, dramatic courtship." He proceeds to tell me about it—the family feuds, the long-distance years, the moment of infidelity.

My eyebrows shoot up at that. "Really?"

"Yeah," Ellis says with a grimace. "But you know, it was so . . . humane. The way they dealt with it. They forgave each other after really letting the other suffer for a bit. I don't know, it feels so radical in a way. They understand that all of this"—he waves his hands kind of vaguely—"is imperfect. That the bad is part of it."

"That's an interesting way to look at it," I say. "I would have run from the drama, I think."

"Really?" He looks at me.

"Yeah. I would have taken all of it as . . . I don't know. Signs."

"Hm."

"What?" I prod. "You don't agree?"

"I guess I don't. People are going to fuck up. You can't predict the future, so you just have to learn to roll with it, you know?"

It's hard not say, *I can predict the future! I know who will make you happy*. But I think about Ellis and his early marriage. How he accepted that as a phase in his life. He has no regrets and it's one of the most attractive things about him. How he feels so secure in himself without knowing what the future holds. I wonder what that feels like. I can't imagine it.

I find my eyes skimming his face, on the brink of reading it. He catches my eye and I flush.

"Heyyy," he says. "Are you trying to read my face?"

I am about to deny it but start laughing. "Sorry. Force of habit."

"I gave you permission already." His eyes are lit up with amusement. Warm in the cold night. And I feel a pang, an ache deep inside. There is something there, there is always something there. He feels it, too. An understanding passes between us in a thick fog of intimacy.

I need to get back.

Then Ellis pulls a tennis ball out of his jacket pocket and throws it across the court and Pickle goes bounding after it. "Wanna play dog tennis?" he asks as he gets up.

"Um, depends?"

"On what?"

"What is dog tennis?"

He runs to the other side of the net to grab the ball from Pickle. "You know as much as I do." And then he bounces the ball hard on his side of the court so that it sails over the net to me. Pickle runs frantically for the ball and so do I. I get to it before him and he starts whining and wriggling his body low to the ground, excited for me to throw it.

"This game seems . . . not tennisy," I say with a laugh as I bounce it back to Ellis. It falls short so Ellis has to sprint forward but Pickle gets it before he does, and when Ellis falls to the ground, Pickle drops the ball and starts hopping all over him, licking his face.

I can't tell if Pickle's on my team or Ellis's, or his own, but it doesn't really matter. We keep the ball soaring through the air. At one point, Ellis "serves" it with very good form only to throw it directly into Pickle's open mouth. We laugh so hard we end up curled into fetal positions on the court. As I catch my breath, I roll onto my back, a sense of peace blanketing me as I lie in the cool night air, crickets chirping, beside Ellis. I stare up at the sky and notice the gauzy clouds have turned the color of sherbet. How long have we been out here?

"I think it's morning," I say, voice hushed.

Ellis rolls onto his back to look up at the sky as well. "Looks like it."

"I think . . . I should try and sleep for a couple hours," I finally say, sad for this bubble to burst.

Ellis gets up and brushes his hands off before reaching down for mine. I look up at him and am hit with the bittersweet realization that Ellis always finds me when I need him. I take his hand, and he pulls me up. We end up standing close, my hand clasped in his strong one. "Thank you," I say quietly.

He doesn't say anything for second, just staying close, his breath warm and mingling with mine. Nervously, I add, "That was a great distraction. Just what I needed."

Something seems to snap back to reality in him and he lets go of my hand, steps back, and gives me that familiar, easy smile. "I'm glad."

We walk out of the tennis court, the birds chirping high in the trees, our footsteps echoing in the quiet early morning just as the lights of the tennis court shut off.

34

I take way too long getting ready for the wedding. This is actually my favorite part—the lazy morning followed by a getting-ready routine that stretches out for hours in some hotel room. Curling irons ready to go, formalwear hanging off closet doors, room service languishing on a table. I think maybe I love getting dolled up because I used to love watching my mom get ready the few times she had nights out. She was still so young and probably itching to remember her old self as she put on a short skirt and fun eyeliner. I used to sit on her bed and braid my Barbie's hair as I watched her do hers.

"I wish I looked like you," I said one time, watching my pretty mother curl her waist-long hair.

Mom raised her eyebrows at me through her reflection in the bathroom mirror. "Why would you want to look like me when you look like *you*? No one else in the world looks like my Cass."

I shrugged. "But you're prettier."

She put the curling iron down and walked over to me, getting down in a crouch so we were eye level. "First of all, buddy, that's not true. Second of all, do you know what makes someone beautiful?" She pulled at my dirty sock playfully.

"No?" I said, wary of what kind of sappy speech I was about to get.

"How stinky their socks get." I laughed. She went on, "How they pick which Doritos to take on a road trip. How many colors they can fit into a drawing. How loud their burps are." And to punctuate it, she let out a *really* loud one. I laughed so hard, I had to roll over onto the bed to clutch my stomach.

She chucked me under the chin before getting back up. "Those are the things that matter, Cassia. Don't you forget it."

Despite having a mother who instilled in me what was really important, I still love a beauty moment. But I'm very aware that Daniel takes a mere twenty minutes while I'm still in my robe, drinking a glass of champagne, and munching on hotel gummy bears (the thrill of being with a man who insists *Life is short, eat the hotel snacks*). He's got the patio doors wide open and is sitting outside reading something on his ebook reader, his bare feet propped up, his tie thrown over his shoulder, sunglasses on. *GQ* would probably style a celebrity exactly like this.

"I swear I'm okay getting ready alone! Go for a swim, catch a movie," I say as I run a thickening lotion through my damp hair.

He throws me a look. "I came here to spend the weekend with you. And I enjoy watching you do all this stuff. The secrets of womanhood."

"Wait until I reach deodorant application!"

Daniel smiles at me fondly before returning to his reader.

Nonetheless, it's two hours later when I'm finally ready. I'm wearing a red satin dress with a corset bodice. The straps are delicate and tie at my shoulders, the ends dangling down my arms. It fits snugly at the bodice and hips, then the skirt falls to my knees, with two slits on either side. It's vintage and more than a little come-hither—both felt right for this venue. My hair is set in voluminous waves and pushed over to one side, a la Veronica Lake.

Daniel's expression when he sees me makes all the effort instantly worth it. "Wow." He pulls me in, his fingers grazing the ties at my shoulders. "You look like a present."

I flush. "Insert bad unwrapping joke here?"

The wedding is taking place in an ornate, high-ceilinged, wood-paneled room in the main building, complete with a stage and a spiraling staircase. Rows of hot-pink upholstered chairs are set up and the stained-glass windows let in colorful, diffused sunshine. I spot Ellis and Avery right away—both dazzling and young and beautiful—and we sit a few rows behind them. The ceremony itself is emotional and funny. Max is Mexican-American and Curtis is Arab-American, so we get a lot of cross-cultural nods. Tears are shed when Curtis's father reads a Mahmoud Darwish poem and both their mothers light a candle. Daniel reaches over and squeezes my hand—because people without parents understand how bittersweet it is to witness such warm family moments.

Cocktail hour is in the lobby by the banquet hall and Daniel and I grab every hors d'oeuvre that passes us. We group together with the other guests from the firm. Which means Ellis finally sees me. I swear a cartoon sweat drop appears on his face as he tries not to have a reaction to my dress. I'm not proud of myself when I say this brings me intense pleasure. Especially when his date looks like a cotton candy confection in pink taffeta and tanned skin, just ready to be eaten up.

I grab something with a pastry puff involved off a tray and pop it into my mouth in an act of self-defense.

"Such a good ceremony, right?" Avery says, breaking the ice without any knowledge of ice existing.

"So heartfelt," I say, brushing crumbs off my face.

"Those vows were so Max," Daniel says with a knowing look to Ellis, who grins in return.

"*So* Max."

Avery looks between them. "How was it so Max?"

I cringe inwardly—making people explain inside jokes is painful. But Ellis does, patiently. I notice, though, he keeps his hands in his pockets, his body distanced from Avery's.

Laura from the firm runs over to us with her harried husband, who is holding her jacket, purse, and heels (she's barefoot now), to tell us we all have to take shots. Oh, god. I look to Daniel for help; he just gives me a shit-eating grin and shrugs. "We gotta." He puts a hand on my lower back and leads me to the bar. I am aware of Ellis behind us and resist moving away from it.

Everyone from the firm is waiting for us and they hoot and holler. "Let's get the boss *der-runk!*" the cute girl with the bob says, the one I remember from Joshua Tree. Her name is Sonya. We're all handed shot glasses full of a brown liquid and I brace myself before throwing it back with everyone else. It burns down my throat and I try not to say, "Gross!" It's mezcal, a liquor I truly hate. The smokiness of it haunts my nostrils long after it's taken. Another round is poured and I tense up. I really don't want to take this nasty shot. When I reach for my glass at glacial speed, it's suddenly swapped out with an empty one. I look up to see Ellis holding a full shot glass and downing it. When I look down at the empty glass and then at him again, he gives me a little wink before stepping away. Oof. I resist clutching my chest.

Soon after, the doors to the reception are opened and I'm relieved. I can't hang with these party animals. I need a meal and a chair.

The firm is all placed at the same table, but luckily, I'm seated at a distance from Ellis and Avery. After we're settled and served champagne, the wedding party comes out to the *Game of Thrones* theme song, setting the tone for the entire night immediately. Max and Curtis dance their first dance to a beautiful acoustic cover of "Last Dance" by Donna Summer and then we're served salads with wedges of beautiful ombre-colored citrus and slivered almonds.

After our table toasts, party-animal Sonya says, "Should we play 'Never Have I Ever'?"

A bunch of us groan, including me, but she powers through. "Come on! We have free drinks, we have to play a drinking game."

"We don't *have* to do anything," Ellis says, taking a sip of water. "We can just eat and be normal people at a wedding!"

"Boring," says Sonya.

Avery nudges him with her elbow. "Come on! It'll be fun!"

Our main courses arrive—mine is a beef bourguignon—and everyone digs in for a moment before Sonya says, "I'll start. Never have I ever hooked up with someone at a wedding."

"Wait," Avery says. "Like, even with your date?"

"No, no, with a stranger you meet at the wedding," Sonya clarifies.

No one under the age of thirty drinks, the rest of us do. Including me.

"Respect," says Avery. "Okay, I have one. Never have I ever been engaged."

All the married couples take sips of their drinks, predictably. And then Ellis does, too. Everyone stares at him.

"Wait, what?" Avery asks, her jaw on the floor. Daniel looks equally confused.

"You guys didn't know Ellis was married?" Parker asks, already drunk as well.

"Married?" Daniel asks.

Ellis shoots me a little knowing look and I feel the intimacy of it sear across my skin for a brief moment. “Yeah. Married my high school girlfriend, got divorced soon after. It’s not a big deal.”

There are so many questions. So many from everyone. But the game goes on and then it’s time to dance and everyone storms the dance floor, incredibly drunk. Well, everyone but Daniel. He shakes his head and says, “I want you to still fancy me. If I dance, the jig is up, as you Americans say.”

I hate when people pressure others to dance so I give him a little kiss on the forehead and say, “Just sit here and continue to look handsome, then.”

Whitney Houston tells us she wants to dance with somebody and all of us dance with each other. I’m in a dance circle with some of the singles from the firm, vaguely aware of where Ellis is on the dance floor at all times. He’s a good dancer in that effortless way, not in the “I can be in a boy band” way, which always intimidates me as a woman who can dance just *okay*. He’s comfortable in his body, which reminds me of what it was like to have him put all his focus on *my* body.

I decide the logical thing to do when having this train of thought is to drink more. Somewhere in the back of my mind a tiny red flag is being raised but I ignore it. Drunk dancing is the best dancing, and I don’t often get opportunities to do that anymore. I am vaguely aware at some point that the song I am dancing to is a slow one—meant for couples. But I just stand with a couple randos from the wedding and sway with them, our arms draped around each other. Suddenly I realize one of them is Ellis.

“Oh,” I say, my voice sounding far away. “Hello there.”

“Hi,” he says in that way that he used to say to me. Is he drunk, too?

Then I see the silver glimmer under the collar of his unbuttoned white shirt. Without thinking, I reach out and loop the chain around my finger. "This thing kind of drives me crazy."

He laughs. "Why, too tacky?"

"Not that kind of crazy."

His eyes get dark and suddenly it's so intimate around us that I let go of the necklace and look anywhere else but at him. Then I ask, to completely break the spell, "Where's your date?"

A flicker of annoyance passes by his features. "Um, Avery went to the room. Too much to drink."

The room. Careful use of words there, Ellis. Also, he didn't go back with her. He does not strike me as someone who would let his girlfriend go back to her room alone. They are clearly just friends and even though Avery said as much, this confirms it for me.

"Where's *your* date?" he asks. And there's something challenging there.

I glance over at a table where Daniel and a few others are drinking and chatting. He's animated and having a good time. "He's fine. He's enjoying himself."

The other people in our little dance circle break off and suddenly it's just us two. We don't touch, but we stay close, our bodies swaying near each other. I ask him, "Are *you* fine?"

His limbs are loose, his eyelids heavy. He's drunk, too. "I'm not fine, Cassia." His voice is low, gravelly.

I swallow, suddenly feeling like this is not a good idea. But I say it anyway. "Why?"

"Because you're in that dress"—his eyes glide down, leaving a searing path in their wake—"with my boss."

Yup. Bad idea. We're in a big crowd, being blocked from Daniel's view. I step in closer. "I know."

"Why did he pressure you to come here anyway? I feel like that was kind of shitty of him, don't you think?" His voice is angry—and I know it's not at me. It's at him.

"He didn't pressure me." But it's unconvincing and Ellis knows. He always knows.

"Well, it's shitty to put you into that position."

"I know," I say, my voice tight.

"You know?" He raises an eyebrow. "You know how shitty this is?"

Tears fill my eyes, surprising me. "I'm sorry."

He looks struck, and he reaches out to pull me into a hug. "Hey, hey," he says against my hair. "I'm sorry. Please don't cry."

I'm mortified and try to pull away. This is all so inappropriate. But he keeps me tightly in his grip and his voice is close to my ear. "I shouldn't have said that. Forgive me?"

Forgive *him*? It hits me then, the full impact of Ellis. Of this walking, talking open heart of a man. A man, who, when he was twenty years old, was so swept up by love that he wanted to marry someone.

"You didn't do anything wrong. I did everything wrong." I pull back to look up at him but he's looking at someone behind me.

"You doing okay there, dancing queen?" Daniel's whiskey-warm voice asks. I turn to him and smile.

"Yeah, getting a little tired, though."

He gives Ellis a look, one that seems relaxed if you don't notice the hard glint in his eye. Then he runs a hand down my arm and holds my hand. "Me, too. Let's get you in bed."

"Night, guys," Ellis says, waving and stepping back, immediately absorbed by the dance floor crowd. As we leave, I look back and can feel Daniel watching me do it. I'm going to have the worst headache tomorrow.

35

The entire drive back to L.A., I am so hungover. Daniel gets us huge iced coffees and doesn't mind when I mostly sleep. He's quiet, too. In some back cave of my memories, I remember him *noticing*. And those small embers of resentment at even being at the wedding start smoldering again, making me feel defensive as I curl up in the seat.

Before I doze off, my phone buzzes. A couple more messages from the Park women harassing me about setting up dinner. And one from Ellis. I glance up at Daniel before reading it.

> Sorry if things got weird last night. Blame the cocktails? Safe travels home.

I swallow back a lump of emotion and close my eyes against the pounding in my head.

My eyes are pried open hours later when we hit the familiar bump of my driveway.

"We're here." Daniel's voice is quiet, like he doesn't want to quite wake me.

I straighten up, adjusting my sunglasses and working out a crick in my neck. "Oh, god. Sorry I slept the entire ride."

"It's fine, I don't know if I was in any condition to have a conversation, either," he says with a self-deprecating laugh.

"You all party hard at Watson and Associates," I say.

"It's really a problem," he says, but it's with love, like he's talking about his misbehaving toddler. "And hey, thanks for being such a good sport. I know it wasn't easy . . . with Ellis and all."

The weekend and all its complications come rushing back to me and I can't tell if my headache is from that or the booze. Ellis's eyes when he was dancing with me.

I can't have this cluttering my brain. I need to excise Ellis and these tiny inklings of doubt once and for all.

"Well, now you owe me one," I say, biting down on my lip, looking at him with big innocent eyes.

His eyes follow my lips then look up at me, amused. "Oh, do I?"

"Yes. Are you ready for . . . dinner with the Parks?"

A flash of white teeth then he reaches out to hold my hand. "Darling. Yes. I'd be honored."

"You sure?" I ask, squeezing his hand. "It's not just my grandparents. It's Sunny and Stu and Emoni. And probably Mar and her family."

"Sounds perfect," he says, not missing a beat.

I appreciate him so much in that moment, I stretch across the space between us to throw my arms around him. "Thank you," I say into his neck. He smells like a spicy aftershave that I've grown used to smelling on my sheets. "It means a lot to me."

"Well, then it means a lot to me."

"Are we on the same page, then?" I ask a little nervously.

He pulls back to look at me, pushing my hair out of my eyes. "And what page is that?"

"I . . . I want a big, grand love story." Saying it out loud takes effort, takes something from me. It's a yearning that, as a woman, you learn to keep locked tight. Because to reveal it would make you feel like you're wearing your organs outside your skin.

Daniel's smile is gentle in the harsh daylight. "You should have a grand love story."

It's the reassurance I need—what I had been hoping for the past few weeks, a yearning I'd been skirting around. "Does next weekend work?"

"On one condition," he says. My heart jumps to my throat and then he says, "Will you help me pick out what to wear?"

"They're gonna love him, he's gonna love them," Mar says over the phone. I'm putting on my jeans, getting ready for the big dinner, and Mar is on speakerphone.

Betty squawks at her from her perch on my dresser. I grab a black leather rope belt and loop it through my white jeans. "You're right. But I feel like vomiting, nonetheless."

"It's just because of the whole wedding thing." Mar knows all about what happened, obviously.

I pull on a white cotton T-shirt. "Ellis made it clear he still cares for me. And when I'm around him, it's hard for me not to feel the same way for him. I need to stop living in this in-between zone and just fully *commit* to this future with Daniel, so that there's no room for me to think about Ellis. I know that having my family together and seeing him with them—it'll confirm that all is right in the world. That we're *fated* to be together."

She's quiet for a second. "You're putting a lot of pressure on this dinner, Cass."

"I know." I look at my reflection, my hair down and loose over this all-white ensemble that I'm hoping will signal a fresh new start or something. "But I've been avoiding it too long anyway. Why? It's time. Just rip it off like a—"

"Band-Aid, yeah. You've said that, like, ten times to me already."

"Sorr-reeee. See you there."

After we hang up, Daniel texts that he's on his way. I put Betty back in her cage and wait for him on the porch, the sky a dusty blue as we approach sunset. As I often do when I sit on our porch—the wind chimes my mom made tinkling from the eaves—I think about my mom. This time, about how she would feel about Daniel.

She'd probably like him. He's basically every parent's dream spouse for their kid. But she'd like Ellis, too.

In fact, she'd probably love Ellis. And that's why she ended up with my dad instead of her fated.

Daniel pulls up in his very clean BMW and I climb in. "Let's see the fit," I say. He preens for me—in a crisp, short-sleeved button-up with skinny brown stripes. He's wearing white jeans and dark brown boat shoes. We look like we're going to an engagement photo shoot. I almost make a joke of it but decide that is a joke best left to myself.

"Oh, look at these," I say when I spot a giant bouquet of hydrangeas in the back seat. Cream blooms edged in sky blue. "They're beautiful."

"Do you think Halmoni will like them?" he asks a little nervously.

I touch his hand and smile. "She'll love them. Don't worry, they already love you."

"I highly doubt that," he says with a self-deprecating laugh. "We barely spoke two words at LACMA."

Oh, if he only knew.

36

He's too good-looking but that seems to be his only flaw."

The water pitcher I'm holding almost slips out of my hands as I laugh. "I'll just have to live with that, Logan."

"Poor you." He's helping me arrange a platter of fried zucchini and we're both in the kitchen. I've left Daniel alone with my family outside on the terrace, and I hope he's not been beaten down spiritually yet. "He was worth waiting a decade for."

A decade. Jesus. "I'm glad he has your seal of approval. On hotness anyway. You're one of three men in my life whose opinion I give a rat's ass about."

"I'm flattered. But yeah, dinner will be all about substantive things like . . ."

"Favorite sports teams?" I finish for him.

He scowls. "What? No. What his D&D alignment is. That sort of thing."

I laugh, again. "Okay, only the pertinent ones."

"Exactly." Logan's smiling when he pauses, then asks, "So, am I right? He was worth waiting for?" The way he's asking suddenly makes me wonder how much Mar has told him about Ellis.

I watch the pitcher fill up with water from the filter in the sink.

"He's really, really great. It just feels so seamless to have him in my life. We have so many things in common and it's just really easy."

He nods. "I'm really happy for you, Cass."

I hug him. "Thanks, Logan." It warms me up inside, because Logan is one of the good ones.

We head out to the terrace where everyone's seated for dinner. The night is warm and I stand for a moment in the doorway, taking in the scene. Daniel is seated near the middle, being plied with appetizers and wine. He's smiling, the charm just oozing off of him, and everyone's attention is on him. Even my fairly stoic grandfather is grinning, opening a bottle of frosty beer for him. Earlier in the week Halabuji had called asking what kind of beer British people like to drink, and it makes me feel warmed from the inside out to see the bottle of Newcastle Brown Ale being handed to Daniel.

My first family dinner with my own fated. Not the odd man out, the single aunt seeking love. There is a tangible relaxing in my body, in my bones. It's like something is being recalibrated in me to just *rest.* Downhill mode.

I seat myself next to Daniel and his eyes lock on mine with amusement. "Hello," he says, and I kiss him on the cheek.

"You hanging in?" I ask in a low voice near his ear.

He reaches over and squeezes my thigh. "It's been an absolute pleasure."

"You're a great liar," I say with a laugh. I catch Halmoni's eye at the head of the table and she holds up her glass of wine to me, her happy expression bordering on smug.

"We were just talking about how much we owe him for his marketing help," Sunny says with a smile.

Daniel actually looks embarrassed. "I just helped Cassia with a few ideas."

"He's being extremely humble right now," I say. "You really lit a fire under my ass."

Mica and Ozzie laugh and I cross my eyes at them, making them laugh harder.

Everyone starts passing around the food—heaping piles of fluffy white rice, crispy grilled fish, ice-cold cabbage and cucumber kimchi, fried zucchini, soy-sauce marinated brisket beef, and big leaves of lettuce from Emoni's garden served with bright-orange ssamjang. It's a lot of my favorite foods and I know Emoni and Halmoni were meticulous in planning the menu.

My heart squeezes with love for all of them.

"Okay, Daniel, we're going to have to ask you a million questions, you know that, right?" Mar says. Logan groans.

"Daniel Nam!" Ozzie cries out. Everyone but Daniel freezes and stares at her.

I force out a laugh. "Ozzie, you're so good with names, good job." Logan immediately starts distracting her with some chopsticks.

"I got grilled like this, remember?" Stu says to Sunny as he pours wine for her. "Sorry, Daniel, it's a rite of passage."

Daniel leans forward, an impish gleam in his eye. "I would expect nothing less."

Mar clears her throat and folds her hands under her chin, all business. "Daniel, tell us about your childhood," she says.

"Well, I was adopted by my parents when I was an infant," he starts, tucking into his food at the same time. "I grew up in a suburb of London called Woodford. It was pretty uneventful and ordinary and I feel lucky for it."

"Were you an only child?" Emoni asks, piling some fish onto Mica's rice bowl. Daniel nods and Emoni looks at me. "Just like our Cassia."

Daniel and I look at each other and he squeezes my thigh under the table again. "Yes. Both of us are such difficult spoiled brats, aren't we?"

Laughter all around, a musical sound in my grandparents' lush garden. Then it's Emoni's turn to lean in, and I know that she's about to get serious. Interrogation mode initiated. "What's your romantic journey been like?"

He drops his head slightly, rubbing the back of his neck before looking up with a sheepish grin. "Well, truth be told, I've been quite the typical bachelor."

Some huffy sounds are made around the table, and I hold back from laughing. Daniel continues, "I have had one or two serious girlfriends. One in uni—college, that is—and then one several years ago. But, like Cassia, I've been building my career and business for the past decade or so. And because of that, I have not had much of myself to give until recently."

Everyone has questions, but Emoni is not done yet. "And how did it feel when you met Cassia?"

Daniel pauses and looks at me, his heart in his eyes. "When I met Cassia, I felt everything in me still," he says, not breaking eye contact with me. "I had been going-going-going my entire life. Reaching for the next thing, the next goal. It's quite American of me, really." His amusement makes him pause. "And, really, I knew the next big step was finding my partner. And I felt something in me just click the first second I met her. I felt like, ah, there she is. You can stop now."

Because we're meant to be. Because we've met in one or many lifetimes past.

A sigh comes from Sunny. "It's the best feeling. Cass, what about you? What did you like about Daniel?"

"Well, I had to get over his hideous looks first," I say. More laughter. Mar laughs a little too loudly. "But once I was able to overcome that obstacle, I found myself so impressed by his passions and drive. How much he notices the natural and designed world. His confidence that makes him a strong leader. So well-respected by everyone in his life. And just . . . we're so on the same wavelength. We know what we want and the kind of life we envision."

"And what kind of life is that?" asks Stu.

Again, Daniel and I look at each other. "A partnership built on respect," he says.

"With lots of good food, books, and nineties movies," I add with a grin.

"Always," he says. "Growing old together in the sunshine."

"Sitting on a deck made out of sustainable wood." I smile at the vision of it.

Emoni is beaming. "And a house full of grandchildren? You have a family business to carry on after all."

I turn to Daniel, smile still on my face, but find his wavering. "Ah," he says with a nervous laugh. "I think I will make an incredible uncle, for now."

The silence after that is like a physical presence. It sits on my chest and makes it hard for me to breathe.

What the fuck?

Someone somewhere clears their throat loudly—I think it's Halabuji—and everyone starts talking at once, trying not to put us in the spotlight anymore. Then, maybe reading my mood, Logan asks Daniel to help him get something from the kitchen and he gets up, giving me an apprehensive glance before doing so. I smile, trying to act cool.

Only when he's gone does everyone look at me, again.

"Did he say what I thought he said?" Emoni asks in a loud-hushed voice.

"He did," Halabuji says grimly, meeting my eyes over the table. "You guys never talked about this, Cassia?"

Mar flinches for me. "It's not her fault."

"Everyone, calm down," Halmoni says, finally. "Don't make this a bigger deal than it is."

"It's a big deal!" Emoni says. "He cannot be serious!"

Everyone starts bickering and I sink back in my seat. When I look up, I see Sunny staring at me intently. She mouths, *Sorry*, and I shake my head. How could she have known?

37

It doesn't mean he doesn't want children!"

I shake my head, my bike helmet jostling my brain. "Be fucking *for real*."

It's the morning after the fateful family dinner, and Mar and I are coasting downhill, weaving through Pasadena. The streets are wide and lined with majestic mature trees of all kinds. It's both peaceful and menacing here—a quiet suburb where nary a human being can be seen in their yards or walking the perfectly clean sidewalks.

But it makes for a beautiful and zippy bike ride. We ride over an old, small bridge that crosses a leafy arroyo and after a few more stretches of tree-shaded residential streets, wind up at the Rose Bowl, a giant historic stadium home to the best flea market on the second Sunday of every month.

"I'm just saying," Mar says as she locks her bike on a stand. "He said 'for now.'"

I grab my giant IKEA tote bag that I've refashioned into a backpack for the ride home. "He was literally sweating. Like, pit stains. This man is *meticulous* about hygiene."

We pay to get in, briskly making our way to our favorite vintage-clothing stalls. The sun is beating down on our capped heads even though it's only eight a.m. The law of the universe is that any Sunday morning you decide to hit up the Bowl will be the hottest morning ever in the history of mornings.

"Well, he was put on the spot!" Mar says as she beelines to a stall only selling embroidered dresses from Mexico. "Your entire family was just staring at him."

"That might be true, but '*for now*'? Sir, you are *forty-two* years old. You don't know if you wanna have kids yet? Wake the fuck up!" My voice is loud but the woman running the stall just gives me a look like, *I feel you*.

Mar is somehow carrying three dresses already. "All right, slow your roll, Gloria Steinem. Up until *very recently* you didn't one hundred percent know that you wanted children."

"What do you mean? Of course, I've always known," I say, taken aback. "I froze my eggs!"

With zero self-consciousness, Mar whips off her tank and pulls the dress on. Her voice is muffled under the hot-pink fabric when she says, "Yeah, because Halmoni was on your ass. But you didn't actually know if you wanted kids until you slept with Ellis."

My mouth drops open. "What!"

The dress falls to right under Mar's butt and she inspects herself from behind. "Yes. Until you made up that excuse to break up with Ellis, you didn't definitively know you wanted kids. Remember? You even said it."

I want to argue with her, but I replay that weekend in my head. How, when he said, "I go where the wind takes me," I had felt a panic seize me.

My throat seizes up in response and I can only nod.

Sensing my emotional state, Mar immediately strides over to me and gives me a hug. “Oh, Cass.”

“I always thought maybe . . . maybe I was assuming I wanted kids to keep the family business going. Because, you know, only the women are born with the gift. And with Emoni’s family being freaks and only having boys, it was on me. And I resented that for a while. But now, I think having felt myself fall for Ellis, a twenty-eight-year-old *dude*, made it all so crystal clear. I can’t mess around, because I know I want kids. And I want them for *me*, to love someone like my mother loved me.”

Mar pulls back and nods, her eyes teary. “That makes sense. And hey, you are allowed to change your mind or feel however you want about this. There’s no ‘right time’ to know when you want kids. Sometimes it hits you like lightning, sometimes you just think, ‘Why the fuck not, what else do I have going on?’”

I start laughing through my tears. “Get out. You planned the birth of your children with a financial advisor.”

She shrugs. “But not because I felt some longing inside of me. It’s because I could see a future with college-aged kids talking down to me about politics around the kitchen table and suddenly I wanted to start making that future happen.”

“And sometimes you’re twenty-three and get pregnant with an absolute zero of a man,” I say as Mar pays for her dress. My voice sounds petulant even to my own ears.

“Trust me when I say that the second your mom saw your little scrunched-up newborn face, she had no regrets,” Mar says.

I let that sit with me, I try to believe it as we make our way through the aisles of the flea. We end up at a stall selling little charms and trinkets. The seller is an old white man wearing a black velvet vest and we make some chitchat with him as we peruse the trays of oddities. I pick up a tiny turquoise penis. "I'll fashion you a charm bracelet with this," I tell Mar. Mature until the end.

"Please do."

"Those are a deal right now, five for ten dollars," the seller informs us.

My Emoni-training kicks in. "Hm. Can you do a little better on the price?" I can feel Mar dying next to me. She has not been trained in the fine art of haggling like I have.

"Eight is the lowest I'll go," he says.

I make a noncommittal noise and peruse the other trays. Mar rifles through a bowl full of stone fetishes that claim to be from a local Native American tribe. I glance at the seller. Highly doubt it. "Hey, did you figure out the liquor-license thing?" I ask her. This has been the restaurant's latest battle.

Mar shakes her head. "I swear the licensing department in this city is a scam. The steps required are so convoluted even Logan gets a headache puzzling it out."

"Bastards," I say. "What happens if you can't get it before the restaurant opens?"

She holds a charm midair. "Why would you say such a thing?"

"What!"

Mar looks around frantically until she spots a wood tray and knocks on it. "Don't say that! An oyster bar without booze might as well be a fish market."

"Sorry!" I say, looking around for more wood to knock on, too, finding a nearby chair. We move on to another stall selling old movie posters.

"So, what do you think you're going to do?" Mar asks. "About Daniel, I mean."

The question that's been turning in my mind since dinner last night. I've been avoiding the Park women, who have been equally concerned and optimistically dismissive. Emoni threatened to have a talk with him but I convinced her not to, luckily.

"I don't know," I say. "I mean, if he's my fated, shouldn't we be on the same page about this?"

"Hm, that's what I would think," Mar says.

There's something in her tone that makes me stare at her. "What?" I ask.

"Nothing."

"Mar."

She pauses and looks up at me behind her cat-eyed sunnies. "Maybe you need to . . . ignore the fated thing while you deal with this."

"What?" I shake my head. "What do you mean?"

"That maybe, maybe the fated thing is putting too much pressure on you. That maybe you need to take a beat, and make sure you're really sure about this guy before freaking out about your future children and your bloodline and all that."

"But . . . the fated thing. That's the *whole thing*." And even as I say it, I realize how wrong that sounds. To think of Daniel, this wonderful man, as *one thing*.

Mar hears it, too. "Maybe you need a little break from the nonstop Daniel dating."

"Well, tomorrow's his park opening so I can't avoid him forever," I say, feeling the morning sun get hotter. Or maybe I'm just sweating because of, oh, general *life panic*.

"Oh shit, right," Mar says. "Well, just think about it, Cass. That's all I ask."

And for the rest of that morning as we buy vintage bits and bobs, and later as we lug our goods home on our bikes, I do. I hope that by tomorrow, my head will feel more cleared. That I'll have more assurance in what I need to do next.

38

I want to fly into space and forget about Daniel and Ellis, fateds, and men in general. But I absolutely can't miss the opening of Daniel's biggest project. The mayor, city council members, and press will be attending to cover the event. Also, my family and Marcella's will be attending as well. It's sweet, this show of support for Daniel.

I wear a grass-green linen maxi skirt with a white tube top, a chunky black beaded necklace, and delicate black leather sandals. My hair is pulled back into a messy braid and I opt for a rare bold lip in coral red.

"You look ready for a vacation," Daniel says when he sees me. "Let's book one to Greece this fall."

It's already August and nothing sounds better than the idea of a for-real vacation that requires a passport. "Drown me in olive oil, please," I say. But a small voice in the back of my head is asking, *Will we be together long enough for a vacation?* We haven't had time to talk since the big "uncle for now" bomb, and I've decided to wait until after the event for the breakdown since it's sure to be a doozy. I just need to get through today.

We arrive at the park at four, a little earlier than the other guests so that Daniel can make sure everything is set up correctly. I walk around and take in the completed park. It's beautiful. Tall native grasses, majestic sycamores, and flowering sage are all planted alongside a paved gravel path that winds through the gentle slopes along the river. There are benches and water features seamlessly integrated throughout, creating an inviting space that dares you not to be relaxed. And the river is bordered by boulders and plants, restoring it back to its former glory when it ran naturally through Los Angeles, before it was rerouted in cement.

"Do you like it?" Daniel asks when he finds me wandering one of the small paths along the river's edge.

"It's so beautiful," I say with a happy sigh. "You should be over-the-top proud."

He hugs me from behind, burying his face into my neck. "Thank you. I'm so glad I can share it with you." I close my eyes and take it in. *This feels steadying. This feels nice.*

People eventually start trickling in and music is piped in through speakers scattered throughout the park. I made the playlist because if it had been left up to Daniel, it would have been a "Today's Hottest Hits" list off Spotify.

I chat with various firm employees, being drunk BFFs with some of them now, and try my damnedest not to be on alert for Ellis. Marcella and her family arrive and I show them around the park. The kids eventually run down to the riverbed and take off their shoes to go wading, which they probably aren't allowed to do but I take liberties as the girlfriend of the designer.

"They did such an amazing job," Marcella says to me as we grab some bites from the buffet table.

"Right? I'm so proud," I say, taking in the gorgeous views again. I spot Sunny, Emoni, and Halmoni in the distance and wave them over.

"Beautiful park!" Sunny says brightly as they approach. "This used to be such a shithole."

"Sunny!" I say with a laugh and Mar almost chokes on her falafel ball.

"Daniel is very talented," Halmoni says matter-of-factly, pleased like he's already her grandson.

"And Ellis and the others," Mar says pointedly.

Of course, that's when I spot Ellis. He's wearing a vintage Western shirt, with the short sleeves cuffed, his hair a little wet from the shower.

In sharp contrast to my reaction to Daniel, I feel everything in me tilt toward him and completely destabilize. What I can't figure out is whether that's a good or bad thing.

Two older people join him and I openly stare—they must be his parents: an Asian woman with salt-and-pepper hair pulled into a youthful ponytail, wearing cool wide-leg jeans and a block-print top. Next to her is a white man towering over her, his hair thick and dark and his posture relaxed in light blue chinos and sandals. They are looking at Ellis with what could only be described as adoring pride.

I am staring at them for so long that I eventually make eye contact with Ellis and jolt. When we lock eyes, I feel it in my entire body. I can't even be embarrassed at being caught staring so I just smile and wave. He gives me a cautious smile back.

"Do you think those are his parents?" I whisper to Marcella, trying to look subtle.

"Yes, and they are so young and stylish," she says. "As if you needed another reminder that he's twenty-eight."

"I *do* need that reminder," I say before I grab a glass of champagne. Mar looks at me sharply.

Before she can interrogate me, the music stops and Daniel taps the mic. "Hi, everyone. Thank you so much for joining us here for the opening of the Frogtown River Park." People start applauding. He smiles that devastating smile. "I'm Daniel Nam-Watson, the head of Watson and Associates—" Here, everyone at the firm starts cheering wildly and he gives the crowd a second as he grins. "The best landscape architecture firm in all the land, obviously. Please take a look at the people around you and give *them* a round of applause for creating this brilliant, beautiful place."

We do, heartily, as the crowd is made up of mostly friends and family of the firm, alongside the official folk. Marcella shouts, "Hottest architects *ever*!" to nervous laughter. Who needs embarrassing Korean aunts when you have this kind of best friend?

Daniel talks about the design choices of the park and then a few city officials declare how important this park will be to the city and future plans for the community. Again, I feel a surge of pride for Daniel and the entire firm. I try my best not to look around at the crowd, not wanting to risk eye contact with Ellis again.

Then Daniel gets back on the mic and says, "We're so proud to unveil the park today because, as many of you know, this has been quite the journey. This firm and our clients have put up with my endless ideas and my, ah, fastidious vision." His employees laugh knowingly. "Like with everything else, I had very specific plans for this park and could see the future so clearly in my mind." He looks straight at me, the corner of his mouth lifting up, his eyes twinkling. A look that would normally set my pants on fire. But this time, when my heart is beating, it's not with romantic anticipation. I find my gaze moving—roving over the crowd until it finds Ellis. He seems to feel my eyes on him, because he looks up.

I go where the wind takes me.

Who is the person to best navigate the chaos of life with? Do I want a relationship that feels like a slow, steady burn—one full of shared passions and big plans? Or do I want one that feels electric and unexpected—digging my bare hands into the dirt and accepting life's surprises?

The music comes back, snapping me out of it, and the Park women start making their way out.

"I can barely hear anything," Halmoni complains.

"And I have to catch the shuttle to the casino," Emoni says as she grabs a shrimp skewer.

Sunny gives me a hug. "Enjoy tonight, okay?" She pauses a beat. "Don't overthink it, just go with how you feel."

I nod and hug her back. "Thanks, Sunny. And thank you all for coming, it means a lot."

After they leave, we start the cocktail portion of the evening just as the sun sets. There's a dip in the temperature and the heat lamps are turned on. While I'm grabbing some drinks for myself and Daniel, I feel a tap on my shoulder. It's the woman who was with Ellis earlier.

She smiles warmly at me. "Hi, I just wanted to say hello. I'm Ellis's mom, Christina. Are you Cassia?" she asks, holding out a hand. Christina has one of those faces that has seen a lifetime of smiles and sunshine. Age spots on her high cheekbones, fine lines by her eyes and mouth. She's beautiful.

I fumble to put the drinks back down to shake her hand. "Yes! Nice to meet you."

"We've heard a lot about you," she says. Then she adds, "All good, by the way. Ellis would kill me for saying any of this to you."

It should be awkward but everything about Christina exudes a warmth that puts me at ease, as if we've known each other forever. I guess this shouldn't be a surprise, Ellis had to get it from somewhere. "I'm flattered," I say. "I have nothing but good things to say about your son as well." And then I do catch his eye—he's across the courtyard where we're gathered, in conversation with some coworkers. He freezes when he sees us talking. "He's helped me a lot."

Christina seems to catch something between us, her bright eyes taking on a curiosity, so I quickly say, "You should be so proud of the work he's done on this park. It's beautiful."

"Oh, I am. This entire firm—they do such great work," she says. "We were over the moon when he got the job. Speaking of 'we'"—she motions to the man who was with her earlier—"this is Ellis's dad, Greg."

Greg gives me a firm handshake and a warm smile as well. "Hi, there. You must be Cassia?"

I can't even pretend that I'm surprised by him knowing who I am. "Hi, yes, nice to meet you, Greg. We were just talking about how proud you must be of Ellis."

"Oh yeah, but we can't show it or he'll turn into a pile of mortified dust," says Greg. "That hasn't changed since he was a teenager."

"Never could handle a compliment," Christina says with an eye roll.

I feel a greediness rise in me to hear more about Ellis from his parents. To know what he was like when he was younger, how he is with the people who know him best. It bothers me, this greed, because I've never felt it with Daniel.

"Uh-oh, here he comes," Greg says under his breath.

And he is coming over—big steps, a little bit of panic in his eyes while his expression stays relaxed.

"Hey," I say, trying to reassure him with my smile, my so, *so* relaxed posture.

"Hey," he says back, his eyes bouncing between me and his parents. "Why have my parents cornered you?"

We laugh. "They're just showing me naked toddler photos of you, calm down."

"What?" His head whips to his mom but when he realizes I'm fucking with him, he relaxes. "Honestly, wouldn't be surprised."

"No, we were talking about what a great job you guys did here." My voice is wrapped in cautious warmth, putting a barrier between us. "It's so perfect."

A blush creeps up his neck and he ducks his head. "Thanks, it's a great team."

Christina and Greg shoot me looks as if to say, *See?*

"What did you work on, specifically?" I ask, genuinely curious.

"Ah." He looks around. "Well, the planting, but the trees are my favorite. So, the newly planted seedlings, but also working with the arborist to preserve the established mature trees that are native to this area."

"You always loved trees," his mom says warmly. "Since you were a baby."

"Oh my god," Ellis says under his breath. "I did not show a tree aptitude as an *infant*, Mom."

"You did!" she exclaims. "You were colicky and ruined my life but the only thing that calmed you down was stepping outside under the trees. You would look up at the leaves and instantly calm down."

He's beet-red now, and this entire interaction is so adorable that I have to look away. "Well, A-plus on the trees. Would hire you for sure."

"You should prune that sycamore in your front yard," he blurts out suddenly.

"What?"

"Ah. If you want, I mean. But the upper limbs are getting heavy and might pose a danger if we get heavy winds this year." It's said in a rush, as if he's been holding this opinion for weeks. Which, he probably has.

"Oh, okay. Good to know," I say. And suddenly it *is* awkward.

The acknowledgment that he's been to my house, the familiarity of it in front of his parents.

A small moving object runs into my legs at that moment and I shoot a thankful prayer to whoever just sent Ozzie to me.

"Auntie Cassie! I skipped a stone!"

"Oh wow, did you?" I rub her hair affectionately. "That's a really difficult skill, my bud."

Mica comes running up, too. "She didn't!" he says scornfully. "It just hit another rock, so it looked like it."

"I *did*!" Ozzie screeches.

But Mica isn't paying attention to her anymore. He's jumped into Ellis's arms. "Ellis! Ellis! My arm is better now!" He holds out his arm.

"Look at that," Ellis says seriously. "You wouldn't even know that a swan monster attacked you." Both kids giggle and I feel that familiar spark of yearning inside of me. Then Marcella and Logan join the kids and we introduce everyone to each other. Food is passed around, stories are exchanged, and all of it feels so natural. But instead of making me happy, it makes me feel choked up.

39

I take a few breaths and splash some water on my cheeks, then reapply my makeup. My hands shake. The extreme reaction I'm having to seeing Ellis's family with people I love is distressing. I close my eyes and take some breaths—concentrating on my feeling earlier with Daniel. The rightness of it. The steady effect on my soul.

When I feel ready, I leave the restroom—running straight into Ellis. "Oh," I say stupidly.

He looks at me, his expression inscrutable. "Are you okay?"

"Yeah, totally."

But my little smile feels flimsy even to me. He steps in close. "Sorry if my parents bombarded you."

"No, don't be sorry. They're lovely," I say. "As they would be. And hey, you *should* be proud of your work. The trees—that's a huge deal. There are, like, a billion of them here."

He laughs, but it's edged with self-deprecation again. "I had a lot of help from Daniel."

I frown. There's something about him that is shrinking into himself when he talks about his job that is at odds with the confident, easy guy that I know so well. "Daniel tells me that everyone at the firm has a lot of ownership over their specialties. He's really proud of you, too."

This doesn't land in the way I want it to, and I point over our heads. "Tell me about this tree."

"Come on," he says with an eye roll.

"I'm serious. I wanna know about it. And why you decided to plant it here." It's not quite a mature tree, but it's tall enough to provide a leafy canopy over us and the bathrooms. The bark is textured and light brown, the leaves are fernlike, and it's full of gorgeous yellow blooms.

We both tilt our heads back. "Well," Ellis starts, his hands in his pockets. "This is a Cassia leptophylla, otherwise known as a golden medallion."

I shoot a look at him. "Another Cassia?"

He smiles. "Yeah, same family. It's evergreen, so it'll never be bare. They get these beautiful blooms so are mostly used as ornamental sidewalk trees in Los Angeles. Not an obvious choice for a park, and definitely not native. But they are really hardy, drought-tolerant, and I thought would be a nice splash of color and texture here by the restrooms."

I stare at him. "*Okay*, Bill Nye of trees!"

"Anyone with Wikipedia could have told you that," he says with a headshake, his necklace glimmering in the sunlight.

"That's not true. What you told me was your reasoning behind planting it here. Knowledge and experience went into that, buddy. Hate to break it to you, but you're good at your job."

Something sparks in him, I can feel it diffuse from his body, subtle but there. His smile is genuine, free of self-deprecation. "I'm not fishing for compliments!"

"That's nice, you just caught a juicy trout anyway."

"Juicy?" he says with his eyebrow raised. "Dork."

A yellow blossom drops from the tree and lands on my shoulder. I'm about to get it when Ellis reaches out and catches it between his fingers. He holds it between us for a second, twirling it between his thumb and middle finger. I watch his elegant fingers and feel my limbs go heavy with longing.

His eyes scan my face intently as if he can hear my thoughts, and I feel myself warm under his scrutiny. "Ellis," I say softly.

He waits for me to say more, but I don't. I step closer to him and our faces are inches apart. "We need to stop doing this," he says, his eyes intense.

I swallow. "Yeah." But I inch closer because I can't deny the pull of this man. Our bodies are always in tune with each other, circling and circling—restless until we're close.

And then my lips brush against his, and he doesn't move. I pull back immediately. "I'm sorry," I whisper. *What am I doing?*

But he shakes his head. "I don't want to be sorry anymore."

And he pulls me in, quick and assured, and we're kissing again. In earnest, for real. No tentative brushes of our lips, just a need to be closer, to swallow each other whole. It feels like relief and punishment at the same time. His hands run down my sides, and suddenly I'm hauled up against his solid body.

We both make noises into each other's mouths and the kiss turns primal as I find myself pushed up against the wall of the bathroom. I am aware that this hides us behind some greenery, and somewhere in the back of my mind I'm admiring Ellis for this maneuver, for his thoughtfulness even as we're both completely out of our minds.

His hands touch the skin between my top and skirt. Then they climb up my ribs, gentle and possessive, and I'm lost in the press of his lips, the slide of his tongue when a toilet flushing jolts me out of it. I pull back immediately and so does he. We stare at each other, catching our breaths. We don't speak as I adjust my top, my hair.

"Fuck," he says under his breath. "What are we doing?"

"I don't know," I say. But maybe I do. "I think we need—"

"Hey, there you are." Daniel strides into the clearing. "I've been looking for you." He looks between us and smiles for a second before it falters. That's when I notice my lipstick smeared all over Ellis's mouth, his neck.

Fuck, indeed.

40

Everything happens so quickly.

Daniel swings his arm back and punches Ellis square in the face. My hands fly up to my mouth. "What the hell?!" I screech. "Daniel!"

Ellis quickly recovers and tackles him around the belly, his arms wrapped around Daniel's lower back as they both topple to the ground.

"Oh my *god!* Stop it, you two! Stop!"

They look ridiculous. These are two men in fine physical shape, but they do *not* know how to fight. They're kind of swiping at each other with both fists and openhanded slaps. Kicking on occasion.

"You are *grown. Ass. MEN!*" I yell, throwing my hands up in the air.

But they exist somewhere outside of me at the moment—in some adolescent macho zone that I'll never understand. I want to pull them apart, but I'd have to get down on the ground and dodge their flailing limbs.

"You little *asshole!*" Daniel yells at one point when his arm is braced across Ellis's neck in a chokehold. Ellis starts coughing dramatically and Daniel looks taken aback for a second, loosening his hold. "Bloody hell, are you okay?"

Ellis responds with a yell and grabs Daniel's ears. His *ears*. Daniel howls at the top of his lungs and people come running at the commotion.

I am about to sink into the earth and die. These idiots!

When I see Ellis's parents and Marcella's family, I further want to die. Because I'm standing there with my head in my hands and Ellis's face is still smeared with my lipstick, and it's obvious to anyone with eyes what's happened.

"*I'm* the asshole? *Me*? What kind of boss *are* you? Dating *my* girlfriend!" Ellis yells as his grip on Daniel slips a little bit, letting Daniel escape and slam his body into Ellis's again. The crowd gasps and Ellis is on his back with Daniel standing above him, panting so hard he's wheezing. Ellis is rolled into a fetal position. Good lord.

"She *dumped* you," Daniel says. "Why can't you just let it go?"

"Also, technically she wasn't your girlfriend!" someone calls out.

All of the coworkers have gathered, too, and Laura says, "I'm *so* Team Daniel."

"No way, Team Ellis," Parker says.

"There are *no* teams!" I yell.

Greg, Ellis's dad, breaks through the crowd to help Ellis up.

"Fucking sleazy-ass Korean Hugh Grant," Ellis spits out as he stands up.

"Oh my god," Greg mutters under his breath.

Marcella chokes on a laugh next to me but then Daniel lunges forward and catches Ellis with a left hook to the side of his head that kind of misses but infuriates Ellis enough for him to swing at him in turn, which turns into yet another grappling match. At that point, Greg and a few of the other coworkers manage to break the two apart.

Once it's clear they don't need to be restrained any longer, Daniel looks at me. "Are you guys fucking *kidding* me?" he gasps out, wiping blood off his face. And then suddenly, none of it is funny anymore. Something crushes inside me.

And it just comes out: "It was a mistake."

Ellis's head swivels toward me, his hair in disarray, his shirt untucked. Betrayal flashes across his face.

"Daniel—" I reach for him, but he turns and walks away, practically running. Everyone is dead silent around us until someone says, *"Damnnnn."*

Marcella looks at me once before saying, "Okay, everyone, let's leave them to it." As she and Logan start dispersing the crowd, I catch a glimpse of Sunny. What is she doing here? But before I can register that, Mar has led her away, too, and I'm left alone with Ellis.

His hands are on his hips, staring down at the ground, and I see his heavy breaths through the heaving of his strong back. I don't even know what to say—confusion courses through me, I feel so rattled and sick inside.

"Are you okay?" I ask quietly, not daring to get close to him.

"No," he grinds out, still looking down, his body coiled as if he will lose his shit if he looks at me.

"What I said—"

His head whips up then. His eyes red-rimmed as if he's going to cry but also filled with so much regret. "I want to be okay with this. Because Daniel deserves someone great like you. But I just . . . can't seem to be okay with it." Blood is dripping off his cheekbone when he says, "And at the wedding, you didn't seem to be okay with it, either. With Avery, especially." His words land with a violent thud. The truth of it too big to ignore.

I take a deep breath. "Yeah, I guess I'm not."

"You almost murdered her in a swimming pool."

Laughter bubbles out of me, a sweet release. "I'm sorry."

"No, you're not." But he's smiling a little, too. "You have nothing to be jealous of, you know."

"I have no right to be jealous anyway," I say quietly. "I'm being one of those selfish assholes who wants everyone to love her as some sort of concept."

The word "love" hovers above us like a curse and I keep talking to make it evaporate. "What I mean—"

"I think I love you."

My entire being stills, the blood freezes in my veins, my heart stops beating, my lungs stop expanding. "What?"

Ellis reaches out, his hands gripping my arms. His eyes don't leave mine. "I love you, Cassia."

I shake my head. "No, Ellis. No, you don't. We've only spent a weekend together, really—"

"Who cares? We've seen each other more than that. *We keep seeing each other*," he grinds the words out. "There's something bigger here, something that could be so great. And you won't let it happen because of my age? Or is there some other secret thing you won't tell me?"

Other secret thing. I know he's not trying to be dismissive, that he's just frustrated. But it stings, that offhand reference to something that is the biggest secret thing. The most special thing about me. The thing that has built a legacy for my family. One that we protect generation after generation.

"Ellis, I don't know." It's whispered, my eyes filling up with tears. I am so, so tired and confused and unsure about everything. Something dims in his eyes and we are far apart, again.

He's shutting down. Organ by organ, until his heart is locked up tight. "Okay. I have a scrap of pride left. I won't bother you anymore."

Something close to despair fills me, and I say, "Ellis, I wish—"

"That I was ten years older? Yeah, I know. All of this was a mistake. I get it now." He walks away and I want to walk after him, but I know the kind thing to do is stay where I am and let my heart break right along with his.

41

Minutes, maybe hours, pass before Marcella finds me.

"Can you take me home?" I ask her, trying not to cry.

I'm quiet on the drive home and Marcella doesn't press me for details. When we get to my house, she follows me in and immediately opens up a bottle of wine and guzzles it straight from the bottle. "You're going to turn me into an alcoholic," she finally says. "Do you want to talk about it?"

I lie down on my rug and groan. "I can't believe myself."

Betty is squawking so loud that Marcella lets her out of her cage and the chaotic flapping of her wings is a nice distraction for a second. We both stare at her as she swoops overhead before perching on the back of the sofa, near but not on me. I feel her judgment.

"So, am I right in assuming that Ellis and Daniel were fighting over you like two macho losers?"

Somehow, I manage to let out a huff of laughter. "Yes, you are correct."

"And am I right in assuming it's because Daniel caught you two in a compromising position?" She is keeping her voice even, to her credit. As if this isn't the juiciest shit she's ever heard.

"Kind of. We had just . . . finished. Making out! That's it!" I say quickly before Marcella can spontaneously combust. "But it was clear what we were doing."

"You chose today of all days to go for a bold lip," she says sadly. "Years of me trying to convince you and this is how it happens."

The hilarity of the situation cannot be avoided and soon we're laughing so hard tears are coming out of my eyes, the kind of manic laughter that can turn into true tears on a dime. I take the wine from her and take a gulp. "Ellis said he loved me."

"Oh my god. This guy!" But she's not mad, she's in love with him, too. "And?"

"And . . ." I stare off into the distance, my eyes catching on the sycamore tree that needs pruning in my front yard. My chest clenches. "And I didn't say anything."

Mar's quiet.

"And then he left."

A sigh as big as the world leaves her. "Damn."

"Yeah. I think I like Ellis more than Daniel. Actually, I think maybe I love him."

Marcella nods her head. "This is . . . obvious to me."

I throw a pillow at her head. "But was it just because he was there first? Maybe because I can't have him, knowing my fate, I keep getting tempted?"

"Tempted? Who are you, Jesus?"

"No, but I would have to be to resist Ellis."

"Okay, wow." Marcella sits up straighter, her back against my Danish armchair, and runs her hands through her hair. "I am seeing how deep your feelings for Ellis are if you are acting *this* chaotic. Cass, you need to—"

She's interrupted by a knock on the door. Mar gives me a

questioning look then walks to the door and looks through the keyhole. "It's Sunny."

I sit up as she opens the door. Sunny rushes in, looking strangely disheveled despite her usual impeccable outfit. "Is everything okay?" I ask her, alarmed.

Her eyes stay on her feet as she takes off her slingback heels. "Not really. We have to talk."

The serious tone makes me panic. "Is it Halmoni? Stu? You?"

She waves her hand in the air. "No, no, everyone's okay. But . . . well." She glances at Mar. "Can we have a moment alone?"

Mar looks surprised but nods. "Of course! I'll head out actually, to give you two some privacy." She grabs her bag and then gives me a tight hug. "Call me later, okay?"

When she leaves, Sunny sits on the sofa and pulls her legs up into herself, making herself into a tiny ball. Her unease is palpable, and I nurse a tiny kernel of panic as I sit in my armchair. "Okay, what's going on?"

"I really don't know where to start," she says, her voice low and shaking a little. She's twisting her fingers in her lap. "Um, maybe I'll start with how your parents met."

A prickle up my spine. "My parents?"

She nods. "Yes, your parents. You know how they met, right?"

"Yeah." I'm trying to make heads or tails of why Sunny wants to talk about this right now. "They met at art school."

Even though my mom never loved talking too much about my dad, she did tell me the story of how they met and would bring it up casually at times. Maybe she was avoiding the topic of my dad being this fraught, angsty thing in my life. They met their first week at ArtCenter, a top art school in Pasadena.

"Yes, they did," Sunny says. "And you know your mom had to be won over by your dad, right?"

"Obviously. Mom loved that part of the story."

She smiles, but it's sad. "I'm sure she did. But do you know why she resisted him?"

"She thought he was annoying," I say automatically. "He came on too strong."

"Maybe he did," she says, her voice quavering again. "But the real reason was . . ." Her voice trails off and her gaze goes to my bar cart. "Can I have something to drink?" She gets up before I can answer and walks briskly over to the cart, grabbing the first bottle she can find—whiskey. I watch as she pours herself a very full glass. With nothing else. "Whoa," I say.

After tossing half of it down, she looks me in the eye, still standing. "Your mom didn't like your dad because . . . because she knew he was her fated."

"Sunny. What are you saying?" I ask, my voice sounding way calmer than I feel.

After my mother died, her life was a cautionary tale. When I was ten, my ballet class was performing *Swan Lake* for our big recital, and I was deeply disturbed by the story. The couple weeks leading up to it, I had fallen into a melancholy that my grandparents couldn't snap me out of.

Then, as Halmoni helped me get ready for the recital, I confessed to her that I was afraid of being left behind by everyone in my life. I thought of the prince who plunged to his death once he realized he couldn't be with his true love. How they could only be together in death.

"People who find their fated don't die alone," Halmoni said to me firmly while plaiting my hair into a braid, then pulling it up into a tidy bun. "We are fated to find our person." The unspoken words were that my mother, having abandoned her fate, had died without a person.

My father.

Sunny looks like she might throw up. "I am saying that, when your mom met Matthew, she knew who he was. Because Halmoni had read Evette's face when she turned eighteen and given her his name."

"No, no that can't be right," I say. "Mom rebelled—she rejected all of this!"

"Yes, she did. But Halmoni insisted Evette should know so that she didn't end up with one of the bad boys she was always drawn to. So, Evette knew who Matthew was when they met, and wanted nothing to do with it. With him. But he was persistent. He was completely smitten by her." Her voice softens and I don't know how to feel. What the hell is this? "They started dating a couple years into school and then she got pregnant with you."

I clutch my chest. "But . . . but he left."

Her eyes fill with tears. "He did. He couldn't handle having a kid that young, and your mom, she wanted to have you. She told me she knew you were special, and you are!"

I ignore her attempt at kindness. "But it makes no sense! How could he leave her if he was her fated?"

Sunny looks miserable when she sits down next to me. "I don't know, honey. We were all shocked. It was beyond comprehension that this could happen, and that it could happen to Evette, who was so rebellious about it in the first place. Their relationship already so hard-won."

"Sunny. Everything . . . *everything* I believe about life and love is based on fated matches." My voice gets louder, angry. "Have you all been *lying* to me this entire time?"

"No!" She pauses after she says it. "I mean, in a way yes, but not about fateds and past lives. You have the gift, you see it for yourself!"

"Then why lie about Mom? And why tell me now?" I get up and

start pacing the room. As if sensing something, Betty follows me, swooping back and forth. It's oddly comforting.

"Because of Ellis!" she cries out, emotional in a way that is so unlike Sunny. "I saw that fight and then I saw you talking to Ellis after. And I realized we've made a huge mistake keeping this from you. Not to mention your reaction to Daniel saying he wasn't sure about being a dad. I saw how it shocked you. And I just . . . I don't want you being with someone just because he's your fated!"

"My god, Sunny—that is *the entire fucking point!*" I am yelling now, my heart thudding in my chest, my skin feeling itchy and hot.

She drops her head into her hands. "I know, Cass, I know. But I owe it to your mom to tell you. I can't let her daughter make the wrong decision because of this!"

The anguish in her voice mellows my anger and instead fills me with intense sadness. I stop in front of her. "What do you mean you owe it to Mom?"

"Do you think Halmoni would have let me wait until I was in my late forties to meet my fated if it wasn't for Evette?" she asks.

"You mean, Mom dying?" I ask, so discombobulated.

She shakes her head. "Halmoni always regretted Evette staying with your dad," she says, her eyes shiny with tears. "She thinks because she forced her fated on Evette that Evette . . . Well, all the things that went wrong were because of that. And so, with me, she gave me room to figure it out. And we decided to make it a rule that we wouldn't read faces without explicit permission. See? If it wasn't for your mom, I would have also been coerced into finding Stu much earlier. Much earlier than I was ready. I owe my happiness to her."

I take in a breath, on the verge of tears. "Sunny. This is so much to take in."

She stands up and grasps my hands. "I know, I'm so sorry Cass.

I really thought once you met Daniel, it would all be fine. But that dinner . . . I got scared. Then this fight between Daniel and Ellis. And when I saw you and Ellis together the morning of your birthday, I don't know, something about it rang true to me. I could tell that when you found Daniel it wasn't an easy decision."

I'm shocked by this. "You . . . you've been skeptical of Daniel all this time?"

She shakes her head. "Not skeptical. Cautious. And I was really, truly happy that things seemed to be going so well between you two."

"But you think now it's not?" My voice is grim.

"No, not necessarily. I just want you to have all the facts," she says. "Matthew would want you to know, too."

Something about the way she says my dad's name makes me sit up. "Do you . . . Do you keep in touch with him?"

I can tell she wants to lie to me, her eyes cagey. But she slumps. "Not really. Just . . . sometimes he reaches out to me to ask about you."

"Oh my *god!*" I truly cannot handle all this information. "Sunny, this is beyond fucked up."

"He didn't want you to know!" she says. "It's not like we're close! But he's your father, Cass!"

"Only by blood," I say viciously fast.

"Yes, of course," she says. "I'm not defending him, okay?"

"Does this mean you know where he is?" I ask.

She nods, hesitant. "Yes. He lives in Michigan."

"Wow." It's all I can muster right now. "And you have his phone number?"

"Yes." Then she pulls out her phone, an idea forming. "I'm giving you his info, okay? I think it would help you to talk to him."

My phone vibrates when her text arrives and I almost recoil. "Are you out of your mind? Why would I want to talk to him?"

"There's only one other person in this world who knows what

went on in their relationship," she says. "Don't you want to know more? To help you figure things out with Daniel?"

My head swims. "I don't know what I want, Sunny. This is all so fucking much. And it's hard for me to even believe you."

She looks hesitant for a moment before she reaches into her bag and pulls out something. "Maybe this will convince you." She hands me a wood box inlaid with mother-of-pearl and abalone in images of cranes and flowers.

"What's this?" I am suspicious of everything.

She puts it in my hands. "Open it."

I open the little metal latch. The box is lined in hot-pink silk. Lying in it is a single item—a piece of paper. I pull it out. It's our handmade paper.

On it is a name, stitched in thread: *Matthew Lee*

The breath is knocked out of me. Until this point, there was the possibility of Sunny lying to me. That everything remained as I thought.

But here's the truth. Sitting in the palm of my hand. Then I notice the thread color. It's black, not white. "Why . . . why is it black?"

Sunny shakes her head. "We think it's because their connection broke. We've never seen it before or since."

I look up at Sunny with tears in my eyes and she pulls me into a hug. I start sobbing into her shoulder.

"I'm sorry, Cass," she whispers. "I love you. I want you to have the world."

42

When Sunny leaves, a wild feeling comes over me.

Before I can think too hard about it, I grab my weekend travel bag and throw in some underwear, toiletries, and a change of clothes.

Then I text the girl next door to see if she can check in on Betty tomorrow—she can. With that confirmed, I put my stuff into my car and make the drive to LAX.

Ann Arbor. That's where my dad lives. A city I've even been to once, with an ex whose family lived there. A leafy college town that looks like something straight off of a postcard. My hands clench the steering wheel.

I start dictating a text to the Park women group chat. "Sunny told me everything. About my parents and how they were fated. I can't believe that my own family lied to me my entire life. I can't see or talk to you guys right now. I'm taking a week off from work, please don't try and contact me." I'm glad they can't hear the trembling in my voice.

Then I turn off my phone so I don't see their responses. When I get to LAX, I do something that people only do in the movies: I book a one-way trip to Detroit, the best option to get into Ann Arbor, on a red-eye. It's not for a couple hours, so I decide to walk through the sprawling hellscape that is my city's international airport.

There's a comfort to my anonymity, the chaos of everyone else's plans not touching me in any way, acting as white noise for my thoughts. People from all over the world finding themselves in this one place. The news I'm processing is life-changing, and seeing the rest of the world go on, business as usual, calms me.

I don't even know why I'm doing this. All I know is, I can't be in L.A. right now, I can't be near my family. If I saw Halmoni, I would lose my shit.

As I walk through the terminals, I keep replaying Ellis confessing his feelings to me after the fight. The hurt on his face when I didn't reciprocate. The hurt on Daniel's face before it turned to anger. This revelation about fateds—it should release me from this indecision. I'm free to go running to Ellis!

But instead, it makes it one million times more complicated. Do I really want to be with Ellis, or was it just me having second thoughts about Daniel? Even without the fated aspect—Ellis doesn't make sense for my life. My very tidy, peaceful life that I've spent forty years building. A life I love. Throw a twenty-eight-year-old into the mix and it just goes upside down. Will I have to teach him how to deep clean a fridge? I'd rather get a root canal. Learn to "go with the flow"? Will I always worry that he'll leave me for a younger woman? What if I'm out there doing CrossFit and dieting at sixty to keep my young man close? I'd rather die.

Will he even want children? Will *Daniel* ever want children?

I get in about thirty million steps before I'm on my flight. As the plane ascends, I look out the window at the dark, deep blue of the Pacific. I think about my dad leaving L.A. to move to Michigan. There are so many questions I can finally ask him. Why did he leave us? Was it just the freaked-out-by-fatherhood thing? Wouldn't the strength of his fated love to my mom be strong enough? A thought sneaks in like a whisper, a hiss low in my ear. Why was *I* not enough?

I feel exhaustion drop over me like a weighted blanket. I give in happily, easily to sleep.

When I wake up, we've landed and a single line of drool has dried on my face. I wipe it off with my hand and look out the window. It's dark and overcast but the pilot says it's eighty-four degrees and humid. The sun is just starting to rise.

According to the navigation in my rental, the car ride to Ann Arbor is another forty-five minutes. I blast the AC as high as it will go because my cotton T-shirt is already stuck to my back, the humidity an assault on my California body. As I drive away from the airport, the enormity of what I'm doing hits me. What am I going to say to him? This man is a stranger to me. But I do know that he's the only one outside of my family who *knew* my mom and knew about our family secret. An outsider and an insider at the same time.

I'm not ready for this talk, but I've never been.

The landscape starts to change from city highways to industrial to more suburban landscapes. I drive through Ann Arbor proper, which is quiet in the early morning and as charming as I remember it—brick buildings, tree-lined roads, local cafés. Then Google Maps takes me into a neighborhood filled with different architectural styles—some Gothic Revival, Tudor, and Craftsmans. It's not fancy, but it's lovely, especially with everything framed by huge, stately trees. You feel the age and history of the area immediately.

I come to a stop in front of a modest, sage-green two-story Colonial. There are tall maple and beech trees planted around it, and blooming lantana and petunias lining the brick pathway through the green lawn.

I park on the curb and stare at the house. This is where my dad has been living. Halfway across the country in this quaint neighborhood that feels like a different country from L.A. What's his life like? I don't even know if he has another family, or what. Or if he's even home. It's early, what if he's still sleeping? I finally muster the nerve to get out of the car and walk up the path, my heart beating in my throat every step of the way.

This is surely the most impulsive and nutjob thing I have ever done in my life. And if I think about it too much I will chicken out and will have flown out here for fucking nothing. So I reach out and ring the doorbell.

43

He answers the door.

I know it's him despite not having seen a picture of him since I was six. He's still got a head of dark hair, thinning but dark. He's wearing black-framed glasses that remind me slightly of Stu. He has the square face of an older, handsome Korean man. In fact, it's the benign-ness of how he looks that fills me with absolute devastation.

He looks like an average Korean dad. But I never had that dad.

I take this all in as his expression goes from curious to shocked. "Cassia?"

His recognition of me catches me off guard. "Yes. Are you Matthew?" I manage to croak out.

His expression turns from shock to what I can only describe as astonishment. His eyes widen, his mouth drops open, and he makes a small, instinctual movement toward me. "How . . . What are you, I mean—"

"Sorry to surprise you so early," I say, annoyed that I have to begin with an apology. "But I just found out something and needed to talk to you. Sunny gave me your address."

"Are you okay?" he asks, his eyes flying over me, as if checking me for injuries. Something about it makes me want to cry.

"Yes. I mean physically," I say with a weird, tortured laugh.

After looking at my face with the same stunned shock for a few seconds, he shakes his head and steps aside, holding the door open. "Please, come inside."

I kind of don't want to but of course I should. Even if he's not a great dad, I doubt he's also a serial killer on top of all else.

I step inside and look around curiously. It's a very normal house, shoes piled up in the entry. Men's and women's. No children's shoes. But why would my dad have little kids at this age even if he had kids? I don't know, honestly I know nothing.

There aren't any family photos or anything in the entryway, just a table topped with mail and keys and other normal life things. A woven rug that runs along the narrow entry, and stairs that lead to the second floor. Some coats and jackets hang on a row of pegs nearby. It smells like food and coffee.

"Um, did I interrupt your breakfast?" I ask as I take off my sneakers.

He shakes his head, watching my every movement with wonder. "No, we just finished up." It's almost eight a.m. and I note that maybe I've caught him on the way to work. But I don't mention it because he doesn't, either.

"Do you . . . Is your family here?" I ask, way too tentative for my liking.

Sadness flashes through his eyes. "I—uh, I'm married but have no children. Didn't Sunny tell you?"

I shake my head. "No. I didn't have time."

"What's going on?" he asks, his voice gentle.

Suddenly, I feel like I might pass out. "Uh, could I possibly sit and have a glass of water, please?"

"Oh man, of course," he says, slapping his forehead. I can instantly imagine him as the former skater kid who grew up in the Valley. "Here, take a seat." He leads me to the living room, which has a large picture window with green curtains, lush indoor plants cluttered onto tables by the window, and a series of black-and-white landscape photographs hung around the walls.

I take a seat on a cozy sectional, placed opposite a large TV over a fireplace. There's a basket full of knitting next to a leather armchair with a dog in it. It's a beagle that looks about a hundred years old and is snoozing like it's been drugged. "Your dog doesn't seem to mind I'm here," I say without thinking.

"Oh, she's gone completely deaf," he says with fondness. Then he hovers for a second. "Well, let me go get you some water, okay? Be right back."

He rushes off and I hear voices. A woman. They must be in the kitchen because I can also hear some dishes being washed. Before I can take stock of everything in the living room, he's back, holding a tray with a glass of water and two mugs—one with tea and the other coffee. There's also a carton of half-and-half and a jar of sugar. "I wasn't sure what you would be in the mood for," he says nervously as he places the tray on the coffee table in front of me.

"Thanks," I say as I reach for the water first.

"Rachel, my wife, is home but I told her to give us a little space. That's the only reason why she's not coming in to say hello," he says as he picks up the dog and sits in the armchair, keeping it in his arms. "But of course, you can, ah, meet her if you'd like."

I nod, unable to make any kind of decision about that yet. "What's your dog's name?" I ask instead.

"Walnut," he says, giving her a scratch behind the ears. "Old girl's been around sixteen years now."

Matthew talks with a mix of California and Midwest accents that I find amusing. "She's very sweet."

"She's very senile," he says with a grin. Then there's silence because we've talked about the dog as much as we possibly can.

I put my glass down. "I'm here because Sunny told me about you being Mom's fated."

His hand stills on Walnut. "She what?"

My body starts to feel hot again. "Sunny told me that you were Mom's fated. Because I didn't know."

"What do you mean?" he asks, slowly and carefully. "All this time . . . Who did you think I was?"

"I knew you were my dad," I say, agitated. "Obviously. But my grandparents and Emoni and Sunny . . . they told me you weren't Mom's fated. That you left because you weren't meant to be."

Matthew has stopped petting Walnut and she gets annoyed and hops off his lap in a loud huff. She waddles out of the room indignantly. He stares at me. "They told you that?"

"Yeah."

"Oh my god," he mutters under his breath, sitting back. "That is so . . . that's so like them."

Instantly, I am defensive. "You don't know them."

The sharpness of my voice sends his eyes flying over to mine, and he looks regretful. "I don't mean to insult them. But, Cassia, there's so much I don't think you know."

"Well, that's why I'm here," I say, my spine snapping straight with the mission at hand. "Tell me. Everything."

44

I met Evette at freshman orientation." My dad has a faraway expression, and I can tell he might be in some unreachable place right now. "I spotted her immediately—not just because we were the only Asian kids there, but because she was so beautiful." He looks at me then. "You look so much like her. It's . . ." His voice trails off as he glances away and takes a deep breath. "It's a trip."

I know I look like my mom and it's something that I've always been grateful for—to have her features live on in me. But now I look at my dad and see some of myself in him, too. And *that* is a trip, as well.

"I remember what she was wearing that day," he says with a smile. "It was the early eighties, you know? Everyone in art school thought they were either a hippie or a punk. I veered toward punk myself. A suburban kid with something to prove. But Eve—she was uniquely herself. She wore this oversized T-shirt that she had hand-painted herself, with little red shorts. It's really hard to explain. Her hair was so long—like yours—and wavy and glinted in the sun. It was difficult not to notice her."

Photos of Mom when she was young are all around my house,

so I can picture this outfit exactly. A cold clenching feeling comes over me. I suddenly feel her absence so acutely that it's hard to breathe normally.

"Anyway, I felt like I was pretty cool, so I swaggered over to her during our lunch break. We were outside and she was fanning herself under a tree with a paper fan she made. It was hot out. So, I brought her a pop from the vending machine. At first, she was friendly and maybe even flirty with me. But when I introduced myself—Matthew Lee—she suddenly turned ice-cold."

"Because you were her fated," I said weakly.

He nodded. "And she iced me out for weeks. I had no idea why. I had such a crush on her. I thought, maybe she didn't want to be hanging out with one of the only other Asian kids in our program. Or she thought I was too dorky. Not talented enough. Because Evette was just so cool, man." For a second, he looks boyish, lost in time. He leans forward, his hands clasped together, his voice low and urgent. "But she couldn't deny our chemistry. And I was persistent. It would probably be considered a 'red flag' on TikTok today." I laugh without thinking, and there is a twinkle in his eye in response. He continues, "So after a few weeks, she gave me a chance."

"Where was your first date?" The question slips out, I can't help it. I am sucked into the story, thirsty for every drop of new information about Mom.

He groans a little. "Oh, I was so embarrassing. I was trying to impress her, so I invited her to my . . . show."

"Like, an art show?"

"No." He can't even look at me. "My . . . band's . . . rock show."

"Oh. Oh, no."

We make eye contact for a second and start laughing. It loosens me up. I realize that I've been absolutely still—coiled, and tense.

"Yeah. Despite that, she somehow went on a second date with me. And then a third . . . and, well, we . . . our feelings got big fast. Soon after that, she told me everything—all about past lives and fateds and all that. And I believed her, because everything was great for a while. We spent four years together at art school—grueling schedules that required so many all-nighters. Being broke and eating saltines and butter for breakfast. You bond with people when your relationship is forged in fire, you know? I thought we could face anything . . . Then Eve got pregnant. It was earlier than planned, clearly, and we weren't married so your grandparents were furious. But once you were born, they were all in."

Then comes the pause.

My voice quakes. "But you weren't."

His head drops down. "Cassia, I know there's nothing I can say or do to make up for . . . anything." He finds the courage to look up, and his eyes are red-rimmed. "But what I can tell you is that I was young and freaked out and didn't have the tools to become the man I needed to be. And that when I was gone long enough, I felt like I no longer deserved a place in your life. Then when Evette died, it just seemed cruel to attempt to take her place."

Both of us are crying now.

"I did love you both. I still . . . I still think about you all the time. Cold comfort, I know. But it's true. You were never forgotten. And neither is your mother." He pauses to look at me, his eyes roaming over my face again. "Seeing you is such a gift. It's like time travel."

I need to take giant gulps of air to breathe, and he watches me with misery before standing up. A few seconds later, he returns with a box of tissue. I take one and wipe at my eyes. "So, it's true? You were her fated and despite that, you still left us. Her."

He nods, suddenly looking all of his sixty-plus years. "Yes."

"Did being fated mean nothing to you?" I shake my head. "I know the dad aspect freaked you out, but what about the fated part? You knew it was real. You were willing to break up life after life of fated love?"

What he says next is careful, deliberate. "The thing is, Cassia . . . Fated loves? That's your family's religion. It isn't mine. I just loved your mom. And that love was so intense—I believe that we loved each other in other lives. But in *this* life, I wasn't brave enough to stick around."

The honesty floors me. He's not trying to make excuses. There's still so much I want to ask him, but I am completely drained. My eyes feel sticky, my skin dry as a bone, and my brain has left planet Earth. He must see it in my face because he asks, "Did you fly here overnight?"

"Yeah. I slept a little on the plane, but I probably need to find a hotel to crash at for a bit."

"No, no. Stay. We have a guest room. It's always ready because Rachel is . . . She's like that," he says with a smile.

"I couldn't impose," I say automatically, absolutely mortified at the idea of wearing out my welcome. "I have a rental car and am fine with a hotel." I'm already up, grabbing my purse.

But he's up, too, and he looks at me with urgency. "Please, Cassia. I couldn't . . . I can't send you out like this, so upset. I want to know you're close and safe."

The sturdiness of that statement throws me off-balance. It's so dad-like. "Are you sure? What about Rachel . . ."

"She wants you to stay," he says. "I've already talked to her about it. She's put out towels and a scented candle by now."

I laugh, a kind of laugh that comes from delirium and a softening of resolve. "Okay. I'll stay."

The happiness in his eyes feels like a gift.

Rachel does indeed have the guest room ready for me. The spare but cozy room has a small bedside sconce with an adorable gingham-patterned pleated lampshade. The comforter is fluffy and white and there is an abundance of pillows on the bed. A set of plush sunny-yellow towels are set on the end of the bed. There's even a bud vase with a single daisy in it on the nightstand. It's complicated to think of my dad's new wife taking care of me.

After a quick routine in the adjoining bathroom I fall into bed like dead weight. My phone has been on Do Not Disturb and I finally look at it. Unsurprisingly, I have a slew of missed texts and calls from my family. A conspicuous lack of any from Daniel. I put my phone face down on the nightstand, plug it in.

These are all tomorrow problems.

When I wake up, I am completely disoriented. Sunlight is streaming in through the shades, and I feel like I've slept one hundred years. I look at the time—it's five p.m. Holy crap.

After I put myself together, I head downstairs. It's quiet and I wonder if Matthew and Rachel are home. It's Tuesday, they might be at work. But when I step into the kitchen, I see a woman sitting at the kitchen table, on her laptop. She doesn't notice me right away, so I clear my throat. "Hi."

Her eyes fly up to me. "Oh, hi!" The woman, who I'm assuming is Rachel, is around my dad's age. And whoever I imagined set up my cozy guest room is not this woman. She's got a graphic tattoo on her right bicep and bone structure that would make a sculptor cry, dark brown skin, and a bleached-blond pixie cut.

In other words: She looks way too cool to be married to my dad. She gets up quickly, wearing a vintage Stones tee over black jeans. "You must be Cassia. It's so nice to meet you. I'm Rachel." She is warm and comfortable with me, but keeps her distance, a little indication of good boundaries.

"Hi, Rachel, thanks so much for letting me crash upstairs. I'll be out of your hair soon," I say, rubbing my suddenly sweaty palms on my jeans.

She shakes her head. "Not at all, please stay as long as you'd like. Matt—he'd love that."

"Is he around?"

"He's just on his way back from the pizza place—he went out to grab some dinner for us." She walks over to the fridge. "Would you like a drink? Water or wine? Beer?"

"I'll take a glass of wine, thanks," I say, still hovering in the doorway, really needing that drink.

"Please sit," she says. "Red or white?"

"Red, please." I take a seat at the round wood table set into a nook in the sunny kitchen. I look around and notice more photographs—cityscapes and portraits of people. "Are you the photographer?" I ask in an attempt at polite conversation.

Rummaging in a cupboard, Rachel says, "Oh, no. That's Matt. You didn't know . . . ?" But the question trails off as she realizes that Matthew and I don't know each other at all. She's spared more awkwardness because he comes in through a back door then. He's carrying a pizza box and my mouth literally waters at the scent of cheese and meat. He looks between Rachel and me with a small smile.

"Sorry I wasn't here to introduce you," he says to me, placing the box on the counter.

"It's fine, we're adults," I say more sharply than I intend. Rachel slides a glance at Matthew before handing me my glass of wine. I thank her and she smiles at me, squeezes Matthew's arm, and ducks out into the backyard. Through the window, I can see her walk across their lawn to a large shed out back.

"It's her studio," Matthew says, answering my question for me. "Rachel's an artist."

"Like you," I say. "She told me these photos are yours."

He nods. "Yup. That's what I studied in art school. I teach it now at the local community college."

"They're good," I say in a voice that's more matter-of-fact than complimentary.

"Thanks." He moves the pizza onto the table and sits down across from me. "Did you sleep okay?"

"Like the dead." I reach for the box, feral with hunger. He gets up quickly and grabs a couple plates and napkins to bring back to the table. We sit and eat for a bit before he asks, "You're not married yet, right?"

This question is startling. "No, I'm not."

"Have *you* found your fated?" he asks, his eyes searching mine. "Is that why Sunny told you about me?"

"I'm not married," I say. "But I did meet my fated. I knew about him for ten years, but I only just found him a couple months ago. His name is Daniel."

Matthew smiles slightly. "Daniel. Is he . . . a good guy?" He's testing out his dad reach here, I can tell.

"He's a great guy," I say.

"But?" he asks, gentle.

"He doesn't know if he wants to have kids."

"Ah," he says softly, his eyes dropping. "That old story." I know he's thinking about himself.

"When Sunny found out, she felt like she owed it to Mom to tell me the truth about you guys," I say, emotions bubbling to the surface again. "She's been feeling guilty, and she thinks that I shouldn't be with Daniel if I don't want to be."

Matthew's quiet, eyes still on the floor, looking at his striped rug. "And do you? Want to be with him?"

My eyes fill up with tears. "I don't know. I thought I did. Everything I've done . . . my entire life—it's been circling around this one promise. That I would end up with the love of my life. But look at what happened with Mom? The saddest fucking ending to the saddest fucking love story."

I hear him get up and suddenly I'm being engulfed in his arms. I want to push him away, but I don't. I sob into his shirt, and over and over he says, "I'm sorry. I'm sorry." I imagine this is what having a dad is like and it makes me cry harder.

"I don't want to make the same mistake," I whisper into his shirt.

"Oh, Cassia," he says sadly. "Your mom didn't make a mistake—I made the mistake. *I* left. *I* got scared. But your mom? She got you. The best ending."

I don't forgive him. But I let myself be comforted by him this one time. Once I stop crying, he hands me some tissues.

There's a part of me that wants to lash out at him like a petulant teenager, to rage at him and defend my family business—our entire belief system. But other than Mar, there's no one outside my family I can talk to about this. Freely and without any emotional ties to my family's feelings.

And here's my long-lost dad, who knows all about it.

"Things with Daniel are good. But."

He waits for me to finish patiently. I appreciate it. "They're good. But . . . not only did the whole baby thing throw me, but . . . there's also someone else."

I wait for shame to flood me, but I'm sitting here with someone who will never have any moral high ground over me. There's something freeing about it. He nods and keeps his expression neutral, teetering on sympathetic.

"I am finding myself . . . questioning things. Nervous. It's the first time since Mom died, where I feel like . . . my world has destabilized. I've always had this one thing, you know? This knowledge about my future, who I would end up with. Who I would be *happy forever* with."

The "forever" hangs between us. He was supposed to be forever.

"And what would happen if you didn't end up with Daniel?" he asks. And there, I see it, another flash of what he would have been like as a dad helping me through something. Homework. Friend drama. A broken heart. I wonder why he never had kids after me.

"I have no fucking idea what would happen," I say with a broken laugh. "That's the problem."

For the first time, he allows himself a real smile with me. "Or maybe that's the adventure."

45

For some reason, I want to see Betty when I get home.

I drop my bag on my dining room table and open her cage. She must sense something in my mood because instead of screaming at me and flying away in indignation, she hops to the back of a chair. I pet her, her feathers soft like velvet.

"You have no idea what the past twenty-four hours have been like," I say to her. She tilts her head and just stares at me with her beady little eyes. I scratch under her chin fondly. I remember Betty loving my mom. I was a little nuisance in Betty's life, loud and fighting for her favorite person's attention, but my mom was her entire world. It occurs to me that she probably also knew my dad.

After pouring myself a giant glass of ice water, I walk out onto my back deck. The night sky is a little hazy, but the moonlight is still bright. I call Mar.

The sound of jackhammering greets me before Mar shouts out, "Cass? Hold on a sec." Some more noise and then it's quieter when she says, "Sorry, I'm at the new space."

It's almost ten p.m. "Still? Are they even allowed to do that loud work this late?"

"No, but they're behind so . . . they're cutting corners, now." Her voice is tense.

"If this is a bad time to talk I can call you later."

As if sensing something, Mar says, "It's fine, are you okay?"

"Yeah, I'm okay," I say, looking out into the scrubby canyon below, catching the movement of some small animal between the bushes.

Her silence prods me to be truthful. "Kind of. How long are you going to be at the restaurant?"

"All night," she says with a sigh. "We found something majorly wrong with the plumbing."

"Do you mind if I come by then?"

"Right now? Isn't it past your bedtime already?"

I think about all the times she's driven straight to my house the past couple months to deal with my bullshit. "Yeah, I can bring a midnight snack?"

Less than an hour later, I arrive in Abbot Kinney with tacos from a nearby taco truck. Marcella and I sit in the room that will soon be the main dining area of her new restaurant. The beautiful casement steel windows facing Abbot Kinney are covered in butcher paper, and the space is lit by the overhead lamps. The tables have finally been set up and we're sitting down in the very middle of the room. Most of the workers have left for the night.

While Mar starts opening up the foil packets I blurt out, "I met my dad."

The color completely leaves her face. I have never seen Mar look like this before. "What?" she whispers. "When? And are you okay?"

"Yes." I nod firmly. Then my eyes fill up with tears. "No. Not really. I found out . . . Oh my god. Can I have some wine, too?"

Mar rushes over to the kitchen and comes back with an open

bottle of red and two glasses. After taking a sip, I say, "Sunny came over to tell me that my mom's fated *was* my dad."

"Wait . . ." Mar is processing. "But that can't be?"

"I know. Apparently, despite him being Mom's fated, my dad still left and the romance didn't work out. Which means what the fuck even are fateds? What does any of this mean? Oh, and my dad has been in touch with Sunny over the years to ask about me and she never told me? And because of all that—she gave me my dad's info and I went to go meet him."

It's a lot to take in, I should know, and Mar needs a second, running her hands through her hair. "Okay, so . . . your dad, then. Did he confirm all of this?"

"Yeah, I literally showed up to his house in Michigan—"

"What!"

"I know, I know. I flew to Michigan and came back home within twenty-four hours."

"Christ, Cass!" Mar is looking at me, again, with concern and wonder. "You've never ever done anything like that in your entire life."

"Yeah. Did you know same-day flights cost *so much* money? Anyway. I showed up to his really nice, normal house in Michigan that he shares with his wife. Rachel. She's an artist, too, like Mom was. And really cool despite me showing up totally unannounced."

"I want to know so much about Rachel, but I understand we need to get to the point."

"Yes, we do." And I give her the rundown—the confirmation of my family lying to me all these years.

When I'm done, she's staring off into the distance. "Oka-a-a-y," she says slowly. "Well, this must happen, right? There's no way that all fated matches end in happily ever after."

I stare at her, my mouth falling open. "Mar? *THAT IS THE ENTIRE POINT.*" How many times must I say this to people?

"Huh." She falls back in her seat. "I honestly always thought that was just, like, rounding out the averages."

"What!" I feel literally insane. Nothing in my life is making sense anymore—everything, every truth I held dear is crumbling around me. "Knowing my fated was out there, that everything would go right when I found him—that's been *everything.*"

Mar seems to sober up immediately. "Oh, babe. I know but I was always hoping you would see the light."

I scoff. "That's not condescending at all."

"I'm just saying, I thought once you met Daniel, or reached a certain age or *whatever*—I thought you'd find some flexibility within this . . . prophecy." She reaches over and squeezes my arm.

"Flexibility? What would that even look like when *fate* is involved?"

She looks at me with concern. "Cass. It means you find out who it is, you meet them, and then *you* decide, as a *free-will-having* human being, whether or not you want to be with them."

It's like being knocked over the head. "I guess I was a true believer. There was no wiggle room for me. It was the most concrete, steadying force in my life. And then my dad . . ."

She gives me a beat. "Do you want to talk about it? I mean . . . that's . . . huge."

It takes me a second to know if I want to talk about it. With my dad—it's all so many things at once. "It was surreal. And. I don't know. Sad."

"And shocking, too, I bet."

"Yeah. It was a lot. And he left the door open for getting to know each other."

"How do you feel about that?"

"Not sure. I feel like, first, I have to sort out this fated puzzle with my family. With Daniel and Ellis. Oh my god, what is my life?!" I take a couple deep breaths. "I don't know. After that, then, maybe . . . I can think of accepting him back into my life?" I pause. "He didn't have kids after me. I think, in some ideal version of the world, I would just forgive him and start a relationship. But I have no idea if I want that. It feels like a betrayal to my mom." I poke at my carne asada. "But he knew Mom when she was younger, I would love to know more about that. And, well, he is my only living parent now."

She nods. "But don't forget, you always have your grandparents, too."

Their betrayal stings deeply and my anger at them rushes through me again. "I'm so, so mad at them."

"I get that. But don't you think you need to give them a chance to explain themselves? They love you. That kind of love—they would throw themselves off a cliff before hurting you." A wry smile. "Intentionally, anyway."

"I've been avoiding them, but I know I have to face them."

She finally takes a big bite of her taco. "Soon," she says through the food in her mouth.

I take a breath. "I know. There's just something else I need to do first."

46

The next morning, I text Daniel.

I'm sorry it's taken me so long to be in touch. I've been dealing with some big family stuff.

He doesn't text back. I wait for a bit before sending another one out:

Can we meet after you're done with work? I'll come to you.

Finally, he says:

Ok. Let's aim for eight.

When I pull up to his house that evening, he's standing outside in sweats and a fleece zip-up. It reminds me of Joshua Tree and it makes me sad. When I park, he opens the passenger-side door and says, "Can we go on a drive?"

"Sure," I say, feeling uneasy.

When he gets in, it's silent and uncomfortable. It's my job to power through. "Daniel. I'm so sorry. About everything." I look over at him, his profile sharp and serious. He's not looking at me. "I am. I truly am."

He nods. "Well, glad that's squared away." His hands are clenched together in his lap, and I feel so profoundly bad for putting this resilient, confident man in this state. But then he seems to remember his manners. "Is your family okay?"

The sear of anger I feel surprises me every time I think of my family. "Yeah . . . There was some drama. *Is*. I still have a lot to deal with, but . . . that's not your problem." And it hurts me to say that, to admit that my family really is no longer his problem. And that they have no idea I'm doing this because I don't want to hear any more of their thoughts about my love life.

He nods in response. Okay. This is going to be painful. "Um, did you have a destination in mind or . . . ?"

"Wherever you want, Cass."

I drive us west on Franklin, past Griffith Park, then south until we hit Hollywood Boulevard, where I make another right to keep going west. I have no destination in mind, either, and the car is silent except for the sound of the wind coming through our open windows. The cold night air keeps us tense. We pass streetlight after streetlight, hitting traffic when we're in Hollywood proper. The car creeps forward, and we're in front of the TCL Chinese Theatre, formerly Grauman's Chinese Theatre. It's packed with tourists and people in costumes and I'm happy for the visual distraction.

A light flashes on him for a second and I notice the bruises. My hand automatically reaches out to his cheek. "Are you okay?" He flinches away and I drop my hand, embarrassed.

"I'm fine," he says. "It's my ego that's battered." That dryness.

I decide to make a right on the next street, to get us out of this crush. I keep steering us north, until we're driving up into the Hollywood Hills. Even though I have no plan in mind, my body knows where to go. A lifetime of living in L.A. and going on alternate routes to avoid traffic are programmed into me. So, we end up on the twisty, precarious hillside path of Mulholland Drive.

"I thought I was over Ellis," I finally say.

"Why did you need to get over him in the first place? That's what I don't understand," he says, something finally opening up in him. "Why break up with him and start dating me? It's not adding up no matter how hard I think about it."

He's right and I'm not sure how to answer him without revealing everything. "Ellis and I don't make sense. You and I make sense."

"Brilliant. I'm the *sensible* choice? Like a pair of orthopedics." His voice is quiet when he says this, not showing any real anger and I am grateful for it. We're driving on scary dark roads; I don't need this to be the moment Daniel decides to yell.

"No, not sensible, not like a pair of orthopedic shoes," I say, letting myself feel it all. Explain my brain. "You're, like, a beautiful pair of Italian loafers. Made for my feet, exactly."

He's quiet. "This metaphor might become silly."

Again, that dry sense of humor. So layered and intelligent and Daniel. "Ellis and I were nowhere near serious. Breaking up with him wasn't fun but it wasn't heartbreak. I want you to know that. But I don't know. Somehow the feelings between us have grown."

We approach a familiar gate so I park the car. Daniel looks around. "Where are we?"

"Lake Hollywood," I say as I unbuckle my seat belt. "Want to take a walk?"

The gate is locked but I know how to get in. Having been a teenager in L.A., I know how to find every crack and opening in public spaces at night. We slide through a gap created by a too-long chain and end up on a trail.

A little up the trail, the lake appears. It's more of a reservoir, but it glimmers in the moonlight and looks beautiful anyway. We walk side by side in silence for a while, crickets literally chirping, when Daniel says, "I guess I didn't think you and Ellis were serious, either. So, I squirreled away the guilt I felt about stealing my employee's—*mate's*—girl. But it was clear he was never really okay with it. And that's on me."

"It's on both of us," I say, my voice little in the large space.

"But you broke up with him, you didn't do anything wrong when you dated me. I, however, broke the 'bro code.'"

"Come on," I say with a little laugh. "That's not real."

"It is, though," he says. "It's just unspoken. Not only that, he made it so clear that he wasn't over you. I just ignored it."

I nod, not really knowing what to say. He glances over at me. "I liked you too much to acknowledge it. I was being incredibly selfish."

"It's not selfish," I say. "My line of work . . . it's finding people love. Because to want love is one of the most human things about us. You wanted that and there's nothing wrong with it. But there's another thing. Aside from Ellis and anything else."

His shoulders instantly hunch up and I swear he winces. "I think I know what it is."

"Yeah." We stop walking and look at the lake together. "The whole . . . having children thing."

A sigh goes through him. "It's not that I'm *certain* that I don't want children. It's that I'm still uncertain."

I nod. "And that's totally fair. And I was in the same boat as you until recently. And, well, unfortunately I can't wonder about having kids for another decade."

"Yes, and you deserve someone who knows what they want." He runs a hand down his face. "Ah. I'm always so sure of what I want."

"I know," I say. "And I thought I was also so sure of it all, too. But . . . maybe I want a little more room for the unexpected. And what are kids if not totally unknowable chaos?" I reach for him and this time he doesn't move away from my touch. We fold each other in a hug, fierce and tight.

"I'm sorry. For . . ." My throat closes up, tears sliding down my face, and I duck my head and wipe them off so that he can't see. What kind of jerk cries when *they* break up with someone? "I'm sorry for everything, I guess. What we had was special and real to me, I want you to know that." My voice is a whisper, filled with grief for everything that could have been. For everything that we had planned for. Everything my family had dreamed of.

He strokes the back of my hair, a hand so familiar to me. "It was for me, too. It really was."

We stand like that for a long time, the moon bright in the sky, the night dark all around us.

47

I can't seem to remember the last time I went to bed at my normal bedtime, with my usual bedtime routine. After dropping Daniel off, I drive home on surface streets—my windows down, blasting Max Richter, letting the summer night air wreak havoc inside my car. When I get home, it's well past midnight and I'm wide awake.

I brew myself some chamomile tea and mix in a generous dollop of creamed honey. Betty perches on the edge of my armchair as I take sips of the steaming drink and look out into the dark hillside. I can't help thinking about Ellis, even as Daniel's sad eyes linger in my mind. I need sleep. Just one night of normal sleep, please, before I decide what to do.

Instead, I wake up in the middle of the night to the world moving. Shaking.

Betty is screeching and I fumble out of bed, my body on autopilot in its half-asleep state. I've been doing earthquake drills since preschool and head straight under my vanity table. The room continues to shake in a queasy, swaying way. Sometimes earthquakes are like being shaken hard in a box, other times it's like being tossed around in the sea. It feels like it goes on forever, and I start to panic slightly. Will my little house fall apart around me? Is Betty going to be okay? Are my grandparents okay? I think of the giant chandelier they have hanging in their master bedroom and feel serious regret at letting them install that years ago.

But then the earth stops moving. I think. For a few seconds, it still feels like it is, but it's just a case of vertigo post-quake. I wait to see if there are any aftershocks. When there aren't, I immediately run into the dining room to check on Betty. Other than being annoyed as hell, everything is fine. Her water bottle is crooked and some of the shavings in her cage have fallen out, but that's the extent of the damage. I give her a treat for her troubles and her feathers stop ruffling indignantly. I take a look around the house, checking on ceramics, shelves, and light fixtures. Some books have fallen over, and things have shifted in the cabinets, but otherwise all is well.

Back in my room, I pick up my phone to check in on my grandparents. Even if I'm furious at them, I will always need to know they're okay. There's the usual slew of omg earthquake??? texts from friends and I'm going through them when my phone starts blaring at me, startling me so badly I drop it. It's a series of alerts from the office's security system app.

I open the alert to see that there's smoke detected in the office. Oh my god. For a second I am stuck in my body—my brain screaming at me to do something but my muscles and bones are incapable of movement. The surface of my skin feels like it's buzzing, my hands feel like claws as I hold my phone, staring at the flashing alert.

Then I realize something: I have a plan for this. Of course I do. My heartbeat slows down as I tell Siri to open my emergency file in my notes app. It pops up—a folder of plans for all emergencies in my life. I open "Office Fire," and there are my step-by-step instructions. It immediately calms me. First step: *Call 911 in case the app doesn't send an alert to the fire department.* I do that and my hands and voice shake as I give the operator the address, which I've also typed out in the note in case my mind goes blank under pressure.

I throw on a jacket over my pajamas and get in my car, headed to Beverly Hills, heart pounding. The rest of the instructions involve calling various people, including my family. And even though I am still feeling betrayed by them, hurt and angry, I find that at three a.m. after a fucking earthquake and our family business on literal fire, it doesn't matter as much. I call as I drive.

"Hello?" Halmoni answers instantly, her voice worried over my speakers. "Cassia? Are you okay? Did something happen in the earthquake?"

The panic in her voice is a shot to my chest. "Yes, I'm fine. But I got a notification that there might be a fire at the office. I think we need to meet there."

"Oh my god," Halmoni says. I've never heard her sound like that. "Okay, we're going now."

I call Sunny and relay the same message.

As I drive over, I think of all our family photos. The furniture and heirlooms handed down from generations. The altar in our reading room. The pictures of Mom going up in flames. The air in the car feels choking and oppressive, and I roll down the windows to take large gulps. At this point, I am running on pure adrenaline. I don't know how many life tests I can handle in one week.

I make it to the office in record time in the early hours of the morning. The small window of time when L.A.'s freeways are empty.

I hear the sirens before I get there. Helicopters are flying overhead and the street is blocked off before I can reach the office. When I see the flames, a sob gets caught in my throat. I park quickly and wrench the car door open and approach the police cars, fire trucks, and ambulances. The blaze has engulfed the entire second story—where our reading room and Halmoni's office are. I am absorbing the horror of this when someone calls my name.

I find Sunny and Stu in the crowd that's gathered and rush over to them. Sunny's in glasses, a sweatshirt, and no makeup. "Cassia!" she cries out when I get close, her face etched with despair. She pulls me into a fierce hug. We're both crying, holding on to each other tight.

"I can't believe it," I choke out. "Do you know what happened?" I ask when we finally pull apart.

"I spoke with one of the firefighters and they think the earthquake made something electrical spark? The fire is contained upstairs," Stu says. "But that's . . ."

We look at each other silently. That's everything. The cupboard with everyone's fates, our reading room. The family altar.

My grandparents and Emoni rush up to us through the crowd. I haven't seen them since I found out about my dad, and for now, all of that is put aside. I need to see them, to be with them. It's Halmoni who I want first, and we both push through the people to reach each other. Her hands are outstretched, her expression desperate. I run to her, like I've run to her my whole life. My safe space. My protector.

We fold into each other, her smaller, frailer body tucked into mine.

She pets the back of my hair as I start crying again, comforting me, as she always has. "It's okay, it's okay," she says soothingly. "We're all okay and that's what matters."

I nod, even though I'm too old now to believe that everything will be okay. I let myself be comforted by her, and I feel Halabuji rub my back, too.

"Did anyone get hurt?" Emoni asks tearfully. My bighearted Emoni, who always, always looks out for other people first.

Sunny shakes her head. "No, luckily it was too late for the cleaning staff. And no other buildings have been affected. Just . . . ours."

We all turn to watch as the fire rages—our entire life's work going up in flames against the night sky.

A couple hours later, the fire is put out. We've all been sitting across the street, watching. As soon as it seems safe, I find the fire chief and ask him about the damage. He wipes his forehead, parts of his skin covered in a sooty layer. "Well, we managed to stop it before it came downstairs. We think it might have been an electrical issue upstairs."

"Our server room is there," I say, thinking about the small room off to the side of Halmoni's office.

"That was probably it, we found a lot of equipment near the origin of the fire." He shakes his head. "Unfortunately, the damage upstairs is substantial, even if the first floor has remained pretty untouched."

We all exchange looks. "Can we check it out?" I ask.

"I'm sorry, but no, that would be incredibly dangerous."

Everyone nods in understanding, and we make our way back to our cars, past the trucks, firefighters sitting down with bottles of water, and caution tape. We thank them profusely. My eyes tear up as I impulsively hug one of the firefighters, not knowing how else to show my gratitude.

Before Halmoni gets into her car, she says, "Let's all go back to our house." I must look as conflicted as I feel because she says, "Please, Cassia." Her voice is shaky and I can't say no.

"Of course, Halmoni."

After they drive off, I walk over to the fire chief again. "Is there *any* chance that I could take a quick look? We have things in there that go back generations."

He looks conflicted but I implore him. He sighs. "I have to come with you and it's gotta be quick—five minutes tops."

"Yes! Thank you."

We head toward the office. The smell of smoke and the chemicals used to put out the fire is intense. I'm handed a mask before I step in.

Other than some smoke damage I see near the ceilings, the first floor seems to be intact—the waiting area, the kitchen, intern bullpen, Sunny and Emoni's offices, and my office.

When we get upstairs, I can sense the destruction before I see it. The long hall leading to the conference room, the reading room, and Halmoni's office is missing huge chunks of wall and I can see the burnt wood framing of the building. It smells like firewood and chemicals as I pick my way through the hall, following the captain's cautious footsteps.

The conference room is a shell of its former self—our beautiful walnut table and leather swivel chairs burnt and melted. The big glass windows overlooking the city are smoke-tinged and smashed. I swallow down the pain of seeing this level of damage.

We move on to the reading room and it's in a similar state—the windows smashed, cold air whooshing in and lifting the ashes of what is left of our sofas and beautiful art and sculptures. I try not to linger too much on the damaged tapestry that has been in our family for centuries, on the scorched altar. It'll make me sick.

And finally, we get to the room at the farthest end of the hall—Halmoni's office. The captain approaches it gingerly, already a bad sign. I gasp when I step inside. It is completely and utterly destroyed. If I hadn't known the room like the back of my hand, I wouldn't even know what I was looking at. Halmoni's antique redwood desk is burned down to its metal brackets. And most importantly, the cupboard is almost completely charred and falling apart.

"I'm sorry, we couldn't save any of this," the captain says, his eyes full of regret.

I can't even reply, I just stand in the middle of a destroyed history with consequences I can't anticipate.

"All right, we should head out now, ma'am," the chief says.

"Okay, just one more thing." I rush over to the cupboard, finding my drawer through the damage, and pull out the scrap of paper with Daniel's name on it. The thread is black.

48

When I get to my grandparents', I sit in my car for a minute. With the adrenaline of the fire receding, I am exhausted. The family dinner with Daniel and then Sunny's revelation feel like a million years ago. Before going inside and facing whatever will happen, I complete step #6 of the "Office Fire" instructions. I send out the bad news to Shreya, Lila, and Matteo and there's a deluge of shocked and condolence messages. I decide to close business for the rest of the week until we figure things out. The responsibility of their jobs weighs on me, and I hope we can get back up and running soon.

Finishing this step makes me feel more grounded, but I wish I had a checklist for "What to do when you learn your entire family has been lying to you your whole life." Step one would probably be getting out of the car.

There's food and coffee spread out on the kitchen island when I get inside, and Halmoni, Sunny, and Emoni are already sitting around the table. Stu and Halabuji are in the kitchen, being very busy.

Stu hands me a cup of coffee and I take it gratefully before sitting down with the Park women. Their eyes are all on me as I take my first sip. "I let Shreya and Lila and Matteo know what's happening," I say uselessly.

Murmurs around the table. "Good, good," Emoni says.

Then it's silent and I feel all their held breaths, the moment I've been avoiding for days. "As you know, Sunny told me about Mom and my dad. That they *were* fated."

Something crashes in the kitchen and we whip our heads to see Stu fumbling with a pan. "Sorry!" he says, as flustered as I've ever seen him.

When I turn back, Halmoni is clutching the edge of the table and Halabuji steadies her from behind. "You were never supposed to know," she says in a whisper. Emoni looks stricken.

"No shit," I say bitterly.

"Cassia." My grandfather's voice is booming, stern. He never ever talks to me like that and it only drives home the seriousness of the situation.

"So is it true?" I ask, my voice miraculously calm.

Everyone, including Halabuji and Stu, are silent. That's confirmation enough.

When my mom died, I prayed for any kind of sign that she was still with me. That her spirit had remained on the earthly realm even after we scattered her ashes in the Pacific. I would lie in my new bedroom at night and stare intently across the room at my vanity mirror. Hoping for a glimpse of something translucent and spectral. I was never scared of ghosts. I would have loved to be haunted by my mom.

This fixation eventually faded, but I was always looking for magical signs anyway. And when you look for them, they're easy to find.

The random car backfiring in the street when you want a sign that you should get bangs. The friend who texts you the morning after you had a dream about them.

And eventually, I didn't need to look for magic. It found me. When I was thirteen, I realized that I could read people's faces. The first time it happened, I was in geometry class. I couldn't pay attention because I found the subject to be complete nonsense. Instead, I stared lovingly at the back of Jeremy Zaid's head. The cutest boy in eighth grade. When he turned to me, and I got a good look at his face while in this crushy trance, I suddenly found myself in a courtyard full of olive trees and saw Jeremy carrying a jug of water on his head. I was so freaked out that I screamed in class and was sent home by the principal. It was that day that I learned of the gift in our family. Ever since, it's been the guiding principle of my life: Through this ability to read faces, we find past loves—the *fated* match for everyone.

Believing in true love since the age of thirteen got me through life. I knew my fated was waiting for me at the end of this journey—that even if everything else was unpredictable, this one thing was preordained. It's a powerful assurance for someone who lost their mom at a young age.

A kid's entire life and sense of security are wrapped up in the proximity of their parents. Their mother. When I lost her, the earth beneath me fell apart. Even with my grandparents, Emoni, and Sunny—I felt alone in the world. Broken and cursed with a tragedy that made me feel separate from the kids at school, from my cousins. But when I found out I had this ability, this *superpower*, I felt equipped to take on the world again. It was a gift I shared with my mother, and I felt closer to her and all the women in my family because of it. I had found the key to not just love, but happiness.

I stare at my family sitting around the table. "Does this mean that there are no fated matches?" My voice is shaky, my entire body turning clammy. This is the question that's been haunting me since I found out.

Halmoni closes her eyes for a second before answering. "No, of course not. We *do* find past loves. That's what the red thread of fate shows us in our visions. That's real. Your souls are drawn together life after life. And at some point in our family's history, hundreds of years ago, we realized that we could find that person in someone's current life. And that when they met, they almost always fell in love again."

"Almost," I say, pinching the bridge of my nose, my head starting to throb incessantly.

Halmoni looks at me. "Before your mom, a fated match had never failed. At least in my lifetime. We thought it was a fluke. There were no records of such a thing."

"Because you were the first to keep records," I say out loud, mostly for myself. Before Halmoni, matchmaking was done in village homes. There were no offices, our family business was intimate, a whispered secret between women. Halmoni was the one who brought it into the future. All my lists and organizational systems—they come directly from my grandmother, the most meticulous person I know.

"Exactly," Halmoni says.

"Then, Evette . . ." Sunny says, her voice shaking. "When your dad left you both, we thought, no this can't be. They'll get back together. They have to."

"When he didn't come back, we thought it was because *he* was flawed, not the system." Halmoni sits back, looking very small, suddenly. "We built our business on this concept. On the belief that you were meant to meet your past love, that it was the way to happiness."

"And you couldn't face the truth and, what, lose all the money you've made?" I say, my voice getting loud, waving my hand at their beautiful house.

"Hey." My grandfather again, and this time he's angry. "You're allowed to be angry, but you are not allowed to disrespect us."

A hush falls over the room. I say my next words carefully. "I just need to know why my entire understanding of how the world works was built on a lie."

"To protect you!" Halmoni cries out. "To protect everything!"

"I'm forty fucking years old!" I shout back. "You couldn't tell me before this?"

"And admit that it was *my* fault that your mother died alone?" my grandmother says with a wrenching sob.

I do start crying then. "She didn't die alone. She had me."

Halmoni gets up from her chair and stands next to me. Then she gets on her knees. Through my tears, I stare at her. Shocked. She grabs hold of both my hands and I try and pull her up. "Halmoni, stop it. Get up, please. You're going to hurt yourself."

But she just shakes her head and clasps my hands tight. "Forgive me, Cassia. I never wanted you to find out about your father. I didn't want you to hate me. Like your mother did."

Silent tears are falling down her face and it's breaking my heart. "Halmoni, she didn't hate you, what are you talking about? She loved you. She loved all of you until the very end." I look at Sunny and Emoni, who are in various states of crying as well.

Halmoni shakes her head. "No, she never forgave me for telling her your dad was her fated."

"Listen to me," I say firmly. "She loved you guys so much. Even if she couldn't show it all the time. She had the part of rebellious daughter to play."

Sunny laughs through her tears. "She really did."

Halmoni still looks at me mournfully. "If she had a partner who was a quality person, she might have . . . might have not had the aneurysm." And it's like she's uttered our shared secret—one bigger than our magical gift. A dark belief that has lived in both of our minds for more than thirty years. It's only in that moment that I realize how wrong both of us were. Seeing my grandmother heart-broken in front of me—this is wrong. We were both wrong to carry this burden.

"Oh, Halmoni." I get down on the floor and wrap my arms around her. "I met him. I flew to Michigan and met my dad."

She pulls back in shock. "What?"

Before anyone can react, I say, "I had to talk to him myself. Confirm all of this. And you know what? After we talked . . . after he told me about how they met and what their relationship was like—none of what happened feels so dark and wrong anymore. Their love story not working out isn't some cosmic tragedy. It was just . . . human."

"But . . ." Halmoni trails off. "He *left* you. He ruined your mother's life."

"I need you to let that go," I say gently, remembering the way Matthew talked about my mother, the way he looked at me with a lifetime of regret. "Because it's not true. Mom had a great life. It was way too short, but she had a wonderful family," I say, looking at everyone. Halabuji is sitting down now, crying into his hands. Stu is holding tight to Sunny's hand, and Emoni is smiling through tears. "She loved me so much and showed me every day. I was so lucky to have her for those eight years." My voice chokes up, my chest hurts. "She never ever made me feel like Matthew leaving ruined her life. Mom was always honest with me about him. How he couldn't handle the pressures of fatherhood because he was weak and young. And she let him go. She always made me feel like we were better off without him, because we had all of you. How your love meant more to me than having a father."

Sunny and Emoni join us on the floor. And as we sit there in a pile of arms and grief and unburdened souls, I feel like myself again. Whatever crisis of faith I had, it's being bolstered by something newer and stronger. As always, it's my family.

49

I broke up with Daniel."

No one seems shocked. Emoni nods, solemn.

Stu pours fresh coffee for all of us as we sit around the table. Sunny squeezes his hand in silent thanks, and he drops a kiss on the top of her head. "How did he take it?" Sunny asks.

"Fine," I say as Halabuji walks back into the room with a pale pink throw that he puts gently across Halmoni's shoulders. "As well as someone could take that kind of news anyway."

"But he's your fated," Halmoni says. "I saw it myself and . . ."

I give her a look. We *just* had this conversation.

"He's a gentleman," she concedes. "A good person. He understands."

"Yes, he'll make a good partner for someone. Just not you," says Halabuji as he takes Halmoni's empty plate.

I watch how these men silently take care of the women in my life. And I think of Ellis. Ellis who blocks the sun from getting in my eyes. Who takes a shot for me when he knows I don't want to drink it. Who is always watching, always taking care of me. Even when I'm not his.

What am I doing? My chair scrapes loudly against the tile as I get up. "I need to talk to Ellis."

"Ellis-euh?" Halabuji exclaims. Everyone else looks extremely confused.

"Are you sure?" Halmoni asks, her voice betraying nothing.

I nod. "So sure."

Sunny gets up and hugs me. "You got this. We love you."

"I love you guys, too," I say, choking up again. And out of habit, I look at Halmoni for reassurance. She nods, her eyes shining. That's all I need.

In seconds I'm in my car. It's not quite ten a.m. I'm afraid to go home first in case I lose my nerve—this rush of adrenaline. So I head east on Beverly and take it straight to Silver Lake, really wishing Ellis could be anywhere else.

When I park in front of Watson and Associates, I register what I look like. My pajamas—a white cotton two-piece—are dusted with a fine layer of soot. I flip down my visor. So is my face. I take out some Kleenex and do a cursory wipe but it's kind of a lost cause.

Pride be damned. I get out and walk into the office. The front desk is manned by Parker, the guy who knew Ellis had been married before at the wedding dinner. He looks up at me with surprise. "Oh! Hey." Then he looks me up and down. "Whoa. Are you okay?"

"Yeah, fine," I say with a wave. "Is Ellis in yet?"

His forehead crinkles with confusion. "Ellis?"

"Yes, Ellis."

"Not . . . Daniel?"

I close my eyes briefly. "Nope."

"Yeah . . . he is," he says, his shoulders raised a little in a defensive stance. "But I'm not sure you going in there is a good idea." That's when I notice the wall of glass behind him, which gives me a good look into the big open space full of desks. With all the employees of Watson and Associates sitting in them, milling about, chatting with each other.

I see his point. I don't feel like making a public display of this, yet again, in front of Ellis's coworkers. And I'd rather not run into Daniel, either.

"Would you mind . . ." I start to ask.

Parker takes a good, hard look at me. "Are you about to rip his heart out? Again?"

"No. The opposite, I hope."

Without taking his eyes off me, he picks up the phone. After a beat, he says, "Hey, can you come out and meet me in reception?" His expression stays neutral. "Okay, cool." He hangs up. "He'll be out shortly."

The formal language almost makes me laugh but then it doesn't, because I see Ellis get up from a desk. He looks like a mirage after a long summer spent in the desert. He's in a plain white tee and beat-up jeans. A classic.

It's been days since I've seen him at the park opening and I know at this very second that I no longer want to spend days not seeing him. That seeing him, being near him, is essential to my being. As he walks toward us, the surface of my skin starts to tingle. I get both lightheaded and more grounded.

The moment he notices me, he falters. We make eye contact and confusion washes over him. He takes me in, registering my bedraggled pajama-state. The confusion on his face grows as he gets closer, but there's also concern there. He opens the door and is in the lobby now.

"Uh, you have a guest," Parker says, his eyes whipping between us.

"I see that," he says, his eyes on mine. "Cass, are you okay?"

That *Cass* is electricity through my body. "I am. Now. Can we talk?" I glance behind him, and notice that a few of the coworkers are looking at us, having noticed that I'm out here.

"Maybe outside?" I say.

He nods, short and curt, and we make our way out, him close behind me. Even though we're not touching, I feel him with every step.

We find a private spot tucked in an alley, and a warm breeze ruffles my hair as I take a breath.

"What's going on?" Ellis asks when I stop. Then he takes another good look at me. "Why are you in pajamas?" He reaches out and touches a sleeve that has a line of soot on it. "Is this *ash*?"

His concern, despite everything we've been through, is a reminder of everything that made me fall for him.

"After the earthquake, our office caught on fire," I say.

"What!"

"Everyone's okay, but the second floor's been damaged. It's been . . . a long night. And morning." I laugh weakly.

"I'm so sorry," he says. He means it but he's also confused. "Why . . . why are you here after all that?"

Emotion bubbles up inside my chest, making it tight. "I . . . I needed to see you. To tell you everything."

Something shutters in his expression, and I need to make things right as quickly as possible. "I'm sorry. That's the first, most important thing. I am *so* sorry. For putting you through this roller coaster of . . . me, I guess. And I really needed you to know, as soon as possible, that I broke up with Daniel."

This lands less explosively than I wanted. His eyes flicker, and his body flinches, but that's it. I go on. "Kissing you at the park opening wasn't a mistake. I shouldn't have said that. I don't regret kissing you, but I do regret hurting Daniel. And that moment with you that was so true and real turned into something sordid."

His jaw clenches as he nods his head in jerky movements. I wish so much that I could undo all the hurt I've inflicted on him.

I pull something out of my pajama pocket. "You deserve an explanation. The real one, for why I turned away from you, why I denied the connection between us." I hold it up and he steps in closer to look at it. When he registers what it says, his eyes fly up to mine, confused. "What is this?"

I hold up the scrap of paper with Daniel's name stitched in it. "This piece of paper is ten years old. When I was thirty, my grandmother read my face and told me I would end up with someone named Daniel Nam."

His eyes flash. "What?"

"This is our family secret. We don't just read faces, we can see past lives. And in these past lives, we can find past loves." I say these words slowly, knowing what they sound like. My body tenses, waiting for him to laugh hysterically before fleeing back into his office.

But this is Ellis. And Ellis has always taken me seriously.

"You can see past lives?" His voice is even as his eyes search mine for more information.

I love his eyes—the hint of amber when the light hits them. The long lashes and the wide way they hungrily take in the world. I nod. "Yes. And in mine, my grandmother found Daniel. He's my fated. I'd been searching for him for ten years that morning I dropped you off at work."

He's looking past me now, a million emotions playing across his face. I give him time to sit with this. Letting it all sink in. Then he finally looks at me and asks, "What happened, then? Why did you guys break up?"

"My whole life I believed the reason my dad left, that my parents broke up, was because my mom chose not to be with her fated. Since I can remember, I was warned of what happens when you don't choose your fated," I say, my voice getting stronger as the emotions stirred by all these revelations surge through me. "My mom was that warning. My family told me she rebelled and didn't choose her fated, and that's why my dad left her. Us. But then . . . a few days ago, later on the night of the park opening, in fact, I found out that wasn't true. He *was* her fated. And despite that, it didn't work out."

Ellis looks completely overwhelmed. "Cass . . ."

"So that's why I'm here. Like this." I wave to myself. "I found out about my parents. Then I flew to Michigan to meet my dad." His eyes widen. "I know, long story. But I met him. Then I broke up with Daniel. And then the fire."

I step in close to him and reach for his hand. He looks down but doesn't pull it away.

"What came out of all that is—is this *absolute* clarification: that I want to be with *you*. That even when I met Daniel, it was always you."

My voice cracks. I can feel my heart reaching out between us, begging his to open. But Ellis is still looking down, face hidden from me.

"I believe in fated love," I say, still trying to make him understand. "But I also believe in making your own fate. It used to scare me, the idea of veering off course. But I've been off course since the day we met."

He finally looks up. His expression is guarded. "But you and Daniel *did* have a connection. Everyone could see it."

"Yeah, we did. He's a wonderful guy, as you know. I connected with both of you." I take a breath, my heart fast but steady. "But there's only one of you that I fell in love with."

His head shoots up. "What?"

It's hard to talk around the lump in my throat, the beating of my heart. "I love you, Ellis. I'm in love with you." I get lightheaded with the release of it. "I used the age thing as a reason to ignore all the glaring reasons why it's so easy to love you. The way you never hesitate to help. The bigness of your heart. How you make me want to soften the hard edges of myself and all my routines. The spontaneity of your joy and how you spread it to everyone around you. How, in moments, the magic and wonder I feel with you reminds me of my happiest moments with my mother."

He looks up at that, his eyes filled with an emotion I can't place. Time stills as I wait for his response to my declaration. In the summer heat of L.A., with the breeze wafting over us—this love feels inevitable.

But.

He backs up. Takes his hand from mine. He won't look at me, keeping his eyes lowered. "Cassia. I just . . . this is a lot. I'm sorry, I—"

"It's okay!" I say instinctively, devastated. If I just keep talking, he can't say it's over, even as it feels like walls are shutting down inside of me, one by one. I feel like I'm dying. "This was too much. I get it. Um, let's just start from the beginning . . ."

But he shakes his head. "I don't know. I haven't had enough time to think about all this."

Each word is a tiny tragedy, but I smile. I owe him a buffer from my heartbreak. "I understand." Suddenly I am aware of what I look like—a forty-year-old woman in her pajamas, no makeup, in glasses. Confessing her love to a twenty-eight-year-old who has the entire world at his feet. "Just forget this happened," I say, as my heart cracks in half.

Ellis looks at me with concern. "No, I don't want to forget. I just . . . need time. Is that okay?"

"Of course!" My voice feels a million miles away. "I'll just . . . you should get back to work." And I spin around and walk briskly away, not wanting him to see the tears I frantically wipe away, feeling as foolish as a deluded lovestruck teenager.

50

The fallout from the fire keeps me blessedly preoccupied for the next couple weeks. Calls with our insurance company. Rescheduling everything from the days we closed. Researching contractors with Marcella's help—she does not recommend her own—and stress breathing into a paper bag when the first estimates come in. We set up a remote-working situation for everyone and fumble through our first few Zoom meetings. We hold readings in Halmoni's home office, and we slowly get back on our feet as we wait for the insurance company to approve our rebuilding costs.

It takes all I have to keep it together during the day. The nights, however, are given over to despair. Lots of Elliott Smith on my record player while drinking wine and scrolling through Ellis's Instagram. Betty even feels bad for me—she stops biting me when I feed her and has gotten into the habit of perching on the back of the sofa while I camp out there evenings and weekends, the Park women under strict instructions to give me space.

After about a month of nonstop work and evenings ruminating on my mistakes, Mar convinces me to go on her family summer trip to Catalina Island in late August.

"Being forced to hang out with kids on a vacation is the best distraction," Mar says on the beach as she slathers Mica with sunblock as thick as frosting. "There is no relaxing, no time for your brain to obsess. You are, instead, in a tornado of chaos."

Mica kicks sand into my face as he runs off down to the water. I spit it out and can't help laughing. "I hate you."

"I love you," Mar says matter-of-factly.

We spend the next few days getting sunburned, eating copious amounts of ice cream, and spending evenings playing Go Fish by the bonfire. All of it reminds me of Ellis for no reason.

But then, on our last morning there, it's raining and we stand together on the hotel wraparound porch, staring at the downpour.

"This is so weird," I say. "I can't remember the last time it rained in the summer."

"It's what I miss most about Minnesota," says Logan fondly. "Thunderstorms and rain to cleanse the stifling hot summer days."

"Remember when we used to streak through the quad?" Mar says with a grin.

"What's streak?" ask both kids simultaneously.

Before anyone can answer, I tag them and yell, "You're it!" Then I bolt out into the rain, running through the meadow. I feel the water wash over me like a new beginning.

After coming back from Catalina, I start to spend some of my evenings at Halmoni's or bringing dinner to Marcella at her new restaurant, where she has declared she may have to live until it actually opens in a month. And my playlists no longer exclusively make me want to weep. A couple weeks later it's Saturday and I hop on my bike for the first time since the fire. But when I'm almost to the coffee shop, I decide to take a detour. I pass by the spot where Ellis and

I met and feel a familiar pang in my ribs. Rolling down a concrete culvert on a bike as my meet-cute should've been a more obvious foreshadowing.

When I near the gates that lead to the park, I slow down. I hop off my bike and lock it against the fence.

Even though it's a little uncomfortably warm out, the park is full of people. I see two teens reading a pile of manga on a bench. A couple walking together, holding hands, deep in animated conversation. Three older Asian men walk by briskly holding hiking poles, decked out head to toe in North Face. Kids running through the meadow, dogs happily sniffing blooming sage blossoms with butterflies flying overhead.

I take a picture and type a text to Daniel. Your legacy, bro. I don't send it, but maybe someday. I like to think we'll get there.

I slide my phone back into my pocket and head to my bike. With Mar out of commission getting ready for her opening, I decide to ride by myself that day. And I go where the wind takes me.

"I swear my stapler was moved," I hear Lila say with a suspicious sniff.

"Everything was moved," Shreya says as she places a potted plant on her desk. "Can you please help Matteo grab the files?"

The office is open again, after the most blessedly hiccup-free renovation ever experienced in L.A. I've been plying Marcella with wine and time in Halmoni's massage chair to assuage my guilt. It's well into September, but summer shows no signs of slowing down. But we're finally settled in and the AC is blasting.

We all head upstairs together, passing by the newly constructed reading room and conference room. At my insistence, we've made necessary technical and design updates. No more stuffy floral patterns and heavy furniture—instead everything is furnished in blond wood with pops of warm colors. More rugs, less carpet.

It's a makeover signaling a shift into the future. A future that will always include fated loves, because that is still real. I may have chosen another path, but this is a path that will work for clients the same way it has worked for hundreds of years. In the end, I guess I am still a believer.

Halmoni's office has also been updated. If mostly because, well, it's my office now. My desk sits in the middle of the spacious room, with two overstuffed and bright chairs placed in front of it. The big window behind my desk looks over the newly landscaped garden—beautiful and meadow-like.

"Ready?" Halmoni asks as she sets her purse on the desk. Everyone nods.

We stand in front of the refurbished apothecary cabinet tucked into the corner of the office. It's still damaged, but Halabuji managed to put it back together so that the drawers are all intact and working. He spent weeks meticulously replacing wood, sanding and staining it so that the damage was fairly well hidden.

We all step back and look at Halabuji's handiwork and then at the office. The shift in the air, the next chapter of our agency—it is all palpable.

"Ready to fuck some shit up?" I say.

"Oh my god," Emoni says with a headshake. Halmoni smacks my arm while Sunny cackles. Forty or not, I'll always relish playing the brat of the family. I am my mother's daughter, after all.

We call Matteo, Lila, and Shreya into the conference room.

Halmoni takes the seat at the head of the table and I sit on the other end, which has been left empty for me.

"We're so happy to finally have the office back," Halmoni says. "Thank you all for being so patient."

Then Halmoni makes eye contact with me over the table. "And now that the office has been renovated, we also have a few changes we'd like to introduce."

Curious looks are exchanged by everyone. Halmoni says, "This new office is a new beginning. As of today, I'll be stepping down as president of One & Only, and Cassia will be taking my place. Emoni has also decided to retire." Emoni smiles at us all.

Shreya gasps and even though I knew it was coming, hearing the words sends a thrill through me. Everyone starts talking at once and Halmoni shushes them with one stern look. "It's been a long time coming. But it's clear that Cassia is ready. You're all in the best hands. And, Shreya?"

Shreya straightens, looking dazed. "Yes?"

"You'll be the new director of operations. Sunny will stay in her role, but my sister and I will be leaving the rest up to you."

Shreya's mouth drops and I reach over to squeeze her hand. "You will be amazing."

"I'm proud of everything we've done together," Halmoni says, her voice perilously close to cracking. Lila and Matteo clutch each other. Seeing Halmoni cry would turn them into dust, I think. "I want to thank you all for being integral to One & Only's success. We couldn't do it without you."

Before we can all burst into tears, Emoni and Halmoni stand up and give everyone hugs and goodbyes. "We still have to do casino night," Emoni says to Matteo.

"If I hear any of you treat Cassia differently from me, I *will* ruin your life," Halmoni says as her last words.

And then I'm left with a room full of staring employees. I tell them to get back to work and we'll have time to adjust to everything soon enough. It's a lot to take in—this level of responsibility. I sit by myself in the conference room and feel the weight settle on my shoulders as I stare out the window overlooking the courtyard.

When we rebuilt the second story, Sunny and Emoni petitioned to also rehab the landscaping. Thanks to them it's been transformed into a tranquil space with blooming pale-barked palo verde trees and blue-green grasses lying low to the ground. A water feature has been added, a little babbling creek running alongside the picnic table and benches set up there.

I go outside and sit down on one of the bright-yellow benches, its metal back rounded gracefully. It's insanely comfortable and I find myself lying down on it, stretched out with my sandal-clad feet hanging off the end.

I gaze up at the fluttering desert willow leaves where sunlight filters through. The sky is that hazy powder blue specific to late summer in Los Angeles.

Something glimmers in the corner of my eye under the tree. I walk over to it and find a small stone statue of a bird sitting in front of a low bush of yellow flowers, Feathery Cassia, almost obscured by the happy blooms. Not just any bird. Betty. The combination of both these things makes my eyes water. And I know it even before I see the words written under Betty's little figure.

IN MEMORY OF EVETTE PARK

51

Venice is bumper-to-bumper on the Friday night of Marcella's new restaurant opening. I've got the Park women in my car, all grumbling about the traffic. As if it's a surprise. But they never leave their little corner of Hancock Park anymore, becoming true fixtures with the Korean ladies who lunch at Larchmont. Especially now that two of them have been retired for weeks.

"I can't believe Marcella actually opened a restaurant all the way out *here*." Sunny says it like we're in Antarctica. "Her commute must be a nightmare."

I steer us down Abbot Kinney Boulevard, past various boutiques selling very cute but expensive goods. "Well, she's only going to have to do it for a couple months. Hopefully, it'll manage to run itself after that."

We pull up to the valet stand and pour out of the car. Halmoni looks up at the black-and-white-striped awning and the cheery lights draped across it. She gives a curt nod of approval. "Nice spot."

"*Great* spot," I say as we walk into the restaurant, the door left open to let people stream in and out.

It's bustling in the beautiful space. There's a U-shaped oyster bar set in the middle of the restaurant with little tables and cozy booths placed around it. The lighting is dim and the walls are painted a pale blue. It's warm and welcoming and feels like Marcella.

"Auntie Cassie!" Ozzie finds me across the room and runs to me. I swoop her into my arms.

"Hi, bud. Where's your mom?" I ask her. She points to the bar and I see Mar squeezed into a group of people. We make eye contact and I make a kissy-face and she returns it, her face glowing. I'm so proud of my friend I could burst.

Logan and Mica find us and I grab drinks for everyone before we get seated. It's a friends and family soft opening, so we'll be eating everything off the menu and I seriously can't wait. I didn't eat all day in anticipation of this.

I'm carrying a French 75 and a glass of wine to our table when I stop in my tracks. Seated next to Halmoni is Ellis. He looks heartbreakingly good in a soft-cream polo sweater and black jeans, no socks, and black moccasins. His head is bent toward Halmoni's as he listens to her with a smile on his face, his hair falling forward in front of his eyes a little bit.

I try to keep my composure as I walk over.

He looks up and only his eyes register that he sees me. From the flicker I see there, I'm very glad I decided on the clingy dress with the flattering neckline. I place the drinks down. "Hey there."

"Hi." He straightens. "Your grandmother and aunts invited me." There's a nervous note in there, the quickness in its delivery.

"Oh, did they?" I bore holes into the heads of the Park women, who are suddenly *quite* busy looking at the menus. And the only seat open is next to Ellis. So, I take my drink and sit next to him. "I'm so sorry that they pressured you. I know you needed time," I say in a low voice.

"They didn't," he shakes his head. "And I did, but—"

We're interrupted by a glass being clinked loudly. I tell my stupid nerves to stop jangling and that annoying flash of hope to die a quick death, focusing my attention on my best friend, whose night this is. Marcella's standing on the bar, absolutely gorgeous in emerald green trousers, her curly hair piled on her head, her lips a fire-engine red. She grins and says, "Before we all start gorging ourselves, I wanted to say thank you to each and every one of you. You've all helped me and this restaurant in one way or another. Please eat, drink, and be merry. This is for you."

The first dish is ferried out by smart servers wearing crisp black-and-white gingham aprons. It's a fish ceviche, filled with slivers of onions and a tart lemony marinade. A plate is placed between Ellis and me, and we both politely insist the other start first.

"Oh, for crying out loud," Sunny says before reaching over and scooping a spoonful each onto our small plates.

I bite back laughter and look up to see Ellis doing the same. Soon the food keeps us all occupied, unable to talk about anything but how good everything is, even as I remain hyperaware of Ellis's every minute movement.

"I didn't know kimchi could be used this way," Emoni says with wonder as she holds up a clam boiled in a kimchi and chorizo stew.

"You can thank our family's influence for that one," I say with a wink.

At one point, Ellis gets up and gets a round of drinks for us. When he returns with a tray full of champagne, he says, "As a thank you for being my first client."

Again, the women in my family are suddenly very busy eating. "What?" I ask.

Ellis looks at me, then at my family. "Ah . . ." He gives my grandmother, specifically, a *look*.

Halmoni takes a genteel sip of her champagne. "Ellis and his new firm designed our garden."

I think of the Feathery Cassia. Of the Betty statue and Mom's plaque. My throat tightens with emotion. Of course he designed it.

Wait. I look at Ellis sharply. "What do you mean, new firm?"

"I started a new firm with a couple other designers," he says, not quite meeting my eyes.

Oh. Guilt twists me from the inside out. "Ah, congratulations." *Sorry. Congratulations and sorry.*

"Hey," he says, reaching and touching my arm briefly. It's electric. Some things never change. "It's not what you think. I'd been thinking of striking out on my own for a while. I have Daniel's full blessing. He's been a huge help, actually. Once a mentor always a mentor."

The sweetness of that assuages some of the guilt. Daniel, what a guy. Just not my guy. "Well, that's huge. Really, congratulations." I hold up my glass.

He touches his with mine. It feels so intimate. "Thank you. And thanks to you all," he says, looking at my family. "It was our first project and it helped get the company off the ground," he says. Then he pauses. "I overcharged quite a bit."

The Park women laugh as if he's the funniest person on the planet and I am suddenly aware of how symbiotic and *right* this all feels. And when I look at Halmoni, she gives me that little nod. I know it's her way of approving. Of letting go of Daniel.

For the rest of dinner, I watch him charm the pants off my family and fall for him more and more with each passing second. It feels like torture. I have no idea what any of this means. The way he keeps an eye on everyone's drink levels, the way he listens to Halmoni talk as if she's the only person in the world, the way he makes Sunny laugh so hard she snorts, the way he makes Emoni beam so hard I think she might cry. The way I can feel him completely tuned in to me during all of it. Like I'm the center of his universe, but it's not a big deal. It's the most natural thing in the world. Has he had the time away that he needed? I want to be patient, but my heart feels like it's about to *Alien*-burst out of my sternum.

At one point, we brush by each other—me on the way to the restroom, him coming back from the bar. "Hi," he says.

"Hi," I say back, and it reminds me of our first night together. "Are you having fun?"

"Oh, yeah," he says. "This food! And I'm so happy for Mar. This place is just . . . wow. What a badass."

The warm fuzzies threaten to spill out of my eyeballs. I clear my throat. "Hey, thank you so much again for creating that beautiful garden. I . . . it's a special place for me."

Something in his eyes sparks, but he keeps his face composed. "I'm glad. And you shouldn't thank me, your grandmother and aunts took a chance on us."

"Not really, they knew what they were doing," I say before I can help it. The drinks I've had, the coziness of the space, the dim lighting and the din of the bar—it's all conspiring to make me loose-lipped.

He seems to sense this and leans in close. "Want to get out of here?"

Ellis is quiet on the drive, and my heart pounds. With his nearness, with anticipation, with the anxiety of not knowing what's happening. I play it cool. It's only when I notice where we are that I ask, "Are we going to my office?"

"Yup. Hope you don't mind."

"I'll only mind if you make me open up my spreadsheets." The innuendo lands with a thud in the car and I flush and look out the window. My phone buzzes with a text from Marcella, which I glance at. It's in response to mine telling her I ducked out with Ellis.

Good fucking luck!

We pull up to the One & Only offices and he cuts the engine. "Look at that beautiful lighting," I say, gesturing at the lit-up gravel path winding between the feather-soft grasses. "Like someone very talented designed it."

Ellis laughs then lifts a brow at me. "Ready for an official tour?"

It's silent for a beat as he looks at me in that way he looks at me. I look back. "Yes."

We walk along the gravel path, our arms nearly brushing but not quite. It's so hard for me not to reach out and hold his hand. The nearness of him has grown unbearable throughout the evening. "So, tell me about this," I say, waving my arm at the landscaping done in the small yard in front of the office.

"Well, even though we were working with limited space here, we wanted the office to feel like an oasis set back from the formality of Beverly Hills. So, we added this path, forcing people to meander through before getting to the front door." Our feet crunch on the gravel, and I move gingerly because of my heels. He slows to match my pace immediately, making my heart grow two sizes.

He tells me about the plants and why they were chosen, everything so considered and smart. Just like the man himself. And even though I had felt it before, I fully see Ellis as someone whose compassion and intelligence are the true measures of what kind of man he is. Not the years he's lived.

"I actually need to thank you," he says when we enter the garden in the back of the office.

"Me? Why?"

He's shy suddenly, hands tucked into pockets, shoulders up near his ears. But then he slides a glance at me and says, "I don't think I could have set out on my own if I hadn't met you."

A soft warmth spreads through me. "What do you mean? You could have done it anytime."

He smiles. "See? There it is. That unshakable confidence in me. That's it."

I think of his parents, their concern about him. But their pride and love, too. "You have tons of people in your life who believe in you."

"I'm sure I do. But you were the person who stepped in at the exact time I needed the nudge to think bigger." His shoulders relax and his smile turns intimate. "Just watching you and how you move through the world, with so much assurance—it's inspiring. The last thing I want to do is point out our age difference here, but you kind of gave me a new definition of adulthood. One that is filled with people you love, a job that invigorates you—just full of pleasure and meaning."

This leaves me speechless. I feel my cheeks flush, my body warm from the inside out. To be so seen by this man. In the face of such a compliment I can only joke, "Maybe you need more forty-year-olds in your life."

"I like the one I have, thanks."

We look at each other in the soft light of the courtyard. He clears his throat. "So, yeah—all that to say, thank you."

"You're welcome," I say quietly.

He leads me to the middle of the courtyard, by the walnut tree. "Did you . . . Did you think of the Betty statue for my mom? And her favorite plant?" I ask.

A flush creeps up his neck before he nods. This man, this man who *blushes*. "Feathery Cassia," he says softly.

"It's . . . perfect," I say quietly.

His eyes soften. "I didn't just come here to show you the garden."

My blood rushes through my ears. "Oh?"

He gets in close. "When we first met—I felt like someone literally hit me over the head with a cartoon hammer." A smile hovers over his lips.

I laugh but am on the verge of crying. "Um, that's because you saw a grown woman fall off her bike."

"Yes, and it was the best moment of my life," he says quietly. "I drove to *Beverly Hills* to find you. Casual."

"The west side and everything."

"And everything," he says, his voice low. "Then, when you asked me to come over . . . I couldn't believe it. I was so happy. It was the best weekend of my fucking life. And, I think it might have been one of yours, too."

It's bold and he knows it, his face flushing a little. But of course he's right. "But then you walked away from that, and right to Daniel. And yet, we just kept being drawn together. And I kept getting hurt." He meets my eyes then and I wish I could undo all the things that caused that look. "When you showed me the paper with Daniel's name, it explained so much, but it didn't take away the hurt or the doubt—I mean, what if you changed your mind again? You told me you loved me, and it was so exactly what I wanted to hear, but I needed time . . . I needed to sort through it all. And then instead I just kept remembering. Remembering all the things I love about you," he says.

I take in a sharp breath.

He pulls me in close. "I love how confident you are when you walk into a room. I love the insane way you organize your vinyl and that you taught a seven-year-old how to load a record. I love your terrible Yoda impression. I love how well you take care of the people in your life and your beautiful home and your cranky bird. I love pretty much every physical part of you to the point of craziness. Even that mole that you're self-conscious about. I haven't been able to think of touching anyone else ever since I touched you. And . . . I love the way you . . . believe in love so much that it's your job." Our faces are so close now, I can feel his breath on my skin. "I love you, Cassia. I really fucking do."

It's hard to talk around the lump in my throat, the beating of my heart. "I love you, too, Ellis."

"Say it again, please," he says, his mouth curving up into a smile.

"I love you." I pull in closer. I kiss his neck. "I love you." My lips graze up to his ear. "I love you," I whisper into it. And finally, I drag my lips to his mouth, and they hover right above his when I say, "I love you."

When Ellis presses his mouth to mine, I feel his love in the tender brush of his lips, the sweep of his tongue. He pulls me into his arms and the kiss deepens. A breeze kicks up and he wraps his arms tighter, cocooning me as we make up for lost time.

When we finally pull apart, he rests his forehead on mine, catching his breath. "I have a lot of questions about this past-life stuff by the way."

"I would be surprised if you didn't."

"I mean, you realize you're kind of a witch?" he says, and I can feel his smile against my cheek.

"I prefer 'shaman.'"

He lets out a cute snort-laugh and there's nothing more perfect than this moment. I feel the potential of it all—the love that overwhelms everything else. In Ellis, I *do* feel steadiness—it's in the unwavering way he loves me. He's steadiness mixed with the recklessness of entrusting someone with your entire heart. He's home and he's adventure.

"So, when are you going to read my face?" he asks as he tugs playfully on a lock of my hair.

I look into his beautiful face. My eyes caress every part of it. "There's no rush."

"We *do* have a long night ahead of us," he says, tucking my head under his as I stay wrapped around him.

My lips brush against his throat. "We have an entire lifetime. And maybe more."

His grip tightens. "I'll settle for this one."

52

The Next Year

I get the phone call on my birthday.

Betty squawks and I hear Ellis soothing her when I grab my phone off the kitchen counter. It's messy—bits of parsley and splashes of olive oil staining it. Signs of a kitchen well loved and used. The sight of it makes me smile before I notice who's calling.

I answer. "Hello?"

"Hi, is this Cassia Park?"

"Yes, it is."

Something in my voice must alert Ellis, because he walks into the kitchen. My eyes take in his soft yellow T-shirt and navy shorts. His messy hair, his long-legged, rangy grace as he steps in next to me.

Our eyes meet and his go wide.

"Ms. Park, I'm calling from the Eastside Fertility Clinic."

"Hi." My voice sounds comically breathy and Ellis laughs. I elbow him.

"We received your message and are happy to go ahead and set up your first egg-implantation appointment."

I do just that and then I circle the date on my wall calendar (something Ellis makes fun of me for, endlessly). We step back to look at the visual symbol of what's about to be a huge journey.

"Did you just start *sweating*?" I ask.

"What! No!" He touches his forehead frantically.

I start cackling and he tackles me. Then he lets go immediately. "Oh, god, I should be more careful."

"Okay, nothing has been implanted *yet*. Also, you better not be this precious with me when and if I do get pregnant."

He makes a face like, *Okay*. And I know that he will take care of me like the most fragile of Fabergé eggs. Pregnancy and beyond.

Betty flies to his shoulder, and Ellis starts rooting through the refrigerator with her while I go back to chopping vegetables for the barbecue. By the time the marinated lamb chops and veggies are on the grill, the doorbell rings with the first guests.

It's my family, of course. Early because they're already hungry.

"Get that bird away from me," Sunny says as she hands me a bottle of Scotch. Stu valiantly steps between her and Betty. I give them both hugs.

"Happy birthday, darling," Sunny says, kissing my cheek.

Halmoni and Halabuji are right behind, with Emoni, holding giant Tupperware containers. "I told you guys not to bring anything!" I exclaim.

"Give me a break," Halabuji says. "Now, where's that leaky faucet you told me about?"

Before I can answer, Halmoni swats him. "Dinner first. Enough with the fixing everything all the time!"

Since the Big Mom Reveal, my grandparents have been visiting more often. They stay for meals, spend time with me in my garden. Watch movies in my living room. I think it's their way of moving through their grief. They're finally able to face it head-on and be in Mom's old home. It's been healing. For all of us.

Everyone's on the deck and Stu is serving up drinks when Mar and her family arrive. It's noisy but Betty is in heaven, preening under the kids' attention. Pickle runs around all of us, his chaotic puppy energy taking it to the next level. The kids are so excited to show me their gifts—little cacti in hand-painted pots. Mica's has Spider-Man on it and Ozzie's has, inexplicably, a meticulous drawing of a skeleton. I love them.

Mar stops in front of my calendar and points at the only date that is circled. "Explain."

I raise my eyebrows and take a sip of my gin and tonic, maybe my last one for a while. She raises *her* eyebrows. "It begins?"

"It begins."

She bursts into tears.

My mouth drops open. "Mar!"

"Oh my god, I don't know what's wrong with me," she says, wiping her face with her kaftan sleeve.

"Are *you* fucking pregnant?" I ask, only half joking.

"NO!" She yells so loudly that everyone outside stops talking.

I wave them off. "Wow, really looking forward to motherhood now."

She laughs and then brings me in for a fierce hug. "You're going to love it. Every damn moment. I'll make sure of it."

I shake my head. "I doubt it, but I love the optimism. And I love you."

"And I, you."

The food is being served when the youth arrive in a pack of checkered patterns and natural wine: Shreya, Lila, and Matteo.

"Your house is, like, *so* real," Lila says.

"Right?" Matteo says, pushing up his sunglasses to get a better look. "It's, like, *Mad Men* meets cottagecore."

Shreya stops at a photo hanging near the entrance. "Oh, wow, is that your mom?"

I look at it with her. It's my mom in college—she's asleep in a pile of jackets next to an easel with a half-finished painting. She's curled up, her face at peace in the studio. This single shot captures that reckless and easy way it was to be young and willing to put your body through hell for your passions. My dad sent me the photo for my birthday present.

"Yeah, isn't it cool?" I say with a smile.

Shreya knows about my mom's early death, and she looks at me with big eyes before squeezing my arm. "It's really cool." Matthew had called me that morning and we had a nice chat about his plans for the summer. It might even involve a trip to L.A. We've been talking more and more and I think maybe we're ready for him to visit. Maybe. Ellis reminds me I don't have to make that decision until I feel like it.

Like this birthday. I decided out of the blue to skip my yearly road trip. Maybe I'll start new traditions.

"Make yourself at home and eat up," I say, pushing Shreya onto the deck.

Soon after, Josh and Brian and their families show up and the house officially becomes way too small for the amount of people in it. We spill out onto the deck, where tiki torches and string lights keep it lit and cozy as the sky turns pink, and everyone is seated on various chairs and stools. Music pipes in from my speakers in the living room and I take a moment to take it all in.

I will not think about the future or the past. This is the moment.

And I feel her here—my mother. She's in this house with all

these people I love, but most importantly, she's with me. Always. Because she loved me in *this* life. And that kind of love, it transcends time and space. It finds you life after life.

Ellis meets my eyes and his gaze scorches me. It doesn't get old, this feeling. I lift up my glass and he lifts up Ozzie, who laughs hysterically and throws her arms around his neck.

He's going to be a great father. I am as sure of this as I am that he loves me and I love him.

What a beautiful, scary, exhilarating thing: knowing this one thing in an unknowable future. A future spread before me to make my own.

53

Another Life

The mist settles in the green valley and makes everything brighter, full of teeming life. A small herd of horses gallops, one of them ridden by a young man who leads them across the gentle hills. His tall form creates a dark silhouette against the brightness of the clouds.

When he comes up over the hill, he stops the herd and spots the house at the base of the valley. Its low wood buildings are set around a dirt courtyard filled with chickens and jars of fermenting vegetables. He can see the women that live and preside over the home—they shake out straw mats, carrying babies in wraps on their backs. The matriarch sits at the edge of one of the rooms, the mulberry bark paper door pushed back. She's sifting through a basket of vegetables, snapping off stems. But she looks regal while doing it and no one dares bother her. A bird squawks from its perch on a tree in the courtyard. It's bright green and its wings flap when a younger woman walks by.

This woman, oh this one he knows well. She walks through the courtyard laughing, holding a bundle of laundry on her head and saying something to the bird that makes it flap its wings more. Her face is lovely, one that makes him catch his breath every time. High cheekbones, eyes that shine, and a wryness to her beautiful mouth that alludes to a secret that only she knows.

She kicks the gate behind her as she balances the bundle on her head; he resists rushing over to help. It wouldn't be appropriate, she's married. Her husband is a noble and respected man in the village, one that has shown him kindness many times. The young man tries not to watch her, but he can't help but follow her path as she heads to the nearby creek nestled in the woods behind the home.

He's about to turn when one of his horses bolts. It runs down the hill, into the valley, toward the woods.

Cursing, he spurs on his horse, and they gallop after it. He can't lose a single horse or his parents would give him hell. He's already lost one due to staring up at the clouds too long. And he cannot let his parents down again—they are growing older and more impatient with him with each passing day for not getting married. But how can he get married when his heart no longer belongs to him?

He follows the runaway to the creek, and the young man is embarrassed to see the woman standing beside it, petting its soft ears.

"Apologies," he manages to get out, never having spoken to her before.

She beams first at the horse, then at him, and it's like being hit with a cannon. "Oh, that's quite all right. This one just wanted to say hello."

Her laundry is piled on a boulder next to her and she's rolled up her sleeves for the task. He tries not to notice the smooth skin of her arms, the way her muscles work under her fine bones when she pets the gray dappled horse. He has never been more jealous of a horse in his entire life.

The horse finally trots back to him, and he throws a bridle on it and takes it by the reins. "Well, good afternoon," he says stiffly before he turns, needing to run out of there before he makes a bigger fool of himself.

But he's only a few steps away when he hears a splash and a cry. He lets go of the horse immediately and runs to the sound.

The woman has fallen into the creek, her laundry floating downstream. The creek isn't deep, but she looks distressed as she tries to grab the laundry, swimming awkwardly in her billowing dress. Without thinking, the young man dismounts and runs into the water to pull her out, his hands strong and assured as he grips her under her arms.

She holds on tight to him for a few seconds once she's out and she seems startled by their close proximity. He steps back and lets her go, but he can feel the press of her hands burned into his skin.

"Oh, there go all our linens!" she exclaims, distraught.

He immediately jumps into the water, wading through the shallow parts and swimming assuredly through the deeper parts. The water is ice-cold, coming straight from the mountains, which are still capped with snow. He grabs every piece of laundry—some straight out of the water, some lodged between rocks. But as he trudges back upstream, his arms heavy with wet fabric, his foot slips on a rock and he falls forward, the laundry flying.

The woman lets out a startled cry. "Oh!"

He wants to reassure her that's he's fine, but he's fallen into a deeper part of the creek where the water runs faster. The heaviness of the current pushes against him, and he finds himself being moved quickly, his head dipping below the water. A flash: *If I die helping her, it is worth it.* But then he sees the faces of his parents and grimaces.

Willow branches whip at him as he moves downstream, impossibly fast. He tries to grab on to something, but his hands slip past the grasses, the slender branches. This peaceful creek has turned into a nightmare.

Then he sees a flash of pale blue and gray ahead—the color of the woman's skirts. She's lying, belly-down, on a log that has fallen across the river up ahead. Her pretty, strong hands are stretched toward him. Before he can think, he's right there beneath her and she grips him firmly.

It gives him enough time to pull his upper body up against the log, and once he has that leverage, he's out of the water. He rolls onto his back, staring up at the cloudy sky, catching his breath.

"Are you okay?"

Her voice brings him back to reality and he wishes he *had* drowned. He sits up quickly, feeling vulnerable lying down. When he does, they are both facing each other—her perched on her knees, staring at him with concern, him with his legs loosely crossed. Drenched.

"Thank you," he says with a laugh. "For saving me from saving you."

Her eyes are serious for a moment before laughter bubbles up inside of her. The sound lights up the entire forest, and the wide smile she shoots him feels like stolen treasure. "We're very bad at this."

The "we" reverberates around them, the sound of the water carrying it away.

The woman snaps to standing, wringing her hands as she sweeps her gaze over him. He burns under it. "Oh, you must be freezing. Please, come with me and dry by our fire and let me give you a change of clothes."

But he knows he can't. Once he follows her, he won't be able to leave without ruining his life. "Oh, I'm okay. Please, you go inside and dry off. You'll get ill." He sees her glance at the laundry. "I'll get the laundry. And wait for you."

She looks at him sharply, and for the first time, she is seeing him. A flush creeps up her cheeks and she twists her wet skirt in her hands. "Well, okay. Thank you, that is very kind."

And she makes her way back to her house, her steps slow as if she's weighted down by her wet clothing. He watches her, making sure she doesn't trip or fall. Then, as if feeling his eyes on her, she stops and looks back.

He waves a hand in the air, as if to say, *I'm here.*

Because he is. And he always will be.

ACKNOWLEDGMENTS

I don't know if I believe in past lives, but I do believe that you connect with people in *this* life in ways that are magical and fortuitous. Thank you to the following people for being on the other end of many red threads:

To Faye Bender, my queen of queens. Thank you for guiding me out of a familiar world into a new one. There's no one else I would follow.

To Tara Singh Carlson, an absolute wizard. Thank you for loving my book and caring about the characters as much as I do (maybe more?!). This book really became the best version of itself in your magical hands and I am so grateful.

To everyone at Putnam for helping bring this book into existence: Molly Donovan, Ivan Held, Lindsay Sagnette, Maija Baldauf, and Andrea St. Aubin. To the publicity and marketing teams for sharing this book with the world: Alexis Welby, Ashley McClay, Katie McKee, and Brennin Cummings. Sandra Chiu for the knockout of a cover. To Lorie Pagnozzi, Kristin del Rosario, Lara Robbins, Graham Clark, and Susan Schwartz for the final and crucial polish.

To Olamide Olatunji-Bello at Penguin Random House UK—thank you for your editing expertise and making sure Hot Daniel was firmly Hot British.

To Jenny Meyer and Heidi Gall for getting this book out into the whole wide world.

To Mary Pender, Carolina Beltram, and the entire WME team for supporting my stories beyond the page.

To Adele Gregory for so many epic saves to my sanity and social media presence.

To Kira Appelhans for her expert eye on all things landscape architecture and plants; to The Baby Mudang for the shaman read; to Meredith Hewson for all things floral. (All inaccuracies as far as plants and shaman rituals are my own.)

To Lauren Mee, Taylor Cyr, and Nick Folkman for the Instagram comments that reflected Actual Youth. Thank you to the entire story team at IG for making me a better, faster, less precious storyteller. Love and miss you guys.

To Kate Hart for the early read. Thank you for cheering me on and assuring me that I actually wrote a novel. To all the brilliant and generous authors who blurbed this book, I so appreciate your beautiful words of support. Special thanks to Rebecca Serle who knocked out a blurb with a newborn baby! Plum, your mom rules.

To Wednesday for your wisdom, cakes, and pool. To Adele Griffin, in particular, for making it all happen.

To the Cauldron for being there since the beginning. Growing up with you guys in this industry has been a gift.

To Friendors for the exact rage vibration I need every Friday. Rohan will always answer.

To Sarah Enni, Morgan Matson, and Veronica Roth for being there for everything. If fated friendship was a thing, it'd be our thing.

To the staff and families at WCC, for taking such good care of my child and fostering such a supportive community. Invaluable.

To my family: The Goos, Appelhans, Appelwats, and Peterhans, for being the stable and loving foundation for everything I do.

To Alexander and Chris: For being the family I dreamed up for my happily-ever-after. I love you both in this lifetime and in every single one after.

ABOUT THE AUTHOR

Photo of the author © Sela Shiloni

Maurene Goo is the author of several acclaimed and award-winning books for young adults, including *I Believe in a Thing Called Love* and *Throwback*, which was a Reese Book Club YA winter pick. Several of her young adult novels are in development for film, and her books have been translated into twelve languages. She also writes for screen, games, and comics. She writes and lives in Los Angeles with her husband, son, and two cats. *One & Only* is her adult debut.

VISIT MAURENE GOO ONLINE

maurenegoo.com
maurenegoo.substack.com
MaureneGoo